What I Remember Most

CATHY LAMB

KENSINGTON BOOKS
www.kensingtonbooks.com

KENSINGTON BOOKS are published by

Kensington Publishing Corp.
119 West 40th Street
New York, NY 10018

All Kensington titles, imprints, and distributed lines are available at special quantity discounts for bulk purchases for sales promotion, premiums, fund-raising, educational, or institutional use.

Special book excerpts or customized printings can also be created to fit specific needs. For details, write or phone the office of the Kensington Special Sales Manager: Attn. Special Sales Department. Kensington Publishing Corp., 119 West 40th Street, New York, NY 10018. Phone: 1-800-221-2647.

Kensington and the K logo Reg. U.S. Pat. & TM Off.

eISBN-13: 978-0-7582-9507-1
eISBN-10: 0-7582-9507-3
First Kensington Electronic Edition: September 2014

ISBN-13: 978-0-7582-9506-4
ISBN-10: 0-7582-9506-5
First Kensington Trade Paperback Printing: September 2014

10 9 8 7 6 5 4 3 2 1

Printed in the United States of America

WHAT I
REMEMBER MOST

Books by Cathy Lamb

JULIA'S CHOCOLATES

THE LAST TIME I WAS ME

HENRY'S SISTERS

SUCH A PRETTY FACE

THE FIRST DAY OF THE REST OF MY LIFE

A DIFFERENT KIND OF NORMAL

IF YOU COULD SEE WHAT I SEE

WHAT I REMEMBER MOST

Published by Kensington Publishing Corporation

For Brad

1

I hear his voice, then hers. I can't find them in the darkness. I can't see them through the trees. I don't understand what's going on, but their horror, their panic, reaches me, throttles me.

They scream the same thing.

Run, Grenadine, run!

It's them.

2

I needed to hide for a while.

To do that, I had to change my appearance.

I went to a cheap hair salon and had them cut six inches off, to the middle of my shoulder blades, then I had them cut a fringe of bangs. I went home and dyed my hair back to its original auburn color, from the blond it had been the last ten years. I washed it, then dried it with my back to the mirror.

I turned around and studied myself.

Yep. That would work.

For the last year I had been Dina Hamilton, collage artist, painter, and blond wife of Covey Hamilton, successful investor. Before that, for almost twenty years, I was Dina Wild. Now I would be Grenady, short for Grenadine Scotch Wild, my real name, with auburn hair, thick and straight.

Yes, I was named after ingredients in drinks. It has been a curse my whole life. There have been many curses.

I am cursed now, and I am packing up and getting the hell out of town.

Central Oregon was a good place for me to disappear from my old life and start a new one.

I drove south, then east, the fall leaves blowing off the trees, magenta, scarlet, gold, yellow, and orange. It would be winter soon. Too soon.

I stopped at the first small town. There were a few shops,

restaurants, and bars. It had the feel of a Main Street that was barely holding on. There were several storefronts that had been papered over, there were not a lot of people, and it was too quiet.

Still, my goals were clear, at least to me: Eat first, then find a job.

I had $520.46 total. It would not last long. My credit and debit cards, and my checking, savings, and retirement accounts for my business and personal use, had been frozen. I had the $500 hidden in my jewelry box and $20 in my wallet. The change came from under the seat of my car. To say I was in a bad place would be true. Still. I have been in far, far worse places than this. At least I am not in a cage. Sometimes one must be grateful for what is *not* going wrong.

I tried not to make any pathetic self-pitying noises in my throat, because then I would have pissed my own self off. I went to a park to eat some of the nonperishable food I'd brought with me.

I ate a can of chili, then a can of pineapple. When I was done, I brushed my hair. I pulled a few strands down to hide one of the scars on my hairline. I put on makeup so I didn't look so ghastly. I put extra foundation on the purple and blue bruising over my left eye, brushed my teeth out the car door, and smoothed out my shirt.

I was presentable.

I took a deep breath. This would be the first job I had applied for in many years. I started selling my collages and paintings when I was seventeen, and I had not required myself to fill out an application and resume.

I looked into the rearview mirror. My car was packed full of boxes, bedding, bags, and art supplies. My skin resembled dead oatmeal. "You can do it, Grenady."

My green eyes, which I've always thought were abnormally and oddly bright, were sad, tired, and beat, as if they were sinking into themselves.

"Come on, Grenady," I snapped at my reflection. "You got a moose up your butt? Get it out and get moving."

* * *

I went to every business up and down Murray Avenue and asked for a job. I hoped they would not be thorough in the criminal background check department. That may have been a foolish hope.

I heard the same thing again and again. "We're not hiring." They were all kind, though. A woman at a café offered me a coffee and pastry while I waited to talk to her. I was hungry, again, so I ate it. She told me, "This town is dying. We're on our last gasp. Ya hear it?"

A man at a hardware store said he would hire me but his "no-good, big-footed son-in-law needs a job because he got my daughter knocked up. I would like to knock him up with my fist, but The Wife says I can't because it'll make Christmas awkward."

I looked for a job for two hours—up and down the street. By the time I dumped myself back into my car, the sun was setting.

I drove to a rest stop. I scrubbed my pits, face, hands, and teeth in the restroom before I went back to my car. I changed into sweats, then ate a can of corn and a peanut butter and jelly sandwich.

I don't like living out of cars. I've lived in cars before, many years ago, many times. Sometimes the car was mine, sometimes it wasn't. I can do it again, but I don't like it.

The car I have now, an Acura MDX SUV, where the back two rows were collapsed for my stuff and could also provide a cramped but doable bed, is much better than the cars I've slept in before.

The other cars were small and tight. The seats were broken on one, so they wouldn't recline, and the passenger door wouldn't lock on another, which made me nervous in the middle of the night.

Oh, and then there was Clunker. Clunker was a long, black beast and the most comfortable to sleep in, but the steering was loose and sometimes the brakes would lock up. Made for an exciting ride.

I rolled out my sleeping bag and blankets and lay down, my mind reeling as if someone had stuck a firework in it.

I hardly slept. Fall is cold outside, and rest stops are not restful, even late at night. There were sixteen-wheeler trucks roaring in and out, people in and out, and a group of teenagers partying.

I finally went to sleep around three in the morning, after watching two drunks duke it out with each other. They hit each other so hard they both collapsed flat backward onto the grass, exactly like in the movies. *A perfect outcome,* I thought. Now they'll shut up.

There was a family with a baby a few parking spaces down, and the baby woke me up twice. Two semis roared in way too fast around four. I woke up with a start and had a vision of a snake wrapped around a knife. I have had this vision since I was a kid and I don't know why.

Sometimes I don't want to know why.

I missed sleeping in a bed. I didn't miss who had been in it with me, but I did miss the mattress part of it.

The next morning I drove south, colorful leaves flying through the air, as if they were racing to get off the trees. I stopped at several towns. The last one was called Silver Village. I had the same poor result as I schlepped door to door, trying to hide my desperation.

I applied in a factory, restaurants, four bars, the library, and two gift shops. I did not apply at the strip club. I am not there yet and probably never will be. I am way too old, anyhow. Strip clubs usually like women whose boobs are in the right place, preferably large. I was stacked on top, but they weren't young boobs anymore, and my ass wasn't exactly as tight as a whiskey drum. The scars on my back would not be seen as sexy, either, unless their clients were into S and M.

The people I talked to were all polite, except for one scraggly lady who told me there was no way she'd hire me, ironically, "with a big rack like that. My husband works here, too. I only hire ugly women."

There were no jobs. I spent another night in a rest stop. Once again, I hardly slept because two women truckers blared the entire sound track to *Phantom of the Opera* while they played cards at a table lit by a lantern. I drove away from them, but then a mentally ill man pounded on my windows and yelled, "The CIA is chasing me!"

I felt sorry for him. I handed him two chocolate candy bars. He said, "Cupcake Man thanks you and so do I." He took off again, waving the candy bars and shouting into the air, "They're coming!"

Three teenage girls sat near my car and cried because their car wouldn't start. I called AAA for them and gave them a pack of gum. They hugged me when they left. They were way late getting home and said, "Our moms are gonna kill us. *Kill us!*"

I thought they should be grateful to have moms who would be so worried that they would "kill" their teenage girls for being late, but I didn't say it.

I ran to the bathroom when I saw two other women going in at four-thirty in the morning, so I wouldn't risk getting attacked, then tried to sleep again. A barking dog woke me at five-thirty in the morning.

This was not good.

I looked at my face. Car living is never good for the complexion.

3

Lincoln County Police
Incident Report

Case No. 82-9782

Reported Date/Time: June 10, 1982 12:30 a.m.
Location of Occurrence: Hwy 43, mile marker 15
Reporting Officer: Sgt. Joey Terrerae
Incident: Found Girl

On Friday night, trucker Alan Denalis saw a girl running along Highway 43 about midnight. He stopped the truck, then ran after the girl. She screamed and kept running, like she was afraid of him, so he kept a distance until she became too tired to run. He estimates that they ran close to a half mile.

When he caught up with her she was hysterical and crying. Her head was bleeding profusely. Mr. Denalis has children and said it was as if she was caught up in a night terror and didn't know where she was.

He tried to calm her down, then carried her back to his truck. She kept pointing at the forest, but he did not know what she wanted him to do. She was too upset to speak. Twice she tried to get out of the truck when he was driving.

He brought her to Helena's Café on Highway 99 where he met police. The waitress, Darlene Dilson, brought the girl a hamburger and shake, but she began screaming again. The waitress said it was like she wasn't inside herself, like she wasn't there. She kept trying to run out the door.

We worked with county and state police, as we thought that maybe she'd been in a car accident and had managed to escape. We also thought that perhaps she'd been running from an abusive home or situation, perhaps she'd run from a car, but there are no homes where she was found and we found no one who was looking for a lost girl. We didn't know whether she spoke English.

She was brought to St. Clare's Hospital, where she was examined. She has a concussion and a deep cut near her hairline that will probably scar. The doctor put in fourteen stitches. She continued to scream on and off and was not able to talk for a long time. She has green eyes, and they were blank, like she was staring off into the distance.

We will be working with local media to see if we can figure out who she is and who her parents are and what happened. We'll be sending her photo to the FBI to see if she is a kidnap victim or missing child . . .

Lincoln County Police

Chief Liovanni,

I know you wanted me to keep you up-to-date about the girl who was found on Highway 43. She says her name is Grenadine Scotch Wild and she is six years old. When I talked to her after a couple of days in the hospital, she was still almost hysterical and begging me to find her parents. I told her we would.

We have not been able to locate the parents, despite help from city, county, and state police and the FBI. (For once I didn't get any back talk from Jerry.) Grenadine doesn't remember what happened. She said she remembers they were at a festival, she and her parents; they were going to fly her red kite, there was another man, and that's it. Zip. Nothing else. She described her parents but could not describe the man except to say that he had curly brown hair and a big forehead.

As you know, her picture has been on local and statewide TV, but no one seems to know who she is. We are unable to locate any relatives. We asked her if she had grandparents, and she said no. A huge part of this problem is that she says her parents' names are Freedom and Bear Wild. There is no record of anyone named Freedom Wild or Bear Wild.

The parents most likely made the names up. Plus, they named their kid Grenadine Scotch Wild? Who does that?

There is no record of Grenadine's birth anywhere in America or Canada. It's like she appeared out of the fog that night.

Grenadine is in a foster home and under the care of the Children's Services Division. We will continue our search and work with CSD.

She seems like a good kid. It's a terrible situation.

Sgt. Joey Terrerae

4

I stopped in a town named Pineridge next.

Pineridge is surrounded by mountains. Brothers, three mountains in a row, tower in the distance, lined up like mountain soldiers. Ragged Top, with a jagged peak, and Mt. Laurel round out the incredible view. The view would not buy me a job, but it's always better to be broke in a beautiful place than an ugly place.

Pineridge was designed to resemble the Wild, Wild West. It had 4,500 people. It was a small town, but not too small. I could be there and not be noticed much. It was also almost four hours from my home and no one knew me, which is exactly what I need.

The 1850s buildings lining Main Street were somewhat fakey, with their cowboy and Indian days façades, but still appealing. There were balconies and boardwalks, brightly painted store fronts, old-fashioned lampposts and hanging flowerpots. A steel statue of a cowboy on a bucking horse divided the main street. You could almost see the horses, carriages, women with bonnets and bustles, and gunfights in the middle of the street, if you had an imaginative imagination.

Pineridge was charming, but within the charm I needed to find a job. I brushed my hair and pulled it back into a braid. I changed my shirt, as the other one had chili on it. I changed my jeans, as I'd worn them for two days. I pulled on my cowboy boots. I put on mascara, liner, blush, and lipstick to hide the gluelike color of my skin. I applied foundation to the purple and blue bruises.

I started at the grocery store. The manager said they weren't hiring now, but she had a lot of employees, some of them teenagers, and said, "You never know when they're not going to show up in favor of a kegger."

I went to a quilting and crocheting shop. In the back corner they had shawls. I saw a red, crocheted shawl. I ran my fingers down it, and my eyes burned. I scooted out of that shop before I became too emotional about the red shawl. I could not work in a shop with a red, crocheted shawl, anyhow. Heck, no.

I turned the corner and sat down in a park on a bench in front of a fountain. The fountain's base was a wagon wheel. I picked up the newspaper beside me for distraction. It told the usual—wars that shouldn't be fought, budget issues, and another serial killer guy on death row appealing his sentence. The thought of the serial killer made me nervous.

I stood back up. Restaurant. Café. Hardware store. Another restaurant. A bookstore. Pawn shop. Antique shop. A sign shop and a copying place. An optician's, a dentist's, a doctor's office, pharmacy, art galleries. All said no, in a friendly way. Hours later, I trudged back to my car, tired and discouraged. Rejection made me feel stupid, a familiar feeling.

"Lose the whine, Grenady." I drove out into the country as the sun went down over Ragged Top, parked my car off a deserted street, and ate a can of pineapple and a peanut butter and jelly sandwich. I peed out the side, brushed my teeth with bottled water, then climbed into my sweats and sleeping bag in the back.

I hoped an ax murderer wouldn't come along when I was sleeping. Couldn't have been more than two hours later and I was woken up by cars flying by, engines roaring, music blasting.

Apparently I'd parked on a strip where kids from town like to drag race. They flew past, whooping and hollering. I moved my car. The next place was quieter. So quiet it was creepy and scary. I tried not to remember what happened that other time, years ago, under a bridge. I felt sorry for him.

The next morning—a whopping four hours of sleep under my belt—I went to McDonald's and used their toilet, then quickly pulled my washcloth out of its baggie, rinsed it, added some hand soap, and cleaned up my face, my neck, my pits, and my chest. I wanted to strip, straddle the sink, and clean up my Big V, but that would have gotten me arrested if anyone came in.

With my luck, someone would have snapped a photo and my straddling butt and I would have ended up on YouTube.

I dried off with my handy-dandy hand towel and pulled my hair out of its sloppy ponytail. It looked simultaneously greasy and as if I'd been electrocuted. I brushed it out and braided it.

My eyes appeared almost drugged, I was so wiped out. "Well, now, shoot," I said out loud. I was pale. Sickly. Cement and hay mixed together—that was the color of my complexion. "My, aren't you gorgeous."

I shut the door of a stall and changed out of my sweats and into a red cable knit sweater, jeans, clean underwear, a white-lace bra, and knee-high boots. My figure, as he said, "Curves. You're not fat, Dina, but you have enough to put in a man's hands. Put yourself in my hands."

I stamped down a well of sweeping hatred that bubbled up like a volcano. I would spit volcano fire, lava, and smoke at that man's ferret face if I could. I would kill him and hide his piggy body if I could.

I bought a large coffee and settled into a stall. I put in six creams. I wished they had liquid whipping cream—that's what I like in my coffee. There is a lot I will give up when I am broke, but I will spend my second-to-last dollar on coffee. I will spend my last dollar on paint. Call me crazy and reckless, but I'll do it.

I would try the other half of the street today for jobs, and if that didn't work, I'd move on.

My cell phone and e-mail were burning up with their messages. Crying. Swearing. Yelling. Cancellations for my paintings and collages, deafening outrage.

I didn't blame them at all.

*   *   *

"Hello. Can I talk to the manager?"

"I'm the manager. And the owner. Can I help you?"

"I'm Grenady Wild, and I'm looking for a job." I shook her hand. It felt so odd to use the name Grenady, but right, too.

"Tildy Green. What kind of job?"

The woman staring back at me looked like she could wrestle a bull to the ground and win. She had thick, straight gray hair and a white streak arching from a widow's peak in the middle of her forehead. She had strong features and broad shoulders, and was cleaning a hunting rifle behind the bar.

I didn't know you could clean guns in a bar/restaurant, but there were only about ten other people in there at the time and none seemed to be bothered by it. I sure wasn't. "Anything you have."

"I don't have anything. You're new in town."

It was a statement, not a question. She could meet someone and know she was new? I thought this town was bigger than that. "Yes. I am."

"You came to town without having a job." She peered down the barrel of the gun, searching for any problems, then waved me to a barstool so we could talk.

"Yes, I did." I sat down. I could hardly stand anymore. I had been up and down the entire street asking for jobs. There were none. Or no one wanted to hire me. That was a distinct possibility.

"You missed the quilt show."

"The quilt show?"

"Yes. Quilts all over the place. I love quilts."

It was almost funny that a woman cleaning a gun with such care loved quilts.

This restaurant/bar was called The Spirited Owl. It had a lodgelike atmosphere with both log and brick walls.

It was a two-story building with a faux balcony on the second floor. There was a covered boardwalk out front with several Adirondack chairs on it. The original wood floors had been scuffed by thousands of cowboy boots; white tablecloths covered circular tables, each with a small bouquet; leather booths lined the walls; and a huge rock fireplace with a hearth warmed up the place.

It had the longest bar I'd ever seen—an exquisite, shiny piece of wood, built to seem old, with curves and scrolling and a gold foot rail. Behind the bar, a huge mirror reflected the expected, vast array of bottles of liquor. Above the mirror was a row of stuffed owls. The owls wore aviator sunglasses. It was a quirky touch.

There were fishing poles and black-and-white photos of the Wild West on the walls, and two canoes hanging from the ceiling, amidst several fishing nets. Comfortable, classy, not cheap.

I read part of the menu posted outside before coming in, so I knew a little about the cuisine: Tildy's Wild Steak, Hail to the Hamburgers, Lusty's Lasagna (I wondered who Lusty was), Cowgirl Calzone, Shooting Straight's Chef Salad, Home on the Range Soup and Salad, I Won't Club You Club Sandwich, Kickin' Chicken, and Buckin' Bronco Salmon. It also had an extensive alcohol offering, and the desserts, especially the pies, made me hungry thinking about them.

It was the gun-slinging west meets "I want my steak medium rare and I'll have the house red wine with that."

"If you don't have a job, I'll take a beer," I told her. "Please."

"What kind of beer?"

"What do you recommend?" She told me what they had, at length, with questions about my tastes and preferences. So complicated. But this is Oregon. We're particular about our beers. "I'll have a Sisters Pale Ale."

"Coming up."

I put my head in my hands for no more than five seconds. My spinning and fuzzied-up brain needed a rest. Good golly God, my face was horrendous.

"Here ya go."

"Thank you." I sucked some of that beer down and enjoyed the hell out of it. I did a Personal Financial Calculation. I was under $450 now because of gas costs and my coffees. I could not afford a hotel. If I was hired, I would probably not be paid for at least two weeks unless I had a job where I received tips. Like this one.

"Where ya from?"

"I'm from . . ." I'm from I Don't Want To Tell You. "Portland."

I could feel her sizing me up. "Born in Portland?"

I didn't know where I was born. No clue. Two people knew, and they were long gone. "Near there."

"Why you here?"

"I like central Oregon."

"Why?"

She was trying to figure me out. I got it. "This is a nice . . ." What was it? "This is a nice town. I like the mountains. I like the space. I like the open air and the views."

Her expression said, "Yeah, right."

"You're cagey, aren't you?" She went back to cleaning her gun again. "Really, why are you here?"

"You don't quit, do you?"

"Why would I? It's my bar."

"And it's my beer, and if I wanted to answer twenty questions I'd put myself on a game show."

"I haven't asked you twenty questions yet, now, have I? I'm on number seven. Besides, you asked me for a job, so I can ask you some questions."

"You said you didn't have a job."

"Maybe I will soon. So quit dodging around and tell me about yourself."

Tip money would be helpful. If I ran out of money, I'd be out of coffee and cream. That would be bad.

"I need a job. I was a waitress for eleven years and tended bar for four of those. I can handle multiple orders at one time and multiple assholes. I make an excellent martini. I prefer to shake them, but I'll stir it if it must be done. My specialties are mint juleps, cosmopolitans, Singapore slings, blood and sands, and black bombers. My Bloody Marys are outstanding, and I make a pretty tasty Ginger Rogers, Galapagos, and Sex on the Beach, which is the most asinine name for a drink on the planet. People order it so they sound cool, and I think they're idiots. Not a bad drink, though.

"The bars I've worked in had rednecks and convicts, millionaires and college professors. I can handle anyone who comes in here, sit them down, shut them up, and get them their order on time. Sometimes I even smile. I don't take any crap from anyone, even the customers, so if you want some sweet little thing in here who will smile even when some slovenly, sweaty-palmed creep is trying to grab her ass, you don't want to hire me. Someone pulls that on me, I will punch first and ask questions later."

I saw a slight smile. "Sugar, I don't expect any of my employees to take any crap. None. You could swing if you want, and I'll back you up with the baseball bat behind the bar."

I wondered why she didn't say she would use the gun instead of the bat, but I didn't ask. "I work hard and I'm on time. I'm efficient. I know how to listen to people who want to bend the ear of the bartender back one hundred and eighty degrees. I'd like the job." And I needed the money. I didn't want to resort to Dumpster diving again. I will if I have to, I'm not above it, but I'd rather not.

"I might hire you, but I don't need anyone right now." She smiled. It softened her face.

"If you do need someone, will you call me?" I scribbled my number and e-mail on a napkin. "My bartending and food handlers licenses are up-to-date."

"Any drug problems I should know about?"

"No. None. I don't do drugs."

"You have a criminal record?"

"No." Not quite officially. Not *convicted*. Only arrested. Done only a small amount of time. Innocent until proven guilty, and all that is American and red, white, and blue. I went back to my Sisters beer and studied the suds. She heard the pause, I know she did.

"What happened to your face?"

"A woman decided she didn't like me."

"Stole her husband?"

"If you knew me, you would know I'd sooner swing a rattler than take someone's husband."

"I don't mow other women's grass, either. Why'd she hit you?"

"Because I hit first."

Tildy raised her eyebrows.

"She called me Barbie Princess."

Tildy made a hissing sound. "That would tick me off, too. How insulting."

"It was. There's no need for that kind of trash talk."

"Absolutely not. I would have slugged her."

We were interrupted by a crash.

The crash was so deafening, it sounded like a bomb had dropped through the roof and we were caught in the center of the explosion. Glass from the windows went flying. Tildy and I hit the floor. I heard wood splitting, a car horn blaring, and, strangely, country music.

A light fell from the ceiling and shattered. Two picture frames fell and broke. I covered my head again.

When the noise stopped, except for the horn and the country music, I turned, my heart pounding, to figure out whether I needed to run for my sorry life.

The hood of a blue truck was *inside* the restaurant. *A truck.*

It was old, I'd give it thirty years.

Another plate of glass came straight down, and I covered my head again as it split and went flying. A table wobbled and toppled over. The vase broke.

Tildy stood up and swore. "Damn that crazy mother shit drunken alligator head." She slapped the bar with both hands. "Lunatic. Rotten breath, brainless idiot!"

She stalked out of the bar, her cowboy boots crunching glass. She did not have the gun. Probably fortunate.

I stumbled up and ran over to the truck to make sure no one was underneath the wheels. My legs trembled. When I saw no one was under the front tires, I raced outside to check the back ones, hoping the thing wouldn't blow.

The hood of the truck was four feet in. Tildy yanked open the driver's door as other people ran toward us, including several police officers.

"I am going to skin you alive, Reuben!" Tildy shouted, pulling the young man out by his arm and his collar. She let him crumble to the ground. "Skin you alive like a dead skunk!"

I bent over him to check for damage, surprised at Tildy's rough handling of the driver. There was blood on his face, but it wasn't gushing. Liquor emanated from him like waves of shame. Whew. Reuben had a skull tattooed on his upper arm. I have always hated skulls.

"Am I . . ." Reuben stuttered from the ground. "Ding. Dang. Think I ding danged my own darn head . . . am I . . . uh-oh . . . owls and spirit . . . late for work, Aunt . . . Aunt Tildy?" His eyes rolled back in his head and he passed out, drunk as could be.

"Hello, Tildy." A police officer tipped his hat to her, two more coming up behind him.

"Do you see what this lousy slug of a raving, drunk nephew did to my restaurant? I think my sister must have dropped him too many times on his head, because he is dumber than a dead toad." She kicked a tire, twice. "Now I'm off my rocker! Off my bleepin' rocker!"

"He gave us a chase," one of the officers said. His name tag said Lieutenant Mark Lilton. He was a six-three African American and wore horn-rimmed glasses. "I believe he's drunk once again. This is his third. Some people learn slowly."

Tildy pointed at Reuben. "Now, you arrest this drunk slug. Lock him up for a long time. I'm not paying no bail—never have, never will, you know that, Mark. Being locked up is the only thing that's gonna sober him up. I'm pressing all charges I can possibly press. Teach him a lesson."

"Will do, Tildy."

"And I'm going to get rid of his truck," Tildy declared. "He is not fit to drive."

"I didn't hear that, Tildy." A police officer named Sergeant Sara Bergstrom spoke up. She had dark hair, gray streaks. "Not one word of that reached my ears."

"Me either," the third officer, Justin Nguyen, echoed. Justin had black hair, dimpled smile.

"To get rid of the truck, that's a fine idea," Lieutenant Lilton mused, then adjusted his horn-rimmed glasses. "Not that I'm encouraging it. It would be illegal to steal a truck, destruction of property. Etcetera, etcetera, etcetera. Even if it's an excellent idea."

"Oh me, oh my!" Tildy threw her hands in the air. "My heart beats in fear of the law." She toed her nephew, not gently. "Thank God he didn't kill anyone. I'm glad he didn't kill himself, either, cause when he wakes up, I'm gonna kill him."

"I didn't hear that either," Sergeant Bergstrom said. "You can't kill people. It's illegal. Jail time. Blue scrubs. No beer. No wine."

"That would be an unfortunate decision, Tildy," Lieutenant Lilton said. "And now that you've made the threat, if that boy ends up hanging by his ankles, we'll have to come to you first, and I don't want to do that. You make the best bleu cheese burger in town and I would miss that like the dickens—by the way I'm reading Charles Dickens right now—but I will uphold the law."

"Right," Officer Nguyen said. "So if you commit a crime, Tildy, don't get caught." He grinned. Dimple, dimple. Darling. "Do you have raspberry pie today? No? What about peach? Great. Can you save me a piece? Last time you all ran out, ruined my day."

Tildy told Officer Nguyen she would save him a piece.

The officers turned to me and smiled. "You're new in town," Sergeant Bergstrom said. "Welcome."

The other officers shook my hand, smiled, and I introduced myself.

Tildy swore up a storm again at her "tiny-dicked, tiny-brained nephew," then turned to me. "You got yourself a job, Grenady. Start tomorrow. Wear black. I'll get you a Spirited Owl apron. They're red. I gotta get this glass cleaned up, damn this damage. We may open late, but I'm openin'. I've got a

Middle-Aged Women Gone Wild group comin' in, and they will not like it if I'm shut. It's their only night to relax."

"I'll be here. Thank you." Oh boy. I sure could be here tomorrow. Tips! Immediate money!

His drunken loss, my gain.

Whooee. I had a job.

That night I thought of my interview with Tildy. The "Tell me about yourself" request always throws me. What should I say about myself? What should I not say about myself?

I'm a crack shot and can hit damn near anything.

I'm a collage artist and painter.

I used to have a little green house. I sold it. That was a huge mistake.

I can smash beer cans on my forehead.

I fight dirty. Someone comes at me, and my instinctive reaction is to smash and pulverize. It has gotten me into trouble.

I love to decorate. Things must be pretty around me or I feel like I'm losing it.

I have a temper, my anger perpetually on low seethe, and I have struggled with self-esteem issues and flashbacks for as long as I can remember.

I can wear four-inch heels and designer clothes like wealthy women, make social chitchat, and pretend I'm exactly like them. I am not like them at all.

Some of the kindest people I have ever met were missing a lot of their teeth and loved their guns and pickups.

Some of the worst, most narcissistic, uncaring people I've met drove Mercedes and belonged to country clubs.

I survived my childhood. Now I'm trying to reinvent myself to survive once again.

Who am I?

Where did I come from?

Those questions I can answer easily: I don't know.

5

She never should have gotten away.

That was a mistake. He had not expected things to take so long. It had always bothered him. He liked things neat. Planned. Perfect.

He wanted to see her again. Before.

He would do it! He would think of a way. He pulled four strands of hair out of his head, then made a design on the table in front of him.

He giggled. He twitched in his chair.

He told himself a nursery rhyme. He changed the words to create a new rhyme. He sang it out loud. He wrote it in his rhyme book.

He giggled again, then he hurdled his rhyme book across the room, tilted his head back, and screamed.

6

When I left Portland, all my prior packing and survival skills came flooding back, as if I'd never left that helter-skelter life. I brought blankets and a sleeping bag and threw my clothes—warm sweaters, jeans, boots, coats, tank tops—into duffle bags. I brought soap, shampoo, toothbrush, washcloths, towels, makeup, a small cooler, and two large boxes of food.

I have food issues. I always have to have a full fridge and pantry, or it makes me anxious. I am now extremely anxious.

I brought art supplies in boxes: My paints and brushes, pastels and colored pencils. My jars of buttons, beads, Scrabble letters, ribbons, patterned scrapbook paper, folded fabrics, old and sepia photographs, peacock feathers, vintage stationery, modern flowered stationery, Victorian gift cards, fortune-telling cards, art books, and books with maps, nature, and birds that I used for my collages. I brought my old but reliable sewing machine and threads. I figured I'd go back for the rest later.

I brought plastic bags for trash and laundry. I like to be neat, especially when I'm living in a place with an engine.

My front passenger seat was packed, and the entire back was packed, too. I barely had room to sleep.

That evening, after a gourmet dinner of cold, canned clam chowder and canned peaches, I peed in the only big-box store this town had, and scrubbed my face, pits, and teeth once again.

I do not want to attract attention, especially the attention of police officers who might tell me to move along, so I parked in the back lot of what appeared to me to be an out-of-business furniture store.

I changed into two pairs of sweats, two pairs of wool socks, and two sweatshirts, and curled up in my sleeping bag and blankets. I needed a shower so bad. So, so bad. I was grimy and gross. I do not like to be unclean. Ever. I vowed I would find a shower the next day. Maybe I could sneak into an athletic club. The thought of a hot shower almost gave me a hot shower orgasm.

My .38 Special was nearby, just in case. I learned a lot about guns years ago, from a few men and women who knew their way around them. I'm a heckuva shot. When you learn how to shoot squirrels, possums, and beer cans off downed tree trunks when you're a kid, the skill never leaves you.

I was so relieved that I had a job starting tomorrow, I almost cried.

I had to pee again about three in the morning, so I scrambled out of the car and squatted in the dark night, the moon obscured by shifting clouds. I peed at the passenger side of the car purposefully, so I wouldn't step on it tomorrow.

That's important: Never step in your own pee.

The call from him came early in the morning.

"Come home now."

"No." I stared out the car window. There was fog on the mountains, amidst the trees. I peeked out the other window. Same thing. I took a deep, trembly breath; burrowed deeper into my sleeping bag; and shut the trees and fog out.

"I need you home, Dina. Where are you?"

"That's none of your business. Call my attorney."

"I'm calling you." His voice was razory, demanding, and sharp. He likes to get his own way. "I can explain everything. We can work together on this. It's all going to be fine, but I need you here."

"No." Fry me a pig, I wanted him on a spit. "You have lied from the beginning, and you're lying now to save your skinny, flea-ridden, stenchy butt."

"Don't go back to your trailer trash talk, Dina, it's unseemly. Sexy, too, but unseemly at the moment. I will save both of our butts, you have to trust me."

"Don't go back to my trailer trash talk? How dare you say something like that to me. And I would sooner trust a maniac with a .45 pointed at my face than you."

"Dina"—his voice rose—"I'm warning you, come home. If you don't—"

"If I don't, what?" I heard his tone. I would not let him scare me.

"Things are going to get bad for you—"

"They're already bad. If I had a dead possum, I would throw it at you."

"More trailer trash talk. Things are going to get worse for you if you push me."

"What do you mean by that?" Now I was scared.

"I'll tell you when you get home."

"Tell me now. What else are you hiding?"

"Home. Now."

"Don't order me around, asshole. I'm hanging up."

"You had better not—"

I hung up, even though I knew him and knew he'd make good on his threat.

He called back. I ignored the call.

There was something else coming down the pike with him, I knew it in my gut. I shivered and wrapped my arms around myself. It was colder than a cow's tit in December inside my body. Outside it wasn't much warmer.

I could not go back to sleep.

I paid five dollars to be a guest at the local YMCA. I took a long, hot shower. I'm sure if someone was watching, they would have thought I was asleep in there. I washed my hair twice, then let the cream rinse sit. I scrubbed up twice. I shaved. I let the hot water stream this way and that, working the kinks out of my back.

It was worth the five dollars.

*   *   *

"Ma'am, I'll take another beer."

I nodded at the man at the end of the bar.

"Me too, honey," his friend said. The friend was middle aged, balding, with a stomach that mirrored a nine-month pregnancy.

I leaned over the bar and glared at the pregnant man. "I've told you three times over the last two weeks. My name isn't honey or sexy lady or sweetheart or tight cheeks. It's Grenady."

He smirked. "Okay, dumplings."

Some men like the power. You tell them not to do something and they do it to show you that you can't tell them what to do. They want to get in your head and control your brain.

Tonight I smiled, displaying all my shiny teeth, then I tipped his beer right onto his crotch. He jumped up, ticked off, flustered. His buddy laughed.

I stood my ground, smile gone, beer dripping off his pants. "My name is Grenady. If you have a problem, you can wear your beer on your crotch." My voice arched over the conversation at the bar, and it became quiet. I didn't care. My temper was out and rolling. "Every night. Until you learn. You're a slow learner, aren't you?"

He glared at me, then he suddenly started to laugh along with his friend, who about fell off his stool he laughed so hard. "Yes, ma'am."

"Say you're sorry." I slammed the glass down.

"I'm sorry, Grenady."

"Women do not like your smirks or your snarky comments." I pointed my finger right at his fleshy face, his bulbous red nose. "Each time you open your mouth and say something derogatory, they think you're vomit. Want to be known as vomit? Treat me with respect or don't come in." Sometimes the middle-aged, balding fat men are the worst. It has not caught up with them that they are not attractive and women do not want their sexual attention and are, in fact, repulsed by it.

"Yes, ma'am." He shook off his pants, red faced.

Several men at the bar applauded. I ignored them.

Tildy said, "Do I have to get the bat out, Val?"

"No, ma'am."

"Sit down and shut up."

He sat. He shut up.

I went back to work. Why are men such cocks?

"Took care of that one, didn't you?" Tildy said. "Smooth, quick as a lick."

"Thank you." I adjusted my red Spirited Owl apron and pulled my black T-shirt down beneath it. I never missed the irony of working in a bar with a name like mine, no, I did not.

I made martinis, strawberry daiquiris for a bridal party, cosmopolitans for three women who told me they "all hated men," and what seemed like hundreds of beers. At the same time I kept the bar clean, took the money, made sure we had ice, took the trash out, and pulled orders from the kitchen and delivered them to the customers at the bar. There were ten waiters and waitresses, two hostesses, a gang of cooks, and Tildy and me at The Spirited Owl.

The bar and restaurant were packed. A band played in the corner. The noise was constant, blasting. I was having a surprisingly good night in tips. Being new to town, I hadn't realized how popular The Spirited Owl was. Now I knew.

I was making minimum wage, which was unlivable, but the tips made it something. When I could afford first and last month's rent, and a security deposit, and had enough to continue paying my divorce attorney, Cherie Poitras, the monthly amount we'd agreed on, I could find an apartment. I could have my own roof, toilet, and shower.

With an apartment, I could get back to my collages and paintings, too. I was withering without my art. I was lost. That feeling of being nothing was skating on in. I did a Personal Financial Calculation as to how long it would take to get an apartment and tried not to swear out loud like a raccoon caught in a trap when I had my answer.

"Guys at the end of the bar have had too much," Tildy yelled over the noise. "I told 'em they're cut off. They must have been slammin' 'em down before they got here, because I've served them only two drinks each." Two minutes later, when she disappeared to talk to the cooks about the sautéed mushrooms, they called me over.

"Grenadeeeee, we need another round and round beers here for us good mens."

"Nope. Tildy cut you off."

"Ah, come on," another drunk pleaded, then sang part of a song by the Beatles—"I wanna hold your hand"—and held out his hand. I stared back at him.

"One more for the road to paradise," he begged. "Paradise and round beers for the mens."

"No," I said, "the road doesn't need you driving drunk and killing someone."

"Hey!" Third drunk friend. "We have ourselves here a designated driver! Designated! We picked him. A nomination. Like for president how we do that. He brought us here on his motorcycle!" One of the men pointed to a man who had his head on the counter.

I walked around the bar and pretended to check on the "designated driver." I picked his pocket and came out with his keys, which I slipped into my apron. I have many skills, some of them the criminal variety.

"Your designated driver is passed out," I told them. "No more drinks."

They groaned and moaned but were too drunk to care.

One of the men, for some odd reason, took a pair of lady's purple panties out of his jean pocket and pulled the panties over his head. He then began a serious discussion about the engine in his truck. His friends laughed and laughed. About fifteen minutes later he pulled out a second pair of purple panties and pulled them up over his jeans. He went to the bathroom wearing those panties.

"Now, that is drunk," I said to Tildy.

"You got the keys?"

"Yes." I had dumped them in the trash. He had about twenty keys, but anyone who drinks that much intending to drive should have a consequence. I do not have tolerance for drunk drivers.

"Good. Then panty man and his gang won't hurt anyone. They can stumble on home on their drunk feet, crash into lampposts, and bang up their tiny jewels."

I went back to the bar and served drink after drink. I never thought I would be bartending again. I thought I'd left that part of my life behind. Goes to show you, you can't count on not falling back to where you were before.

The fall can be long and hard. I remembered what a woman who could wring a chicken's neck without thinking about it once told me: "Don't ya ever get too big for your britches or someone's gonna bust your britches wide open and then they'll find out you got a butt like everybody else. Nothing special about it."

That night I left with a hamburger; a salad full of mini tomatoes, because I love tomatoes; and a piece of chocolate cake. I was also able to take a medium-sized take-out carton of fruit and four strips of leftover bacon for breakfast. For me, it was a haul.

Tildy says that during each shift we can have one free meal worth less than ten dollars. We can have all the lemonade we can guzzle. In addition, the staff can take whatever food she won't be serving the next day. She sets it on the counter.

It's a deal for me, as it's essentially two meals for free. Eating peaches and pears straight out of the can for breakfast has lost its appeal. Plus, Tildy's food was outstanding. She knew how to cook, and so did her chef, Andy, who had trained at two fancy-schmancy schools.

I drove through the night and the deserted streets of Pineridge to the same parking lot by the out-of-business furniture company that I'd slept in for the last two weeks. I parked at the end of it, as usual. I did not want the police here to know that I was temporarily homeless.

I ate my dinner, the only thing I'd eaten since my cans of fruit, used a water bottle to brush my teeth, squatted to pee outside the passenger door, and went to "bed," so to speak.

It was so dark, so deserted, it made me nervous, but I'd been safe on the other nights and I would be safe tonight.

Sure I would. No problem. In five hours it would be getting light anyhow. "Don't let your fear eat you, Grenady," I said out loud.

I suffer from anxiety. It's always lurking inside of me, has been for as long as I can remember. Sometimes it spikes, seemingly for a long time, and other times I'm able to push it down and live somewhat normally. I hide it at all times, as best I can, but I have named my anxiety Alice, My Anxiety, to bring humor to a situation that has none.

Alice, My Anxiety, was not happy now. She was not calm, and I was pushing her down as hard as I could.

It was cold, and I put on two sweatshirts, two pairs of wool socks, two pairs of sweats, and my jacket. I brought one of the blankets into the sleeping bag with me and put the other over the top. The silence was so loud. What I wouldn't give for a neighbor's barking dog . . .

My fitful sleep was broken by someone breaking into my car.

Glass shattered on the passenger side window. I sat straight up, absolutely and instantly terrorized. I tried to move, but my legs were stuck in my blankets and the sleeping bag.

I heard two men outside the window laughing. Evil laughing.

"Come on out, sweetie!" one called out. "Play with me!"

"We're gonna have some fun, lady. We seeeeee you! Don't try to hiiide!"

"Aren't you a pretty little bitch?"

Through a rush of searing panic, I could tell by their slurred voices that they were drunk or high, or both.

I saw a hand shoot through the broken window, running up and down the side of the door, searching for the automatic lock.

"Hey! You were fuckin' right, Turley. She's got red hair."

"How are the tits? Titty tit tits."

I kicked out of my sleeping bag. By shots and by fire, I was not going to get stuck here.

"Here she comes!" The passenger door opened, and a man wearing a black knit hat poked his head in. The driver's side door, now unlocked, opened too, and a second man with the same horrifying black knit hat poked his head in also.

My breath caught when I saw them, those black masks freezing my blood.

"Come on out, baby. We're gonna have some plain fuckin' fun!"

"Fuckin' fun!"

I swallowed hard, hysteria closing my throat. I was behind the two front seats, but they had all the advantage. I could try to escape out a side door, but they'd be there in a second. I'd left the keys in the ignition, and I'd left the gun in the glove compartment. Stupid. Why am I so stupid? I had had the gun next to me every night before this one.

One of them burped. The other giggled and burped back, then his expression changed. "Get out of there, bitch! Move your ass!"

"Don't make us come get you!" he singsonged.

They reeked of pot and liquor, sweat and mortal danger.

The one on the right opened the side door, near to where I was. He had a rope—*a rope*—linked around his neck. I hate ropes. Oh, my shouting spitting Lord, I hate ropes.

I instinctively moved back. I could scream, if my throat would move, but it wouldn't help, no one would hear.

"Give me a second," I said, my voice strangled.

"Give her a second," the one near me said, his voice mimicking mine, his black head bobbing. "A second for what? You want to put on some lipstick or something? Grab a condom? We don't use no condoms, lady. I wanna feel you."

"Feel you, feel you," the other one sang. "Feel you. Me first this time."

"No. I'm first."

They started to jokingly argue with each other, as if I wasn't a person, a woman, but a bull cow they were bidding on.

"I..." I tried to think through a haze of tingling fear that was rapidly turning into rage. I was about to be attacked by two stoned, violent men wearing full black masks. My blood was curdling, my body stiff with fright, but who the hell did they think they were? I currently hate men. All of them. I do. I hated *him* most of all, but these two were right there with him.

Another wave of liquor and pot rolled through. I wanted to gag. I hate pot and its skunklike smell.

Get the gun.

It was them. I knew it.

Shoot it.

I heard their voices, louder than my fear, in my head.

"I have some pot, hang on," I said, breathless.

"Pot!" One of the vermin laughed. "Hey, bring the pot. We'll stick it to you, a threesome, ya know? And we can all light up together. We can put the joint in your vagina slit and smoke it. We can flip you like a sausage and smoke it from your butthole. Butt. Hole."

I kicked my legs from my sleeping bag, then scrambled into the front seat. The man who had opened the side door, shut it, and went to the front. "Where ya goin', Miss Titties? I want a titty in my mouth."

"Titty!" the other said. "Bite it! Titty bites."

Shoot them, Grenadine! I heard them again, as if they were sitting right by me.

The masked men were so scarily stoned. I put my fingers on the handle of the glove compartment. "It's in here. We can get stoned together. You're right. It'll be fun. Right up my vagina."

The one next to me, inches away now, his breath rancid, said, "This be my night, this be my night, how about yours, Jason?"

"This be my night, too. We got a redhead and we got free vagina pot. And don't call me, Jason, Turley."

They laughed.

Both of them stopped laughing when I pulled the gun out and put the barrel smack on Turley's forehead.

"Shit!" they both screamed simultaneously.

"Back the fuck off or I will shoot," I said, rage ripping through my body. I wanted to kill them, I did. I don't come from much, but I've been taught to fight, and shoot, and survival instincts are as much a part of me as my intestines.

The man, high as a kite but slow, tried to grab the gun. I

moved the gun to his shoulder, although that was a gift he did not deserve, and pulled the trigger. He fell straight back.

I turned the gun on the second one as he lunged through the driver's side at me and shot him, too. He fell straight back, screaming, like his demented, violent buddy. Too bad for them.

I yanked the passenger door shut, the glass that was still stuck to the rims of the window crashing to the seat and pavement. I kept the gun in one hand, then whipped over to the driver's seat. I slammed that door, transferred the gun to my left hand, turned on the car, and reversed like a bat out of hell.

Both of them stood up, yelling and swearing, each holding onto their wounds. They stumbled back to their car. I didn't like the looks of that. They would come after me, I knew it.

I hit the brakes, turned to the right, rolled down the window, steadied my shooting hand, and shot out the back tire. The car heaved, then flattened out, listing to the left.

They both flattened themselves to the ground.

I shot out the driver's window, which clipped through the front window, too, glass splitting into that otherwise silent night. I shot a bullet toward the engine.

In between I heard those sons of bitches swearing to "fucking kill you!" as they lay facedown, cowering on the ground. For fun, I shot again, close to Jason's head, then Turley's.

I heard them scream again. They deserved that. They were lucky I didn't kill them, but I didn't want the mess.

I took off.

Damn.

They'd wrecked the window of my car.

They'd wrecked my house. It wasn't much of a house, but still. It was all I had at the moment.

I desperately needed my own roof and my own toilet.

And a locked door.

I was truly pissed.

I parked my car in a neighborhood for the rest of the night, teeth gritted, nerves shot. I put the driver's seat down but didn't sleep. I reloaded the gun and left it on my lap.

I could call the police, but I wouldn't. It was self-defense, no question, even though I had shot off a number of "excess" shots. I liked the police, sometimes, but I didn't always trust them, or their "procedures," or the government, especially now. I also didn't want the publicity, the press, and I didn't want *him* involved, or his henchmen.

I did, however, worry about those stoned creeps doing that to another woman. That was a major problem. They tried it with me; they would go after someone else. Clearly, I was not their first victim.

Would being shot teach them a lesson? I hoped so, but I doubted it. I had not shot to kill, they should be grateful for that. I could so easily have put them six feet under, and when I thought of their future victims, I wished I had. It's not in me to kill anyone, and that's what had prevented me from shooting them both through their brains.

I would not blame someone else for shooting them through their brains, though, not at all. And it could be argued that I had failed The Sisterhood. Had I killed them, this wouldn't happen to any other woman.

I didn't like failing The Sisterhood and I sat in that bleak failure for a long time. We women do have an obligation to each other, especially against vomitous and raging men.

I also thought about the police tracing this event to me.

I had had the .38 for years, same with the bullets. The man who gave it to me, Timmy Hutchinson, who I have known since I was a kid, was not exactly enamored with law following—none of the Hutchinsons were. It was unlikely that he had bought the gun from a legitimate dealer, but if the gun was traced to him—highly unlikely—there was no way he would tell a police officer he had given it to me.

But I didn't have only a gun problem. This was a small town. If my attackers told police that a red-haired woman shot them, it wouldn't take long to find me. If they went to a hospital, the doctors would call the police, as they do with all gunshot victims, unless they could concoct another story.

I wasn't too worried about their going to the police. I'd bet

my pounding heart that each of those monsters had a rap sheet.
If they went to the police and told on me, they knew I would tell
what they had done. Black masks. A smashed window. Pot, alcohol, attempted rape.

They'd be arrested, tried, and jailed.

They knew that. So what would they tell the doctors? It was
an accident?

Would they later track me down on their own? Would they
try to take revenge? That made my spine stiffen. They might.
And if they were following me, I wouldn't even know. I hadn't
seen their faces. They could even live here in town and start
stalking me once those shoulders were bandaged up.

I climbed into the backseat of my home-on-wheels. I opened
up the sleeping bag's zipper so I wouldn't get trapped again and
climbed in. It was too cold to sit in a car without covers. My
body shook, from cold and shock.

The black masks and that rope taunted me all night long. The
sound of my car window breaking into a million pieces played
again and again in my head, their singsong, vicious voices ping-
ponging through my fear.

I tried to think about painting or creating a collage.

All I saw was a blank, white canvas with bullets shot clean
through.

I ate the bacon and fruit at six in the morning. When
McDonald's opened I washed up as best I could in the bathroom. I brushed my hair and ignored the two light, white scars
near my hairline.

I wrapped my hair into a braid and put on makeup. My
bruises were almost completely gone, so I was glad about that.
My eyes looked exhausted, the lids heavy, the skin puffy. Even
the green color seemed dimmer. Whatever.

I wet my washcloth, added a little soap, and closed the door
of the bathroom stall. I washed the Big V and my rear while
squatting over the toilet. I had to. I had been so scared last
night, I squirted pee and I could smell it on myself. When no one
was in the bathroom, I pulled up my pants, rinsed out the wash-

cloth, went back in the stall, rinsed off the Big V over the toilet, dried off, then put my washcloth and towel back in their baggies. Gross.

You know you're on a slippery edge when you're cleaning your privates in McDonald's.

I would have to go to the Laundromat immediately.

I dried off, then put on fresh underwear, socks, jeans, a thick white sweater, and hoop earrings. It's extremely important to me that I don't appear homeless, washed up, and poor. I can't do it again. I washed my hands one more time, then headed out to the counter.

I bought a huge coffee, dumped in six creams, and sat in the back, hoping to disappear. I decided I could not eat another can of peaches, and I also deserved a treat for surviving last night, so after my coffee I drove to the grocery store and bought yogurt, with a coupon, milk, and two bananas, and I felt better. I also bought duct tape.

I used the plastic bag from my groceries to hold the glass I picked out of my car. I put one of my black plastic bags over the window and secured it with the duct tape. I poked a small hole through the center of it so I could see to the right, then drove around town, trying to find another place that might hire me. I needed a second job because I needed an apartment pronto.

I received my first check from Tildy, which was not large, but she'd told me in three months I'd get a two dollar an hour raise. "If you last that long with some of these turd mouths."

Waiters and waitresses are taxed at their regular tax rate and then another 8 percent of all the food they sell. This means our checks are pathetic. I did, however, have my tip money in my glove compartment, and it was adding up.

I drove about ten minutes outside of town and saw a sprawling brick building with corner-to-corner windows and a peaked roof, surrounded by lawn. The sign above two red barn doors said HENDRICKS' FURNITURE in black block lettering. There were pine and maple trees around the building, the leaves of the maples red, burgundy, and brown.

Aha! I knew about Hendricks' Furniture. They made high-quality, hand-carved, exquisite wood furniture. Built for log cabins, rustic mountain retreats, hotels, upscale fishing lodges, higher end restaurants, and homes whose wealthy owners could afford it. Hendricks' Furniture had been featured in many magazines and newspapers. It was expensive but totally worth it. It was furniture you would push out if your house caught fire.

I hadn't known that their headquarters was out here. This was dandy news.

I parked in the parking lot at the farthest end. I would wait until ten o'clock, then I would walk in and apply.

What could I tell a furniture store owner that I could do? I could sell their furniture on the floor. Did they do that? I could be a receptionist. I could take orders over the phone. I could . . . I could . . . could what? I could do marketing for them . . . advertising. Maybe. I could learn. I could cold call companies and see if they were interested in the furniture. I could not handle a saw, though—that was a fact, Jack—but I could learn.

I leaned back in my car seat thinking about my plan of attack so I could get hired. A day job and a night job, and soon I'd be paying off Cherie, my divorce attorney, and, more important, I'd have an apartment and would not have to worry about masked people crawling through my car doors intent on attacking my Big V.

As I no longer had a window, and no money to replace it because of the cost of my insurance deductible, my current disastrous financial/safety situation went up about ten dang notches.

I yawned. I was so tired. Shooting people takes a lot of energy. Rushes of spiking fear exhaust a body. Rage like what I felt last night strips one of all reserves. Fear that one could be stalked is also knee knocking.

But I was in front of a business. People were around. It was safe. I was wiped out.

I could sleep. For fifteen minutes. I could sleep.

7

This time when I heard the rap on my window, I automatically reached for my glove compartment with one hand and grabbed the door handle with the other. I was instantly awake, ready to fight.

The man rapping saw the stricken, perhaps murderous expression on my face, threw his hands up, and said, "It's okay, it's okay! I didn't mean to scare you!"

I exhaled. He was not one of the two previous diabolical devils. This one was tall, lanky, and blond. About forty years old.

I turned the ignition key and rolled down the window, trying not to pant.

"Ma'am, I'm sorry. I wanted to check on you. I've been eating lunch out here and you haven't moved, you've been still, and your windows are up, so I was wondering if you could breathe. I was worried. You okay? Can I help you?"

I took in a deep, deep breath, my heart hammering. "Yes, I'm fine. Thank you. I was . . . I was going to go in and apply for a job here, but I arrived too early and fell asleep." I pushed my hair back and forced myself to smile. "How embarrassing."

I didn't want him to peer in my backseat and see the sleeping bag and all the boxes, so I opened the car door rather quickly and climbed out.

"Hi. I'm Grenady." I stuck out my hand to shake his and shoved the door closed with my other hand.

"I'm Sam Jenkins." We shook. "It's a pleasure to meet you. You're new in town."

Sheesh. Was this town smaller than I thought? "It's a pleasure to meet you, too, Sam, and yes, I'm new in town." Sam seemed nice. Maybe he could help me get a job. Maybe he was the manager. He seemed confident, authoritative.

"And you're . . . I'm sorry. What did you say your name was?"

"Grenady Wild."

"Ah." He looked into space for a minute, then grinned. "I like it. Reminds me of grenadine. My kids love Shirley Temples. So, you need a job?"

"Yes, I do. Do you know if they're hiring?"

"I don't know. We might be. Hardly anyone ever quits here, though. The owner returned from fishing in Alaska with his buddies a couple days ago, so I know he's busy today, but come on in and I'll have you meet Bajal. She'll get you an application. She's hugely pregnant, though—over eight months today—so if she all of a sudden can't talk, don't worry. She's been getting Braxton Hicks contractions.

"She married a former NFL football player. He owns the quilt shop in town, but he's huge and she's only five two. A bitty thing. We've told her to take time off—Kade has, too—but she won't. Her husband insists she take time off. Every day, he comes in here and says, 'Quit, Bajal, right now,' and they have a fight in the lobby, but she won't do it. He's carried her out, twice, in his arms, but she's back in an hour."

I nodded. He talked fast, like he had to rush all his words out or they'd be taken away.

"Looks like your window decided to take off. Go to Billy and Billy's downtown. Husband and wife team. They're both named Billy, obviously. We call them Billy Squared. As in squared, the math problem?"

I smiled nervously. He smiled back. "Now, don't worry if you meet Kade Hendricks. He's not as scary as he looks. Everyone is petrified the first time they meet him. Maybe the second and third time, too." He pushed his hair back. "Okay, for a while they're petrified. He's tall, a few scars, and he doesn't smile much, but he's a good guy. Looks like a mafia man, but he's not."

A mafia man. Well, what did I care? I wanted a job.

As for the scars. Hey, I had more than a few, all over my body.

And I remembered how I got every one of 'em.

I sat down with Bajal, at her desk in the lobby, who did indeed have to stop talking for a minute while she leaned over and had a contraction. "Sorry about that."

"It's no problem at all," I said. But it was. I do not like seeing people in pain. It makes me ill. "Can I get you some water?"

"No, I'm fine." Bajal had black hair and huge dark eyes and was wearing a black, sleeveless maternity dress even though it was cold out. "This baby's gonna be huge. She's going to have a head the size of a tire. No, the size of a globe. No, the size of a watermelon. I'll have a watermelon-head kid."

"Your first?"

"Heck, no. It's my third. Can't keep my husband off me."

While she searched for an application, I took a quick peek around. The lobby had one full wall of windows next to the door, which let in a ton of light, and Bajal had a stunning wood desk—pine trees carved into the legs, a buck's head and antlers carved into the front—but the room was plain, functional only.

To the left of the large lobby was the factory. There was a door between us, and it muffled the saws somewhat but not completely. To the right of the lobby were offices and what looked to be an employees' lounge.

"Okeydokey, here's an application. I don't know if we're hiring, but we probably are, because this sucker baby is going to pop out any minute and Kade knows it. I may not come back at all, but don't tell anyone I said that." She wriggled her fingers. "I take it back. Everyone knows I'm not coming back. Kade does, too. I'm going to have three rug rats. I told my husband if I have to work after having this baby I'll be too tired to have sex, so he says I have to quit. He wanted me to quit a long time ago."

"Smart husband."

"This baby kicks my uterus like it's a punching bag, and she sits right on my bladder and I gotta go all the time."

I put a hand to my slightly sweating forehead as I pictured a kicked uterus.

"Fill out that application. You can do it here, sign it, and I'll have Kade look at it when he gets a chance. We don't put applications online because we get so many resumes all the time. You're new in town and you work at The Spirited Owl. I know that because my husband's friends told me there's a 'hot-looking'—their words—new bartender, and that's you. Welcome to Pineridge."

"Thank you."

"Too bad you weren't here earlier. You missed the quilt show."

"I heard that." They sure liked their quilt show.

"So you want two jobs?"

No. "Yes."

"That will be a lot of work."

I felt worn out thinking about it. "I can do it."

"Saving for something?" Bajal tilted her head. "I'm saving for a boob job. After nursing three kids, I think my boobs are gonna be in my armpits."

"Uh. Well. Good for you." I'm saving for my own toilet! "I'm saving for a home."

"Here I go again, here I go! Whew! Watermelon-Head Baby is moving. That head must be the size of a troll's—"

"Can I help you?" I so wanted to help her. I walked around the desk and put my hand on her back. I bent over with her. Her pain was making me dizzy. I dropped my head.

She didn't answer for fifteen seconds. "Thank you, but there's not much you can do to help unless I have the baby right here. If I do, don't let any of the men look up my crotch. You do it. Or get Rozlyn, the chief financial officer, to help you, or Eudora, love her, but no men. And not Marilyn." She said that name with dramatic angst. "She's been here a month. I can hardly stand that woman. She's like a blood-sucking tick who smiles at you before she sucks the life out of you. I can say that now because I'm quitting."

"Yes to Rozlyn and Eudora and no to all men, and Marilyn the tick, if you have this baby right here in this building."

"That's right. I could never look Kade in the eye again if he saw my vagina, especially with a head coming out of it. I mean, I love my husband, but Kade is, well, Kade is Kade."

"Got it. Never fear. If I have to push your dress up and take your underwear down on the first day we meet to help you get Watermelon-Head Baby out of you, I'll do it." She was clearly hurting. I wiped my forehead.

"Thanks," Bajal exhaled. "I think we're gonna be friends. Do you like to play Scrabble?"

"No." I was bad at Scrabble. Truly bad. I only used Scrabble letters in my collages. "How about if I take you to the hospital?"

"Not yet. I hate hospitals. They make me get the willy-jillies. Make sure you sign that application. I'll tell Kade you offered to help me give birth here. That'll help you. Shows initiative. Helpfulness. Courage. I mean, what woman truly desires to see a strange woman's vagina?"

"It's not first on my own personal list, but I would do it for you."

"You're a pal."

"Thank you."

Later that afternoon, I reached inside my glove compartment, pushed my gun aside, and pulled out a ceramic, shiny pink box with three dark pink roses on the lid. The gold clasp was in the shape of a heart. I had bought it for three dollars at an estate sale when I was twelve. It was in the home of a ninety-nine-year-old woman. I opened the box.

I called it the lily bracelet for the simple reason that there were lilies—purple, pink, and red with green leaves and a fake crystal in the center of each one. Each flower was surrounded by gold and clasped together.

When I was a little girl, my mother gave it to me. I remember the day clearly. My parents and I were at a lake, near a mountain. We had hiked in, leaving our VW yellow bus at the entrance. This was what we did most days. We camped. Often in a tent; sometimes in our bus. We stayed in different state parks and national parks and often in the middle of nowhere. In the winter, we drove to California and lived near the beach. My dad sang in bars and my mom sold her paintings out of the back of our van.

After we went swimming, my mom braided my hair and said, "I love you so much, Grenadine, and so does your daddy. We want you to have something special." I called her Mommy, but other people called her Freedom.

"It's your mother's, hummingbird daughter," my dad said, strumming his guitar, "but she wants you to have it." He liked to call me the names of animals and birds he loved. I called him Daddy, but other people called him Bear.

My mother took the lily bracelet off her wrist and wrapped it around my wrist three times. "See how it sparkles?"

"Hang on to it, unicorn girl," my dad said, giving me a kiss on the cheek. "Don't lose it."

That night we located the Big Dipper as we always did, unless it was cloudy, and ate pink cookies.

I knew later, as a young adult, that it was a pretty piece of costume jewelry, probably picked up at a street fair or a drug-store, but it was all I had of them.

I touched each lily. They had weathered well over the years. I loved the bracelet—it was my most treasured possession—but what I remember most about that day was my parents' love for me. Their hugs, their kisses on my cheeks.

I heard their voices again.

Run, Grenadine, run!

What happened to them?

Run, Grenadine, run!

I had not enjoyed my stay in the downtown jail at all.

The FBI came to arrest me at my home, Covey's home, hand-cuffs and all, and I was read my rights. They were polite but firm. They put me in the backseat of one of their nondescript cars and tried to talk to me in a conference room downtown. I have a low trust level for the police and authority figures, and I asked for an attorney. Twice. My exact words were, "If you think I'm talking to you without an attorney, then you are stupider than you look."

Then I went to jail.

I spent ten days there because of a small fighting problem.

It felt like a claustrophobic lifetime. A lifetime I had lived before, although technically I had not been in jail before, only Juvenile Hall, which is its own sticky, black, dangerous nightmare.

The intake area was light green. Think of a slimy light green. That is the color. Walls and floor, with a darker slimy green around doors.

I arrived in handcuffs. I was told to remove my jewelry and valuables and check off what I left there on a long yellow sheet. I took off the $10,000 wedding ring Covey gave me and checked off "ring." I checked off "earrings" for a pair of diamond studs. I also had silver bangle bracelets with tiny rubies, and my lily bracelet, which I wanted to kiss before I dropped it in the envelope but didn't because I didn't want to appear insane.

There was a white ribbon running through my white lace shirt, and I was told to take that off so I wouldn't use it to kill myself. Same with my belt with a silver buckle.

I signed the paperwork.

Another set of paperwork was filled out by one of the officers who brought me in. It listed all my vital stats: name, age, address, vehicle, height, weight.

I was fingerprinted. There's something about the way they roll your fingers that makes you feel like you're giving up on yourself right there. I was led to a small table by a sergeant with brown curly hair and gold hoop earrings and told to look straight ahead for my mug shot. I was then photographed after being told to look to the right at the red X.

While I had my photograph taken I listened to a man in one of four tiny cells screaming the f word every third word while he demanded his "American rights." I later learned those cells are for people who are flipping out; are filthy, as there's a shower in one cell and used by many homeless people; or have a contagious disease like tuberculosis.

I was then led to a person who was called "Medical," who asked many questions: What medications are you using? Have you ingested any drugs? Have you ever taken drugs? Were you raped or assaulted on a previous visit here? Is there someone we need to keep you separated from while in jail? Did I have any injuries or health issues?

While I answered questions, two gangbangers came in yelling, mostly at each other, and were forcibly separated. A woman was brought in with pink and blond hair and a bird tattoo on her neck. She was humming and wouldn't stop.

A man was dragged in front of me, head back, voice on full throttle, hair matted, vomit down the front of him. It was obvious he'd been out on the streets. They dragged him into the tiny cell with the shower. "Come on, Jeffy," one of the officers said, kindly. "Ya need a shower, dude, ya stink. Let's get you cleaned up."

Jeffy didn't want to get cleaned up because he knew the water was poisonous. He struggled again, then started crying and asking if his mother was here, and if not, could they call her. "Her name's Nance. Nance. My mom."

It was sad and pathetic.

I could not believe I was here.

I was told by the sergeant in charge of me to follow the black stripe on the floor to a large closet where they stored prison clothes. I was led to an open cubicle and told to strip. She was a no-nonsense, don't-mess-with-me sort of woman.

I took off all my clothes, my hands trembling so hard I could hardly manage. I was given a dark blue bag with a black zipper to put them in. She examined me front and back, then I was told to bend over, spread my butt, and cough.

I hesitated for a second, and she told me, again, "Turn around, bend over, spread them, cough."

It is impossible to describe how demeaning and vulnerable it feels to be naked, bent over, pulling your butt cheeks apart, and coughing while someone watches, so I won't try.

"People put all kinds of things up their human suitcases," she muttered.

Swing me a cat! "Up their *butts?*" She allowed me to turn around again.

"We see it all the time. Sometimes they hide it behind a tampon. That's why we don't allow tampons here."

Oh, gross. I hoped the curse would hold off another week. She gave me prison-issued light blue clothing, a top with a V, and pants. They looked like scrubs but were heavier, rougher. I also received a pink T-shirt, a pair of beige rubbery sandals, pink socks, pink underwear, and an ill-fitting pink bra. All had clearly been used a thousand times.

Each piece was stamped with the word JAIL.

When I was dressed like an inmate, she handed me a baggie with a toothbrush and toothpaste, paper, a flexible pen so I couldn't "use it as a weapon," deodorant, shampoo, and maxi pads.

She gave me two beige blankets, a bedroll, two sheets, a towel, and a pillowcase.

"Do male guards do this with women inmates?"

"Nope. Gender to gender. Let's go."

We walked back out. A TV was on. Men and women, inmates like me, were sitting in chairs, waiting. There were officials everywhere, in beige, in uniform, with stun guns and pepper spray containers. There was little air flow. No windows. The whole world was now gone.

There were cameras covering each inch of that building. You could not fart without someone knowing.

We stood in front of a steel, light green door. It did not open immediately. We had to wait for someone else to buzz us through. I heard the buzz. The door opened.

I thought about how much I hated Covey, then I put my shoulders back, put my tough lady face on, and gathered up my alpha personality. Jail is like the jungle. The weak are preyed upon.

I would not be weak.

I would not be prey.

* * *

My divorce attorney, Cherie Poitras, called me.

"How are you, Dina?"

"Not joyful."

"No, I don't suppose you are."

Cherie wears four-inch heels, animal prints, and black leather. Men fear her. She likes it.

She rides a motorcycle and currently has four foster kids, which made me like her from the start. She has an edge and had a lousy childhood. We got along.

I met her when she commissioned a mural from me. I showed her a design I thought she might like. It was a woman holding a bow and arrow. The bow and arrow were authentic. I'd attached it to the canvas and to the plywood under the canvas. Surrounding the bow and arrow were flowers I'd made out of beads, as if they were flowing gracefully through on a wind stream. The whole ethereal effect was an interesting juxtaposition to the man running in the distance, away from the bow-and-arrow-shooting woman.

Most of her clients are divorcing women, and they are unhappy. Perhaps that explains the collage best.

She put the collage on the opposite wall from a sign stating her company's motto: Poitras and Associates: We'll Kick Some Ass For You.

Cherie told me about her strategy to "rack Covey's genitalia."

"I will get this done for you, Dina. This is gonna be fun. You know, fun like you and I have when we go to target practice. Shooting fun."

Shooting fun. I knew who I wanted to shoot.

On Saturday morning, jittery, anxious, I grabbed my sketch pad and a black charcoal pencil and drew a girl in a closet, her arms over her head, semiburied behind clothes and shoes, a rat in the corner.

I drew another picture of her with a leash on her neck, being dragged.

I drew her alone in a forest.

I drew her in the hospital, unconscious.

I drew quick, angry, panting, biting my lip.

When I was done, I felt like there was nothing left in me.

I have tried burying my past.

It doesn't work.

This is how I push it back.

They had all called and e-mailed many times.

"It's our Grenadine!" I heard her shout when she picked up the phone. "On this here telephone, by hell! That Covey is a sick possum, and I want to run over him with my truck. You come on home to us. No one can come and get you here. We'll hide ya. Right, boys?"

I heard them shoot off their guns in the background, yelling their agreement that Covey was a "dead man" and a "skunk-shooting loser" and "By shots and by fire, we're gonna smash him with the tractors when he's not lookin'!"

I made the second call after the first. She cried when she heard my voice. "I love you, baby. Come here and live with me."

I told her I couldn't. I needed to be out of town, and I didn't need her, or them, harassed by the press. It wouldn't look right for me to hang out with felons, either, unfortunately.

I bent my head and sobbed. Love will do that to you sometimes.

There were a lot of martinis and daiquiris ordered on Monday night at The Spirited Owl. Plus beer. Rivers of beer.

Two men hit on me. I actually saw one eye me up and down, smile, then, when I turned away, he took off his wedding ring and slipped it into his coat. I saw what he was doing via the mirror behind the bar. What a jerk. When he said to me, "How about dinner, Miss Green Eyes?" I said, "Get your wife on the phone. Let's ask her first. If she says yes, my answer is still no, because I find you sneaky and weasel-like, but I am curious about her opinion."

The men around him laughed. He weaseled off that barstool.

The other man was polite, asked to take me to coffee. "Ah, coffee," I said. "So you don't think I'm worth dinner?"

He backed up, asked me to dinner. I smiled. "Thank you, but no. And remember, if you want to impress a woman, ask her to dinner. And pay for it."

It's degrading to be hit on all the time as a bartender. It's not flattering. It doesn't boost my ego. These men, for some asinine reason, think that a bartender is easy game. Probably because I serve them drinks and listen to them. To them that equals, for some ball-knocking reason, that I must be attracted to them.

Men are so clogged in the head sometimes I want to bang their heads together and let their brains crawl away.

I also heard the usual complaints from various men:

One slug of a man said, "Women are so picky. If you don't look like Brad Pitt or you're not rich, they don't want you."

I said, "No, they don't want you, Marley, because you look like you have a baby in your stomach, you're unshaven, you drink too much, and all you want to do is talk about yourself and whine in that whiny voice of yours. Would you be attracted to you? No? Then why would a woman be?"

He stared at me, eyes wide in his big, bald head, then said, slowly. "By God, you might be right, Grenady."

"I am right."

The next complaint was a ringer, to which I showed a boat-load of compassion: "My wife's always complaining because she don't get no free time cause of the kids."

"How many kids do you two have?"

"Five."

I slammed a pitcher of beer down. My anger is always simmering. "You're here every night and you're complaining about your wife because she says she needs free time? You must be joking, Selfish One. What do you think you're doing here? Working?"

"Uh. No."

"You're having free time. I dare you to let your wife come sit at this bar and you go home and take care of the kids."

"I don't want my wife here! There's a whole bunch of men here."

"Why don't you go home and love your wife before she discovers there's a whole bunch of men here and chooses one to live with who is not *you?*"

His face paled.

"You think she won't do that? You think she won't fall in love with some other man simply because she said 'I do' to you years ago when she was young and not thinking rationally? She said a vow and you think that will keep your wife from leaving some jackass husband who goes to a bar like a liquor leech and talks behind her back?"

"Uh."

"Uh yourself. Ask yourself an easy question: What are you doing to keep your wife in love with you? What?"

"I'm her husband!"

"Big deal. I can assure you that part is not impressive. All you have to have to be a husband is a marriage license and a dick. Yours is probably small, but she signed the paper, poor woman. You should do what you can to prevent her from signing another piece of paper saying you are now her ex-husband because her life would be easier without you. Now, good-bye." I took his beer. "Tip first, Selfish One."

He gave me a five and scuttled on out.

Tildy came up behind me. "I believe you're teaching the men some life skills."

"Never too late to learn." I took a deep breath and buried my flying temper.

"I grew up on a ranch, and I'd call some of the men we deal with in here Buzzard Kill."

"As in buzzards would kill them?"

"As in that's about what they're worth." She knocked on the bar with her knuckles. "You know, Kade Hendricks made this bar for me. It's my most prized possession. Kade himself gave me a deal on it because he likes my Blue Stallion Crunch. I always make his burger myself, to thank him for this." She bent and kissed the bar. "Exquisite."

"I hope he hires me."

"Betcha he will, Grenady. You work hard." She crossed her arms and laughed. "But do not try to cut that man down to size like you do with some of the men in here. That man's a man, and he would not take kindly to that."

"Thanks for the insight."

"My pleasure." She got her gun out to clean it again.

That night, buried under my blankets and sleeping bag, I thought about my little green home, the house I owned before I met Covey. I sold it after we were married, when he pushed, because I was in love and grossly irrational.

It was small, maybe a thousand square feet, in a Portland neighborhood that was somewhat edgy, on the poor and ramshackle side here and there, but many of the houses were being remodeled and repainted, and new shops were going in nearby, so it was up and coming.

My home was about eighty years old, with old-fashioned built-in bookshelves, a built-in dresser, and a white fireplace surrounded by shiny, emerald green tile. When I ripped up the stained, gray carpets I found untouched wood floors.

There were three tiny bedrooms downstairs, in addition to the family room and kitchen, but I had walls knocked out to open it all up, leaving one small bedroom in the back for me. I painted all the walls white. I painted the kitchen cabinets azure blue; added beige laminate counters; and put in two blue, red, and yellow pedestal lights that resembled stained glass.

My studio was the whole upstairs under a peaked roof. I called it my attic studio. I filled it with two long work tables and two easels. I painted two tall bookcases turquoise and filled them with books on art, artists, and artists' studios, which I rarely read, but I loved the photos.

I painted two shorter bookcases red and pushed them up against the two large windows on either side of the room. They were perfect for my flowering plants and bonsai trees. I had two wood dressers—one pink, one green—for supplies; two small wood tables that could be moved as needed; and three wood

chairs in purple, green, and yellow. I had a few of my own collages on the walls, the ones that didn't disturb me.

I also had boxes, jars, and plastic containers full of paints,
brushes, pencils, pastels, buttons, coins, chalk, sparkly jewelry
from Goodwill, sequins, beads, yarn, string, shells, dice, game
pieces, wood letters, dollhouse furniture, rocks, broken glass,
lace, and a bunch of other things. (No rope. No bits of rope. I
don't use rope in my art, ever.)

I had fabric stacked up and wicker baskets filled with sewing
supplies next to my sewing machine. I had a comfy red chair
and a flowered footstool by one of the windows so I could sit
and think and sketch. I had a stack of newspapers, magazines,
sheet music, old books, and colorful wallpaper.

I lit candles with names like Blueberry Dazzle, Cinnamon
Crunch, and Tangerine Apple on cool days.

I had two skylights put in when I had to replace the roof after
the rain came through like a waterfall late one night. I had recessed lights in the ceiling, but I also bought three lights and
decorated the lampshades in red and yellow fabrics and ribbons.

My canvases were stacked up against a wall. I don't work
small. My smallest canvas is four by four, a perfect square; most
are much larger. It is not unusual for me to create collages and
paintings on eight-by-ten-foot canvasses.

I would work on my art for hours each day. I'd wake up in
the morning, not bother to change out of my T-shirt and flannel
pants, and work until the sun went down. I would be lost. All
else—my past, my problems, my anxiety—gone.

I had clients come to my home, and we talked in my studio
about the painting or collage they wanted. I had tea and coffee
and cream (whipping cream, regular cream), sugar, and cookies
out. They loved coming. One woman said, "You are living the
life I always wanted to live." They would write me a check and
return when their collage was done. I never had a client who
wasn't delighted.

I painted the exterior of my home green, like the inside of an
avocado, with white trim and bought a white picket fence for
the front. I had always wanted a white picket fence because it

said Home. For two days after the fence was in, I sat on my front porch and cried. My own home!

I had a huge oak tree in the front yard and three maples in the back. So many of my collages had those trees in them.

I planted roses for him, daisies and lilies for them, and I filled clay pots with petunias, marigolds, and geraniums in the spring and summer and mums in the fall. My neighbors gave me clippings, and I planted those, too. I loved gardening and watching plants, trees, and flowers grow.

My green home had a porch out front, which is how I met the neighborhood kids. They would come and watch me paint and draw. Pretty soon I was setting out paints, colored pencils, and pastels for them each Wednesday. They'd run to my house after school, I'd serve milk and cookies, we'd head up to my attic studio, and I'd give them an art lesson.

They loved it. Their parents loved it. A few started coming by each week to help me.

I missed my little green home. I missed my roses, lilies, and daisies; my picket fence; my studio. I missed the funny, happy kids and how much they loved the art lessons.

Leaving my green home was a Herculean mistake. I had created my own world in that house, something I was often not able to do as a child, and I went into someone else's world.

I think it's important to be able to look back on your life and figure out where you blew it all to hell so you don't do it again.

I blew it there.

I heard thunder roll overhead and saw a flash of lightning. The mountains and the forest weren't far away. I tried not to think of the forest, those tall, shadowy trees, the maze within them. My back tingled in remembrance and I pulled the sleeping bag over my head.

8

He pulled on his hair. He liked pulling his hair out, one or two strands at a time. It released the pain.

He decided to write another nursery rhyme in his rhyme book.

> Hickory, dickory, dock,
> The lady ran up the clock.
> The clock struck three,
> The woman screamed,
> Hickory, dickory, dock.
>
> Hickory dickory dock.
> She's dead.
> No head.
> He's dead.
> No heart.
> Hickory dickory dock.
> That's all there is to start.

He drew a picture of a mouse with a woman's head and red hair. He put one of his own hairs on the woman's head. He giggled. He was so funny.

9

I picked up an old newspaper left on a table at McDonald's. I'd had my morning mini-wash-up in their sink, and in their stall, and was holding my morning caffeine blast, my body slouched like an old sloth in a booth.

I scanned the headlines but did not try to read them closely: a storm on the East Coast; the same serial killer and his appeal of his death sentence, which made me oddly nervous; and Washington, DC's continual problems because the politicians don't do what's right for America but what's right for them and their campaign contributors. The usual.

I found what I didn't want to find, however. There was a police report about my incident with the masked attackers the other night.

In summary, shots were heard at night in a deserted parking lot, where Sylvester Family Furniture used to have their store. By the time police arrived, there was no one there. Police recovered a stolen vehicle with shots through the windows, the side of the car, and a tire. There were other bullets. There were no cameras on the property, as the furniture business was long gone. If anyone knew anything, please contact the police, etc.

I used my phone to look up other articles. I Googled two men, shot, hospital.

And there they were.

Those masked terrors had gone to a hospital in Marvelle River, an hour away. Who knows how they arrived, as their stolen car was disabled. Maybe they hitchhiked. That made me laugh. The suffering would have been intense. They probably thought they were going to die. They might have, too. They could have bled out. But they had time to concoct their story.

The article said that the two men, Jason Halloren and Turley Alquar, addresses unknown, got into a fight and shot each other after a struggle over a gun. The article said that they had been arguing over the gun and it had gone off first at Jason, then Turley. Turley admitted to throwing the gun in the river so "Jason couldn't shoot off his other shoulder." I could tell by the way the article was written that the reporter didn't believe it, and neither did the police, who were also quoted and said there were "many, many unanswered questions."

I looked at their mug shots. They were in their midtwenties. They were white with messy brown hair. They were pale, probably from those darn bullets and a drug-filled life. Jason had narrow pig eyes and heavy lids, and Turley's were plain dead, mean.

They were arrested for aggravated assault—on each other. I laughed.

They would be going to jail. There were warrants out for both of them because of long arrest records including, but not limited to: Assault. Menacing. Harassment. Robbery. Drug possession and dealing. They both had restraining orders against them by a total of four different women. Jason had a son and daughter, and Turley had a daughter. Those children would be better off without their fathers, as would the mothers of the children.

This was delightful news. I hoped they would be assaulted, menaced, harassed, and robbed of whatever money they had to buy their cigarettes in jail.

I wondered if the Pineridge and Marvelle River police would put the two together. A shelled car and two men who'd shot each other. They probably would. They might have already. The dead-eyed scum would stick to their story, except they might include that they shot up the stolen car, too. They would not involve me. Attempted rape and kidnapping would be added if they did and they knew it. They were career criminals. They were probably scared out of their pants that I would report what happened.

I felt mucho better. They would not be stalking me. They would be locked up. The Sisterhood was safer.

Tildy had a shower in the back of the restaurant. I was getting semidesperate. I asked her if I could use it. She eyed me carefully, something flashed in her eyes, and I figured she knew I was homeless. She said, "You go right ahead, sugar."

The bathroom was pristinely clean and decorated in blues with a cowgirl theme. The shower was large, the sink sitting in an antique side table. Tildy had obviously remodeled it. She lived above the bar. I had not been up there, but based on the bathroom, and based on the homey, lodgey feel to the restaurant, and because she's a classy, tough lady, I figured it was a haven from the craziness of work.

I washed my hair using the Passion's Delight mango shampoo and strawberry-scented cream rinse she had in there. I felt guilty about using her stuff, but I had worked hard, the night wasn't easy, and I had dried sweat, fried food, beer, and a whiskey sour on me.

I dried off with my own towel and brushed my hair out. I put lotion on my face, brushed my teeth, and left after I said good night to Tildy and the chefs. It was a friendly group, and I was glad.

"You have a minute?" Tildy said.

I braced myself. I knew what she was going to ask. That's why I hadn't asked to use her shower before this.

"Where you stayin', Grenady? I've asked you before, but you skate away like oil on a hot frying pan."

"Why do you want to know? Do you want to sit down and have tea and crumpets?"

She crossed her arms.

"I have a place to stay."

Silence.

"You can stay with me until you get yourself settled," she said, her voice quiet. "I have an extra bedroom."

"Thank you, no." I heard an edge to my voice. I always prickled at "help." I did not need help. I can do things on my own. I can fix my own problems. Besides, help always comes with unwanted, sticky strings. You feel beholden to someone else, like you owe them, or as if you should be eternally grateful and thankful and kiss their butt. They're above you then, too. They have the power and you're weaker.

Been there, done that. No way. It was partly why I didn't see if there was a homeless shelter in town. I don't want to be in a shelter. I don't need charity. I don't need help. I don't want to stay in someone else's home again.

We locked eyes. Two stubborn women. Tildy is a woman who has seen a lot of life, and she would not intrude on my life. When I filled out the application, I had a valid social security number and a bartending license. I don't know if she later ran a criminal background check or a credit check. I don't know what she did or didn't do. My guess is nothing. She knew people.

"Thank you, anyhow." I made myself sound softer, not so ungrateful.

"Anytime. See you tomorrow."

I could tell she understood.

The first painting I sold, for fifty dollars, when I was seventeen, was of lilies. I painted them upside down, the stems hanging from the top. The lilies were golden yellow, lush pink, soft orange, drawn to the tiniest detail. On the bottom of the canvas I painted a knife with a snake wrapped around it stuck straight into the edge of the canvas. Beauty and terror, mixed. I was told a man bought it who owned a knife and gun shop.

When I'm stressed, I draw and paint lilies. I have sold hundreds of paintings and collages with lilies somewhere in them.

In one lily collage, I painted a huge glass bottle. Inside the bottle was a storm at sea. The black and blue paint was superthick, waving like the waves. I added a pirate's ship, listing to the side. I found a miniature captain's wheel and used sticks to form part of the mast, black fabric for the sails, and mirrors for the windows below deck.

I also painted rocks and a lighthouse. The lighthouse was tilting as if it was being blown over, but somehow I drew it to appear threatening, ominous. *Where is that lighthouse,* I asked myself. *Where?* Then I asked, What did it matter anyhow? It didn't. But it did. Lighthouses are supposed to guide and illuminate. My lighthouse offered nothing but darkness. Was it from that night?

Around the bottle I painted lilies. The buyer, who said he had an ancestor who was a pirate, said it looked like the lilies were alive and going to eat the bottle.

Once I painted an eight-foot-tall white calla lily on a nine-foot canvas. I outlined the whole flower with gold, shimmery paint. I put tiny gold flecks of glitter in the center. That was it. One huge lily that looked like it wanted to talk. A hotel bought it when one of their employees saw it at a show I had at the local college and commissioned twenty more.

I lost myself in lilies. Sometimes it was sweet, sometimes it made me emotional, but the world was gone and it was me and the lilies only.

I often make collages in which I put something that is troubling me. Like the knife or the lighthouse or fog or a forest. I feel compelled. I must do it. Sometimes I hate it, but I must add those dark, painful questions to the canvas.

I have many questions.

Bajal called me the next day from Hendricks' Furniture when I was sitting on a park bench like so many homeless people do. I was, however, trying hard not to look homeless. I was wearing my red coat, a scarf with a swirly pattern, and earrings with three silver hoops each. One of the hardest parts about being homeless is finding somewhere to be all day. It's exhausting having to wander. You can go to the library, a mall, or a park. Unless it's snowing. Then the park's a problem.

I had my sketch pad on my lap, drafting the next collage I would make when I had my own table. I drew four glass, rectangular terrariums next to each other. On the inside of each terrarium I drew glass balls that I would later watercolor with vivid colors. The weather in each terrarium would be different—fall, winter, spring, summer. I would use the pages of books I'd bought at garage sales to make cutouts of snowflakes for winter, fall leaves, spring raindrops, and a garden for summer.

"Hi, Grenady!"

"Hello, Bajal." I crossed my fingers. "How are you?"

She was still pregnant. Kade was too busy to see me until next Wednesday at one-thirty.

"You'll be applying for my position. He'll tell you it's temporary, but it won't be. I'm outta here. You'd be great for the job. I already told him I liked you. Oh, hang on, Grenady. Braxton Hicks . . . hold on . . . hold on . . . whoo, whoo . . . popping melon, Watermelon-Head Kid. I hope I don't need another episiotomy. There's something worrisome about a knife so close to my ya ya. You know what I mean?"

"No, but yes." Listening to Bajal holding her breath, her voice tight, made me feel woozy. I put my colored pencils down.

"Anyhow, Kade's a straight talker. Be up-front, honest, tell him what you can do to help the company. You know what you can do, right?"

"Yes." Not really. "I hope."

"Tell him about your office skills, people skills, organizational talents. You have those, right-o?"

"Yes." No. That was a partial lie. I have no office skills. I have never worked in an office. I like some people, others not. I'm instinctually a loner and have major trust issues with other humans. I am rigidly organized, though.

"Computer skills?"

"Yes." Basic. I am quite talented at e-mail.

"Don't be scared of him. I mean, at least try not to be scared. You will, but hide it."

"I'll give it my best shot."

"It's a girl."

"Pardon?"

"It's a girl. She's kicking me all over. It's a rebel. A bloomin' rebel . . . okay, see you after I have my feet clamped in stirrups, a knife an inch from my ya ya."

Whew. That image made me close my eyes in fright for her.

We chatted more about the baby and her pregnancy, then she regaled me with how she gave birth to the first kid without an epidural because he came too quick—"the stinker ripped me wide open"—and the second kid was "butt down." "I was screaming, I thought I was dying, they had to cut me open like a fish."

I doubled over on the park bench. Now I felt nauseated. "Thank you, Bajal, for recommending me. I mean it. I appreciate this so much." My forehead was sweating.

"You seem like a nice lady and I hope Kade hires you. Hang on . . . here it comes again . . . whoo whoo whoo. Good-bye nice, neat vagina, you're about to be shredded and bloody again."

On that, we rung off. I put my hand over my mouth, breathed. Breathed again.

Poor Bajal. Poor, poor Bajal.

10

Children's Services Division
Child's Name: Grenadine Scotch Wild
Age: 6
Parents' Names: Freedom and Bear Wild (Location unknown)
Date: July 5, 1982
Goal: Adoption
Employee: Wanda Turgood

After three weeks in Raymond and Lennie Chang's medical foster home, Grenadine seems to have made a full physical recovery from her concussion except she is still too thin and is having trouble eating because of stress.

Emotionally she is traumatized and cries often, according to the Changs. She is asking for her parents and begging to talk to the police about them. I told her the police were doing all they could.

The police have talked to Grenadine several times. She told the police that they had to search harder to find her parents and she said they were bad at their jobs, then she apologized.

She will be placed with Tom and Adelly Berlinsky.

The Berlinskys have two boys, age ten and twelve, and live in a ranch home in the country. Father is a trucker, mother is a stay-at-home mother. This is their first year as foster care parents, and they seemed pleased to have Grenadine. I know they are hoping to adopt a little girl.

Her new case worker is Connie Valencia.

Children's Services Division
Child's Name: Grenadine Scotch Wild
Age: 6
Parents' Names: Freedom and Bear Wild (Location unknown)
Date: August 8, 1982
Goal: Adoption
Employee: Connie Valencia

I visited Grenadine today at the Berlinsky family home. She seems happy, although she looks kind of thinnish and has circles under her eyes, a purplish color, and bumpy bug bites on her arms.

She wanted to know if we'd found her parents. I said no. I told her the police are still looking. I don't like to lie to a child. Poor thing.

Because of the trauma she has experienced, I am not concerned that she cried when I was there at the house with her and seemed scared and skinny as a skeleton. (Not really a skeleton! That's an expression!)

I tried to calm her down. She was in a pretty pink, long-sleeved dress with a ruffle, white tights, and shiny white shoes. She said she didn't like her clothes because they itch.

Mrs. Berlinsky did not leave her side at all during the visit while I asked Grenadine questions about how she was doing and what she was doing. She said she was making paintings for her parents because they're lost (she thinks). The paintings were actually super duper. One was of three birdies flying. Each of the birdies had one of those T-shirts on with all the hippie colors on it.

The others were of a family of smiley raccoons in a tree, the dad raccoon had a beard and the mom raccoon had a red shawl. And the other painting had a girl deer with lilies around her neck. Pretty!

She showed me her bedroom. She has a pink bedspread and a white table and dresser. I asked her if she was excited to go to school in the fall, but she said she wasn't going to school and that her parents taught her all the school she needed. She is a funny child.

She looked at Mrs. Berlinsky a lot, so I think the happy bond is growing.

I inquired with Mrs. Berlinsky if Grenadine had been to the doctor for a checkup recently, and she said it was on her schedule for 'to do' next week, and I asked if she had made the appointment with the counselor, and she said she would do that, too, that they were getting Grenadine all settled down, welcoming her to the home.

The home looks messy, but Adelly assured me it was because she had been sickly with pneumonia. The father had left for another two-week trip for his trucking job, which Mrs. Berlinsky thought was good because he gives so much attention to Grenadine, the boys were getting jealous. Boys get jealous like that!

Grenadine is flourishing like a sunny flower in this home, except for a few bruises, which Mrs. Berlinsky says is from all of her playing and skipping and hopping around outside that Grenadine is doing. The family has two dogs, a cow, goats, chickens, and three kitty cats.

She is young and will get over her parents leaving her.

Connie Valencia

Children's Services Division
Child's Name: Grenadine Scotch Wild
Age: 6
Parents' Names: Freedom and Bear Wild (Location Unknown)
Date: November 14, 1982
Goal: Adoption
Employee: Connie Valencia

I visited with Grenadine today. She wanted to know where her parents were, if they had been found, and I said no, they weren't found, not yet, but the police were looking. She cried and she still looks thin like a skeleton (That's an expression!) and pale. I asked Mrs. Berlinsky if the child had been taken for her checkup and she said no, so we had a long and prickly disagreeable fightlike conversation about that.

The other two children, the boys, were teasing Grenadine. One of them called her "their pet dog." The other one called her "Ruff Ruff." I told the boys, "Don't be naughty!" Grenadine kept leaning towards me. I think she's still shy of the boys. I had two brothers and I felt shy around them too, sometimes!!

I talked with Mrs. Berlinsky about the teasing, and she told me she would talk to the boys. She says that Grenadine is a good girl but all she wants to do is art projects, so she asked that we buy art supplies for her, but I told her that the supplies can be bought with the money she is paid monthly for the child. Mrs. Berlinsky said she couldn't afford to buy the child crayons, and we had another prickly fightlike conversation.

There are marks around Grenadine's neck, but Mrs. Berlinsky said it was because she'd helped Grenadine make a necklace of flowers and branches and a buzzing bee stung her. Grenadine has bruising on the arms, but Mrs. Berlinsky says the children play and skip around outside a lot, climbing in the loft of the barn, over the fence to the meadow, and playing in the stream.

Grenadine's hair seemed thinner, but I think it's because it was back in a ponytail, like a little horse.

Grenadine is doing well in this home, I think, and this placement is healthy and safe. I am not healthy, though! This darn cold. Sorry I've missed so much work lately! Poor me.

Connie Valencia

Children's Services Division
Child's Name: Grenadine Scotch Wild
Age: 7 (I think!)
Parents' Names: Freedom and Bear Wild (Location Unknown)
Date: February 16, 1983
Goal: Adoption
Employee: Connie Valencia

I visited Grenadine and she is thriving in the home.

Children's Services Division
Child's Name: Grenadine Scotch Wild
Age: 7 (Seven years old!)
Parents' Names: Freedom and Bear Wild (Location Unknown)
Date: May 26, 1983
Goal: Adoption
Employee: Connie Valencia

I visited Grenadine and she is thriving, in this home.

Connie Valencia

Children's Services Division
Child's Name: Grenadine Scotch Wild
Age: 7 (Still seven!)
Parents' Names: Freedom and Bear Wild (Location Unknown)
Date: October 22, 1983
Goal: Adoption
Employee: Connie Valencia

I visited Grenadine and she is thriving in that home Berlinsky.

Connie Valencia

The Oregon Journal
CSD Case Worker Inebriated, Arrested On Highway

November 8, 1983
By Rolando Krawchek

A case worker with the Children's Services Division was arrested at two o'clock Wednesday afternoon by police. Her car was weaving back and forth across the freeway and reached speeds of eighty miles per hour before crashing into a guardrail. She was arrested after she failed field sobriety tests and taken to the hospital in an ambulance when she passed out.

Case worker Connie Valencia had alcohol, pot, and cocaine in her system. She had one of the children she supervises in the car. That child, a seven-year-old boy, sustained a concussion, broken ribs, and a broken ankle. He spent the night in the hospital but is listed in stable condition. His biological mother has said she will sue CSD from her cell in Teal Creek Correctional Institution.

Valencia was charged with driving under the influence, reckless driving, and endangering a minor child.

11

I will never forget how I found out Covey was a lying, cheating scum eater.

I was finishing a collage in my upstairs studio for a woman named Divinity Star, who was coming by that day to pick it up. Divinity is the chief accountant of a computer firm during the day, where she goes by the name Ellen Horowitz, but in her after hours she believes she is living her fourth lifetime. She belongs to a group of ditzy women who also believe they have past lives.

In her previous lifetimes Divinity was a peasant in Russia who inspired a minirebellion and was then burned at the stake (which is why Divinity says she doesn't like fire), a French baker who hid people behind his loaves of bread during the French Revolution (which is why Divinity says her bread-making skills are magical), and a Canadian with royal lineage (which might explain her self-indulgent and entitled personality).

She asked me to attend one of her meetings with other people with multiple lives the first time I met her to plan her collage.

"You're kidding, right?" I said. "I don't want to know what I did in past lives. I've had enough of this one."

She tilted her head, a pained, patronizing expression on her face like, "You are naïve. You are closed-minded," then patted my arm, as if I were a dumb pet. "That's a shame you don't want to know your true self."

"Who are you to tell me what I want and don't want?" My tone was sharp, and I knew it.

"Women should know their true, eternal, ethereal selves." Divinity flapped her hands like she was a magical fairy. "We have to know what's happened before this journey, the dangers and passionate lovers, the adventures and murders and lessons and rendezvous. I want you to know the core of yourself, deep inside, Dina. I'm sorry you won't take that step with me."

"Hey, Divinity," I told her, pointing a purple pencil in her direction. "If you want to believe in this celestial, past-life, fantasy-fluff crap, go ahead, but don't be condescending to me because I don't believe I've been recycled through the last two thousand years."

Her mouth dropped, the ethereal image vanishing. "I'm sorry, Dina. I didn't mean it like that."

"Good." I am sensitive to people trying to undermine me or yank me down to the rung below them on the ladder. My place on the ladder is precarious enough as it is. "If you did, that would be irritating."

"I wanted you to be interested in who you were before—"

"Come on, Divinity. I don't have paint for brains, and neither do you. Cut it with the fairy dust." I took out a handful of colored pencils and tapped them on the table. "I have twenty-six people who have already paid me for a collage and would like to take your place or the place of anyone else, including the Russian and the Frenchman, in your previous lives, today. Do you want to talk about your collage or not?" Like all my other clients she had to write me a check—that cleared—before I even started.

"Oh, no no no! We all want to be here. I mean"—she coughed—"I want to be here." Her shoulders slumped, and she stared at her red heels with the sparkly bows. Right then I knew she didn't believe in her past lives either, but it was part of her identity. How she reached out to others . . . and how she felt superior to them.

"Glad to hear it. So let's talk about your collage like two people in this decade."

"Perfect. Let's," she gushed, her tone suddenly normal, not

light and wispy. "I can't wait. Thank you, Dina. I've been on your waitlist a long time."

Divinity wanted a carousel, complete with bears and lions and fancy horses. "It's what I loved to do in my childhood," she said. "Ride the carousel and dream, dream, dream!"

As in, I thought, you dreamed about who you wished to be, past and future.

On a six-by-four-foot canvas I had painted a grand carousel with gold, shiny paint. I cut up fabric to make the animals, gold satin for the lions, gray and black and white felt for the horses, and brown felt for the bears, so the animals all had texture. The bridles were made from brown yarn that I painted with a touch of gold. The saddles were pieces of cut leather with glitter on the saddle horns.

I found tiny mirrors and attached them, too, along with gold braid, which I used to outline the entire carousel. I glued on shiny, glittery beads and shook on a liberal amount of glitter.

I was almost done.

I was completing the finishing touches, gluing blue beads along a mermaid's tail, adding fake hair for the horses' manes, and placing rows of sequins along the bottom of the carousel. As I glued on each sequin, I finalized my plans to leave Covey. As soon as Divinity picked this up, I would pack up and go. Last night was it. What he'd done was inexcusable. I was done.

When I was in the middle of braiding the fake hair for the brown horse, I turned on the TV. Now and then I'll watch a talk show to prove to myself that there are people crazier than me out there.

The news came on and I hardly listened until I heard Covey's name. I watched, through a fizzy, fuzzy fog of shock as my husband, in one of his six expensive gray suits, hands cuffed behind his back, was put into the back of a police car and driven off.

I dropped the braided tail.

When the police came for me, I was still sitting, the braided tail under my foot.

*   *   *

That night a man named Moose Williams came in again to The Spirited Owl. I met him the first week I was here. When Tildy introduced us he shook my hand, smiled and blushed.

He's come in many times since then. He sits in the same chair, near my workstation, and talks to me. He is quite . . . pleasant.

Moose Williams has red hair and is probably three or four years older than me. His grandfather's father was born here. He has a million cousins. His family owns property in town, and a ranch, according to Tildy.

"He's an honest man, Grenady," she told me. "Gentle. Smart. Wife left him ten years ago because she couldn't tolerate small-town living. I always thought of her as The Princess. He doesn't mess around like a horny tomcat, he's respectful no matter who ya are, and he's employed. Handles his family's business. Most of the time he's on the restaurant side with his family. He only started coming to the bar like a lovesick cow when you arrived."

Moose reminded me of a soft, safe Ferris wheel. The ride was pleasant, exciting at the top, but you didn't need to do it again. I wasn't interested.

"I've seen him watching you." Tildy pushed that white streak back. "He likes you. You gonna say yes if he asks you out?"

"Nope, I won't."

"Don't like men?"

There was no judgment in her voice. I appreciated that. "I like men. Sometimes. Now and then. If you're asking if I like women, no. I don't want a girlfriend. The thought of touching another woman's boobs nauseates me, although I have no problem if another woman feels differently. The nauseated part, though, prevents me from being gay."

"Me too, darlin'," Tildy said, hanging wineglasses upside down on a rack above our heads. "I like men in a physical sense, a roll in the hay settles out my stress and gives me a lift, but anything with a penis is suspect. Their brains lodge down there when they're in their teens and don't rise much higher their whole life."

"You take Moose, Tildy. Go ride that bronco."

"Too young for me."

"Give me a break. He's forty if he's a day."

She winked. "I'm a cougar now and then, I admit it. Growl!" She wriggled her claws. "But I'd send him home packin' in the morning, like I do the rest of them. I need my space, and I don't need a man invading it except to suit my purpose."

Moose struck me as the type of man who was shy with women but tried hard to overcome the shyness. I think I made him more shy. "Hello, Grenady," he'd said the first night I met him. "I'm Moose Williams. Moose is not my birth name."

"I didn't think it was. I cannot imagine a mother naming her son Moose."

"Nah. She didn't. It was my older brothers. They called me Moose because they said I always butted them with my head. Hence, Moose. My name is Beau Williams. It's actually Beau Williams the fourth, but that makes me sound both pompous and ridiculous."

I laughed. "What can I get you?"

He had me get him one of the local beers, then asked me a couple more questions about myself: Where was I from, which I answered vaguely; was I moving here permanently, which I answered even more vaguely; then I switched the topic back over to him. Men are so easily fooled. You're fuzzy in your answers about your personal life, then ask them a question about themselves and they're happily back on their favorite topic: Themselves.

Dumb.

Moose smiled, and I went back to work making a mint julep, Gin Fizz, and a Manhattan.

I knew he was watching me, but I ignored it.

Moose was there for three hours. He ordered another beer, he ordered dinner, dessert. He left me a twenty-five-dollar tip. I liked that because I needed the money, but I also didn't like it because I didn't want him thinking he was buying any of my "special" time in future.

The next night he came in again. Then again. He knew a lot of people, and they came over to say hi to him and he introduced me. I was constantly shaking hands with his buddies, cousins, aunts, sisters, other relatives, and chatting.

One night he waited until it was less busy, then said, "Grenady, it would be an honor if you would go to dinner with me. Please." He waved a hand. "I'm sorry, I should have said please first. I know of a nice restaurant, it's in Bennett City, only twenty-five minutes away, private, and they have the best pasta. How about Sunday night?"

"Moose, I'm flattered that a man like you would ask me out, but I am not dating right now." Or ever again.

"Oh." His face fell. He blushed. "I'm sorry to hear that."

"My life is too complicated." Let me count the ways.

"Maybe I can help you uncomplicate it?"

"Men never uncomplicate a woman's life, Moose. Exactly the opposite." I could count the ways there, too.

"I'm uncomplicated." He smiled.

He was sweet. Like a milkshake or a plum. "No, thank you, Moose. I'm sorry."

He sighed. "You are the prettiest lady who has ever been to this town and you are so easy to talk to and you turn me down." He slapped a hand dramatically to his forehead. "My hope has been squashed."

I laughed, handed him another beer. He still left me a twenty-five-dollar tip.

He asked me out three nights later. "It's not a date, Grenady. But there's a movie I want to see, and I'd like to take you and buy you the biggest tub of popcorn in Oregon. We can sit at opposite ends of the theatre and I promise I won't look at you, not even one time, though I confess I will be tempted."

"No, thank you."

"Hope squashed again," he said, fist to heart. "How will I recover from these blows?"

I smiled. "Ask someone else out."

"No one rivals your beauty, Grenady." He smiled back. "Your wit. Your humor. And I like the red hair, too."

When Moose came in a week later, he said, "Grenady, this is

not a request for a date, but how about if you come with me to a family barbeque this weekend?"

I laughed. "And that would be a no again, Moose. When your date meets your mother, you know where that's headed."

"I think you'd like her."

"I'm sure I would. Ask someone else. She'd be more polite than I would, for sure."

"Why do you say that?"

"Because of what I'm going to say to that mongo lumberjack over there." The mongo lumberjack walked in and swore at Randi, a sweet waitress working her way through community college. Randi was bringing a heavy tray of food out to the dining area. He thought Randi was in his way and said, "Shit. Watch where you're going, missy! You blind?"

His voice boomed in that restaurant.

"Get out," I told him when he sat his floppy haunches on a barstool.

His hairy brows furrowed. "No. Who the hell are you to tell me to get out? I came here for a burger and I'm gonna have my burger and my fries. Get me a beer and none of your sass."

"Get out," I said again. I stood my ground. He wasn't even in my top-twenty most scary people.

He shifted his hefty, farty self on a stool. "When I tell you to get me a beer, you get me a beer." He pointed a finger at me and yelled. "Move your butt, woman."

Move your butt, woman? No one talks to me like that anymore. *No one.*

"Don't talk to her like that," Moose said from the other end, then stalked over to confront the fool.

I grabbed an empty beer pitcher and slammed it on the bar. I grabbed Tildy's bat and shoved it into the pitcher, my temper triggered high and wide. "Here's your beer."

"That ain't no beer, so what ya gonna do now, tight ass?" He gave me the once-over with those slitty eyes. "How about you spread those pretty legs and—"

I took the bat out, the pitcher went flying across the bar, and I took a swing at his head.

He pulled away in the nick of time. The men on either side of him had already moved, knowing what was up when the bat first made its appearance.

"Let me show you what a tight ass can do, you fat, drunken, dirty son of a bitch." I came around the bar, wielding the bat around my head like a samurai warrior. I could feel myself losing control, diving into my latent fury.

"Shit!" He stumbled off the stool. Ignorant and drunk. He fell to the ground. *Splat.* Like a wallowing pig.

It was almost as if the room shifted. All I could see was him, a bully and a loser, picking on people he thought were defenseless, like all bullies. I wanted to smash him. I advanced, bat above my head. "Apologize to Randi! Apologize!"

"Whoa, okay!" He put two hands up. "Sorry, Randi! Sorry!"

I felt Moose right beside me. He grabbed for the bat, to protect me from getting arrested, I later realized. "Don't come in again. Ever," Moose said. I was surprised at how deep and threatening his voice sounded.

"Leave before I bash your head in," I said. I hate men. "Don't you ever get too big for your britches or someone's gonna bust your britches wide open and then they'll find out you got a butt like everybody else. Nothing special about it. Now you get your fat butt on out."

He stumbled out, shocked that someone stood up to him.

I ignored the other customers' clapping and Randi's grateful expression. I took a deep breath, tried to control myself. I rolled my shoulders. I tried to think of something pleasant. Like pie.

"See what I mean, Moose? I don't think I'm polite enough for your mother."

"You're wrong there. My momma used to compete in rodeos, and she would love you." He grinned. "Are you sure about the family barbeque?"

It was raining after my shift at The Spirited Owl. I drove past the steel statue of a cowboy on a bucking horse, through the faux Wild West town, parked in another neighborhood, and tried to breathe in the dark, icy solitude of my car. It had been a busy night, even without the samurai sword attack.

I ate a bowl of tortilla soup, cheese bread, and a stuffed baked potato with butter and sour cream. Then I had a piece of apple pie. I had not stopped to eat during my shift and had only two bananas and half a can of chili before work, so I was as hungry as a bull on charge.

When I was done, I peed in a pop cup, dumped the pee out the back passenger side door so I wouldn't step in my own waste, and washed my hands with bottled water and soap. I brushed my teeth, then changed into my sweats, two sweat-shirts, my jacket, a hat, and two pairs of wool socks. Before I went to bed I opened the pink ceramic rose box and put my lily bracelet back on. I did not want to wear it to work. I was worried I would lose it.

I wrapped myself in both blankets, but not tight in case I had to move quick, and wriggled into my sleeping bag, my gun only a foot away.

The rain turned to hail, and it pounded my roof and clattered on the black plastic. I hoped the black plastic would hold through the night, but I wasn't counting on it. Soon it felt like the inside of a refrigerator in that car.

Being broke never gets easier.

The poor girl mentality has never left me. Even when I was living in that obnoxious semimansion with Covey, driving a $50,000 car that he gave me, and wearing designer clothes and heels and a bag that cost five hundred dollars that, again, Covey bought and insisted I use over my twenty-dollar black purse, I was poor in my head.

Covey used to laugh at me with such derision. "Dina, you can buy anything you want, with your money or mine. I gave you a credit card. You could buy a slew of thousand-dollar purses. You can buy designer anything, but here you are, cutting out coupons before you go to the grocery store."

He was utterly baffled. My coupon cutting offended his man-liness, his ego. I found it sensible. Why pay full price when you can cut out a coupon and pay less? I would go to the store for paper towels and seriously debate which package to buy based on a savings of fifty-nine cents.

I never wanted piles of money so I could buy a yacht or a sports car or a huge house. I never wanted it so I could show off. I never wanted it so that I could feel better than anyone else. I wanted the money so I could feel independent, not scared and vulnerable, open to anything the world could throw at me.

Having money, to me, meant protection. Safety. Another day.

And to me, now, with my accounts frozen, with little savings in the new bank account I'd set up in town, I felt like I was waiting to be shot.

Waiting for the bullet.

I dreamed that night of a red crocheted shawl. It wrapped around me as I slept, snug and warm, over my head, down to my toes. I felt her hand on my cheek, his arms hugging me, keeping me safe.

Sleep, Grenadine . . . sleep, love.

Was it them? Was it my imagination?

Did it matter?

I slept.

My federal public defender, Millie Sanchez, called me the next morning at eight o'clock. I was already awake because the plastic on my car window had come off at six-thirty, after also coming off at three. I'd had to find the duct tape, hit the ice off the plastic, and retape it, all in the dark.

Millie was born in Mexico and moved to the United States when she was fifteen. Both neighborhoods were rough. She'd told me she learned how to box from her brothers. One brother was currently in jail for boxing someone's face in.

She is the one who will keep my butt out of the slammer, if she can, which is unlikely, due to a ginormous mistake on my part. She explained to me, when I was in the slammer, about the FBI, IRS, postal service, and the U.S. Attorney's Office investigations that had gone on for months against Covey and me.

There were judges involved, search warrants, a secret grand jury, and an indictment; our bank had handed over our statements without telling us. Covey apparently had secret accounts and shell companies, and had lost millions in investor money. There were a hundred other things my blown mind could hardly handle.

The bottom line: I had been charged with theft, fraud, embezzlement, and money laundering, though I had zero clue how to do any of those things even if I wanted to, which I didn't.

We dispensed with the pleasantries quickly.

"Hey, Dina. Bad and badder news. The assistant U.S. attorney has already built a solid case against you, although the case is infinitely stronger, more egregious, against Covey. It's those five different documents that you signed that are making you look guilty as sin."

I put a hand to my forehead. "Millie, I told you that Covey had me sign papers that were part of his business."

"That's why you're screwed to Mexico and back right now. Why didn't you read them?"

Why didn't I read them? I didn't even want to go there. That would have me diving headfirst into shame. I was stuck in a beer bottle. "I told you. Covey pushed, said they had to be signed right away, since I was an officer in his company, there were tax reasons, banking reasons, government rules and regulations, investment protocol...it was for our clients. I didn't know. He sounded official and confident, and when I asked for time to read them, he started throwing fits, saying I didn't trust him.

"When we married he said he wanted me to be a part of his business life so we could share it together. I didn't want to be a part of his company, I wanted to do my art, but he pushed and I gave in."

"Isn't that romantic?" Millie is not a romantic in her public life. In her personal life, she has been married for twenty-five years to a man who used to be a race car driver in Europe but now has an organic garden and sells fruits and vegetables to grocery stores.

"Come and join my lucrative company, new and innocent wife,

Dina," Millie mocked, "and sign these papers. Double cheater. Your signature is on documents that transfer money into differ- ent accounts, then that money went through complicated chan- nels and was shifted out of the business to shell businesses on the devil's evil tail."

"I didn't know. I'm stupid. I get it." Stupid. I'd heard that so many times in my life, "Stupido Grenado . . . she's stupid . . . she's retarded . . . she can't read . . . what's wrong with that stu- pid head?"

"You're not stupid, Dina, are you kidding? Married couples sign papers between each other all the time and they don't know what they're signing. When most of America signs their tax re- turns, which were prepared by their accountants, they don't even look at the numbers. It's too confusing, anyhow. The tax accountants could have their clients signing away their rights to their uteruses and grandmas and no one would know." She sighed.

"I should have known, Millie. I shouldn't have let him push me into this. I trusted him."

"I remember when I was younger, my mother handled all the finances, and she would go over to my dad, who would be sit- ting in his lounge chair drinking a beer and watching a football game, and she'd say, 'Sign this, Pablo,' and without looking up from the game he'd sign the paper, then pat my mom on the butt and say, 'Come sit with me and watch this football game. I'm lonely for you.' She'd put the papers away, drink a beer, watch the game with my dad while they ate quesadillas, and he would never even ask what he signed."

"Looks like I'm your dad." Sheesh. It was so cold in my car, my fingers were numb. I noticed the scars on my hands from the fire. Hardly noticeable to anyone, but they were noticeable to me.

"You're not the first wife to get wrapped up in something like this, and that's what I'm harping on with the FBI, the U.S. Attorney's Office, blah blah and blah. Problem is that your maggot-brained husband isn't clearing you."

"Not at all? Still?" I wanted to castrate him. Two quick

whacks. I'd recently blocked Covey's home, cell, and office phone numbers—and blocked him from my e-mail. Unfortunately, he called me from different numbers, and I had to block those, too. I'd already shut down Facebook and my website. I didn't want to talk to him, and Millie told me not to under threat of "mean punishment."

"I've called his attorneys—those two are slick mothers, aren't they—and Covey is refusing to tell the assistant U.S. attorney and the rest of the governmental gang that you had nothing to do with his flaky, shaky business at all."

"I think he made sure I signed enough papers so he could have something to hang over my head like a guillotine if I ever dared leave him."

"I think you're right. That gutter dweller wanted your name on something incriminating."

"Control issue. Then he could always threaten me with jail if I left." That knowledge floored me. He was so devious, I could hardly grasp it in my frozen brain.

"Yep and yep. He should be the only one taking the fall here. I would like to fry him in hot sauce."

We talked more. I was depressed when I hung up. *Depressed.* I could feel it moving in like black clouds. The black clouds had been with me for years, long ago. I had gotten rid of them by fighting them off. But now they were back—heavy, tight, relentless.

I did not see an end to them on the horizon.

I went to a Laundromat. I didn't want to spend the money, but I didn't have a choice. When I was there I sketched a collage. I drew lilies, their long, green stems inside a circular glass vase with a twisty neck. Inside the vase was an entire country village. Cobblestone streets. A church steeple. White picket fences. A city park and gazebo. People on bikes. Idyllic. Warm.

I drew a jagged crack in the vase.

During my shift, two nights later, I felt myself getting sick, as if my body was breaking down a piece at a time. I remembered a woman from years ago who told me moonshine could cure anything, and gave me a shot of whiskey to get better. I was thirteen. It helped me sleep.

In my car, a light snow falling, I felt the flu taking over, starting with my throat, which burned as if it were on fire. I ached like a poked rat, my head throbbed, and I was soon coughing and sniffling. It grew worse and worse throughout the night. I soon was chilled to the bone and knew I had a fever. I put it at about 100 degrees. As I usually run about 97.6, this was not good. I tried to picture my fever burning up all the germs. Didn't work.

I had to get better. I had to be efficient and not temperamental at The Spirited Owl and I had to pester Hendricks' Furniture to give me a job. Until then, I would fake being healthy, chug medicine to get me through, and spring for orange juice.

I put on two sweatshirts, a sweater, a jacket, both sweatpants, three socks, a hat, gloves, and a scarf. I snuggled into my sleeping bag and both blankets in the back of my car. I nearly froze to death that night. I shook and shivered. The freezing air, and a few snowflakes, blew through the black plastic bag over my window like it was nothing, which it was, nothing. I felt my feet go numb and my fingers tingled.

I cursed those black-masked criminals who busted my window and wished for their testicles to wither and drop from their bodies and for a large snake to invade their rectal cavities.

About an hour later I could feel my fever rising and along with it a spreading, bone-jangling chill. I struggled into the front seat, turned on the heat in the car, and drove around. I parked and went back to shivering. When I was drifting in and out of a nightmare-filled sleep, I thought to myself: I understand how people die from the flu. I get it.

Then the plastic dropped off the window.

I groaned. Snow flew in on a wind gust. I heaved myself out of my sleeping bag, took off my gloves, and used the duct tape to get the plastic back up.

I was shaking harder when I crawled back into my sleeping bag like a dying rat.

My insurance would pay for the window to be replaced. I would tell them that someone smashed it when it was parked in a parking lot. That was true. If I told the full truth, it would trigger an investigation. My problem was that I needed to put up a $1,000 deductible and I could not do that yet. The $1,000 would put off my being able to get in an apartment.

Should I suck it up and be cold and get into the apartment sooner? Or get the window fixed and not freeze outside at night? Would an intact window help that much in the depths of winter? Doubtful. I did a Personal Financial Calculation in my head. I was in poor shape, but not as poor as when I first flew out of Portland. I would get my next paycheck soon, and I had tip money. I needed first and last month's rent, a security deposit, and Cherie's monthly payment for the divorce. That was a lot, but I was getting there.

Thoughts of what to do with the black flapping plastic versus a roof went pinballing through my pounding head until I finally went to sleep, or passed out, the flu flattening me like a rabbit under a steamroller.

I woke up at seven in the morning, cramped, my head stuffed, my cough deep, my body aching and trembling. It took a long time to get my sweats off. I grabbed my pee cup and peed. I was totally dehydrated. I wiped, threw the tissue in my handy-dandy plastic baggy trash bag, and dumped the pee onto the ground on the passenger side. I noticed the fog was back in the trees in the mountains. I did not need to see that suffocating stuff this morning.

I washed my hands and scrambled back into my sleeping bag. I hate peeing like this. It is one of the worst things about being homeless. The no-toilet disadvantage.

I put my hand to my head. My forehead was sweaty. I thought I might toss my cookies. I did not want to pay for a hotel at all. I wanted to save the money for my car window and an apartment, whichever came first.

It was Sunday, though. I didn't work today, and wouldn't

work again until Tuesday at five-thirty, so I had some time to rest, if I could.

Hail pounded on the roof. I could hear the plastic taking another beating. I watched it start to slide again.

I groaned. My body shook. My throat burned. My sneezes made me pee in my sweats.

"Oh, my shoutin', spittin' Lord. You're gonna freeze to death, Grenady," I said out loud. "Move or die."

I went to McDonald's but did not bother to get out of my sweatshirts, jacket, a red knitted hat, and sweats. I was too sick to care what people thought. I'm sure I looked homeless. I am homeless. That was a hard one to come to terms with. It had been before, too.

I had to spend a lot of time on the toilet as I now had diarrhea, the butt curse. I tried to go only when I heard the other toilets flushing because I was embarrassed. I tried not to moan at all.

When I could stand up, leaning heavily on the door handle, I washed my hands and sweaty face and pits with my washcloth and brushed my teeth.

Two little girls bopped on in and didn't seem to find anything odd about watching me brush my teeth. One even said, "Hey! I use that toothpaste, too!"

I said, "Fabulous."

She said, "My sister and I have big teeth in our mouths. See? You think we have big teeth? Show her, Carissa."

The two girls opened up their mouths as wide as they could, eyebrows shooting into their blond bangs.

"Those are some chompers," I told them through my toothpaste.

"I bite my brother."

"Good for you, vampire kid." She giggled, thought that was funny.

"I don't bite," the other one said. "That bad."

"Yeah, it is."

They chatted more about their tongues, which they thought

were long, and I agreed when they showed me. "Maybe you're part frog," I said. "They have long tongues."

I think they took me seriously, and seemed pleased by the frog thought. They hopped out.

I used a wet, somewhat soapy washcloth on my Big V and privates in the stall, dried off with tissue, buttoned up, waited until no one was in the bathroom, rinsed out the washcloth, went back into the stall and rinsed off. I felt disgusting. My self-esteem was in the toilet. I looked in the toilet. Yep. Right there.

I brushed my hair but left it down. I had no energy to braid it, and my hands refused to do anything else. I didn't bother with makeup. I felt so ill, I could hardly stand.

I left the bathroom with my bag, bought a huge coffee, dumped six creams and sugar in, then hid in the back in a booth, leaning against a wall. I downed the coffee with four Advil.

I could feel myself nodding off, the flu slaying me like a stuck pig.

Before I humiliated myself, I noticed a man with thick black hair walk in. He was the tallest man I'd seen in a while, with shoulders that seemed to block light from the door. He looked my way.

Holy Mother of fire and brimstone.

I would not want to meet that badass on a deserted street. He had the squared-off jaw of a fighter and a couple of scars on his left cheek. Lines fanned out from his eyes and from nose to mouth. He also had a hard and steady gaze that warned, "Don't mess with me. You'll lose." He was hellaciously handsome, though—compelling, like how a sexy bad guy would be in a movie.

I couldn't look away. He stared right back at me. I blinked and wondered if we'd met, but then knew we had not. I would not forget some bull-kickin' stud like that.

Another time, feeling healthy, I would have smiled. I like the tough, bad-boy type. The testosterone and manliness is a megaton turn-on. But there was no smile in me today. I thought I saw him smile, a small smile, but I wasn't sure.

Another round of sickness seemed to invade my body at that unfortunate moment, and I bent my head and drank more cof-

fee, then shut my eyes for a second. I put my coffee on the table
and forgot about the badass. *One second,* I told myself. You can
sleep for one second. Or one minute, two minutes. Three. No
more than three. Don't be a homeless person asleep in the back
of a McDonalds. Don't . . . be . . . homeless . . .

I woke up to a young girl, maybe three, grinning at me. She
was in my booth, leaning over the table, watching me. "You
sleepy!"

"Yeah, I am." What was with the kids here today? Why did
they keep talking to me? I sat up straight and reached for my
bathroom bag, which also held my black twenty-dollar purse
that Covey hated. Relief swept through me. It was still there.

"You take nap." She was wearing a hat with a monkey on
top of it, a blue frilly dress, and red and green striped Christmas
tights.

"Yes, I did."

"I take nap."

"Good. Then you won't get bratty." I don't know why kids
like me, they just do.

"You sick?" She pointed at my nose. "Red."

"Yes, I'm sick, so you probably shouldn't get too close."

"Here's my lizard." She held out a stuffed purple lizard. "It's
Tipper Lizard."

"She's floppy."

"She a bad lizard."

"Being bad can be fun." I blew my nose. "Why is your lizard bad?"

"She eat snails."

"Ah. Gross. That's a dumb lizard."

She giggled. "Ya. Dumb lizard. And poop. She eats poop."

"I didn't need to hear that right now."

"But I tell you about the poop."

"Yes, I know." I felt like death.

Her mother called her over. The girl with the Christmas tights
waved at me. "Bye-bye."

"Bye-bye."

Her mother gave me a funny look. I didn't blame her. If I had a kid and she went over to talk to a homeless woman dressed in layers of clothes and a red knitted hat who was asleep in a Mc-Donald's booth, I'd get antsy, too.

I checked my watch. I'd been asleep for about two hours and was frozen cold. Obviously the coffee hadn't helped keep me awake. I headed back to the bathroom to handle another round of Cursed Butt. I scrubbed my hands and rinsed my sweaty face, brushed my teeth in hopes of getting rid of the putrid bile taste, then wobbled out to my car, where I ate a can of pineapple. I crawled into the back, squeezed into my sleeping bag, covered myself with my blankets, and conked out for three hours.

12

I woke up when my phone rang. I didn't recognize the number. I knew it was Covey calling again from someone else's phone. The son of a gun would have about lost his stupid head when he couldn't reach me from his own phone. He left a message. Pleading. Yelling. I blocked that number, too. I went back to sleep.

I woke up feeling worse. The flu had settled on my body like a thousand tons of germs.

Snow floated down. My plastic crackled. I gave up.

I drove to a hotel with a statue of pioneers in front called Pineridge Pioneer Hotel, which I thought might be moderately priced, and asked for a room. When he said $140 a night, I said, thank you, but no, and limped out, arms around my churning gut.

I went to two more hotels—too expensive. I drove into town, then off a side street into an area of well-kept homes. I saw a sign outside a light blue Queen Anne home with a white porch and white gingerbread all over it. It said Talia's Bed and Breakfast.

I stopped the car and stared. It was glorious. It had personality, grace, and class. I coughed. Blew my nose.

I didn't fit in that home. I was grimy. Exhausted. Sick. I had spent weeks in my car. I was doing my best to keep my chin up, but the flu had knocked me down and almost out. Physically and emotionally I felt totally beat up.

The B and B would be way too expensive. I knew it. Plus, I shouldn't be staying in someone's B and B. I was sick. But. If I could afford it, I could go to my room, keep the windows open a bit to get the germs out, and not come out to infect anyone else. I climbed out of the car like an old and creaky woman to check the price, wondering why I was torturing myself.

I climbed the steps slowly, my body a swirling mess of virus, and for five blissful seconds I pretended that I lived in that house. The yellow chrysanthemums in the pots on each step were mine. The porch swing with the red pillows was mine. The attic room on top with the pointed roof was mine, as was the window seat. I rang the bell and waited.

A woman answered, about my age. She had blond hair in a ponytail, one of those huge smiles that took up half her face, and brown eyes. She was wearing an Indian sari in red and gold.

"Hello," she said. "Looking for a room?"

"Yes, I am." I crossed my arms over my layers of sweatshirts and my coat.

"Come on in."

I didn't want to waste her time. She seemed cheerful and I'm sure she had better things to do than chitchat with me.

"I don't want to take up your time." I made sure I did not get too close to her. "How much is a room for one night?"

Her eyes did a swift assessment of me, from my red knitted hat to my boots. I saw it, and put my chin up. Inside I quivered. I knew this judged, "less than others" feeling. I'd felt it for years of my life. Not good enough. Outsider. Dirty. A burden. Not wanted. *Stupido.*

For years I'd built a life for myself so I could put my chin up and feel equal. Now I was back to the first life, but I would not put my chin down again. Unless I had to vomit into the dirt like I had last night. Then I'd put my chin down.

"How about eighty dollars?"

"Are you kidding?" I could hardly breathe.

"Not at all." She looked out at my car. "And I'll tell you where to go to get that window fixed, too. It's called Billy and Billy's."

"Thank you." Second recommendation for Billy Squared. This was a good sign. "One thing, though. I'm sick. I came down with it two days ago. Do you still want me to stay here? I could go somewhere else." No, I couldn't.

"Don't worry at all. I'm immune to germs. I have two boys, they had the flu last week, so did my husband, Lyle. You probably have the same thing. Germs are all over, no matter what I do. I'm Talia Kallelemoto. My sister's in India, and she sent me this sari. Whaddya think?"

"I think it's colorful and sparkly." I had judged her too quick. I thought she was judging me based on my sweats and multiple sweatshirts, my yucky appearance. She wasn't. And, if she was, she met it with compassion and invited me into her home. For a second I wondered how many times I had assumed someone was judging me harshly who wasn't judging me at all . . .

"My sister's always traveling and bringing me back scarves and jewelry and stuff. I live vicariously through her. Most exciting thing I do is book group. Partly because one of the ladies drinks too much and tells us about her raunchy sex life, which I like hearing about, and two of the women hate each other. Makes for an exciting evening. Bring your stuff in. Welcome."

"This is your room."

I gaped. It was like walking into décor heaven.

"Is it okay?" Talia wrung her hands.

"It's a room out of the old movies." I stepped in and away from her, keeping my germs to myself. She had decorated it in the style of the 1900s. A pink-and-white canopy decorated the top of a four-poster bed, a footstool next to it. Pillows were piled high on a pink flowered bedspread, with a thick, white down comforter at the foot. A comfy beige chair and a rocking chair were in front of the gas fireplace. I love rocking chairs. They're my image of a peaceful home. I've never had one, but it's on The List.

Wallpaper with red camellias gave the room a feminine touch, as did the lace curtains on all three windows. There was an antique roll-back desk.

"I don't think I'll ever leave," I muttered.

"Okay," Talia agreed. "I could do with more women around here. I'm surrounded by testosterone. And you don't need to leave tomorrow until one, because I don't have time to clean the room until then, anyhow."

"Thank you."

She laughed at my heartfelt thank-you, and I handed over the cash.

I was still freezing, weak, but being in this room, knowing I could sleep in it, be warm, tucked in bed, with a fireplace, I started to feel less like a corpse.

I brought my bags in, then stripped and stepped into the white, deep tub. I turned on the hot water, dumped in bubble bath that spelled like cinnamon spice, and sank right in.

I let the water soothe my tight back muscles and my banging head. The shampoo, cream rinse, and soap smelled like cherries. I was in the bath for an hour and a half and pumped more hot water in twice. I used a fluffy white towel to dry off, then brushed my hair.

I caught a glimpse of my back in the mirror. The scars had faded over the years. Still there, but not glaring anymore.

I moved so I wouldn't see them and that particular memory.

I tumbled into bed and pulled that flowered bedspread and white comforter right over my body. I think I was asleep before I covered myself.

I woke up from my nap at eight o'clock, starving. I pulled on two sweatshirts, sweats, and my jacket. I knew I couldn't walk far, so I planned on opening up another can of chili and some peaches.

I almost stepped on a plate of lasagna, a salad, and bread outside my door.

I was so grateful I about cried.

* * *

I slept for another twelve hours at Talia's. Twelve hours of sleep, particularly if you're not squished like a slug in your car, will do wonders. I put in a load of laundry, as Talia said I was welcome to, then took a bath as I was still cold, but not as cold as I'd been before.

I padded down the stairs in my sweats and heated up the breakfast that Talia made me. I hadn't even heard the kids or her husband last night.

There was a note on the kitchen counter to me, saying that my breakfast was in the fridge. Eggs Benedict, a cinnamon roll, bacon, and fruit in a pile.

It was the prettiest piece of breakfast art I'd seen. I ate all of it, starving like a pig, then made coffee, dumped in whipping cream that I found in the back of Talia's fridge, and drank two glasses of orange juice, then more coffee and cream.

Talia and Lyle's home was a family home. She had a true talent with decorating, but it was friendly, too. Yellows, blues, green, and tons of soccer and football equipment lying around.

I could feel my fever coming back, so I cleaned up the kitchen, then climbed the stairs and went back to bed. I set my alarm for twelve forty-five.

At one o'clock, I padded back down and paid Talia for another night.

"I'm delighted to have you. Thanks for cleaning up the kitchen. You didn't have to do that. That was so nice. Want a sandwich?"

I sure did. It was egg salad. Delicious. I thanked her for the lasagna. Talking to Talia was a ton of fun. She was irreverent and funny and said being a mom was the best thing she'd ever done, but the woman in her was gone. She was going to go on a "woman-finding journey" someday. "When football and soccer are over with and the kids have graduated."

"Yes, hunt your womanhood down," I said, "and when you find it, shoot it with an arrow and bring her on home."

When she left to shuttle her sons around, I cleaned up the kitchen again, swept the floor, and put in another load of laundry. I felt so much better getting my clothes clean.

I then went back up for a nap, my body's tiny burst of energy now completely gone.

My appointment with Kade Hendricks was the day after tomorrow at one-thirty.

I wanted that job.

I would learn how to use a saw if I had to and I'd damn well like it.

That night I took another hot bath as I was freezing again, my fever moving up and down. I would sweat, then freeze, then back to sweating.

I almost fell asleep in the tub with the cinnamon spice bubble bath. I dried off and crawled like a beat chicken to my soft bed with the soft pillows. I was so glad I wasn't spending the night in my car. It was now hailing. I had to get out of my home on wheels immediately.

I had brought my pink ceramic rose box with the lily bracelet in with me. I attached the bracelet to my wrist but couldn't sleep. I felt too sick to sleep.

I closed my eyes, concentrated. I needed the oblivion. This frustration went on for an hour.

When another roll of ghastly sickness overwhelmed me I heard, *Sleep, Grenadine.... Go to sleep, hummingbird daughter.*

It was them.

I knew it.

Sleep, Grenadine. We're here.

I put my hand on my lily bracelet and slept.

I had a nightmare about prison, which woke me up a few hours later. The fear of a forced vacation in a *cage* made my whole body shake as if a warden were standing on top of my liver, electrocuting me.

I will never forget the smell of my stint in jail. So many women, crammed together, hormones, tempers and all. Some unwashed, most of us sweating at some point, poor food, thin mattresses, little air ventilation, no open windows, the pungent aroma of fear and desperation, and a faint whiff of unwashed vagina. The smell of cleaners, particularly bleach, was heavy and nauseating.

The women at this jail, downtown, were in and out, some for only twenty-four hours, or a weekend, then released. Others were there for weeks or months as they awaited trial.

One woman was screaming with anger; one was muttering to herself. A few argued with each other; one argued and swore at the prison staff, and was put back in her cell

Some were talking, being cool; others were ready to take your head off if you peered cross-eyed at them. Some were quietly crying.

I shared a cell with a woman who said her name was Jane. Then she said it was Hecks. Her third name was Prime Number. When she asked, I told her my name was Dina.

"I'm Dina now. You are Prime Number," she told me. "I've got a kitty cat under the bed and a pig on the shelf."

I peeked under the bed to humor her. She meowed at the imaginary cat and snorted at the pig. She smelled like urine. She was bony and had straggly brown hair and a face that looked as if she had been surviving on the streets for a long time, worn and tired. I put her at about thirty-two, though the lines made her seem older.

"Cat's name is Pickle. No. Now it's Ed. No. I think its name is Amoeba Plus Vector Calculus. Pig's name is Quantum Physics. No. Now it's Cylindrical Shell Method. Pig changed his name. It's Derivative."

I nodded.

Jane was in for robbery. Apparently she walked into a 7-Eleven wearing a red, furry cape. She put a whole bunch of Hershey's candy bars into her bag, then went up to the checker, pretended she had a gun under the red, furry cape, and said to him, "I'm going to talk to you about the surface area of a revolution while you hand me nine dollars in quarters, then I'm going to shoot a quadratic equation."

The clerk, who did not speak English well, as he was from Vietnam, only understood the word "shoot" and handed over the cash. He handed over three hundred dollars, in bills and change, which made Jane mad. She had asked for quarters! She started counting out nine dollars in quarters, and was still counting when the police arrived.

She had no gun. She did have a cat under her red, furry cape and was extremely upset that the cat was taken from her. Apparently she kicked at the police officer who took the cat, which was probably Amoeba Plus Vector Calculus, but it could have been Pickle.

She told me this whole story while waving her hands, wriggling her fingers, and swaying. At one point she stroked the imaginary cat in her arms and bent down and petted the pig, Derivative, aka Quantum Physics.

As I watched her I couldn't help but think how screwed up our money situation is in this country: Billions for weapons and invading countries, and we have Jane in jail with her imaginary pig and cat because we don't have a bed in a nice, safe, warm mental health care unit. She has pneumonia in her head and we think that because she robbed a 7-Eleven of nine dollars, her best placement is in jail.

Our cell had two bed platforms and four-inch mattresses. The floor was concrete. There was a small rectangular window with a crack in it.

The noise in jail was almost constant. Even in the middle of the night, someone was crying or throwing a fit or detoxing. The doors were steel, and during the day they clanged and banged and buzzed all the time as people came and went, inmates and staff. It was like being stuck in a beer bottle with a hundred other people without the smooth cool of the beer.

The fluorescent lights were bright and harsh, and on sixteen hours a day. There was a door on my cell to lock me in, but there was a cutout window in it, so there was no privacy at all. I had a silver toilet in my room, which was attached to a silver sink. Anyone could see when I was using the toilet if they looked in at that special moment. A silver built-in shelf held my toothbrush and toothpaste. A mirror, that was not made of glass, was above the whole thing.

I was a dangerous animal that needed to be contained. Claustrophobia made my heart palpitate, my hands tremble. My phobia about being stuck in a cage again took my breath away.

The women were in for everything: assault, murder, robbery, drugs, prostitution, street crimes. A lot of them were coming off drugs, and it was not pretty. They shook and trembled and cried and had trouble breathing. The nurses would come in and check on them, and if they gasped for air, passed out, convulsed, or vomited, they were taken to the infirmary.

One woman, who was not more than twenty, was covered in scars up and down her arms. She talked about her childhood. Attacked by her stepfather for years, addicted to coke when she was fourteen, she'd been in and out of juvie and jail since. It was not surprising that she'd reached for coke to numb the pain. I understood how someone would want to numb pain. I understood her choice.

"This time, though, I think I gotta stay for a while in Jail Hotel. I don't got healthcare, and I need a doctor down there in the privates bad. Can you smell me?"

Another woman, short and angry, said she was innocent. "Only shot him once. Once! He cheated on me. I supposed to take that shit? He lived, too. Only hit him in the butt. Left cheek. Butt cheek." She stood and pointed at her right butt cheek. "He'll think of me next time he's a pushin' on another woman's cushion."

A third woman, in her forties, was in jail because she tried to burn her house down. "I didn't do it. I don't even know how to light a match. I don't even know how to light a lighter. Man, I need a cigarette."

Another inmate found out more about cigarette woman's case and learned that she'd actually started the fire in her own home and tried to burn the house down with the kids in it. Her oldest son, twelve years old, jumped from the second story with the baby in his arms.

He broke both legs. All three kids lived because once the boy was on the ground with his broken legs, he put the baby on the grass and then caught his three-year-old sister, breaking his left shoulder.

Cigarette woman had the hell knocked out of her in the shower and ended up in the infirmary. I didn't know who did it. I wouldn't have told, anyhow. I don't advocate shooting a cheating husband, but I get it. Robbery even when no one gets hurt? Hey, numbskull, don't. But I'm not beating anyone up for it. Burning down your kids? Hurting children at all? No. Go die.

Jail brought my past rushing back until I choked on it in my own throat, the bars closing in on me tighter, tighter, tighter, till I couldn't breathe and Alice, My Anxiety, was screaming, hands over head.

I woke up Tuesday morning at ten o'clock. Talia was gone. I ate the bacon and mushroom omelet and toast she made for me, which was high-ranking delicious; drank two glasses of orange juice and three cups of coffee with whipping cream; then cleaned her kitchen. I had already washed one of my blankets, so I washed the other one, then climbed into the deep, white tub one more time, the bubbles brewing as if I were in a cauldron. I was cold to the bone, that fever still stubbornly clinging to me, but I felt like I could function again.

When I was done, I put my blanket in the dryer and dropped my sheets into the washer so Talia wouldn't have to do it, then went back to bed and passed out under the comforter for another hour. I put the sheets in the dryer and put on my white cable knit sweater and a white turtleneck, a red and beige scarf, dark jeans, and my cowboy boots. I wore gold hoops and two gold bangles. I put my lily bracelet on, too, for luck.

I pulled my hair back in a ponytail. I didn't miss being a blonde at all. Auburn, my natural color, was more me. I added a little more blush than usual because I was pale and sickly looking, then liner and a smear of eye shadow.

I made my bed with the clean sheets, wrote Talia a note and told her they were washed, then almost cried as I walked down her porch at one o'clock with my bags. I was still sick and I wanted to stay. I wanted my pink flowered bedspread and the white comforter. I wanted that deep, white tub and hot water and a toilet always at the ready. I wanted to be able to throw away my pee cup for good.

I did not turn around for a last glimpse at that light blue house or the yellow chrysanthemums or the porch swing with the red pillows or the window seat. I couldn't.

I climbed in my car, my body stiff and old, and headed down the street, the black plastic crackling.

At least your clothes and blankets are clean, I told myself. That was a relief.

I wanted to bang my head against the steering wheel.

13

He would write about the nursery rhyme with the sheep. It was one of his favorites.

> Baa, baa, black sheep,
> Have you any wool?
> Yes, sir, yes, sir,
> Three bags full...

He whistled to himself. He had to make this nursery rhyme better.

> Baa, baa, black sheep.
> Have you any blood?
> Yes, ma'am, yes, ma'am
> Two bags full...

What would be the next line? This one was harder for him. He would have to take some time and study it. That was okay. He had time. Lots of time. He pulled a hair out of his head and ate it.

He giggled, then his face flushed.

"Shut up, Danny!" he raged, hurdling his rhyme book across the room. "I don't want to listen to you. Shut your trap! Shut your butt!"

14

I worked my shift on Tuesday starting at five-thirty but was off by ten o'clock.

One of the regulars, a polite older gentleman named Grizz whose white and gray hair reminded me of a white and gray grizzly, said to me, "You gotta get yourself on home now, Grenady, and eat chicken soup and go to bed. Add a spoonful or two or six of whiskey to your tea and you'll feel better soon. My grandma taught me about the whiskey and tea part."

Ah. So someone else was handing down whiskey wisdom.

Tildy said to me, "It looks like death has come stalking," and made me take cheddar cheese beer soup and chicken noodle soup with me. "Anytime, Grenady," she said quietly.

I knew she was offering me a room, but it was charity and she was my boss, too. I was not pathetic. The soups did warm me up in my car that night.

And the plastic stayed over the window.

Both things to be grateful for.

My fever spiked and I shook, then it fell, and I sweated like a poaching pig.

At Hendricks' on Wednesday I was greeted by Sam Jenkins, the same friendly man who had knocked on my window in the parking lot and who I'd almost shot.

"Welcome back, Grenady! How are you?"

"Thank you. I'm fine. How are you?"

We chatted and he talked fast again, as if he had to get all his words out quick. I asked if Bajal had had her baby yet.

"She sure did. She said she bled like a rushing river, poor girl. Hemorrhaged, but she's right as rain now. Her husband about lost it, though, poor guy."

I felt light-headed.

Sam had seen the baby. The baby had black hair. The father had blond hair, so there was joking about the parentage, ha ha ha.

His phone rang. "Good luck, Grenady. I hope you get the job. I think you'd fit in well here."

"Thank you." Oh, how I needed some luck. And health. My fever was still roaming around, but I was jacked up on coffee, orange juice, and four Advils.

I had worn black jeans and knee-high black boots. I had on a thick, dark green sweater with a V collar, a wide leather belt around my waist, and gold hoops. I wore my hair down.

I twisted my lily bracelet around my wrist and studied the rather dull lobby. I started redecorating it in my head to calm myself down. I chose the colors for the walls, then I started designing a mural . . . should it be paintings of the furniture here? The outside of the building? I thought about what kind of photos should go up, what lighting I'd choose, how a sign that said Hendricks' Furniture should look. . . .

I heard a door open at the end of the hallway to the right, then boots coming straight toward me. I took a steadying breath and stood up.

A man strode in. It felt as if he filled up the whole room. Tall, black hair, shoulders back, muscled up under his black T-shirt . . . I'd seen him before.

He was the McDonald's man. Oh, shoot. Shoot. Shoot.

He was in McDonald's when I was hiding in the back with my huge coffee, layers of sweats, a jacket, and my red knitted hat, trying not to sleep but falling asleep in the booth anyhow minutes after I'd seen him. I'd looked homeless.

He may have seen me asleep, leaning against the wall. I had probably been slobbering, or snoring, my mouth gaping open. I hoped my tongue had stayed in my mouth where it belonged.

You should walk out now, I told myself. He's going to think you're stupid. Lazy. Poor. *Homeless.* I wanted to drop my gaze. I wanted to hunch my shoulders. I fought both impulses.

"Hello." He held out his hand and I automatically shook it. "Kade Hendricks."

"Hello. Grenady Wild." I hoped he hadn't seen me in McDonald's—he *saw* me, but I hoped I didn't register with him, that I was invisible in my homelessness. I tried to smile. My smile wobbled. I probably looked like a strange, homeless weasel.

"Nice to meet you. Come on in."

"Thank you." I tried to figure out whether he recognized me, but there was no sign. He put out an arm indicating I was to go first, and I walked down the hallway and into his office while we made small talk about the weather.

As we were talking, I thought, *Well, whew.* What I'd heard was right. Kade Hendricks was scary close up. He was six five if he was an inch. He had thick, black hair that brushed the top of his black T-shirt, dark eyes, two scars on his left cheek, and one between his neck and collarbone. He had that darkened appearance on his jaw that said he should probably be shaving twice a day but wouldn't. He was not smiling, but he did not seem unfriendly.

I was still scared.

And desperate for the job.

Kade's office was the most distracting I'd ever been in, and I have been in a lot of offices because of the painting and collage work I've done for companies and law firms. It was a large corner office with a wall of windows with sweeping views of the mountains and meadows. It was like a three-dimensional postcard outside those windows. How did anyone work with a view like this?

His own furniture was in there, as one would expect. His massive desk had a carving in front of a stream and fly fisherman that was so intricate, so finely detailed, I stopped and gaped at it.

There was an armoire in the corner with two leaping salmon on each door, and a circular table with a carving on top of a grizzly momma, her two cubs wrestling, the forest behind them.

I stared out the windows. "The sunsets must be something else."

"Yes." He nodded and waved at the grizzly table for me to sit down. "They are. So are the sunrises. Please. Have a seat."

I sat down, crossed my legs, and clasped my hands together tight so they wouldn't tremble.

I wondered about the scars on his face. Obviously I would not be saying, "Hey, dude. How'd you get those scars? And why do you look so menacing, like you could pound the life out of someone without breaking a sweat?"

"So, it's Grenadine?"

"Yes. But I'm called Grenady." As of a few weeks ago. Grenadine Scotch Wild was my name in childhood. It was also my official name attached to my social security number and the one I wrote on my application.

Dina Wild became my name when I wanted to escape my childhood and start over. Dina came from Grena-*dine*. Dina Hamilton was my married name, which I never officially changed, though Covey pestered me to do so, and Grenady Wild is the name I'm using now as I escape my marriage and the publicity.

But, well, shoot. He didn't need to know all that.

"Okay, Grenady, I was looking over your application. Looks like you're an artist."

"Yes."

"I couldn't find a website."

"I took it down." And . . . the website was in the name of Dina Wild.

"What kind of art?"

"Collage. Paintings. A combination of both." That man was intimidating. Huge, unsmiling, serious. "It's a mix. I like working with large canvases."

"How large?"

"Four foot by six foot. Three feet wide by eight feet. Six foot by ten foot. Sometimes larger. I like them big."

He blinked.

Had I just said I like them big? As in carnal big? I rushed to save myself. "I like large canvases. All my canvases tell a story, of sorts, so I need room."

His expression didn't change. "How do you decide what to paint?"

"I paint what's in my head. I paint whatever I'm thinking about at the time. I'll twist it up, spin it out, add color, add layers, add collage items, and I keep going until it feels done." I felt myself relax a teeny bit. "I was recently commissioned by a national bird-watching group to make a collage for their headquarters. I used a three-by-eight-foot canvas and painted one eight-foot-long branch horizontally. I painted seven different birds on the branch, all native to the community. I added wood sticks to the branch and feathers to the birds."

"I can picture it," he said quietly. "What other kinds of collages?"

"I made a collage for a winery about two months ago. I used a lot of their corks. Hundreds of corks." I chuckled thinking about those corks. "I painted their wine bottles on a table overlooking their land, and I used the corks for the frame."

I told him about Divinity's carousel and her past lives. "She has a lot going on in her imagination."

"Sounds like it." He laughed, and I relaxed.

He asked a lot of questions about my art. That was a safe topic for me.

"Are you going to continue your art?"

"Yes. In the future." Not now. Hard to do so in a car. This time he waited until I started speaking again.

"I closed my business." My clients dried up. Suspected criminal activity makes clients run away. Especially when they believe you ripped off their life savings.

"Why?"

"Because I needed a change." That change was forced on me. I could not live in a city where people wanted to see my mug be-

hind bars and my name was in the paper. Nor could I live anywhere near Covey.

"What kind of change are you looking for?"

"A new life. A quieter life. Less stress." Not being convicted
would be helpful.

"And a break from your art?"

"Yes." Heck, no. I couldn't wait to get my hands on my
paints, my button collection, my sheets of music, and a history
book I'd found at Goodwill with people dressed in top hats and
bustles. Without my art I am lost. I am nothing.

"So you drove out to central Oregon."

"Yes." Away from jail and a soon-to-be ex-husband I didn't
want to talk about.

He was quiet for a second, waiting for me to elaborate. I did
not elaborate. I didn't want to tell him I was separated from that
son of a bitch.

"I understand you work at The Spirited Owl, too."

"Yes, I do. I'm a bartender and a waitress."

"You need a second job?"

"Yes."

"Why?"

"I'm saving for a home." True enough. An apartment is a
home.

"What did you do before you were an artist?"

"I was a waitress from the time I was fourteen—"

"Fourteen?"

"Yes. Then I was a waitress and a bartender when I turned
twenty-one. I waitressed and bartended until I could support
myself as an artist. I've been able to support myself for about
twelve years now."

He dropped the application down on the table and leaned
back in his chair. His eyes narrowed. My application wasn't
complete; there was a missing website, holes all over, and I knew
it. He was no fool. He was sensing something else. "Tell me
about yourself."

I knew Kade wanted the personal info that people can't
legally ask in interviews, but I was going to take a detour and

talk only about the professional end of it. Too much to hide, too much to cover up.

"I want a job in a company where I can learn new things." Actually a job, any job, at this point would be good enough.

"I think I can help you because I know how furniture can, and should, work in a home, and I know what questions to ask your clients in terms of what they need and want because I've worked with clients for years who bought my art. I know how to get to know people and apply it to a project." My clients often drove me insane, and I was forced to tell them that sometimes, but I would be nicer to Kade's clients.

"I like that each of your pieces is personalized. It isn't only a dresser or a bed or a desk. It's special. It's unique. I love how you've paid attention to the tiniest detail in the carvings. I like the types of wood you use. People can hand this furniture down to their kids and grandkids because it's art."

I went off a little longer than I should have, but the truth was that I loved his furniture. Many of the people I had worked for had Kade's furniture in their homes and vacation homes.

Kade listened carefully. He heard what I did not say, which was anything personal about myself or my history. I rattled on and when I finished he let the silence hang between us. I waited him out. I tried to hold his dark gaze. I willed myself not to tilt my chin down or slump my back.

"What job are you hoping for within the company?"

I tried to smile. My smile felt stiff, and I worked to get it straight so I didn't look like I was leering. "I think I could help you in sales, but I understand that you have a receptionist job available."

He nodded. "I do. My receptionist left to have a baby. Her water broke in the lobby here. I drove her to the hospital myself. She hates hospitals. Anyhow, this job would probably only be temporary. She may come back." He gazed out at the mountains, then shook his head. "She probably won't."

I knew Bajal wouldn't. I launched into a short speech about how I knew that as the receptionist I would be the first person people would talk to, how the way I talked to people on the phone could encourage them to buy, or discourage them from buying, furniture; that it was important to be welcoming, friendly, and knowledgeable about the furniture, and to get the customer to someone who could help them more than I could.

He asked me one question after another. I tried to be brief but thorough. He listened closely. I could tell he wasn't buying me, buying what I said. "Is there anything"—he drummed his fingers on his desk—"else you want to tell me about yourself?"

"No." I said that too quickly, but there was nothing else I *wanted* to tell him.

"Where are you staying in town?"

"I'm staying at Talia's bed and breakfast until I figure out where to live." Small lie. I smiled harder. "I think I would fit in here. I work hard. I learn quick and I can talk to people."

"Okay." He turned his head, and I knew things had not gone well.

Did he know? My other name, Dina Hamilton, had been in the newspaper. My photo had been in there, too. A reporter had used one from a golf club party Covey and I had attended months before—a dreadful event—but I had longer, stick-straight blond hair then, and now it was my natural red with a fringe of bangs. I was also not in a ball gown, my boobs pushed up.

"I would like the job. I can start today. Tomorrow. My shifts don't start until five-thirty at The Spirited Owl and I'm only working for them Tuesday nights through Saturday."

"Long day for you."

"I can do it." His dark eyes missed nothing. I would not want to get in a fight with this man for all the tea in China, the Netherlands, and London put together. He was one of the only truly rockin' bad dudes I'd ever met.

I kept my shoulders back. Barely. I knew he wasn't sure about me because he thought I was being cagey.

"I hear that you're pretty tough at The Spirited Owl."

"I don't take any crap." Why did I say that? That did not sound elegant or refined.

His mouth tilted slightly, a tiny smile. "I understand."

"I didn't mean to sound so snappy." I drummed my fingers. "The clientele can get . . . challenging."

"Yes, I'm sure they can." He studied me, then stood up. "I'll call you when I decide what to do about Bajal's job." We shook hands, my hand lost in the warmth of his. Part of me didn't want to let go. "Thanks for coming in."

"I would like the job." My voice came out soft, sort of desperate, which was humiliating.

He was analyzing me, thinking, speculative. I knew he knew I wasn't telling him the full truth. He was trying to figure out how much of that mattered versus how I came off in the interview. Would I be good enough anyhow? We were still clasping hands. I let go; he waited a second, then he let go, too.

I thought I saw his face soften up for a minute. His eyes not quite so hard. His body language relenting, maybe there was even a hint of a smile.

Maybe.

Maybe I was delusional. I was still so sick.

"Thank you for your time. It was nice to meet you."

"You too."

I turned to leave, and that was that.

I could feel his eyes on my back as I left. I didn't think I had the job. In fact, I was pretty sure I didn't. I tried not to cry all the way to my car. I unlocked the door and drove out to the country. I pulled over on a side road and put my head on the steering wheel, the wind blowing in from that blasted broken window, the plastic crackling. I cried and cried until I'm sure my tear ducts were begging for mercy.

I blew my nose, coughed, sneezed twice, and held my head as my whole body started to sweat. My fever was breaking yet again. I chugged more cold medicine.

I hate being sick. I cannot run my life well while sick. I cannot handle what's coming my way like a pickax to my gut while sick. I cannot fix this car-living problem while sick.

And I had to pee. Bad.

I climbed out of the car, peeked around for people, then

quickly dropped my pants. I already missed my bathroom at Talia's. It was getting colder outside, and my butt was going to freeze if I had to live like this for many more weeks. I washed my hands with my bottled water and soap, drank an entire bottle because my nerves and fever had dehydrated me, then pulled out a can of chili and ate it for lunch. I had been eating too much chili lately.

I brushed my teeth, spitting into the bushes, then drove down the street and out of town in the other direction to apply for a job at a lumber yard. I would prefer working for Hendricks', but that was the way it was.

The manager was rude. She was tall, thin, and told me she wasn't hiring. I said thank you, felt stupid, and left. I was almost down to applying at McDonald's, though I'm sure my arrest would probably eliminate me immediately.

Had to cover my bases. I needed more money than McDonald's paid, but if minimum wage was all there was, that was the way it was. I could put on a blue shirt and name tag and flip a burger if I had to.

I thought about what the press would do if they saw me in a McDonald's uniform, and put that thought aside. I had no pride left. Freezing in a car, living in a car, will take it all away. And, at the end of all this, after a jail term, I'd probably move out of state, maybe to Wyoming or Alaska, and disappear. So, who cared? I had one goal: Get an apartment before winter hit harder.

That night, after my shift at The Spirited Owl, I parked in a different neighborhood. I stripped off my work clothes and climbed into my sleeping clothes, then hurried into my sleeping bag and blankets. My clean blankets smelled like powder. The temperature had dropped another ten degrees.

I had made $125 in tips that night, partly thanks to Moose, who left me the usual twenty-five dollars. If I was hired at Hendricks' I would still have Sundays off to sleep and get my mind together and deal with whatever crap came up with Covey and the attorneys.

I have workaholic tendencies. I know this. I always have.

I assumed Hendricks' Furniture would pay me, as a receptionist, slightly more than minimum wage, but I was pretty sure he would have health insurance, which would save me hundreds. I did not have health insurance with Covey's company anymore. I thought of his twelve employees and their families. I felt bad for them. Except for three of the employees—Davitt, Angie, and Victor. Those three were possum scum like Covey.

The cold medicine was wearing off again, which meant that my fever was spiking back up. I shivered, pulled on another sweatshirt, tugged my red knitted hat down, and scrunched farther into my sleeping bag, pulling it over my head. I was wiped out from my cold, my chest ached, my nose was stuffed up, and I was fighting off despair. I could feel it dragging me down, but I had a tiny morsel in me that was still fighting like a raccoon caught in a trap.

I would have a nice house again someday, I told myself. I would. It would be a small home, something I could afford no matter what, something that couldn't be taken from me ever. It would be yellow on the outside and yellow on the inside.

There would be a gas fireplace that I could switch on at any time so I wouldn't freeze my butt off like I am now, and it would have a deep tub so when I was sick I could warm my bones. I would have piles of blankets and pillows and quilts, and I would have cupboards stocked with food so Alice, My Anxiety, wouldn't feel anxious.

I would not live in my car again. This was it. Last time. I would not be a homeless, lost person, even temporarily.

Stupid, stupid, stupid. I had trusted Covey, and this is where it landed me.

I would not be stupid again.

The rain came down like a flash flood.

Please, Kade, hire me.

I woke in the middle of the night to silence. I knew I had been dreaming of the red, crocheted shawl because I felt peaceful. Not so alone.

My fever had spiked again; my cough had deepened, thickened; and I wondered if I was dying. I closed my eyes again.

We love you, Grenadine. Be strong.

It was them.

Hang in there, sweet butterfly.

I knew it. I felt them, felt their love.

Every night for the rest of that week, as I slept in my car, the rain and hail pounding down, I did a Personal Financial Calculation and told myself that I was getting closer and closer to a home that I could not drive. I had paid Cherie our usual monthly four-figure agreement, which had set me back, but I was still moving ahead.

For some reason, each night I had visions of a snake wrapped around a knife shrouded in fog, which woke me up, a sense of impending doom hanging over me.

When the plastic fell off the window, I reattached it.

I was getting admirably adept at using duct tape.

15

Schollton Police
Incident Report

Case No. 83-2285

Reported Date/Time: December 8, 1983/8:30
Location of Occurrence: 6260 S.W. Fisher Ave.
Reporting Officer: Sergeant Trina Orleon
Incident: Found Girl

Shirley Lyn Trumachev, 65, saw a girl walking down her street, Fisher Ave. The girl was wobbling, thin, and pale, according to Mrs. Trumachev. It was snowing, and the girl was dressed in shorts and a T-shirt. Mrs. Trumachev's home is in the country and she has the only home, she says, for a half a mile and did not recognize the girl.

Mrs. Trumachev ran out of her home to check on her, and the child collapsed in her arms. She called 911.

When we arrived, the girl was unconscious. Breathing shallowly. She was wrapped in Mrs. Trumachev's coat and on her lap. She was thin and her chest made a rumbling sound from sickness. She was missing hair and had purple and blue bruising on her face. Her arms and legs looked emaciated. I have never

WHAT I REMEMBER MOST 111

seen a child in such poor shape. Repeat: I have never seen a child that thin.

After we ascertained that the ambulance was on its way, I briefly examined the girl. She had cigarette burns on her chest, stomach, and legs, and she had markings around her neck that might be from a rope. Her heartbeat was weak and slow.

The paramedics arrived, and they determined, as had Lieutenant Ting and I, that the child had to be hospitalized immediately.

Lieutenant Ting held the child in his arms because Mrs. Trumachev was shaking badly, and carried her into the ambulance. He insisted on going with her to the hospital. One of the firefighters rode along in the ambulance, as one of the paramedics seemed to have a hard time getting himself under control.

The girl was so pale and limp and skeletal, I thought she was dying. I have never seen a child in this bad condition.

Mrs. Trumachev was soon hysterical. We called her son when the ambulance left. She started to fall, and Sergeant Pattinser and I caught her. We laid her down and she clutched her heart, and within seconds we called another ambulance as Mrs. Trumachev had a mild heart attack. She kept saying, "That poor dear, that poor dear" repeatedly, as if she were in a trance. She was no longer able to communicate much with us.

Schollton Police
Incident Report

Case No. 83-2285

Reported Date/Time: December 8, 1983/16:30
Location of Occurrence: 27482 N.W. Owl Dr.

Reporting Officer: Sergeant Trina Orleon
Incident: Found Girl

The girl who was found at 6260 S.W. Fisher Ave. this morning is named Grenadine Scotch Wild. She is the foster child of Tom and Adelly Berlinsky, who live at 27482 N.W. Owl Dr. We were not able to immediately talk to the Berlinskys this morning because Grenadine was at St. Clare's Hospital and unable to tell us her name due to being unconscious and, when later awake, in critical condition.

When Lieutenant Ting, Sergeant Pattinser, and I arrived at the Berlinsky home, Adelly insisted that Grenadine was home. She was impaired from drugs and/or alcohol and unable to find the child. She repeatedly asked us if we wanted a beer but said she didn't have any. She also kicked the cat and told her son he looked like a leprechaun. She asked if we had stolen her hair dryer and said her husband was in Hungary because he was hungry.

When asked when she had last seen Grenadine, Mrs. Berlinsky could not remember. When Mrs. Berlinsky went outside in the snow to find Grenadine, screaming for her, her sons led us to a large kennel in the basement with a pink blanket.

We assumed the kennel was for the dog, but the children said that was where Grenadine lived. There were bowls for water and food. Upon examination, the bowl for food was filled with dog food. The water bowl was empty. In a corner of the kennel there were feces and urine.

One of the boys, Kevin, age ten, told us that that was where the human dog, Grenadine, lived. The other boy, Tom, Jr. age twelve, told us that their favorite game was to poke the human dog with a stick and whoever poked her most, won.

There was a rope on the walls. Tom Jr. said that sometimes they put Grenadine on a rope and walked her but mostly not because Grenadine was bad and that was why she didn't get people food and why she had to be locked up.

Grenadine told them that her dad was going to beat them up for hurting her. The boys thought that was funny because they said Grenadine does not have a dad and that he is dead and they told her that, too.

When we asked where Grenadine's bed was, they said she slept in the kennel, too. When we asked where Grenadine got the bruises, the boys said mostly from their mom, and some from their dad, and the belt and the wooden spoon, but some from them because she wouldn't bark when they told her to and whenever she was out of the kennel she snuck food so they were allowed to hit her on the head with their model airplanes.

We arrested Adelly Berlinsky. Tom Berlinsky is on a long-haul trucking job, but we have contacted the company and they are cooperating with authorities in locating Tom. A warrant has been issued for his arrest.

On a personal note, I want to admit now that I was angry with Mrs. Berlinsky. I did yell at her, and the children. She resisted arrest and tried to run, then hit me, and we were able to get her on the ground. Her nose did break as she continued to fight with us. Lieutenant Ting did not have to restrain me for more than a minute. Mrs. Berlinsky said that Lieutenant Ting purposefully hit her head when he was putting her into the police car; that claim is untrue. Again, she was struggling, which will account for the bruises on her face.

Lieutenant Ting and Sergeant Pattinser took her to the Justice Center, and Officers Lenton and Cables and I waited until CSD arrived for the boys. The boys asked if we were going to put them in jail. We decided not to answer them at that time.

To: Laurie Gutirrez
From: Dr. Paresh Chakrabarti
Date: December 9, 1983
Re: Grenadine Scotch Wild

Dear Laurie,

I hope that you and your family are doing well. It was good to see you, Miguel, and the kids on the slopes last weekend. I am very sorry for the loss of your grandmother, Mabel.

On another note. Yesterday we admitted a girl named Grenadine Scotch Wild, who is seven years old. She weighs forty pounds and is suffering from acute pneumonia. She is having difficulty breathing and is limp. She has no color in her face. Her temperature was 105 degrees upon arrival, it is now at 103, but it continues to spike up to 104. She has the worst ear infection I have ever seen. One eardrum recently burst.

She is severely dehydrated and the most malnourished person I have ever seen. Her ribs are protruding. Her hair is missing in patches on her head. She has cigarette burn marks on her body, old and new bruises, and three broken ribs. She has burns around her neck from, I believe, a rope. I don't know if someone dragged her with it, or tried to hang her.

I believe she has been hit with a belt on her back.
There are wounds so deep she will have scars for
life.

She has lice and scabies. She has dog bites on
both arms, one infected, and two of her toes are
infected from what looks like an animal bite, perhaps a rat.

Her eyes are lifeless and she is hardly able to
speak. All she says is that she wants her lilies, but
we are unsure what she is talking about.

She is unable to eat or drink, so we have not been
able to take the IV out.

She does not cry. The nurses are with her
constantly and claim she does not let go of their
hands, though her grasp is weak.

Without medical treatment, it is my opinion she
would have been dead within days. Even now she
is in critical condition. I cannot guarantee you
that she will survive.

Grenadine is a foster child. The foster parents
have been arrested. Apparently, this family was
trying to adopt her. It is unclear to me how a
child in the care of the state could deteriorate to
this point. This was a long decline, not overnight.
Where was her case worker? Where was the over-
sight?

We must act on this, my friend, not only with the
police but with the children's services division and
with the government. A review needs to be done

about this particular situation and other situations where other foster children might be in grave danger.

As you are the hospital's attorney, and someone who advocates relentlessly for the children here, I am requesting your personal and legal assistance with this matter.

Thank you.
Dr. Paresh Chakrabarti

16

Being homeless is bringing Alice, My Anxiety, to the forefront. I am vulnerable in many ways. My physical safety is not assured. I am cold. I do not have a bed or a home. I cannot take a shower when I need to. I am peeing out the side of my car. Sleeping in my car makes me feel claustrophobic. I do not like tight spaces. I don't have enough money.

Nothing is organized as it should be. When things are disorganized I feel scattered and nervous. I need a home environment that is neat and clean with tons of healthy food in the cupboards.

I need pretty around me and bright colors to ward off the darkness so I am not reminded of where I used to be. Any reminder of the chaos of my past, the danger, will set me off. I am now set off.

I need my art, too. There is no "stupid" in art. It can't make fun of me across the canvas. It can't force me to stumble over words. It can't ridicule me. It is mine. I am art. I create and paint, layer, and build. I need my canvases, my paints; my odd, shiny, rough, original, unique, trashy, sparkling collage materials. I need my scissors and my glues.

My hands are not used to not doing art. My mind is not used to being present in the real world at all times, nor does it like it. My heart needs art.

I need a home so I can art it out, so to speak.

Which translates loosely into: If I can't art it out, I will lose my friggin' mind to Alice, My Anxiety.

I am homeless, and Alice and I do not like car living.

"Gren, can you do me a favor?"

"Sure, Chilton." I leaned a hip against the bar. Chilton Weiner was one of my favorite customers. His last name is pronounced Wee-ner.

He has a weathered face, his hair's unkempt, and he looks like he has lived life too hard, too fast, for too long. To me, he is pure kindness. He's polite and always asks how I am, like he truly wants to know, and makes me laugh.

He tears up over love songs, and when he saw a dog get hit by a truck one afternoon, I don't think he stopped crying into his beer all night. He wrapped the dead dog in his coat, found the owners, dug the grave in the single mother's backyard, and gave a eulogy with the crying kids.

He's been friends with Tildy and Grizz for over twenty years.

"You knows I'm a trucker, so I'm leavin' tonight after Tildy makes my burger, and I need someone to stay at my place until I get back in a week. I have pets and they need company." He leaned across the bar. "I'll pay you fifty dollars a day for staying at my house."

I studied those sweet eyes. Tildy told him something was up with me, I knew it. This was his and Tildy's way of getting me into a home, by making me feel that I was doing Chilton a favor. Saved my pride, saved them from poking my pride. "I'll do it for free, Chilton."

"Oh no, young woman, I'm paying you or it's a no-go."

"Then it's a no-go." I crossed my arms. Although I didn't have a fever, I was still as weak as a limp dog from the flu, so I'd play into this charade because I could not stand the thought of sleeping in my car. It was snowing and my window wasn't fixed. But I would not take the money.

He crossed his arms.

I raised my eyebrows in challenge.

He raised his. Then he capitulated and sighed.

"Here's the address, stubborn lady, stubborn as a lady rooster. Don't worry about the snakes. They don't need to be fed, already fed them their mice. They like people around, though. Makes them feel loved and cuddled."

"Snakes?" I swallowed hard.

"Yep. In cages, all locked up. They can't make no escape, now, don't you worry. Sometimes I let 'em out, let the princess and the king out, but they don't bother me none. I keep my eyes on 'em, and then I say, 'Wrap and wallop!' and I gather 'em up and put them back in their homes. Wrap and wallop! They don't give me no trouble, and they ain't gonna give you no trouble, either, because they're locked down."

"I hope not." My spine tingled. I don't know where my fear of snakes came from, but I have it.

He leaned over to me, lowered his voice. "I knows a worried woman when I sees one. You're a worried woman, and I'm sorry for that. It's your business, Gren, and I won't pry, unless you want to share with me your worries one day when you and I have a trust level." He waved his hands between us.

I was touched.

"My late wife, Donna Joey, may her soul rest in peace and comfort and may she have all the tequila she likes without getting drunk up there in heaven, she was a woman who liked her tequila . . ." He wiped his eyes. "Man. Still I cry for my Donna Joey. But she had the same worried eyes when I met her thirty years ago that you do. You be a worried woman, too, Gren. I can tell by them there green eyes, *bright* green eyes. So you get yourself to my place and you rest that head of yours. Here's the key."

"Are you sure?" I figured I could do snakes for a bed and toilet. I didn't think too much about what his home was like. I didn't care at this point. Unless I contracted lice and scabies again. That I would not like.

"Yes, I am. The snakes need you!" He stabbed a finger in the air. "I want to help you and Donna Joey. She's telling me in my head right now to help you, so I am. I do what my woman tells me to do. You go and stay in our home and help me with the snakes. With you around, they won't get lonely." He ambled on out of the bar after his burger, singing a tune about Donna Joey bringing warmth to his heart and to his "nether regions."

Tildy smiled at me when he left. It was late, so she took her gun out and started polishing it. "Take him up on his offer. He is particular about those reptiles, and it makes him nervous when there's no one there. He actually thinks they'll be lonely without a human. You'll be safe. His house is in a neighborhood close by here. Good neighborhood. Here. Take this pumpkin bread for the morning. Made it myself last night. I outdid myself."

I hate handouts, but I had to take this one. It was sleep in a bed in a warm house or get sicker and end up with pneumonia. All I needed was an uninsured hospital bill and I'd be sunk. "Thank you, Tildy."

She gave me a quick hug, her white streak settling on my cheek. "Don't you be thanking me. I'm thanking you. Your antics in the bar are bringing more people in all the time. When you slid four beers straight down the counter tonight and none tipped over, I darn near did a cartwheel. That's skill. And the guys loved it. Same with you pouring liquor from three feet up and memorizing six drink orders at a time." She tapped her temple with the barrel of the gun. "You're smart."

Hadn't heard that one often. I pocketed the key. I was wary about the snakes, but excited. A home. I could stay in a home. I swear I could feel my bones cracking at the thought of another night in my car, my breath forming tiny clouds, my toes stiffening, and the fear that someone else would shatter my window and crawl in, waking me up constantly.

I breathed a huge sigh of relief. Thank you, Tildy. Thank you Chilton. Thank you.

After my shift, about midnight, I drove past the statue of the bucking horse, the faux balconies and boardwalks, and drove to Chilton's home. It was colder than a cow's tit in December, but I was so excited for a bed I was giddy. I told myself I would sleep all night and all day until tomorrow at four-thirty.

Tildy had been right. Chilton's home was in a well-kept, traditional neighborhood. Even though it was dark out, I could see a perfectly mowed lawn, trimmed bushes, the light gray paintwork new and neat.

The tidy exterior picture was an illusion. I stepped into his foyer and was hit with a musty, dusty smell. I thought I heard something skitter, and froze. I reached out a hand and hit a light switch.

I could not take in what I was seeing at first. My mouth dropped, and my breathing, I am positive, stopped.

Snakes.

In fish-bowl-like rectangular tanks. In square tanks. One snake tank was oval. There must have been ten glass "homes" for the snakes. It was a snake house.

"Oh, my shoutin', spittin' Lord," I muttered. In the middle of the family room, or should I call it the snake room, was a battered leather chair and in front of it a huge big-screen TV. I closed my eyes, rocked back on my heels.

If I did not want out of my car as much as I did, if I did not want to sleep in a bed, if I wasn't sick of being scared out of my mind at night, if I wasn't sick of being tired, I would have left, hands in the hair, shrieking. I am familiar with many scary things but not snakes.

I closed the door behind me, dropped my duffle bags and the black plastic bag that held my laundry, and started turning on lights. I tried to ignore the snakes and headed to the kitchen. In the kitchen there was a long picnic table. I clutched my throat. Two more snakes in snake aquariums.

I opened up the windows. Almost instantly the air smelled better.

Could I stay there for the night?

Amidst snakes?

I heard the rain battering the windows. It would freeze tonight. There would be ice covering my car in the morning.

Okay, Grenady. Breathe in. You can do it. Roof. Heat. Bed. Plus, I wanted to wash my clothes, and Laundromats are so expensive.

I grabbed my bags and put a load of dark colors—including all my black work clothes—in the washer. Fortunately, there was only one small red snake in a tank on the dryer. It poked its head up at me. I made sure the lid was on tight, my fingers trembling as I pushed it away.

I closed the windows, turned up the heat, and headed for the bathroom. I stopped when I opened the door to the bathroom, my mouth dropping open once again.

The surprises weren't going to stop tonight, no, they were not. The bathroom was like a miniature Greek bathhouse.

The bathroom was the size of a bedroom. There was a sunken tub for at least six and a tiled shower with two shower-heads. The counters were granite, the faucets were gold, and a bidet waited to clean someone's privates. I laughed out loud. As Chilton did not strike me as a man who liked to clean up, it was a funny dichotomy to see this.

Funny or not, I was going to enjoy a toilet and a hot bath. I brought my duffle bag in with my shampoos and soap, then scrubbed out the bath with cleaner I found under the sink. When it was shiny clean and rinsed, I filled that tub with luscious hot water and settled in, my tight muscles relaxing. The tub was so huge, I could paddle around. I washed my hair, let the cream rinse sit, shaved, and lay like a dead human snake for over an hour.

I didn't want to sleep in Chilton's bed, so after my bath I headed for the room across the hall. There was a queen bed that seemed new. I stripped off the sheets and put my dark clothes in the dryer and the sheets in the washer on hot with extra soap. I sat down and ate my dinner, spaghetti and meatballs, salad and garlic bread, in front of the TV in his leather chair, which was supercomfortable, I had to admit. I ignored the slithering, sneaky snakes all around me.

The beep of the dryer woke me up. I took out my clean work clothes, transferred the sheets to the dryer, and put a load of whites in the washer. When the sheets were done, it was super-late and I'd fallen asleep again. I put my whites in the dryer and my towels in the washer. I made the bed and crawled in with one of my own pillows. It was feathery soft, and I piled on the blankets and went to sleep.

Two hours later my own scream, raw with terror, woke me up. I had a quick vision of a snake wrapped around a knife, fog around the whole thing, then it disappeared. I screamed again when I felt someone on top of me, moving.

Someone *skinny*.

I kept screaming, pushed him away with all I had, and leaped out of bed, my legs tangling in the sheets and blankets. I pitched to the floor on all fours, kicked free, then sprinted into the hallway, thinking at any second a man's hands would wring my breath from my neck. I screamed again, stumbled to the front door in the dark, fumbled with the lock and yanked it open. I leaped out the door to the driveway, the rain pouring down, then stopped. I did not hear anyone pounding after me.

I panted, my heart rate sky high. Had I had a nightmare? Was there no one there? Was I feverish again? There was no one behind me. When my heart slowed, I crept back in, rain dripping off my nose. I peeked in the door and heard...nothing. I reached for my purse by the door, picked up my cell phone, hit 9 1...and crept back to the bedroom. I would hit the last number 1 if I saw anyone or heard a peep.

My knees almost knocking, I touched the light switch and peeked into the bedroom. There was no one on the bed. No one in the room.

The sheets and blankets were in a pile on the floor. I tried to breathe, my heart thundering. It *was* a nightmare, clearly brought on by the snakes in the house.

Of course. That was it.

Then the comforter at the bottom of the bed moved. I smothered another scream. It was not a person, it wasn't big enough... something stuck out the other end. Something black...oh no, oh no. I grabbed my stomach. It wasn't.

Oh no. It was.

Snake.

A huge, black snake. It kept coming and coming out of that comforter, then it slid to the floor, foot after foot after foot.

Go, Grenadine!
Move, move, move!
It was them. Their voices. Insistent.

But I couldn't move. I was so scared I thought my skin would be stripped from my bones, maybe fall off in layers. The snake kept slinking out, then its head, *its head* turned toward me.

Move now! Get out of the house!
That was it. I did what they told me to do.

I hopped, I jumped, I screamed, and I darted out of that room, slamming the door behind me. I rushed to the dryer, panting, and took my dry white clothes out, stuffing them into a duffle bag. I took my wet towels out and stuffed them in a black plastic bag. I ran both bags out to my car, the rain drizzling down my petrified face. I grabbed my other duffle bags, my folded clean laundry, and my stuff out of the bathroom.

I stumbled out of that snake house while keeping an eye out for the snake—it was way too big to squeeze underneath the door, but could it open the door with its face? Could it wrap itself around the handle and pull?

I dumped the bags in my car, then ran back in; turned off the lights; grabbed my jacket, laptop, and purse; and ran back out.

My hands were shaking as I tried to lock the door to the house. I dropped the keys, dropped them again, dropped them a third time, then finally locked the door. I sped off, as if the snake could follow me, my whole body racked with snake shakes.

I did not sleep for one more minute that night. I rocked back and forth in my sleeping bag trying to get the feel of a slithery, giant black snake off of me. I waited in the McDonald's parking lot for them to open, then ordered a large coffee and collapsed in a booth.

I didn't think I'd ever sleep right again.

I decided to clean up my "home" to distract myself so I didn't become a self-pitying mess. I made sure all my earthly belongings were as organized as they could be: All the clean clothes were folded into my duffle bags and a suitcase. My wet towels were spread out to dry out, although I knew that was doubtful in this cold, damp weather.

I rearranged canned foods in one box, dried foods like bread and peanut butter in another, my toiletries in another. I folded the blankets and put them at the end of my sleeping bag.

Then I tried to do something pretty.

I picked up my sketch pad and three colored pencils: magenta, lavender, and orange. I tried to draw, but I couldn't. Not one line, not one curve.

I took the lid off a bottle of buttons.

I tried to lay them out in a pattern on my sketch pad to spark my creativity. No sparks.

I grabbed a box of art supplies with sequins, scraps of famous quotes, and lace, and tried to arrange those, too.

Nothing. No pretty.

I climbed into my sleeping bag. I would not be able to work unless I had a nap. I tried not to sniffle like a whiny thing, but I had wanted a bed so much. And a toilet. And heat. But, daaaaang. That had not worked.

Ah, well. I had not been bitten by a snake.

That was something to be happy about.

I had also not been wrapped in a deathly hug.

Yet another thing to be happy about.

Death by snake is not the way I want to go.

I woke up at four o'clock in the afternoon, cramped and cold. I went back into McDonald's, peed, cleaned up with my wet washcloths, brushed my teeth and hair. I changed into clean clothes and bought another coffee.

While I was there I read the paper.

Buried in the back was an article that I didn't want to read, but I read it anyhow.

My fury flared. My desire for revenge about knocked me over. He was way worse than the snake I'd slept with.

"Hello, Grenady."

"Oh. Hi." I stopped on the sidewalk near the library and

stared up at Kade Hendricks. He smiled. It made him look less like he could knock my teeth out with an expert whack. "How are you, Mr. Hendricks?"

"You can call me Kade, and I'm fine. How are you?"

"Good." The flu was gone. I had received a bone-chilling call from Covey, from a number I didn't recognize, but I was trying to get my courage back. "How is your day going?"

"Busy. I was at work at six, and now I'm starving and need to eat. Want to come with me?"

"Sure." Heck, yeah. Maybe I could impress upon him my faux-wonderfulness and get the receptionist job if he hadn't hired someone else by now.

"Let's go to Bernie's," he said. "He makes some decent sandwiches."

"Okay. Thank you."

I was going to lunch with Kade.

I felt overwhelmed by the man, but he could employ me, so I'd take the chance and try not to say anything inane.

"How do you like Pineridge, Grenady?"

"I like it." I would not say: It's a nice place to hide pre-jail. "I like the mountains, the weather, the town, the people." It would be better with my own toilet. "Have you lived here long?"

"I grew up in California and moved here in my twenties. So about seventeen years."

"Family here?"

"No. I read about it, then drove up."

"By yourself?" Now that was prying. I knew he wasn't married, Tildy had told me, but he could have been then.

"Yes. By myself."

"I drove out here by myself, too." He already knew that. I don't know why I repeated it.

The waitress brought us our sandwiches. I was so hungry I could have eaten a horse and another horse.

"And you had no family here, right?" he asked. "No friends when you arrived?"

"No, I didn't know anyone." I smiled so as to look cheerful and adventurous, not friendless. "Did you have friends here when you arrived?"

"No. I didn't know anyone, either."

We had something in common. I took a bite out of my sandwich. It was like eating turkey heaven. I tried not to inhale it and make moaning sounds. I searched around for something to say to change the subject. "So, tell me something. How do you make your furniture? How do you build, say, a desk?"

He smiled slightly at me across the table, and it softened that face up, but I knew he knew I was changing the subject. He explained how he made a desk. He was patient. He answered my questions about the design, the construction, the woods he used, the saws. I asked how an armoire was built, and he told me. I could sense his enthusiasm, his passion for his work.

Then I wanted to know about his carvings, what tools he used, how long it took, did he draw it onto the wood first? Furniture building, as Kade did it, was art. I like art, so I was particularly interested.

"You ask in-depth questions, Grenady."

"Oh no. Is this annoying?" We'd finished eating an hour ago.

He shook his head. "Not at all. I'm glad you're interested. How's your work at The Spirited Owl going?"

I laughed, rolled my eyes. I soon had Kade laughing when I talked about some of my customers. One who fell right off his stool when a pretty gal walked in. Another who was so drunk he pitched a dart at his friend's head and it stuck. A third who always wore a hat with a Santa on it. Seven days a week. "Something new whenever I walk through those doors." I leaned back. "I should let you go. I'm sure you have to get back to work."

"I'm not in a rush. I know you're an artist. Tell me about your studio."

I told him about my studio, but not the one I'd had in a spare bedroom at Covey's. I told him about my true studio—the one I'd had in my little green home with the turquoise bookcases, the jars of treasures, the long tables, the stacked-up canvases, the red chair to sketch in, the piles of art books, paints, colored pencils, and all of my collage supplies: the buttons, sequins, glitter, newspapers, miniature toys, dice, fake stones. He asked a lot of questions.

I told him about teaching kids art at my home and at their school as a volunteer. He seemed truly humbled by that. "Very generous of you, Grenady." He asked about the kids and their families, and I told him about their home situations, some of which were not happy.

"Don't you have to go?" I asked him. It was almost three o'clock. We'd been talking for two and a half hours.

"Almost."

"Almost?" I laughed. "I suppose your boss won't be upset."

"No. He lets me get away with what I want."

He smiled again. It was a friendly smile, sexy. A little flirty? No, that couldn't be.

"Where did you grow up?"

I studied the saltshaker. I didn't like that question. "A lot of places."

"Moved around a lot?"

"You could say that. And you?"

"Los Angeles. Hard to move around a lot as a kid."

"Yes, it is." A few graphic images skittered on through. Not pleasant ones. I took a deep breath and pushed them out of my head. They nudged back in. I fiddled with my napkin, then willfully shoved them back out again.

"A conversation for another time?" he asked.

"I think it's a conversation I would rather skip altogether. I'd like to hear your story, though."

"I'm afraid it's not pretty."

"Mine isn't either, Kade."

"I'm sorry."

"Sorry for you, too."

He shrugged. "It's the way it is."

"Yes, it is. But I'm still searching for the pretty." I smiled at

him. I couldn't help it. And, holy Mary, his smile came back
again. The mafia man was still there, but it was a gentler mafia
man now.

He picked up the check. I went for my purse. "Grenady,
please. I have it."

"Thank you."

We stood up, and the owner, Bernie, tall and lanky, came up
and shook his hand. "Kade, how are you?"

They chatted for a minute, then Kade introduced me to Bernie.
We exchanged the usual pleasantries. The waitress said good-
bye to us as we left.

"Thanks for having lunch with me, Grenady."

"Thank you for asking. It was fun." I shook his hand.

He held my hand, longer than he should have.

I tingled, which surprised me, as I hate men currently. But I
liked him. I hoped he would hire me.

I called Chilton.

"I slept in your guest bedroom, Chilton."

"My what? Whaddya say, Gren?"

"Your guest bedroom. The one across from your bedroom.
Where guests sleep when they come over. I slept in it."

"The one across from mine? A guest room? Don't got a guest
room. When my brother drinks too much and passes out, he
lays himself flat on the couch. My hunting buddies don't sleep
in that room, either."

"No? But there's a bed in it."

"Comfy bed. Nice new bed. Cost me fifteen hundred dollars.
You didn't sleep in there, didja, Gren? I thought I told you not
to sleep in there."

"Yes, I did." I felt the slinky snake on me again. "You didn't
tell me not to." Now I sounded accusatory, ungrateful. "I mean,
maybe you did and I forgot. I think I forgot."

"Oh no, sugar. Rats! Guess I forgot to tell you that part, now
that I'm remembering. Double rats! I'd had a beer that night.
Beer always plays with my memory. I think it's the hops. They

get in my mind and hop around and make things confusing and fuzzy." He cleared his throat. "Darlin', that room is not for human sleepers. That room is for Hog."

"Hog?"

"Hog the Snake. He eats like a hog, so I call him Hog. That's his room."

Hog the Snake had his own room. His own fifteen hundred dollar bed. I had washed Hog's sheets for him.

"You slept with Hog, Gren?" Chilton asked.

"Only for a few hours."

Chilton laughed. "Rats! I bet you scared the living daylights out of poor Hog."

"I did, I surely did. Probably gave him a heart attack."

Chilton laughed again. "I'm sorry, Gren. Now ya know. That be Hog's room. You can have one of the other bedrooms or the couch by the garter snake village. If you see a mouse, try to catch it and toss it into one of the snake's cages."

"What?" My voice was a hoarse whisper. "Catch a mouse?"

"I'm kiddin', sugar, I'm kiddin'." He laughed. "I'd never have a lady catch a mouse, no, ma'am, specially not one lovely like you."

I thought of Hog the Snake on top of me. I was almost his dinner.

I would brave the weather, marauding scary men, the cramped conditions, and no toilet.

I could not possibly sleep with snakes.

The next morning I woke up nervous. Alice, My Anxiety, does that sometimes. It's as if she can't wait to start shaking me down. I grabbed a sketch pad and charcoal pencil with hands that trembled so much, they might have been electrocuted.

I drew a girl in a kennel, skeletal, eyes closed.

I drew her running down a dark road, mouth open, trees looming.

I drew her sitting alone in a classroom, at the back.

I drew her sleeping in a car, in an alley.

It took an hour.

My tears blurred the charcoal as I pushed the past back.

"Phone call, Grenady." Tildy tilted her head toward the back of the restaurant. I never received calls at work. Who would call me?

It had been three nights since the snake adventure, and I'd had a busy shift. We'd had a group of Red Hat Society ladies come in and sing songs. One was about a woman who kicked that man right out of her house, " 'cause he was a gosh darn louse, with a stick like a mouse," and another was about a lady pirate who rode the seven seas and had seven lovers. They particularly liked that one.

"Hello?"

"Hi, sweetheart," he said.

Not him. Not now. "What do you want, you son of a bitch."

"Let's not talk about my mother that way."

I hated his tone: Reasonable. Rational. As in, don't get hysterical, hormonal woman.

"I can't believe what you've done to me, Covey. I know you're all lawyered up with Goldman and Skiller, but tell the U.S. Attorney's Office and the FBI that I didn't know about your crimes."

"You want something from me but you're not willing to give me anything, Dina. That's selfish."

"Selfish? I'm selfish?" My voice pitched like a banshee cry.

"Tell the truth. I could go back to prison because of you."

"If you cooperate with me, you won't. Goldman and Skiller have a plan, it'll work. They're going after the U.S. Attorney's Office's evidence. They'll shred it, not allow it into court, get us off on technicalities, entrapment, false arrest, blah blah blah, something like that."

"No, they won't, you brainless cow. Do you understand that the U.S. Attorney's Office, the FBI, the IRS, and even the mail fraud unit of the postal service have been investigating your company, us, for months? *Months.* That's what my attorney told me. One of your clients, Tore Shales, wanted his money and you didn't give it to him promptly, and he called the FBI. They started interviewing people. They started following the money, the bank accounts here and offshore, your company, your trips to Vegas, your shell companies, your fake investments and fake accounting sheets." I teared up. I was scared down to my toes and livid. "Tell them I didn't do anything wrong."

"I can't do that, darling. My attorneys will prove that we're innocent. Sometimes investments go bad, and that's what happened here. Stock market risks. Real estate collapse. Economic meltdowns. Not my fault. I'll get us out of this, sweetheart, don't worry your pretty head."

I wanted to hit him so much, my fists were tingling. "I don't deserve this."

"Yes, you do." And there went the reasonable, condescending tone, as icy rage took its place. "You left me. A marriage is forever, no matter what. Times get tough and you leave."

"Times get tough? You are a criminal who is dragging his soon-to-be ex-wife into this mess. How could you?"

But I knew how he could do this. It was a control thing. Covey had sensed in the weeks leading up to this that I'd had enough and was going to leave him. We had been fighting ferociously. He was livid that he couldn't spy on me anymore with the GPS and cameras. His toy and possession, me, was breaking away. His own abandonment issues were flaring like a bonfire in his sick brain.

By not exonerating me, he had control over me, now and in the future.

I did not completely trust Covey when I married him, but I thought that was because it was not innately in me to trust the vast majority of people on the planet. I never expected him to do this.

"You get yourself and that rack of yours home, trailer lady."

"Don't ever call me that." Trailer trash lady. That's what he meant. It only came out when he was steaming at me, his ability to control me slackening.

"If you don't come home and it looks like I'm going down, I will tell the prosecutors about your role in this."

I sucked air in, my body instantly cold, cold, cold. "What are you talking about?"

"You helped me plan all of this, Dina. You were the mastermind. The brains behind it all. I couldn't have done this without you. We went to parties together, even when we were dating, and you met people. The country clubs. The golf club. You smiled sexy, walked sexy, talked sexy. You brought men to me. They followed that rack around wherever you went. We wined and dined them together, then they invested in our company. You were the sales and delivery person."

I opened my mouth to protest, but no words came out. I felt like I'd been hit with a stun gun. "That is not what happened." My whisper was strangled.

"We made the perfect team. Perfect couple. Without you, Dina, I wouldn't be half the man—no, not even a quarter of the man I am now. You were key to the success of Hamilton Investments."

"That's a lie, Covey." I slumped against the wall. The room actually wobbled, as if two giant hands had tipped it back and forth. "Why would you lie about me like that? What did I ever do to you?"

"What did you do to me? Ah, you left me. That's what you've done. And I've got a whole stack of papers here from that bitch, Cherie Poitras, saying you're divorcing me."

I heard that sharp edge in his voice, his obsession, the possession.

"You'll get nothing if you divorce me, Dina, nothing."

"There is nothing. We have nothing. Everything we have will go to your ripped-off clients. We're bankrupt."

"Divorcing me will be a long and torturous process. Your legal fees will hit fifty thousand before you blink."

He would do that. I would have to make payments to Cherie and pay court costs for years to come. He knew exactly how much money I had. He had to win. That's what he wanted. *To win.* When I was broke, when I was smashed, when I was in jail, he would back off, but first he had to punish me for leaving.

"You had me sign those papers to frame me."

"Not to frame you. But to make sure you saw the value in staying with me. I will never give in. I will never let you go, Dina."

He thought he had my future in his hands. He had power over me. I knew he thrived on that. I was at his mercy. It was sexy for him.

"I love you, Dina. It's you and me, babe. And if you don't want to be together then you'll stand on your own and go to jail on your own. I won't protect you unless you come home."

"No. I'm not coming home, and if I go to jail, you will, too."

I could not get air into my lungs. I felt panicky. Move in and hope that his slick attorneys could work something out or that, in the end, if he went to jail he would spare me? Or stay here and risk him frying me alive?

"Exactly—you go, I go. I don't go, you don't go. How do you think you'll fare in jail, Dina? How did you like all your new dyke friends there? How did you like those bars? I know you're claustrophobic. What about isolation? Heard you ended up there. How was that? You like things organized. You're an interior design queen. Jail's not like that, is it? And no art, Dina. No paints. No collages. Art is the only thing that keeps you sane, isn't it? You'll be reminded twenty-four hours a day where you came from: Nothing. White trash. Trailer park."

"Shut up." I pictured Covey. Teeth gritted. Face tight. I heard him exhale.

"I miss you in our bed. I bet you miss it, too, you nymphomaniac. Oh, and how is work at The Spirited Owl? You're back where you were years ago, aren't you, Mrs. Waitress?"

"I hate you. How did you find me?"

"Easy, Dina. A little P.I. work. See you and that tight little ass soon, or I will send that tight little ass to jail. I think my phone is bugged by the government, so be careful what you say to me when you call and beg my forgiveness." His voice lowered. "I love you and I miss you."

He hung up.

I was so angry. If it looked like he was going to jail, he'd take me with him. If he couldn't have me, no one could.

The fear of being locked up like an animal, suffocating, dealing with rules and guards and cavity checks, of not being able to work, or live in my own home, or be independent and free, terrorizes me to my core.

I was scared to pieces.

That night I had a nightmare. I woke up not being able to breathe. I'd heard them shouting again, in horror, panicked.

Run, Grenadine, run!

Carlton Jags fell off his stool and was sprawled on the floor about eight the next night. He was drunk.

Tildy groaned. "Not again. Last time he tossed his cookies in here."

"I got him." I do not like tossed cookies. I might have to clean them up. I went around the bar with Tildy, and together with two men we grabbed Carlton and pulled him outside.

"I served him only two beers, Tildy."

"He was probably drinking away in his truck, crying on his steering wheel, before he even stepped his sorry ass inside."

"This is not gonna solve anything, buddy," Tildy said to him. "Never has in the history of mankind, never will."

Carlton didn't answer Tildy, as Carlton was too out of it. Carlton also did not respond to an eighty-year-old woman named Mrs. Shomoto, who clucked at him and called him a "poor, dear, heartsick idiot."

We put him in one of the Adirondack chairs. Tildy went to call his mother, and the men went back inside. Vaguely I registered that three men were walking toward the restaurant.

I took Carlton's car keys out of his pocket, then made sure he was as comfortable as he could be. I tilted his head so he wouldn't get a crick in his neck.

Carlton, who is about thirty-five, is an online computer technician by day and a musician who wallows in his emotions and sings about them by night. His wife, Chandra, left him three months ago for a lovely woman, and things had gone downhill from there. Apparently he rarely drank before Chandra took off.

Chandra was a cheerful and loving person and an elementary school teacher. The whole town, including Carlton, adored her.

They did not have children, and Chandra and her girlfriend moved to San Francisco. "What a cliché!" Carlton had cried, then pounded his head on the bar. "I'm a cliché!"

I went back in the bar, grabbed two blankets from the back that we keep for this purpose, and put a few slices of cheese bread in a baggie. I don't believe in enabling drunks, and Carlton had to hit bottom to get back up, but I had a lot of sympathy for him and his broken heart. Plus I liked his mother, Joann.

"Hang in there, Carlton," I said out loud, putting my hand on his cheek. "You can get through this." I put the bag of cheese bread in his lap, then covered him with the blankets.

When I stood up I locked eyes with Kade Hendricks. He was with two other men. They were towering giants, like Kade, not a pansy in the bunch. One hundred percent tough male.

"Hello." I wiped my hands on my apron. "Kade."

He nodded. "Hello, Grenady."

I tried to smile. I knew I hadn't gotten the job. It was obvious. Too much time had gone by. It sucked. "How are you?"

"Fine. Looks like you're busy tonight."

"Yes, uh. Well, he had a few too many. Needs some air. He'll be fine. I'll check on him. Tildy called Joann."

Kade nodded. His eyes did not leave mine. I tried hard not to look away or tilt my head down.

"Hello, I'm Rick." The man next to Kade smiled.

"I'm sorry," Kade said. "Grenady, this is my friend, Ricki Lopez, and this is my friend, Danny Vetti. They're visiting from Los Angeles. We've been friends since we were kids."

"Hi. Welcome to Pineridge." I shook hands with both of his friends. They seemed friendly, tough like Kade but not so overwhelming.

"This is part of your job description, then?" Rick laughed.

"Sometimes." I forced myself to keep smiling. I had wanted that job. "Are you coming in?"

They were. I managed to collect myself enough to introduce

them to our hostess, a college girl named Marnie, with dread-locks. She was majoring in Japanese art history, which meant she would probably be working for Tildy after graduation.

Marnie found them a table in the restaurant. A few times, as I smiled and served drinks, I could feel Kade watching me. Not in a weird way, not like Covey did, but definitely watching.

I always worked hard, but I decided to show Kade what he was missing in not hiring me. I wasn't mad at him. I was sad. That would be the word for it. I liked him; he had not liked me. He had seen something in me that wasn't competent enough, smart enough, good enough. And he knew I was hiding some-thing. Smart man. I felt my heart clench and I sighed, then caught myself midsigh and told myself not to be irritating and pathetic.

People were chatting with me a lot now. They were getting to know me, saying hello and good-bye to me by name as they came and went, which made me feel more at home.

We had a bowling team in that night, and they were beer guz-zlers. They had lost. Again. They raised their beers to me before one stood and bellowed out, "To Grenady, best damn bartender to us losers," then clinked their mugs together.

We also had a group of women there who were "sick of baby showers" and had come to divide pitchers full of strawberry daiquiris. The expectant mother was not drinking. "This is my fifth," she told me. "Five kids. I am never having sex again. Never. I told that to my husband before I left and he said, 'Okay, baby,' then he stuck his hand up my shirt!"

I brought her a virgin strawberry daiquiri, on the house. "No alcohol. Just pretend."

About an hour later I was distracted by Moose Williams, who was sitting in the middle of the bar with his buddies and family. Moose had introduced me to many of them. Most were married with kids, one divorced, one widowed. Three were his brothers, six were cousins. His father was there, and so were three uncles. It was Moose's birthday. He'd had a wee too much to drink.

"Grenady, Grenady, Grenady," Moose sang. He started out low and sweet first, then with each "Grenady," his voice grew louder, until it thundered in an operatic, melodious sort of way, all around the restaurant. "Grenadddddy!"

His oldest brother, Chad, put his arms up in victory and yelled, "Sing it, brother!" The youngest brother, Arty, winked at me and said, "We told him when we left he was not to flirt with you. We tried, Grenady."

I rolled my eyes at Tildy.

"Red hair . . ." Moose warbled, standing up, arms flung out. "Green eyes . . ." He held the note, splendid and deep. "A mermaid's body . . ." He hit a high note, pitch perfect, and those easily entertained customers laughed and clapped.

I kept pouring beers and shook my head. I wished he'd keep it down. I knew Kade and his friends could hear him at their table in the restaurant, and I didn't want him to think I was encouraging this.

"You haunt my dreeeeeams!" Moose shot his voice down to a gravelly roar, and I was struck by how on tune he was. The man actually sounded like an opera singer.

"Can't help that, Moose." Oh, please, Kade, don't look over here.

"You follow me around toowwwnnn . . ." Moose put a hand to his chest.

"I never follow you, Moose." I grabbed three wineglasses from the rack over my head.

"Your spirit does!" The word *spirit* bounced along the walls. "It's beeaautifffull to mmmeeee . . ."

I was so embarrassed. I don't like being the center of attention. Ever. "Thank you for the solo, Moose, now chill out." I hurried to the other end of the bar to work. This was Moose's sign to stand up across two stools and continue singing, his cackling cousins holding his legs so he wouldn't fall.

"Grenady, Grenady, Grenady, I want you for my wiiiifee!" His friends hooted as he stood *on the bar.*

"Oh, fry me a pig and shut up," I muttered, and shook a martini.

Tildy said, "Don't fall. If you do, you may not sue me. I am warning you, Moose."

"We could live in the country. We could have chickens and coooows!" The word *cows* was held, his voice reverberating, low and deep, in his chest. "We could have a hundred children," same with the word *children*, "if you'll only say yeeess to meeeee!" Oh, how he held that note.

"No, Moose, sorry. No chickens, no kids." I was blushing. I did not dare peek at Kade. I served the martini to a woman, and she said, "Take him. I'd take him. He looks well hung."

I headed to the other end, and he followed me strutting *on top of the bar.*

Moose puffed out his chest, the whole place enthralled, cheering, as he finished his mini-opera so dramatically with, "You are my laughter, my smile, my love and my desire, please, Grenady, Grenady, Grenady, say yes to me tonight!"

The customers clapped, pounded the bar and tables. I thought his brothers and cousins were going to wet their pants, they were laughing so hard. I rolled my eyes and poured vodka shots.

I turned my head, couldn't help it, and saw Kade staring at me. He was not happy. In fact, the deadly mobster expression was back. I felt myself get hot. Then hotter. Unattractively hotter. As in sweaty hot. I actually felt one bead of sweat run down the front of my chest between my boobs.

Kade's friends were watchful, quiet, too. I turned away and felt like crying. I had wanted to appear professional tonight. Hardworking. Competent. And I didn't.

"Is it a yeeeesss?" Moose sang, almost hitting a high C.

"No," I said again, tight smile. "But thank you for the opera. It was entertaining. Original."

Tildy called out, "You break your butt, Moose, you pay for it."

Moose feigned a heart attack. He crumbled to the bar, then to his stool, then to the floor.

Ah, so funny. Everyone loved it. They clapped again. I could never be with a guy like Moose. He was funny and kind, but not my type. Was any man my type anymore? I thought of Kade.

Moose's family pulled him back up, almost hyperventilating with laughter.

His father said to me, "He has a romantic heart. I've tried to toughen him up. Doesn't work."

I caught Tildy's eye. I could tell she knew I was dying. She tilted her head toward the exit behind the kitchen. When Moose's attention was finally elsewhere and people weren't staring at me, I escaped out the back to the picnic table she had there for staff. There was a white awning over it. I sat down and covered my head with my arms.

I was back where I was when I started, years ago. It had happened so fast, I couldn't even dig my heels in and stop it. I was working as a bartender. I was living in my car. I was struggling to save for rent. My window was gone. Winter was here.

My reputation, as Dina Hamilton and as the artist Dina Wild, was obliterated. I was in the midst of a divorce which would be long, brutal, and costly. Financially I had been stripped of all I had, my accounts on lockdown, and in all likelihood, that money would be confiscated. I would be sued for an enormous amount because of Covey, and be in debt for decades to his poor victims. Maybe my whole life. I could go to jail for years.

Shut up, I told myself after ten minutes of my defeatist self-pity party. *Quit feeling sorry for yourself.* You have enough money for today and next week, and you have a job where you get a full meal on each shift, plus extra.

Buck up.

When I didn't feel like I was going to blubber on, I went back in and started working. I faked a smile. I was efficient, chatty. All a charade.

Moose was too tipsy, but his father and friends left me more than two hundred dollars in tips.

I did not look at Kade and company again.

I couldn't.

Tildy patted my shoulder that night. "Moose's performance was as torturous for you as a cow getting his balls branded, wasn't it?"

"Yes."

"I understand." She leaned against the bar. "You're a tough one, Grenady. You should be proud of yourself."

"Why?"

"Survival instincts. You have them in full."

"Learned those a long time ago."

She pushed back that white streak. "Me too. They've suited me well. Make sure you take a slice of my chocolate cheesecake when you leave. I outdid myself again."

17

He tapped the pencil lead on his tongue a few times, then placed it on a clean, white page in his rhyme book. "I am a poet!" he declared. "A poet!"

He would change things up today, take some literary liberties.

> Rock-a-bye, baby,
> on the treetop.
> When the waves crash,
> the cradle will rock.
> When the rock breaks,
> the cradle will fall,
> And down will come corpses,
> cradles and all.

He thought of her. He thought of her every day. He bopped up and down in his chair. The Getaway Girl, that's what he called her. She would pay for getting away.

They had almost caught him because of her that night. He'd had to hide in the woods. No one had guessed it was him for many years. He had a job and a home and a bike. They thought he was normal.

He giggled into his hands, then bit down on his thumb. It bled. He giggled again.

He was not normal.

18

Children's Services Division

To: Sima, Yolanda, Sam, Quenelle, and Kiyanna
From: Margo Lipton
Date: December 15, 1983
Re: Grenadine Scotch Wild, foster child

I need to see the five of you today in my office at eleven. Cancel all your other appointments.

Dr. Paresh Chakrabarti and St. Clare's Hospital have filed complaints against the Children's Services Division because of the condition that Grenadine Scotch Wild was found in. Their attorney, Laurie Gutirrez, has called several times requesting a meeting. I have met her before, and we will need our attorneys here to deal with her. She is a human pit bull, and she is extremely angry.

The governor's office has been calling, and an investigation has been launched.

The only person talking to the press should be Wilson Deveneaux.

The Oregon Journal's articles about Grenadine have the public in an uproar. We are being besieged by letters and phone calls.

All of Connie Valencia's kids are being checked on. She apparently has not seen many of them in months. There are problems in other homes, and those kids are being moved immediately.

Liel Nover, Lenny Circo, Beth Morris, and Georgie Labelle have been suspended pending a review.

Children's Services Division

To: Margo Lipton
From: Daneesha Houston
Date: December 29, 1983
Re: Grenadine Scotch Wild

Dear Margo,

As you know, Grenadine has been in St. Clare's Hospital for three weeks. I have been to see her every day. Seeing this girl struggle to live has been the most heartbreaking experience of my career.

Grenadine asked why we hadn't come to see her at the Berlinskys' home. I told her we were checking on that, and she said that her caseworker, Mrs. Valencia, never came to help her and the Berlinskys took her out of school so she couldn't tell a teacher.

She told me that she had been treated like a bad dog there.

She said she was not going to be in our "program" anymore. She told me she wants to live on her own. She said we did a "really bad job" last time and that if we put her in another home where she's locked in a cage and gets bitten by dogs and rats and hit by the mom and dad, she's going to call the police on us and have us arrested.

I assured her that we wouldn't do that and that the people who had been in charge of her case were no longer working for the department.

She asked if the Berlinskys were going to jail, and I said yes. She said that we belonged in jail, too, and I told her that, yes, we did. She said that even though her body is starting to feel better, her mind can't stop feeling scared and she has bad dreams and keeps thinking about what happened and can't stop.

We were able to retrieve the lily bracelet from the Berlinsky home. It is all Grenadine wanted. She asked about her parents.

I called the detective in charge of the case, and he knew nothing new. I told her that we have still been unable to locate them.

She told me we hadn't tried hard enough and cried and asked me to get my "big butt" out.

Grenadine is pale and weak still, but her hair is no longer falling out and the IV tube has been removed. She has gained ten pounds. The bruises are almost all gone. I am told she will have scars for life, from the belt and from the cigarette burns.

She is a favorite of the nurses. They say she has drawn them, and her doctor, Paresh Chakrabarti, the most beautiful pictures. They have framed three of her paintings of lilies. She is clearly artistically talented. She handed me a picture before I left. It was a picture of a girl in a kennel, facedown, bruised and beaten, a dog biting her arm, a rat biting her toe. She told me to give it to whoever was in charge here.

I am not embarrassed to say that I cried. Even though she is so angry at us, she reached for my hand and held it and said she was sorry she made me cry.

I gave it to Bruce. He cried, too.

I received your note about placement in a new foster home. I will be at that meeting on Tuesday. Grenadine needs, and deserves, the best place we can find for her. I have a family in mind.

Also, I will set up counseling and future medical services, including dental, as it looks like one of her teeth was knocked out.

She asked for art supplies. I have already brought her one huge box, but I will be bringing her another one tomorrow. I have also bought her new clothes, a backpack, and books, even though she said she can't read.

19

I think a lot about Covey's victims.

I knew so many of them. Many were wealthy and had invested part, or all, of their money with Covey. Some were not wealthy, but Covey, "out of the goodness of my heart," invested their money for them.

They had all lost.

Millions and millions of dollars.

Retirements, college education money, inheritances, savings.

Gone.

The government could take all we had to pay back the victims, and we would be millions short. I didn't know what Covey owed on his home. He told me he'd gotten a sweet deal on it— "no one can wheel and deal like me, baby"—but maybe he was lying about that, too. Maybe he was lying about his other homes, like the one in Mexico, being paid for, too.

I had written him a check for $10,000 to invest, and I knew I'd lost that, too.

I was distraught for the victims. People say that money isn't everything, that it doesn't make you happy.

That's ridiculous and wrong.

If you don't have money, if you can't pay your mortgage, if you have no retirement, if you can't send your kid to college as promised, if you don't have any savings to fall back on when you lose a job or hit a medical disaster, that's a teetering-on-a-financial-cliff unhappy place to be.

It is extremely naïve to believe that people can be happy when they have, financially, lost their footing and are struggling to survive.

Covey had caused that grief, that devastation. I felt wretched for them. I knew what it felt like, and I know what it feels like now, to be financially in a panic.

I wanted a hit man.

How expensive are they anyhow?

Kade came in about ten o'clock on Tuesday night. He was alone, no friends, and sat at the bar.

"Hi. What can I get you?"

And that was that. He wanted a beer and a Blue Stallion Crunch. I put the order in, and it came up quick. I smiled. Couldn't help it. I liked him even if he hadn't hired me.

"That was nice what you did for Carlton the other night."

"I feel for him. Poor guy."

We talked about Carlton missing his wife.

"It's hard when a marriage breaks up," he said.

"Not if he's a blood-sucking maggot who lies like a fiend."

"Would that be your husband?"

"Soon to be ex."

"In the middle of a divorce?"

"Yes."

"How's it going?"

"I wish he'd self-explode. Have you been married?"

"No."

"You're kidding?" This he-hunk had never been married?

"No, I'm not. I've had several serious relationships, but I've never been married."

"Why not?" I figured I could ask all the questions I wanted since the chance of a job was quite clearly zero.

He tapped his fingers on the glass. "I couldn't see a future with any of them for forever."

"Till death do you part?"

"Yes."

"And that's what you want?"

"Yes. Don't you?"

"Marriage is not for me again. Did it once, will not do it again, even if someone's pointing a .45 at my face."

"What if Prince Charming rode up?"

"I would know he was a fake. There are no Prince Charmings. Besides, Prince Charming has always seemed rather effeminate and vain to me."

He laughed.

"What did you do today?" I wasn't even pretending to work as I chatted with Kade. Tildy was resting upstairs, and I knew the customers were fine. Two of them I wouldn't serve any more drinks to, anyhow, and I'd already told them that. Crazy Jeremy hadn't been happy, but he was rarely happy.

Kade told me about his day. He'd been out of town for several days. Went to Montana and met with three new clients and had orders in hand. He was going back to work after he ate.

"How is your art going, Grenady?"

"Oh . . ." Terrible. "Fine."

"Can I see your work?"

Ha! "Not . . . yet."

"When? Tomorrow?"

"Not tomorrow." Well, now, shoot. What was I supposed to do? Show him my "studio" in the back of my car?

"The next day?"

"Only if there's a rainbow over the mountains."

"I'll hope for a rainbow then." He smiled. It was another one of those almost flirty smiles that lit my nether regions on fire.

I smiled back at that dangerous pirate for too many long seconds and let my mind wander.

Kade was bad-guy hot.

Okay, Grenady. Chill out.

I want to run my hands over that chest and those shoulders. Stop it now.

I want to feel his mouth on mine.

Think about something else. Like math.

I want to naked-straddle him and ride him like a cowgirl.

And that is enough.

"You're stubborn, Grenady."

"And you're not?"

"I think I might be, too." He tipped up his beer. "Were you interested in art as a kid? Did you have a parent who was an artist?"

Whew. That question felt like an icy cold shower.

"My mom and dad both liked art. My father liked to sing and draw, my mother painted." Pain.

"Do they still like art?"

Pain, pain, pain. "Not as much."

"Did you get your green eyes from your mom or dad?"

"Mom." Pain. Freedom. Bear. Daisy crowns. Dancing. Painting. Pain, pain, pain. "So. When are you going to tease the fish again?"

I noticed how his face stilled. He knew I had shut him down when I talked about my parents. At that moment one of the men who had been cut off alcohol, Crazy Jeremy, belted out, "Beer."

I went over and told him he couldn't have one. He became belligerent, stood up, and pulled his arm back like he was going to take a swing at me. I ducked, and when I stood up again, reaching for the bat, Kade was right there and Crazy Jeremy was flat on his back on the ground, knocked out cold.

I stood over Crazy Jeremy. "Excellent hit, Kade."

"Thank you."

The dangerous pirate smiled again. I smiled back. Daaaaang.

When Tildy heard what happened, she banned Crazy Jeremy for life, then said, "Chivalry is not dead. It's in the fists of Kade Hendricks. I've always liked him. Everybody likes him. You should like him, Grenady."

Those hands of Kade's could punch and they could . . . oh, boy. What they could do . . .

I woke up only one time that night, about a half hour after going to sleep. I was parked on a road outside of town, the dark forest that triggers bad memories appropriately far off. I heard a truck approaching and burrowed down deeper into the warmth of my sleeping bag. I thought the truck slowed, then stopped, when it went by my car, but I couldn't be sure. I was too tired, so tired, and went back to sleep when it headed down the road.

I decided to take a walk to get the tight kinks out of my body the next morning, and to stretch out the muscles that used to be chock full of flu germs. I felt good but needed to get moving again.

I drove down Main Street, past a fake Oregon Trail wagon in the park, drove about three miles out, and parked on the side of a road with a view of Brothers, Mt. Laurel, and Ragged Top. Central Oregon was postcard perfect that day, but it was deceptive. The sky was a serene light blue, like a baby's blanket, the clouds puffy and white, but it was freezing, colder than a cow's tit in December. I saw my own air when I exhaled.

I pulled on my red jacket and started walking.

I stared at the clouds and let them morph and move into different shapes. When I was a kid I would stare up at those clouds and wait until they turned into animals: Dragons wearing aprons. Zebras in top hats. Lions dressed as kings. It entertained me and took me away from my own life. As I walked past a meadow I saw a falcon reading a Pippi Longstocking book, and a giant snail. To me, the weather was both art and living collage.

I felt, then heard, a horse galloping behind me, and I turned. On top of the horse was a girl, screaming, panicked.

"Stop, Liddy, stop!" The girl was wearing a red cowgirl hat with pink lights that flashed on and off.

I stood in the middle of the road, my hands out, calming. The horse, dark brown and sleek, slowed, neighed in fear, then bucked, came down, and bucked again. I was surprised the girl didn't fall off. I approached carefully, talking to the horse, softly, gently. The horse jittered to one side, then another, its head swooping up and down, eyes wide.

"It's okay, calm down," I said to the horse. "It's okay."

The girl was crying. "Should I jump off?"

"No, no," I said calmly, not wanting to spook the horse again. I envisioned the girl trying to jump off and being crushed by the horse's hooves. I tried to grab the reins, and the horse yanked her head away again, but she wasn't breathing as hard, puffing as hard.

I went back to soothing talk, firm and authoritative, then grabbed for the reins again, this time catching them. I ran my hand along her sweaty neck, showing how safe I was.

When the horse was calmer, I said to the girl, "Get off slowly. Very slowly." I reached out a hand and helped her off, not letting go of the reins. "Go and sit over by the tree." She did, and I walked the horse.

Within two minutes a truck came speeding down the road. I cringed as the horse tensed beside me. I brought the horse to the opposite side of the road, away from the girl, and hoped the pickup would quit speeding. It slowed down about fifty yards from the horse and stopped. A woman ran out of the driver's side and the girl ran straight into her arms. The frozen panic on the woman's face made the earlier panic on the girl's face look like nothing.

"Momma, I'm sorry!" the girl said, hugging her close.

"I told you not to get on Liddy until I was there!"

"I know. I'm sorry. She was spooked by the bees! The bees!"

The mother looked at me, in tears, her arms tight around the girl with the red blinking cowgirl hat, her face grateful, so grateful, unbelievably relieved.

For a second I stood, pain racking my body at the mother's love for her child.

I smiled. It was the way it was.

"Hello," I called out. "I believe I have your horse."

Once Rozlyn, the mother, could breathe again, she insisted I come to lunch. As I was starving, yet again, and had nothing else to do to fill my sweet—homeless—time, I said yes. "That'd be super!" were my actual goofy words.

Rozlyn and Cleo DiMarco lived in an old, light green farmhouse with a white porch about a half mile down the road. A big, red barn was west of it. She had a sweeping view of the mountains, a Christmas tree farm, and an open field.

I felt like I was in a kaleidoscope when I stood in her home. It was filled with color and quilts, as Rozlyn is a quilter. I leaned in closer to study one of them. One quilt had a woman in a skimpy blue dress sitting in a huge martini glass, her legs spilling over the side. Another quilt had a black-haired woman in a red negligee, huge boobs, sitting in front of a computer writing. It was clear she was a romance writer by the covers of the books stacked around her.

"I love 'em," I told her, awed. The fabrics, the colors, and designs were fantastic. "Wow. You are talented."

"Thank you. Quilting is my hobby. You missed the quilt show. I sold ten quilts. My mom and I used to quilt together, but no way could I be a normal quilter making squares and triangles. I had to add the *ooph*. The woman-power, butt-kicking angle. The fun of living and being naughty."

"I think you nailed it." A third quilt had a woman climbing a mountain . . . in a purple leotard and pink tennis shoes.

Rozlyn's home was also filled with plants, books, two huge birdcages with blue and yellow parakeets, colorful scarves on the walls, and art. The mismatched leather, flowered, striped, and soft furniture somehow all worked together.

I felt totally at home.

Rozlyn had a bunch of black curls and was about my height but curved more. "I'm 225 pounds of love. Menopausal love." She had on a flowing, Mexican-style skirt, black cowboy boots, black tights, and a black sweater. She wore huge hoop earrings. She was about ten years older than me. "Don't be alarmed if I start to sweat as if an elf is holding a miniature garden hose over my head. I'm having hot flashes. Only they don't flash. They soak."

Cleo, age six and proud of it, had blue eyes and three blond ponytails under her red cowboy hat, the pink lights still flashing. She said Liddy was her "best friend. I can talk horse talk. I know because Liddy understands me."

She was wearing gold tights and a shirt with a monster on it that said, "Don't Monster With Me, Sucker."

We had taco soup, and it was delicious multiplied by a hundred.

"This is the best soup ever," I told Cleo. "Did you make it?"

"Yup. Me and Mommy. Your eyes are green like Jolly Ranchers."

"Do you like Jolly Ranchers?"

"Yep."

"Good. Don't eat my eyes."

She thought that was pretty funny.

We had hot bread, fruit, and some yummy cheese. Rozlyn had a hot flash. We ignored it, though it did indeed look like she had an elf holding a miniature hose over her head.

Cleo said to me, "I think I'm a descendant of cats . . . I wear my hair in three ponytails because you can catch butterflies better . . . If I don't have a banana in the morning I can't poop."

When she skipped off, Rozlyn and I talked, and she made me laugh about menopause, which meant she was "knee-deep in horny hormones, mood swings from the devil, and night sweats that have me in a pool in my own bed." I couldn't remember where I'd heard her name before, but then she said she worked for Kade and I remembered Bajal saying that Rozlyn would be allowed to help her give birth in the lobby.

"I'm the money woman, chief financial officer. I love numbers. They're my obsession. I love doing math in my head, and I love making numbers work. Kade's great. You applied there? You didn't get the job? I'm surprised. That's too bad. I'll talk to Kade for you on Monday. We have a money meeting. He likes numbers, too, and he's quick."

She was married in her twenties and divorced, amicably. Three years later she wanted a baby and tried naturally, which didn't work, then she tried the usual pregnancy helpers, including IVF, which failed. She decided to give up on having kids and went to Houston for a business trip as the chief financial officer of a social media company. She had a fling with a smart and funny man named Mike.

One month later she had morning sickness and found out she was pregnant. "I cried for a week I was so happy."

She had no idea who Mike was, didn't know how to contact him, didn't want to contact him, and was tested for all sexually transmitted diseases. "That was the asinine part. No condoms. What am I? Fifteen? Nah. I was hopeful." She tested negative and delighted in vomiting into her toilet in the mornings because she knew she had a baby.

"Cleo's my gift." She wiped her eyes. "I love that kid."

"I can see why. She's hilarious."

"I also love, from afar, like a lovesick mini-cow, a man named Leonard."

"Leonard?"

"Yes." She picked up a quilting magazine next to her and started to fan herself as another hot flash hit. "He owns a construction company. He has blond hair. He has eyes that I want to dive into. If I could get him knocked up, I would."

"You would like to get him pregnant?"

"That'd be my dream." She winked.

"Why do you love him from afar?"

"Because he doesn't know I'm alive. I sound like I'm in junior high. I try to run into him. I try to chat with him on my brave days. I want him to ask me out."

We talked about her "aching heart" and her sex drive, which was "shooting up sky high because of menopause," then she asked, "Tell me what work you did before you came here."

"I'm an artist, but I'm taking a break. I'm working for The Spirited Owl."

"I know. I heard you're fun. Word is you can make a tall pyramid out of shot glasses and make a taste-bud-blazing Singapore Sling. Hang on, I'm having a hormonal rush."

"What's that?"

"It means it feels like my hormones are rushing to the surface and I want to cry for no reason."

"I'm sorry."

"It'll end." She burst into tears and I put my arm around her. "Men. O. Pause." She laughed, wiped her tears. "As if I would ever pause on men, especially not Leonard. Tell me about your art."

I did, and she had a host of questions, being a quilt artist. It was a most excellent art conversation.

"Husband? Boyfriend?" she asked.

"Soon-to-be-ex-husband. I wish he'd fall into a hot geyser and burn."

"I can see that serenity surrounds that relationship." We talked about twisty, sneaky men who tangle with your mind-health. "Where are you staying, Grenady?"

Cleo bebopped into their big, red barn to visit Liddy and horse talk with her while Rozlyn unlocked a door on the side. In the small entry were two saddles mounted on sawhorses. One was ornamented with silver, and the other looked like it was about a hundred years old. To the right were stairs to the second story, above the barn. The stairs looked new.

I was expecting to see a people barn at the top of the stairs. As in, rough wood, maybe a stall-like feel. Stray hay. Dusty. One window. We were, after all, above horse stables.

"I had this built five years ago for my mother," Rozlyn said. "I wanted her to have some place nice to stay when she visited us. She died last year. You know where she died? Paris. Seventy-five years old. She said she could die as well in Paris as any-where, and that's what she did. She went to Paris, by herself, for three months. She died the last day of her trip.

"You know who called the ambulance?" She teared up, then laughed. "An eighty-year-old Frenchman. It was one o'clock in the morning. He was fluent in English, had attended college here. Told me she was 'the woman of his soul' and he would see her again soon. Apparently he had a heart problem, so he didn't think he'd be here long." She wiped the tears. "I think it was a gift. A last fling for both of them."

"I'm sorry she died, Rozlyn, but I'm glad she had that time. Romance and Paris. I can only hope for the same for myself."

"Me too. A Frenchman in my twilight years right before I die. Happy bang bang in bed. I'm glad for my mom. We loved having her here. She would visit, then jet off on another trip somewhere in the world. She was a teacher for thirty-five years and always wanted to explore, so after she retired, she took off."

"Good for her."

Rozlyn unlocked the door at the top of the stairs, and we stepped into a room flooded with light. "I had French doors installed front and back and added a couple of skylights so we could get the sunshine in. My mother loved sunshine."

"The sunshine is sure in," I said. "Wow."

The room was not large, nowhere near the width of the barn, but it was plenty large for me. The floors were wood, the walls were white, and the recessed lighting added even more light when Rozlyn flipped the switch.

In front of the entry was the kitchen. It was small, shaped in a V, and charming. The cabinets were white with black cowboy hat handles. There was a large window over the white apron sink. The appliances were stainless steel, and a black granite countertop separated the kitchen from the family room.

A skylight opened up the space in the small family room. A beige couch lay along one wall with a cushy, pink flowered chair next to it. The fabrics were dated, but they looked soft and comfortable and clean. There was a circular kitchen table and two chairs.

Across from the couch was a gas fireplace. My freezing hands felt better already! I almost clicked my heels at the thought of being warm. No more snuggling into my blankets and sleeping bag with a hat pulled low like a bank robber.

The French doors opened to a small deck, wide enough for a couple of chairs and a table. I saw Cleo walking around, Liddy following her like she was Cleo's dog.

To the right of the kitchen was the bathroom with a clawfoot tub.

I made a gaspy sort of sound and covered my mouth.

"That tub okay for you? My mother had a thing for baths, so I bought her a deep one. She said she liked to give her bones a break. Baths settle my mood swings."

"Me too." My bones felt better already! No more showering at work or washing down in McDonald's! The window was low enough so that I could look outside while lying in bubbles. There was a shower, too, and a pedestal sink. And a toilet, of course. My bladder felt better!

On the other side of the bathroom was my bedroom, small but dee-lightful. It fit a queen-sized bed, with a skylight straight above it, a wood nightstand, a dresser, and a chair in front of the French doors. My back felt better now, too!

A second deck overlooked Rozlyn's farmland.

My whole world was better.

"You can watch the sun come up on one side of the apartment and go down on the other. We get some beautiful sunsets, too. Skies on fire. On hot days I want to take off all my clothes and dance out there. I've done it before. Three times. I dared myself. I do that. Dare myself to do crazy things. Might as well. Only live each day once, right?" She handed me the key and grinned. "I'm glad you're staying with us. I like your vibe."

"I like your vibe, too." We fist-bumped, then laughed. I felt like doing an odd jig. Tra-la-la. But with my clothes on. "It's charming, and perfect and warm. Thank you so much."

When Rozlyn had asked me at lunch where I was staying in town, I had hemmed and hawed. Rozlyn seemed puzzled, so I dove quick into my "I'm looking around at apartments" speech, even mentioned Talia's B and B, and Rozlyn said, "You can stay above the barn."

I said, immediately, "Great. Thank you." I think it surprised Rozlyn that I agreed lickety-split to live above a barn, as she had not yet explained to me that the barn had an apartment above it. I had simply, instantly, thought of a plain bedroom above the barn with a roof, and was grateful for the roof.

"How much would you like per month?"

She leaned back in her chair, then named a sum.

My mouth fell open. Holy moly.

"Too high?" she asked.

"Oh, no, not at all. I'll take it."

"That includes utilities, of course, all one bill to me. There's Internet, too. My mother wanted to keep up with all her friends and, I think, a few men friends. The intimate type of man friend."

I grabbed for my purse. "I'll get you the first and last month's rent. How much do you want for the security deposit?"

"I'll take first month's rent only, Grenady. I trust you."

I felt guilty when she said that. She didn't know what I was running from. She didn't know I'd been arrested and had sanity smashing accusations leveled at me and people who thought I'd lost them their life's savings. But I was, selfishly, once again, thinking of myself and getting out of my car before snowstorms hit like a steamroller over a rabbit.

"I know when you leave, you'll let us know beforehand, and you'll clean before you go."

"Yes, of course." I handed her the rent money, in cash.

"Thank you." My eyes burned, but I didn't cry or I'd look like a loon.

"You're welcome. We owe you. You probably..." Rozlyn choked up, too, but not for the same reason I had. She took a swipe at her teary eyes, then fanned her face, both hands. "You probably saved Cleo's life. Liddy was running so fast, then I saw her buck, not once but twice. I don't even know how she held on. You stood in front of a charging horse, calmed it down, got it to stop bucking, and my daughter's safe. I can't thank you enough. I will never be able to thank you enough. "

She gave me a hug, and I hugged her back. It was the strangest thing, but I felt close to her. I do not feel close to women easily at all. I don't trust women. I hardly trust anyone. But Rozlyn? I liked her.

"Thank you, again, Grenady."

"Oh, thank you, Rozlyn, thank you so much. I am so happy to be here."

"We're happy you're here, too. I think it's karma we're together now. I do."

We chatted some more. Cleo bounded up and told me that she was going to make wings for herself so she could be a flying squirrel after she took Liddy for a walk. She gave me a hug before she jumped down the stairs singing, "I'm a wolf, wolf, wolf, and I'll eat you up!"

I growled at her. She growled back.

I could not believe my new home. I touched the shelves in the closet in my bedroom. I pulled out the drawers and cabinets in the kitchen, which were filled with pans, bowls, and utensils, obviously for the late mother who loved to cook. There was even a coffeemaker and a blender.

I stood on both decks and admired the view of the snow-tipped mountains and meadows, then lay down on the couch and on my bed and looked up through the skylights. I sat on the toilet even though I didn't need to go. I climbed into the tub and imagined my bath tonight after work. I washed my face and hands in my own sink. I peered in the mirror and saw my smile. First smile in a mirror in weeks.

I imagined washing my clothes in my own small washer and dryer tucked into the closet by the door. I imagined putting my clothes away, stocking cupboards and my fridge, and getting covers for the couch and chair and a bedspread for my bed.

My new home was small but immaculate. It felt new. There were no broken windows. It was heated. It was dry. The door locked. I felt this bloom of happiness, and I didn't let go of it. I knew what was behind the bloom: cold fear and the danger of being locked up like an animal for years, but I was taking this moment, yes, I was.

I practically skipped out to my car I was so excited. I brought my bags and boxes up and did a load of laundry. I threw out my pee cup. I put my food in the cupboards, then lined up my art supplies on the table, and then underneath it when I ran out of room.

I had missed having my paints and brushes, pastels and colored pencils, jars and boxes of buttons, beads, Scrabble letters, ribbons, patterned scrapbook paper, folded fabrics, old and sepia photographs, peacock feathers, vintage stationery, modern flowered stationery, Victorian gift cards, fortune-telling cards, my art and nature books, and two puzzles all out so I could see them. I put my sewing machine on the table, too.

I could do my art again. I am not myself without my art. I could now escape into my canvases and collages.

I could paint lilies while wearing my lily bracelet and calm down. I could make dragonflies out of beads and netting. I could make birds' nests out of tiny sticks. I could draw the outline of a woman reading against a tree, then photocopy pages of classics and cut them into leaves. I could use my charcoal pencil to push my past back anytime I needed to.

I decided to have two baths today. No law against it.

I sighed as I sunk into the hot water, relieved beyond relief.

20

~

CIRCUIT COURT OF THE STATE OF OREGON
FOR THE COUNTY OF MULTNOMAH

THE STATE OF OREGON,
Plaintiff,
V
ADELLY BERLINSKY and TOM BERLINSKY,
Defendants

Case No. 11-9658
March 28, 1985
JUDGE EMILY CARRADONE

GRENADINE SCOTCH WILD, having first been sworn, testified as follows:

SABRINA SILVERS: It's nice to see you again, Grenadine. You and I have met before, haven't we?

GRENADINE SCOTCH WILD: Yes.

Q: And for the record, who am I?

A: You're Sabrina Silvers and you're the attorney who is going to put the Berlinskys' butts in jail. Yeah, you. You two fat people who put me in a kennel like a dog. Quit smiling, Mrs. Berlinsky, you weasel fart face. It isn't funny.

Q: Grenadine, can you please look at me and answer my questions? This is not the right time to talk to Mr. and Mrs. Berlinsky.

A: Never is the right time to talk to them.

Q: Can you tell the jury how old are you?

A: Nine years and two months exactly.

Q: What school do you go to?

A: Fir Grove Elementary. Furry Grover is our mascot. It's a dog.

Q: What are your favorite subjects?

A: Art. I don't read good. The letters get all confused and flipped. They move around and make me dizzy. And my writing is bad, too. People can't read it. I'm dumb in reading and writing.

Q: I'm sorry. I don't think you're dumb. What do you like to do?

A: I like to paint and make collages.

Q: Can you tell us why we're here today, Grenadine?

A: Yes.

Q: Why?

A: Because Mr. and Mrs. Berlinsky kept me in a dog kennel and didn't send me to school and hit me and didn't feed me and no one helped.

MR. STANLEY OROKOFF: Objection!

JUDGE EMILY CARRADONE: What's the objection?

MR. OROKOFF: She was not asked about her experience yet.

JUDGE CARRADONE: She's nine. Overruled. Sit down.

MISS WILD: What is objection?

JUDGE CARRADONE: It means he objected to what you said; he felt that what you said wasn't appropriate at this time.

MISS WILD: Well I don't care what he thinks is . . . is . . . that other word you said.

MS. SILVERS: Grenadine, when did the Berlinskys put you in a dog kennel?

A: A few weeks after I got there. They said I was bad.

Q: Who said you were bad?

A: Mrs. Berlinsky said I was bad. Mr. Berlinsky said I was a pain in the ass because I kept asking where my parents were and he was sick of saying I don't know, but he doesn't know much, does he? Do you, monkey lips?

MR. OROKOFF: Objection. She cannot address my clients.

MISS WILD: There's that objection word again. I told you I don't care what you think of what I'm saying, so sit down.

JUDGE CARRADONE: There's leeway here. She's a child. Grenadine, talk to Ms. Silvers.

MS. SILVERS: Why did Mrs. Berlinsky say you were bad?

A: Because she said her husband paid too much attention to me.

Q: What do you think she meant by that?

A: Because he would look at me and play with my hair and he was always trying to adjust the buttons on my shirt but I told him I could get dressed myself, and sometimes he'd play spank me, and he wanted me to sit on his lap all the time but he smelled like cigarettes and farts so I didn't want to. Yes, you did, fat man. You smelled like cigarettes and burps and farts. Mixed.

MR. OROKOFF: Objection. Again, she can't talk to the Berlinskys.

JUDGE CARRADONE: Grenadine, please don't address the Berlinskys.

MISS WILD: I don't know what address means. You mean, like write their address down?

JUDGE CARRADONE: No, it means you can't talk to them right now.

MISS WILD: I don't ever want to talk to them, but he did smell, Judge, like cigarettes and farts and burps. Mixed. I'm telling you so that you know what kind of smelly person he is.

MR. OROKOFF: Objection.

MISS WILD: I objection to what you're saying, too.

JUDGE CARRADONE: The jury will disregard Grenadine's last statements.

MISS WILD: What do you mean when you say that, Judge?

JUDGE CARRADONE: I mean, they need to try to forget what you just said about Mr. Berlinsky and his burps and passing gas, and they can't talk about it in the jury room.

MISS. WILD: Why not? It's the truth. You're supposed to talk about the truth here, right?

JUDGE CARRADONE: Yes, we want the truth.

MISS WILD: Then that's the truth. When he made me sit on his lap and hugged me too tight to his chest and rubbed me against him, he stunk. Like vomit, too. I didn't want to play the spank game, Judge; he made me. Or the weird daddy loves me game.

MS. SILVERS: Where did you sleep in their house, Grenadine?

A: The kennel.

Q: What do you mean, the kennel?

A: A kennel. A kennel like, for a dog. Why did I have to stay in a kennel? Do I look like a dog? No. Where's the floppy ears and the tail? See my butt? There's no tail. So why was I there?

Q: Was there a blanket in the kennel?

A: Pink blanket. Had bugs on it. Like spiders and lice that make your head itch.

Q: What did you eat?

A: Me and Spikey ate the same food.

Q: Who is Spikey?

A: The dog. Mean dog.

Q: What kind of food did you eat?

A: Dog food. The type in the purple bag with the gold dog on the front.

Q: So you shared with Spikey?

A: Yeah, but he didn't like to share. He bites. Bites hard.

Q: What did you drink?

A: The water in the blue dish. Not the red dish. They told me to pee in the red dish like a dog. They treated me worse than a bad dog.

MR. OROKOFF: Objection.

JUDGE CARRADONE: No reason to object. Sit down. Overruled.

MS. SILVERS: Your honor, opposing counsel is trying to intimidate my witness. She's a child.

JUDGE CARRADONE: Counselor, sit down, and if there is one more unwarranted interruption, you will be removed from court and your assistant will carry on for you.

MISS WILD: He's bad, too.

MS. SILVERS: Who's bad?

A: That man the judge said to sit down. He told me when I first met him that I imagined what Mr. and Mrs. Berlinsky did to me.

He said I dreamed it. Or nightmared it. He said it didn't happen. He said they're nice people. They're not nice people, you penis, Mr. Berlinsky. You spanked me. I want to spank you back with your belt like you did me.

JUDGE CARRADONE: Grenadine, please don't yell in court, and you can't use the word *penis*.

MISS WILD: I'm sorry.

JUDGE CARRADONE: It's okay, but you need to be polite and answer the questions.

MISS WILD: But he is one. A penis. I didn't dream it. I didn't imagine it. That Orocoughy [spelled phonetically, as spoken] man said the Berlinskys didn't put a leash around my neck, but they did. It happened. His face looks like a fat skull. I hate skulls.

MR. OROKOFF: Objection. Move to strike the comment about my face looking like a fat skull.

JUDGE CARRADONE: Jury, you will disregard that Grenadine said that Mr. Orokoff has a face that looks like a fat skull.

MS. SILVERS: Grenadine, please tell us what happened to you in the Berlinsky home.

A: I will, but you have to promise me that I'm not going to jail and I'm not going to have to live with them again and that Mrs. Berlinsky will never get the chance to cut off my toes.

Q: That's correct. You are not going to jail, ever, for this. You did nothing wrong. You are not on trial, Grenadine, the Berlinskys are. You will never have to live with them again. Mrs. Berlinsky will never be able to cut off your toes. Do you want a tissue?

A: Yes. But I'm trying not to cry. Mrs. Berlinsky said she'd cut them off with a knife or pliers if I ever told what happened. The boys held me down one day, and she put the pliers on my toes and pulled. It hurt. But if you promise, I'll tell you about living with them. You do promise? Okay. I was hungry all the time. I couldn't stand up in the kennel. I had to sit or lay down.

Tom Jr. and Kevin pulled my hair and put a leash or a rope around my neck and took me for walks and they hit me with sticks if I couldn't keep up with them and called me doggy and dog shit. Sorry to you, Judge, for the bad word, *shit,* that's what they told me. They would take me out in my shorts and a T-shirt and it would be snowing and I'd get so cold I couldn't breathe.

Q: Do you need a break, Grenadine, to get the tears under control?

A: No, I don't need a break. I'm going to tell on Mr. and Mrs. Berlinsky so they can never have other kids in their house again. Mrs. Berlinsky used to put me outside even in the rain in the kennel to sleep on a rug and she also screamed at me.

Q: Were you afraid of her?

MR. OROKOFF: Objection. Leading the witness.

MISS WILD: Sit down, dirty penis.

JUDGE CARRODONE: Grenadine, you can't say that to Mr. Orokoff. And no yelling. Here's a tissue. Dry your eyes, take a breath, we can take a break if you want—

MISS WILD: I'm not taking that word back, Judge, but I say sorry to you for my bad words. Mrs. Berlinsky, she told me no one wanted me, but I already know it. My parents did, but they're gone, and they'll come back and then my dad is going to beat you both up.

You called me ugly and weird, Mrs. Berlinsky, yes, you did. Don't shake your head and smile that weird smile like you're trying to be smart and I'm stupid. You hit me, too, on my face and on my head and on my back.

MS. SILVERS: What did she hit you with?

A: Her hand and a belt and a hammer three times when I snuck upstairs for food and the kids were allowed to hit me with their model airplanes on the head and in the face. They didn't feed me. I'm a kid. Kids need food. How come they didn't feed me? Pretty soon all I can do is lay down in the cage and not move and I'm so hungry my stomach is eating me and then I get sick because I got cold one night, and I told them I can't breathe right, but they all laughed like it was funny when I was coughing and I was shaking like this—see how my body is moving? That's what happened. And I got sicker and sicker and my hair starts to fall out on the pink blanket and I'm so thirsty but the dog drinks most of the water first and the boys come and say I'm ugly. I'm ugly? They're ugly. You got ugly kids, Berlinsky butts.

MR. OROKOFF: Objection. Witness is not answering the question. She's speech making.

JUDGE CARRADONE: Overruled.

MISS WILD: I don't even know how to say a speech. You don't like the answer because you want me to sit up here and say I dreamed the whole thing. Why don't you suck in your stomach and sit down and shut up, fat skull face.

JUDGE CARRADONE: Grenadine, calm down. You can't yell in here—

MISS WILD: And they took my lily bracelet and I only got it back after Dr. Chakrabarti told that woman from the department for kids that if she didn't go and get my bracelet for me that he was going to file a report against her. That was from my mom for me, not for you, fat Mrs. Berlinsky, and you, smelly Mr. Berlinsky, and also they laughed at me. They always laughed at me and called me Bugs because of the bug bites and bugs in my hair and sometimes they called me Fleas because they were on me, too. And they called me scabies. Little Miss Scabies. Bug girl. Lice kid. How would you like to be called Lice Kid?

MS. SILVERS: Here's another tissue, honey. Did you ever get a bath?

A: Sometimes they turned a hose on over my head outside in the backyard by the chickens, but that didn't kill the bugs in my hair, and the fleas were on the blanket so I still itched and they ate my hair up and it fell out.

Q: Your hair looks nice now.

A: That's because Dr. Chakrabarti and the nurses got rid of the bugs in my hair and in my ears and in my tummy and all the yucky junk between my toes. And I had worms inside of me, too. You ever have worms inside of you? The doctor had to give me worm killer medicine to get rid of them. They itched my butt. And that's not all the doctors had to do, either. They had to give me other medicine and a needle up my arm to feed me more food. But when I was better I had all the food I could eat at the hospital. Plus milkshakes in the afternoons. Chocolate and vanilla. Two types. And Jell-O, green and red, and pizza.

Q: Were the Berlinskys ever nice to you?

A: Only when Mrs. Valencia came to visit. Then they would hose me off like I was Spikey and put something on my hair for the bugs and put me in a long-sleeved shirt or some weird dress with ruffles to hide the bruises and tell me to be good and smile a lot or they would use the hammer on my knees again and I didn't want my knees hammered. That hurts. Have you ever had your knees hammered? Or they said they would put a black snake in the kennel. They even showed me a picture of the snake.

MR. OROKOFF: Objection.

MISS WILD: Oh, you sit down and shut up. All you want to do is lie and say the Berlinskys were good to me so they don't get in trouble, but I told you what they did to me. I don't care if you believe me or not because you are bad to protect those bad people who hurt me, a kid. I'm a kid. Why do you want to help mean people who hit kids and put them in a kennel and don't give them food? You're a jerk.

JUDGE CARRADONE: Grenadine, sit down. We're taking a break. Fifteen minutes.

MISS WILD: And I may be stupid, Berlinsky butts, I don't spell too good, but I can spell these two words: F.U.C.K. You. That spells *fuck you*.

* * *

JUDGE CARRADONE: Grenadine, we will now begin the portion of the trial where Mr. Orokoff asks you some questions. Please remember what Ms. Silvers talked about with you at the break. You are to answer the questions as best you can, politely. Do you understand?

MS. WILD: Yes.

MR. OROKOFF: Hello, Grenadine.

A: What do you want, fat skull face? And don't tell me that I don't know the difference between the truth and a lie like you did before, because I do.

Q: I'm not going to say that to you, Grenadine—

A: You better not. I'm telling the truth. Even Dr. Chakrabarti saw my whole body when I was in the hospital. I had broken ribs, right here, this side, for a long time. Do you know what broken ribs feel like? They hurt. That's where the Berlinsky boys kicked me. I had scars on my back from that belt and the cigarette burns and a lot of bruises and I weighed only forty pounds and I had papnemonia. He'll tell you.

Q: Yes, I know. Dr. Chakrabarti already testified, but what I want to talk to you about is—

A: I don't know what that tess a fied [spelled phonetically, as spoken] word means, but Dr. Chakrabarti knows and the nurses know I could hardly breathe. He said no one should hurt a kid ever and he was supermad that they—those mean fat people— hurt me. Hi, Dr. Chakrabarti.

DR. PARESH CHAKRABARTI (from the courtroom): Hello, Grenadine.

JUDGE CARRADONE: Grenadine, you can't talk to people in the courtroom, only Mr. Orokoff right now.

MISS WILD: But I don't want to talk to him. Hi, Dr. Chakrabarti. Hi to the nurses, too. Hi, Nurse Susan. Hi, Nurse Debbie. Hi, Nurse Joan. Dr. Chakrabarti, did you tell them how I was in the hospital . . . you already did? Good. How's your wife? How's the baby, Ruchira? You have a picture to show me? I'll see it later when penis man sits down.

JUDGE CARRADONE: Grenadine, I know you don't want to talk to Mr. Orokoff, but you have to because Mr. and Mrs. Berlinsky are on trial.

MISS WILD: What else do you want to know, penis?

MR. OROKOFF: Judge, please ask Grenadine not to use that word.

JUDGE CARRADONE: You can do that, can't you?

MR. OROKOFF: Don't call me, penis, Grenadine.

MISS WILD: No, penis.

JUDGE CARRADONE: Please sit down in the witness chair, Grenadine.

MISS WILD: No. He gets to stand up and he's taller than me and he's trying to scare me by being taller and using a big voice. So I'm going to stand. Sorry to you, Judge. I'm sick of this. What other stupid questions do you have, stupid face?

MR. OROKOFF: Objection. She can't talk to me like that.

JUDGE CARRADONE: Grenadine.

MISS WILD: Why don't you ask me how many times I had to take an ice bath? Do you know what that's like? Especially when someone dunks your head under the water? Mrs. Berlinsky said she was trying to kill the lice. She was trying to drowned me. Can I tell now how Mrs. Berlinsky used to put me in her closet? The kennel was better than the closet. No air, no sun for three days all because I took an apple. There was a rat in the closet.

MR. OROKOFF: I didn't ask about the closet. Please answer only the questions I ask you.

MISS WILD: I'm going to answer whatever questions I want. The rats bit me, too. On my toes. That's why I got the infection that Dr. Chakrabarti had to fix. Hi, Dr. Chakrabarti. Hi, nurses. And you know how I got the bruises on my head? From being hit. And you know why I was all flaky? Because I didn't get enough water. And you know why I had hardly any hair? Because I didn't get good food and it got pulled out and the lice ate it. Now my hair's pretty because my foster mother feeds me all the time and gives me extra snacks in my backpack. Three a day.

MR OROKOFF: Grenadine, how many nights total did you spend in the kennel? Two? Three? And wasn't it part of a game you were playing with the Berlinsky boys if you're totally honest here today?

JUDGE CARRADONE: Okay, that's enough. Do not throw a pen again, Grenadine. Do not throw your shoe. Grenadine, please. No yelling—

MISS WILD: You bald liar penis. I spent almost every night in the kennel, and they would lock me in and you know it. You want to sleep in a cage?

MR. OROKOFF: Did you pull your own hair out?

JUDGE CARRADONE: Okay, Grenadine. That's enough. You've thrown both shoes now, settle down. Please sit down. Stop shouting.

MISS WILD: Why would I pull my hair out? That hurts. It fell out. I remember. Looks like your hair is falling out, too, but not because you weren't fed. You're fed too much. What other questions do you want to ask? Want me to tell you how Mr. Berlinsky stomped on a chick with his feet and made me watch the chick die? He said they were going to do that to me if I told. They made chicken noises at me. Then he killed another one. Six in all. Dead from his boot.

Q: Okay. Calm down. Please.

A: You calm down. You put your hands down. You back up. You stop talking to me like you think I'm dumb. You quit trying to scare me. Why don't you answer these questions: Why did Mrs. Berlinsky put her cigarettes out on my arm? Why did she shake me? Why did Mr. Berlinsky yell at me and scare me? Why did they let the boys poke me with sticks when I was in the kennel? Why didn't they give me a blanket with no lice?

Q: I have no further questions.

A: Good. Go and sit down with the Berlinsky butts who said they were nice to me. If they were nice to me, why did they call me Dog? That was my name, Dog.

Q: Judge, please. I said I have no further questions. She should leave the stand.

A: What stand? I'm standing up right now. I'm not going to sit. I want to tell all you people and you the judge what they did to me. You go sit down. Sit! Sit! Like a dog. That's what that whole family said to me. Sit! Beg! Roll over! Why did I have to beg for food? Why was I put in that home? I kept hoping someone would come and I could tell them about the kennel and ask for a new family, but no one came. Why didn't anyone come get me? Why did they forget about me?

Q: Objection.

JUDGE CARRADONE: Overruled.

MISS WILD: Shut up, penis. I objection to you. When are my parents getting here? The Berlinskys said my parents are dead. Are they dead? My mother had a red, crocheted shawl. Did anybody find that? What about my dad's guitar? I know the police were looking for them. Why won't anyone answer me?

Sentencing Hearing
Tom and Adelly Berlinsky
Judge Emily Carradone

Tom and Adelly Berlinsky, you were found guilty on all charges by a jury of your peers ten weeks ago. I have never, in twenty-five years of being a judge, had a jury come back so fast with their verdict.

Your abuse of Grenadine Scotch Wild is appalling. I am sick-ened by you and by your actions towards a child in your home. You were charged to take care of her, to feed and nurture her, and instead you tortured her in a kennel. You starved and beat her. You burned her.

Your lack of remorse and regret shows you have no conception of the damage you have caused this innocent child.

That you encouraged your own sons to do the same, to degrade, humiliate, and abuse another human being, shows yet another part of your sick, twisted personalities. As you know, your sons are now in foster care, as no one in your families thought they were capable of taking care of them.

Placing both boys with one family has proven to be impossible, I'm told, because they both have severe behavior problems. Adopting them out with their behavior problems will also be near to impossible. They will probably live the rest of their childhood as foster children and then will be moved into group homes if they're not incarcerated for the violent tendencies they have already shown. It's ironic. It's tragic.

What, Grenadine? Yes, the Berlinskys are going to jail. Hang on a minute, I'm getting to that part. I am sentencing you both to ten years in prison. Yes, I said ten, Grenadine. It is the maximum I am allowed to sentence them by law. No, I can't send them away for a hundred thousand years. Mr. and Mrs. Berlinsky, if it were up to me, I would put you both in kennels like you did Grenadine. I would deny you food and sanitation. Then I would take you out back and shoot you like we used to shoot rabid raccoons when I was a girl growing up in the backwoods of Mississippi.

Your sentence will begin immediately. There is no possibility of early parole.

Grenadine, from all of us, every single person in this room, I apologize. This should never have happened to you. You did nothing wrong; nothing was your fault. The system failed you. The Berlinskys failed you. Everyone failed you.

I wish for you, Grenadine, nothing but the best for you in the future. I want to thank your new foster parents, and I want to thank Dr. Chakrabarti and your nurses for all that they have done to help you.

To Mr. and Mrs. Berlinsky, I'm sure you will not be popular in prison. The inmates, I hear, do not like child abusers.

What, Grenadine? Yes, you're right. Mr. and Mrs. Berlinsky are pieces of shit. Is there anything else you want to say to them?

MISS WILD: Yes. I want to spell more words. G.O. T.O. H.E.L.L. That spells *go to hell.*

JUDGE CARRADONE: Thank you, Grenadine. I believe they are headed that way. Court adjourned.

21

That night, after my shift at The Spirited Owl, I turned off all
the lights in the bathroom, filled the claw-foot tub with hot
water, and opened the window so I could see the stars as I
soaked.

I was so grateful for a bathtub. So grateful for a bed. So
grateful for the pans in my kitchen. I had a roof, a door that
locked, and a couch. I had my own Laundromat. I had not one
but two decks, and I was not living in a home with an engine
and headlights.

I would sleep under a pile of blankets. I would not be peeing
out my car door in the middle of the night, or in my pee cup,
waiting for some creepy man to attack me. I would be able to
keep food in the fridge and make hot soup whenever I wanted. I
had heat.

I added more hot water for the third time. Outside, it started
to snow.

I was inside.

I sniffled.

I snuffled.

I slid down so I was entirely covered in hot water in my claw-
foot tub to give my bones a break.

I came up only when I had to laugh so I wouldn't choke on
the water.

*　*　*

I slept in until eleven o'clock on Saturday morning, buried under blankets. I felt like I was getting my energy back, my health back.

I padded to the bathroom in my thick socks, delighted that my first pee of the day did not involve me secretly and furtively squatting like a fool beside my car.

I washed my hands in warm water and played with the soap bubbles like a kindergartener. I couldn't see the scars on my hands with the bubbles all over the place. I made coffee, added whipping cream, then scrambled back into bed with a huge red mug.

My bedroom had a view of the mountains straight in front of me. From my bed I could watch the weather. Watching the weather from bed rather than the back of a car is always more pleasing. I had put my pink, ceramic rose box for my lily bracelet on my dresser, and I opened it up and put my lily bracelet on.

I finished my coffee, then picked up my sketch book.

My art, my creativity, was coming back, too, all in a rush, as if it had gotten stuck in my homelessness. I drew a picture with a handful of colorful pastels of a window. Outside the window I drew a wishing well. The wishing well would eventually have trinkets coming out of it—dice, brooches, faux stones, tiny gold stars, and sequins. A little girl was running toward it wearing a crown of daisies and yellow ribbons . . .

I drew three hummingbirds. I would use sparkly netting and wire for the wings . . .

I drew a double-wide trailer and surrounded it with wild-flowers. . . . I would use buttons and fabrics for the flowers. . . .

Two hours later, I turned on my computer. I vowed I would not look at anything stomach churning, that is, e-mails from Covey coming from someone else's e-mail account, as I'd blocked him, or from my defense or divorce attorneys. I would try not to read any other articles about myself or Covey in the paper. That unpleasantness I'd leave for Sunday.

"Oh, my gosh," I breathed. I read the e-mail, then read it again. "Yippee! Oh, yippee!"

Kade Hendricks had e-mailed me. Moi!

"Dear Grenady: As Bajal is on maternity leave, I have a temporary position available as a receptionist, starting Monday. I would be happy to have you at the company. The position involves answering phones, greeting visitors . . ."

I giggled as I read the rest of the e-mail. Yes, a giggle. I am too old to giggle, but even with my tips, he was offering me much more than what I made at The Spirited Owl, plus medical insurance.

I wrote back right away. I thanked him for the position, told him I understood that it was only temporary and that I would be there Monday at eight thirty, as he had requested. "Thank you," I wrote. "I look forward to working for your company." I read it, read it again, studied the ceiling, walked around, read it again to make sure all the letters were in the right place, then hit send.

I kicked my legs under my blankets. I wiggled with my arms flailing in the air.

I might be going to jail, but I was no longer living in my car and I had not one but two jobs. *Two.*

Because I am an utter geek, I said, "Yippee!" one more time.

On Sunday I went to a thrift shop and Goodwill. I love shopping for used things at bargain prices.

I bought four mismatched, hand-painted china plates and four teacups with saucers for two dollars each because they were so pretty and I need pretty around me badly. I bought a pair of two-foot-tall blue ceramic candlesticks for three dollars for my kitchen table, and a flowered teapot, even though I don't drink tea. I would put it on my stove. I bought three glass vases—one crystal, one stained glass, one huge and blue—for two dollars each. I would put one in the kitchen, one in the family room, one in my bedroom. I also bought light blue Ball jars and two smaller blue vases for fifty cents each.

Then came my splurge: I went to the big-box store at the end of town, used a coupon, bought sale items only, and brought home pink bedsheets, two queen-sized pillows and pillowcases, and a white comforter with tiny pink roses for my queen-sized bed.

I also bought a white slipcover for the couch and a white slip-cover for the chair. I went to a grocery store next and stocked up, my relief at having food again—and somewhere to store and cook it—immense. I sniffled my way through the aisles. I made sure I grabbed coffee and whipping cream.

On the way home, I stopped at a garage sale at a sprawling home in the country. The owner told me that she and her hus-band were downsizing. She had huge throw pillows she'd used on her couch. The flowers on the fabric appeared to be de-ranged. I bought all eight for twenty-four dollars and headed to the fabric store.

I went straight to the discount rack, with another coupon in hand, and got a deal a horse thief would envy. Two of the pil-lows would be yellow with white tulips, and two would have blue and yellow pansies mixed together. One would be candy cane red. I bought enough of each fabric to make tablecloths for my kitchen table.

For the other three pillows, which would be on my bed, I bought pink-and-white-striped fabric.

I felt reckless buying these things, but I had a job at Hen-dricks' and The Spirited Owl! I had not had to come up with first and last month's rent and a security deposit, which I had been saving for, and I had already made another payment to Cherie.

I had to get the scent of homelessness off of me, the clingy cloud of poverty and desperation. I had to. Setting up an orga-nized, colorful, decorated home was the only way I knew how to do it.

When I returned to my home above the red barn, I washed the china and left it out on the counter so I could admire the plates and teacups. I pulled the white slipcovers over the furni-ture. Instant light. I made the bed. Pink and white, sweet and safe.

I set the vases out and decided I'd spring for flowers.

I was relieved to my core to have a home.

After weeks of car living, I am still getting pleasure out of my toilet.

Not in a weird way.

And don't get me started on my shower.

It was like old home week when I was in jail. A woman would come into the dayroom, and she'd be greeted like we were at some kind of family reunion. "Hey, Lonnie. How ya doin'? How's your son?" or "D'Angela. You back in again? What for? Hookin'?" and "Glitter! Been a long time. You still with that shit? How your brother? What about your momma? Saw her last time I was out. She had that hip operation yet?"

They talked, they laughed, they swore together. I didn't know anyone. I wasn't there to make friends, but I wasn't there to make enemies, either.

There was a guard there with a face like a skull, who reminded me of someone else I didn't want to think about. He was bony, thin. He leered at the women. You could tell he took this job because he liked the power trip. I saw him watching me. I said, "Eyes back in your head, skull face."

The survival instincts I had honed for years came sailing right back in, along with the repressed anger and decimated self-esteem. The me who I had become—the artist who had a little green house and taught kids art—was completely gone, poof, as if she'd never existed, and I was back to slamming down my emotions, living with my guard up, fists ready to fly.

I hated it. Hated who I had to become again in there to survive.

I watched one Herculean-sized woman, at least six feet tall, lumber up to me where I sat on the floor, my back to the cold wall. "Now, aren't you a pretty Barbie princess?"

I didn't respond, but I did stand up. I was not going to be kicked in the Big V sitting down, and I could see by the way she was judging me, and how her gaze settled on my crotch, that a swift kick there was not out of the range of possibility.

"What? You can't talk to me, girl? You got in trouble at your country club? What you do, steal the silver?"

"Thought about it, but no." I did belong to a country club, although it was in the city. I hated it. Bunch of fancy, brittle, wealthy people wanting to rub shoulders with other fancy, brittle, wealthy people in their quest to reach the top. They reminded me of vultures in Vuitton. I never fit in.

She stuck her hand out and stroked my hair. I hit her beefy arm away so fast, I knocked her off balance and she stumbled.

"You pussy bitch," she hissed at me.

"You try to touch my hair and I'm a pussy bitch? Don't touch me." I wasn't even scared of Neanderthal Woman. I'd been in fights with worse. Plus I was ravingly pissed because of what *he'd* done to get me in here.

"Fancy lady, aren't you?"

Not at all. If she only knew how not fancy I was.

"Where you from, fancy lady?"

Not much. Less than nothing. "Where are you from?"

"I ain't from your neighborhood, that for sure."

Oh, you have no idea.

She glared at me; I glared back. I felt my temper trigger, like a switch, cold and controlled.

"I asked you a question, Barbie princess. Where you from?"

Barbie princess? Damn. Temper skyrocketed.

She stepped up close to me, her face scrunched like a scrunched-up bag. She reached out a hand toward my chest, and I didn't even think. My fist came swinging out in an arch, and I popped her in the eye. She fell to the ground. She scrambled up, swung, I ducked, and she smashed my cheek with her other fist. I threw a punch at her fat chin. She went flat down again and stayed there.

I ended up in solitary for three days. Neanderthal Woman did, too.

What's funny is that women on the outside think they'll never be on the inside, in jail. I'll tell you, between the women you're in jail with and the women you're at the supermarket with, there's not much difference. In fact, sometimes the only difference between them and you is that they had a weapon available when their life turned upside down.

When I returned from solitary, a brain-mushing experience, Jane and her cat and pig were no longer my roommates.
I missed the cat and the pig.

I bought yellow daffodils with orange centers and purple tulips. I put them in the light blue Ball jars and the two smaller blue vases, then placed them on my window sill in the kitchen.
Instant pretty.
I so needed pretty. It calmed my nerves.

"Hi, Millie." I answered my attorney's call outside the library.
"Hi, Dina. How are you? How's the weather?"
"It's still around. How are things going?"
"The charges have not been dropped, if that's what you're unrealistically hoping for. I'm trying to work with the prosecution guys. They're not giving in, those mules. They believe you were a part of this whole financial scheme."
"I'm not even remotely smart enough to be involved. . . ." She talked me through my semi hysteria. "Millie, is there a chance I won't go to jail?"
"Yes. No. Maybe. Those documents you signed are killing you."
I wanted to bash Covey to pieces.
"A jury may believe you. A jury may also cook you on a spit like a pig. People are pissed off right now about rich people gashing others' savings accounts. Also, Covey is prepared to burn you at the stake on the witness stand, like an accused witch. If you're found guilty, you'll get around five years, probably. If you plea bargain we can make a deal. We can minimize your jail time. The assistant U.S. attorney has offered eighteen months if you plead guilty."
"No!" I semi yelled that. "Hell, no. I will not do time for something I did not do. It ticks me off to even think about it. I will not agree to live behind bars. No way. Never. Let's go to trial. I will tell the truth. No plea."
"Atta girl! You stud muffin! That's what I wanted to hear, but I had to be upfront with you about where this might be

headed. My boxing gloves are off, and I will fight for you with all my legal weaponry. I think you're innocent."

"Thank you. I am innocent. I will not do time for this. I will not plea my way out of this and go to jail for Covey's scheming. I'll take a chance."

"I love a nasty, hair-pulling fight. Raises my testosterone level."

"Maybe you'll turn into a man before my trial."

"Hope not. Women are so much smarter. It would be a detriment in the legal field to be a man."

"Thank you, Millie."

Her voice softened. "You stay strong, girl. We'll get ya through this. Adios."

Sunday night I could barely contain myself. I set out my outfit for Monday at Hendricks': cowboy boots; dark skinny jeans, because the other employees wore jeans; a burgundy silky blouse; and dangly silver earrings. I would also wear a belt with a silver belt buckle in the shape of a rose.

I had talked to Rozlyn. She swore up and down she had not talked to Kade and had planned to do it on Monday. She gave me a hug when I told her about the job, and we danced around her living room with Cleo amidst the women-power quilts. "Yay! A new friend for Eudora and me at Hendricks'!"

I washed my hair, braided it, and hopped into bed at nine o'clock. I would get up at seven o'clock to make sure I was there on time, which was ridiculous as I was only ten minutes away, but still!

I had another job!

And it had health insurance.

"Hendricks' Furniture," I said into the phone. "Yes, he's here. One moment, please." I put through the call that Kade was expecting from a rancher in Wyoming, then I answered the phone again and sent that call off to Rozlyn, money woman and secret lover of Leonard.

Hendricks' was much less physically exhausting than The Spirited Owl. I sat in the lobby; answered the phone, which rang constantly; answered people's questions; greeted people at the door; answered general e-mails from potential clients; and helped clients get the furniture they'd ordered when they came to pick it up.

Another call came through for one of the furniture makers about a particular design, which I transferred to Sam Jenkins, who managed the production end of things, and then poor Dell DeSouza called again, begging to speak to Eudora Ziegler. Eudora dumped him a month ago. She is seventy years old and has been Kade's secretary for sixteen years. She has the most gorgeous bone structure I've ever seen, high cheekbones, huge eyes, arched brows. She has pure white hair and she's an elegant fashion plate. She always wears heels and matching necklaces and earrings. She is sharp tongued and blunt. I like her.

Eudora used to work in Washington, DC, and abroad, she said, until moving here, but she won't elaborate on what she did. She does speak four languages, however, including Russian, French, and Arabic, and seems to know an impressive amount about the history of foreign governments, which is curious, and the Cold War.

It was the end of my second week at Hendricks' Furniture, and I knew Dell and this sorry romantic saga well.

"I'm sorry, Dell, you know Eudora doesn't want to talk to you."

"I know, but I have more to say. My love to express. You gotta tell me what to do, how to catch her. Like a fish. A big fish. A female fish. I need a hook. I need bait. I need a fishing pole!"

"Dell, go fishing in a lake. Go canoeing. Go visit your grandchildren." I once again decorated the lobby in my head. It would be infinitely better with color and a mural that filled a wall. And lighting. Better lighting is key.

"I don't want anything new, I want my Ewie. My Eudora."

"But she's already told you how she feels."

"A woman can change her mind, they always do and that's

what I'm betting on. I'm a betting man, uh—" He cleared his throat. "I'm not a betting man, no betting at the casinos, gave that up ten years ago, but I think I've got this one in the cards. I'm betting on it! I can be a new man for her. An ace of spades. A king of hearts."

We chatted more about his lost love, his aching heart, his shattered soul, then I politely hung up.

Dell is sixty. He's a handsome man. Ex–football player. Wealthy. Tons of land. Totally smitten with Eudora.

She told me she dumped Dell for "being a bad listener and an inability to sit still at the symphony. He also doesn't read books. How can I relate to someone who doesn't read?"

I cringed at the last one.

"Mostly it's the bad listener part. He thinks he should be the only one who talks in a relationship? I told him, 'All you need is a blow-up doll with no brain who nods her head and smiles at you, then spreads her legs. So go get one!' I handed him the name of a company that sells blow-up dolls in Portland. Then!" She pointed her pointer fingers in the air. "I ordered him three. Three different races of ladies. One black, one brown, one white. I told him, 'Here's your United Nations. Pick a woman, because it's not going to be me anymore!' "

Eudora does not strive for political correctness.

"Hi, Grenady."

"Hi, Loren." I looked up, smiled, then went back to work. I knew what was coming.

"So, uh, Grenady . . ." He leaned against my desk.

"Yes . . . ?"

"I was wondering if you would, uh . . ." Loren took a breath, gathered up his courage. He was a super nice man. Tall, thin, built like a candlestick with brown hair. He was an assistant manager for the company, underneath Sam Jenkins. I'd seen him interacting with other people. He was actually rather loud and quite affable and smart. I could see why Kade hired him, but around me he bumbled about.

I heard Kade walking toward the lobby, but Loren was intent on his mission so didn't notice. I hoped Kade would keep walking, back to his office, and would ignore this altogether. . . .

"I was wondering. What are you doing this weekend, Grenady?"

Damn. Kade heard that line and stopped. Loren didn't even know Kade was there.

I wanted to be polite, but I was not interested. I would run this man over like a stampeding buffalo. My personality was way too much for him. It would be like dating a shy dandelion.

"I'm working, Loren, pretty much the whole weekend. I'm sorry."

He looked disappointed but undaunted. "I know you work at The Spirited Owl, but only until Saturday night, right? How about if I see you on Saturday, then take you to breakfast on Sunday?"

My face froze. Did he think I was going to spend *the night* with him? I can't stand men, I can't. Pissants, all of them. My anger sizzled, and I stood up and reached for my stapler to use as a weapon. If he didn't clean up his mouth, I'd clock him. "*No.* That would not work."

Loren put his palms up, waved them frantically, and blushed. "Oh, God. Grenady, not like that. No ma'am. I know you're a lady, and I did not mean to imply that we would . . . we would . . ." He blushed further.

"I hope not, Loren, because that answer would be no." I was so mad I momentarily forgot about Kade. *Crap.*

"Man. I'm sorry, Grenady." Loren ran a hand through his hair. "I meant no offense. I said it wrong. What I was thinking is that I could visit with you at The Spirited Owl on Saturday night—I have friends who go on Saturday night—and then I go home to my house and you go home to your house, not together, didn't mean that. I'm sorry you're a lady.

"No, I don't mean I'm sorry you're a lady." His cheeks were pink. "I'm glad you're a lady. I meant on Sunday morning, maybe ten o'clock, I could pick you up and take you to breakfast at Claudine's Cafe, and we could eat and then I would drive you home and I would go home. Separately. You're a lady. I have messed this up."

"Loren, I appreciate you asking me, but I'm not dating right now, and I wouldn't date you because we work together, but thank you anyhow. Hello, Kade."

Kade was not amused. In fact, his jaw was tight.

Loren whipped around, voice stricken. "Hey, Kade."

"Loren. How's the armoire going for the Hearn family?"

"Almost perfect. I'm following your design exactly perfect. Have the scrolls on the sides done perfect."

"Glad to hear it. I'll come and see it in a minute."

"Right. Okay. I'm getting back to work right now, on a short break here, back to work, and I'll see you in a minute, Kade." He turned back to me, briefly. "Thank you anyhow, Grenady. I'm sorry for the"—he waved a hand, blushed deeper—"misunderstanding. My fault."

"Sure. It's fine. No problem." Poor man. When Loren walked by, Kade thumped him on the back, guy-style.

Kade and I were now alone in the lobby. I felt nervous, as I always did around mafia man Kade. He was wearing a dark green button-down shirt, jeans, and cowboy boots.

"How are you, Grenady?"

"Fine. Thank you. How are you?" I wanted to say, "I didn't encourage that. I'm not trying to date your employees. I don't flirt, I won't cause trouble," but I didn't. I kept my mouth shut. I have learned not to try to explain myself.

"How have the last couple of weeks been?"

"Great." I smiled. They had been great. I had received my first check that afternoon, the job was fun, and I talked to people all day, most of whom were friendly and happy to talk to me about furniture. "I like the people here. None of them are drunk or falling off barstools or ordering too much vodka. Plus, I love the furniture, like my desk. Thank you for hiring me."

"You're welcome." He smiled slightly. "Let me know if you have any ideas for our lobby. I've always found it boring, but interior design isn't my thing. Furniture is, but not all the"—he waved a hand in the air in a circle—"other stuff. I know you're an artist. "

"You mean, you want me to redecorate the lobby?"

"Yes. If you can. Let me know what we should do."

"Oh. Well. As a matter of fact—" I stopped. I didn't want to sound like I was being critical.

"As a matter of fact?" He waited. He did not look impatient.

"I've already figured out what we should do."

He blinked, and I could tell he was surprised.

"What should we do?"

I found myself getting animated. I love colors. Love art. Love transforming a room. When I was done telling him my thoughts, he smiled. "Have at it, Grenady."

"Are you sure?" My voice squeaked like a nut-stuffed squirrel.

"Yes. Tell me how much money you need, what you need to buy, and we'll get it. I'll pay you extra to do it."

"That's not necessary at all. You don't have to pay me extra. I figured it all out while I was sitting here on your dime, so I'll arrange for what I need and get some paint and an electrician in here, and I'll get it done."

"Thank you."

"You're welcome." I smiled. He smiled back. There was something in his eyes I couldn't quite read, but that was typical. He was a private, reserved man. If he had smiled at me in a slightly flirty way before he offered me this job, the flirty smile was now gone. He treated me like he treated all his employees. Respectfully. Professionally. He was The Boss.

He turned and left, and once he was down the hallway, I sunk back into my chair and fanned my hot face with papers and absolutely did not think about stripping off his clothes and running my hands through his chest hair.

No, I did not.

I met Covey at a law firm party.

I had made a huge mural for the firm, and the attorneys loved it. It was an eight-by-five-foot scene of the countryside with a red barn in the background. I had dried wheat for part of it. I used tiny black pieces of wood to outline the barn. I put a gold rooster on the top of the barn for a weather vane. I put white feathers on the chickens. I found two miniature, old-fashioned bikes and attached them, too. I think they wanted something natural and serene to hide the fact that they were sharks.

They invited me to come to their party, and I went for potential clients. I met Covey there. This was the firm Goldman and Skiller, that represented Covey whenever he was sued, I later learned, which was often, so they loved him.

He was nine years older than me and had been divorced for five years. He was a well-known investor. I had even heard of him. He was charming, brilliant, articulate, and dryly amusing. He was also complimentary about my work and my appearance. He seemed relaxed, calm, sophisticated.

He asked me out to dinner. I said no. He was higher up on the social pecking order than me, and I didn't like the power difference. He seemed smart, and I didn't think I was smart. He was educated. I was not. He asked me to take a ride on a boat with him. He asked me to attend a sporting event with him. I said no and no.

Later I realized how much he liked my telling him no. He sensed my rigid resistance, my lack of ability to commit to someone, my lack of trust, so he had a chase on his hands. He had to conquer and tame me. He had to own me.

He commissioned a mural for his office. I had to put him off for three months because I was busy with other murals. That did not please him at all. I could tell in the stillness of his face, the tightening of his mouth. He tried to buy me off my other clients, offered me twice as much. I was flattered then; now I know that Covey couldn't stand it that I was doing anything for anyone else. He had to be first. Three months later, I started his mural. He was not pleased at the wait.

I said, "Too bad."

He laughed. It covered his anger.

Falling in love was not comfortable for me. I was not a virgin, but neither had I ever "made love" with a man. I had "had sex."

Having sex and making love are two totally different things. I liked sex well enough, but there was always something missing. That would be the love part.

I had held back on falling in love. That would have involved trust, and that I could not do. I didn't trust anyone, especially men. When they wanted to get closer, to be committed, I skated right on out of there. But Covey wouldn't let me skate away; he chased me.

He made me feel safe, protected, and loved in the relationship. He called all the time, sent flowers, constantly showed me he cared about me.

And he included me. That would be the word. From the start, he included me.

He was never embarrassed about me, as I had been embarrassed about myself for so long. He wasn't ashamed of me, as I had been ashamed of myself. He didn't want to hide me, as I had wanted to hide. Quite the opposite. He put me on his arm, smiled, and off we went to fancy dinners and trips, skiing and boating. He introduced me to his friends at his country club and the golf club, and they were soon commissioning paintings and collages from me, too.

I borrowed his confidence. I borrowed his easygoing manner. I smiled brightly like him. I learned to control my temper and improve the way I spoke. I didn't swear like a horse thief anymore. I didn't leap into a fight.

But even that side of me, Covey liked. He told me, "I love the rough rider side of you, sweetheart, that ball breaker, but can it when we're at the governor's mansion for another one of those endless charity events, will you? Now hop on top of me, you gun-slinging, deer-hunting, target-shooting, red-necked Amazon woman."

He did not ask many questions about my past. Initially I saw this as sensitive. He could tell I didn't want to talk about my childhood much, the lack of any family. I gave him only the barest bones. I thought he was respecting my silence and privacy.

The truth was, he didn't want to go that deep with me. I was sexy, curvy, mysterious, independent, ran from commitment, challenged him by being a smart aleck, and had a tough side. He didn't see me as intellectual, as bright, so I was no threat to him. I was an artist, which he later told me he thought was an "adorable hobby, sweet cakes. Let's get naked and use your paintbrushes on each other."

He didn't want to know who his Dina Hamilton had been when she was Dina Wild, and he especially didn't want to know Grenadine Scotch Wild.

Oh no. He didn't want to know Grenadine Scotch Wild at all.

22

He had to study the original nursery rhyme for two days. He sang it repeatedly, as loud as he could.

> Pat-a-cake
> Pat-a-cake
> Baker's man.
> Bake me a cake as fast as you can.
> Pat it and prick it and mark it with a B
> And put it in the oven for baby and me.

He pulled out three hairs, then tipped his head back and balanced all three on his nose. He licked them. The licking gave him an idea.

> Pat-a-cake
> Pat-a-cake
> I'm the baker's man.
> I'll bake a person cake as fast as I can.
> I'll knife it, beat it, and mark it with a kiss
> And put it under a rock where I'll take a piss.

Brilliant! He was brilliant! He bit off part of his pencil and chewed on it. It made him giggle. He was a giggler! And a poet!

23

On my first day at Hendricks', Rozlyn came and grabbed me at my desk, as I was too shy to walk into the employees' lounge, stand around, and not know where to sit. It would be like the torture of the school cafeteria all over again. "Get on in here, Grenady," she said. "Come meet Eudora—she's my idol—and Marilyn, who I can barely stand. When I'm having menopausal rage problems I want to smack her."

Eudora stood and shook my hand, smiled, and said, "It's a pleasure. Don't forward Dell's calls to me. I went out on three dates with him and now I can't shake him off. I may have to shoot him." I agreed not to forward the calls. She said something I couldn't understand.

"Pardon?"

"I said, in Russian, I would put him in the gulag if I could, no vodka."

"I'm Marilyn." Marilyn stuck out a limp-fish hand, and I shook it. She did not bother to stand. I knew her already. She was in sales. I had said hello to her that morning. She had stopped when she saw me behind my desk, eyed me up and down, and a sour and hard expression settled on her face like a rock. I knew she didn't like me.

"Marilyn is in a bad mood often," Rozlyn said. "I would like to blame her hormones, but I think it's her personality."

"That's true," Eudora echoed, crossing her thin legs and swinging a black heel with a red sole. "She's naturally petty."

"I am sometimes because of a stressful life." Marilyn sighed before going off on a bunch of piddly complaints about how she was so "overwhelmed" with work at Kade's, her home and garden, her husband. Then she smiled at me, but it was a mean smile, one poised for attack. "You"—she pointed at me with her fork—"are a wife's nightmare."

"Gee. Thanks."

"You're welcome." She tilted her head, examining me as one would a specimen. She smiled again, tight and derisive. "Your contacts are such a bright green! Do you like them like that?"

"I'm not wearing contacts."

I could tell she was surprised.

"She has gorgeous eyes," Eudora said. "Do try to be pleasant, Marilyn, no matter how bad it hurts you."

"Shut up, Marilyn," Rozlyn said. "Get your personality disorder under control."

"I'm sorry! I didn't know they were real."

"Most people's eyes are real," I drawled. "Although there could be people running around with fake eyes. The ones you take in and out of your eye socket. Pop in, pop out. But these are both mine."

Rozlyn and Eudora snickered. Marilyn blushed.

A few days later, Marilyn was at it again. I could tell she had planned how to torpedo me. "I used to own a hair salon, so I know about hair. You do have thick hair, that's a plus, but have you ever thought about cutting your hair shorter, perhaps to your chin, so it's more . . . how shall I say it? Controlled. A better fit for your age."

"No. I don't need controlled hair." I let my eyes drift over her mop ever so slowly. "I don't want hair that is flat and sticks to my head like a sick gopher." I coughed twice, like a sick gopher.

Rozlyn said, "Shut up, Marilyn. You're jealous. Tell Mildred, your meanest personality, to go back inside your head and be quiet."

Eudora said, "Your hair does resemble a sick gopher, Marilyn."

"Let's not get offended, dear." Marilyn patted my hand, ignoring the other two. The word *dear* was so condescending. "I'm simply suggesting that you don't need to flash it."

I put down my sandwich and faced that pudgy and jealous witch, my temper triggered. "What, exactly, do you mean by that?"

I knew her type. Throw mean comments, a slight jab, a fake smile, pretend you are trying to *help* someone improve one of their glaring flaws.

"I mean that some men lust over women like you, and you have to ask yourself if you want that *kind* of attention."

"What do you mean that *kind* of attention? And what do you mean, women like me?"

"You have an image that says ..." Marilyn waved a hand. "I'm available. Anytime."

Rozlyn slammed a hand down on the table. "Damn it, Marilyn. She does not, and why are you so disagreeable? You're like killer gas."

"Vicious and silly woman," Eudora said. "That is enough."

"You mean, I look like a whore?" My temper was now at a dull roar.

"That language!" Marilyn squirmed, lips tightening. "Not *quite* like a whore."

"Not quite like a whore?" Roar again.

"Do you want to know the truth?" Marilyn asked, eyebrow arched.

I hate that question. People preface rude and critical statements with that line. I didn't even answer.

"You're throwing yourself out there for any man. All that reddish hair. That bust. Those eyes. Your lips are ... so puffy. And with you being a bartender, too. Perhaps you need a more restrained style, not so suggestive."

Any man? Man, I was pissed. "Let me tell you what I need. I'll say it slow because you don't seem too bright to me. I need to stay employed. I need to work hard without people like you getting in my way. I am grateful for the job, but I stopped taking shit a long time ago and I'm not taking it from you. I get what you're saying, so shut the fuck up." Roar!

Marilyn sucked in her breath.

"You don't like me because of my hair and puffy lips and boobs. You don't even know me, but you're going to judge me harshly because you feel threatened about your own life, your gopher hair, your husband, your lard butt, or something else. I don't know what it is and I don't care. But if you ever say, or imply, that I look like a whore, I'm going to take that as an invitation for me to shove my sandwich down your fat throat until you choke. Do we have an understanding?"

"Goodness." She flushed bright red. "I think you've threatened me."

Rozlyn crossed her arms in front of her. "Yes, disagreeable one, do you understand?"

Eudora glared at Marilyn and said, "Why so spiteful? In my previous work, people like you ended up in rivers."

"I don't think I'm going to sit here anymore," Marilyn said. She stood up, then paused as if waiting for someone to tell her to stay. "I'm leaving."

I stood up, too. I was taller than her. "Don't ever talk to me like that again."

She waved a hand. "My, you have a temper."

"You have no idea." My temper was flaaaamming.

This time, she backed off. I saw her hand shake as she picked up her lunch bag. I had shocked her with my response. That kind of person lays her power down by assuming no one will challenge her.

I sat back down. "Would you like me to leave?"

Rozlyn hit the table. "No! I can't stand Marilyn! And now she's gone and I'm a happy hormonal woman!"

"You stay right there," Eudora said. "It will be the three of us. A lusty menopausal woman, a woman who threatens to shove her sandwich down an irritating woman's throat, and me, a world traveler who has done naughty things. Cheers to Grenady. Welcome to The Wood Gals Gang."

I wondered what the naughty things were. We toasted our water bottles together.

I ate lunch with The Wood Gals every day from then on. It

was fun. It was entertaining. Eudora was humorously snippy, and Rozlyn lived and thought at full speed.

I liked them.

But what would they think of someone who had been in jail for theft, fraud, money laundering, and embezzlement?

I had my car window fixed. I went to Billy Squared, and they handled things with my insurance company. They were, as I'd been told, the best. Friendly and funny.

When I left they said, "We're coming to visit you at the bar, Grenady!"

I said I would love to see them.

There sure were a lot of nice people here.

But not Marilyn.

My attorneys called. Neither had pleasant news. Swing me a cat, the conversations were downright scary.

On Sunday I slept until eleven, then found a long wood table at the thrift shop for my artwork. The owner's son brought it over, and we carried it up the stairs.

I put it against the wall to the left of the French doors. I set up my brushes and paints: Teal. Amber. Turquoise. Lipstick red. Gold. Deep purple. Magenta. Forest green. Lemon. Pink. Honey. Maroon. Orange. I transferred my art supplies from my kitchen table to this table. My heart felt better, yes it did. I would buy canvases this week.

I made chocolate chip cookies and brought some to Rozlyn and Cleo. Rozlyn was on the couch with an ice pack over her head because of a headache. She whispered to me, "I think I'm getting these headaches because of a lack of sex with Leonard." We both laughed, and I heated her up some bread and minestrone soup she'd made.

While I did it, I studied another quilt she had hanging on her wall. It was the backside of a woman—quite curvy, black hair like Rozlyn's—in front of a lake, a rose in her mouth, a purple lacy thong up her rear. It rocked.

Cleo was singing a song about snails and girls who wear bonnets at the top of her lungs, which couldn't have been good for Rozlyn's head, so I asked her if she wanted to come over and help me sew pillowcases for my pillows with the deranged-looking flowers.

She said, "Yes, yes, cowgirl yes," and jumped up and down. "I do." She was wearing silver sequined go-go-type boots; what looked to be a prom dress of Rozlyn's, which she'd hiked up with a belt; and a hat with a dog on it.

On the way over we greeted Liddy, and Cleo horse-talked with her. Liddy's head actually bobbed up and down, as if she understood the gibberish. "Liddy says she wants to be a space alien, too. Like me."

I nodded sagely. "I'm not surprised."

We cut out fabric, then sewed it up on my old sewing machine. Cleo was pretty good on the sewing machine because of the quilting her mother did. We made the five pillow covers for the family room, then I showed her how to sew buttons on the fabric to make it more interesting. She was a quick learner.

On the candy cane red pillow, we used one large, gold circular button in the center, then surrounded it with five gold circular buttons to make a flower. On the two blue and yellow pansy pillows, we used three white flower buttons in the centers of three of the flowers, and on the white and yellow tulip pillows, we put two fun buttons—a squirrel and a silver horseshoe—in the middle of each one.

As we worked, Cleo kept saying the funniest things:

I wish I had a sixth toe, then I could climb walls better.

Do you think I look like I have a little dolphin in me?

Do you think there are people living on the inside of Pluto but they hide whenever we point our telescopes at them?

"I'm glad you moved into the big, red barn, Grenady."

"I'm glad, too."

Rozlyn's headache hadn't gone away by the time Cleo and I walked back over. I told her to go to bed. Looking at her hurting was making me feel ill. I made spaghetti for Cleo, cleaned up, then I read her three books and tucked her in. She gave me a hug.

"Night, night," she sang. "Don't let the bed bugs bite. If they do, smash them with a shoe in the bumparoo."

"I'll do that, sweets."

"Don't leave until I'm asleep, okay?"

"Okay."

"You can beat back any bad dreams that come."

"I promise you I'll beat 'em back."

I sat there for a full two minutes, her hand in mine, until she conked out.

I turned off the lights, double-checked the stove, locked the doors, and headed back over to my place.

I wondered what it would be like to have a child. If she was a kid like Cleo, I thought it might be darn fun.

"Grenady, can you please, please, please help me with tables seven and eight?"

"Sure will, Monique." Monique is spitfire and honey mixed together. Her mother-in-law has moved in with her and her husband, and World War III had broken out, minus the bombs.

She tells Monique, who is a vegetarian, that being a vegetarian is "grossly unseemly," that she works "too much and will age rapidly at this rate. I can already see it happening," that she does not know "her place as a wife, my poor son."

The other day I said to Monique, in the kitchen, "How are you?" and she picked up a huge knife and killed a cucumber. A week ago I said to her, "Hi, Monique," and she said, "Hi, Grenady," then hugged me and cried. When she was done she cut up *a salad* with two butcher knives.

"Thank you, Grenady," Monique said. "I have to call my husband and tell him that if he does not move that Satan witch out of our house, I will move out." She tipped back a shot glass full of vodka. Tildy does not allow any staff to drink alcohol at any time at work, and Monique knows it.

I took it as a sign of her desperation.

"I'll get the tables, Monique, no problem."

She reached for a second shot of vodka, but I grabbed it. "Go ahead and make the call."

She stalked away, muttering about moving to Guam. I don't know why she chose Guam.

I turned around and grabbed the food from the cook's window and took it to table seven, smiled, and got them ketchup. When I brought the food to table eight, a woman there, all prissed up with blondish hair curling like a bell under her chin, said, "I thought I told you that I wanted my hamburger to be well-done, not medium." She pushed the plate toward me with two manicured fingers as if she couldn't bear to touch it.

"I'm not your waitress, but I'll take it back and have the chef make you a new one."

"You are my waitress. You were just here. Did you forget?" She rolled her eyes at me. "Why wasn't it done right the first time?"

"I don't know, but I'll take care of it." I tried to smile. Her companions, one woman and two men, probably their husbands, looked embarrassed.

"It'll be fine, Anna," one of the men said.

"No," Anna snapped. "It's not fine. You have your food. I wanted to eat *with* you, not *after* you, like a servant. Can you hurry this up?" Her face twisted, red mouth tight.

I studied her for a second. She had that vain, shallow, pampered appearance. The one that says, "I spend an hour and a half getting ready for my day. I don't have anything going on. I don't work, I don't volunteer, but I do have shopping, manicures, and facials to attend to. And Pilates. And gossip."

"It'll be a few minutes. I'll be right back out." I resisted the urge to call her Miss Priss.

"This will affect your tip."

"No, it won't," said the man sitting next to her. He was balding and blushing. "Not at all."

"Thank you." I smiled brightly at him, letting my gaze linger because I knew it would piss her off. He smiled back.

"We're still tipping!" the other woman said. She had a round face and a worried expression.

"Thank you, too," I said cheerily. "That's kind."

The priss humphed.

I turned away with the offending, undercooked hamburger.

I told one of the chefs, Carlos, we had a priss in the dining room who wanted her hamburger well-done. I pointed the woman out. He rolled his eyes. "That's Anna. Rich. Spoiled. Can't stand her. Tildy hates her. I heard she was getting divorced, took her ex to the cleaner and ripped him a new one in back. I don't know who the guy next to her is."

I returned to the bar and made two gin and tonics, two Kahlúa and creams, and poured a few beers. When Carlos hit the bell and yelled, "One hamburger ready for the priss," I laughed and brought the hamburger out to her.

"Okay," I said. "Why don't you check it and see if it's to your liking."

The woman took the bun off, then cut into the meat. "No." Her voice was nasty, furious. "This is not *well-done*. See? There's still a line of pink."

"No, there's not," said the man who I thought was her husband but wasn't. "It's fine. Give it to me. I'll eat it."

"It is not fine." Anna the priss shoved the plate toward me so hard, it skidded across the table and I had to catch it before it went straight over. "Well. Done. Do you know what that means? It means cooked. I don't want to get sick from any bacteria you all have lurking in that kitchen."

"We don't have any bacteria lurking in the kitchen," I said. "We asked all the bacteria to leave last night. They got on their roller skates and took off." The men laughed, and so did the other woman, who put her hand over her mouth. I had a feeling she was enjoying watching the priss get her comeuppance.

The prissy woman was livid. "I did not ask you to make fun of me. What's wrong with you? High school degree, or did you drop out? And the job is still too hard for you, isn't it?"

"That's enough, Anna!" the nonhusband snapped.

"Stop it," the other man hissed. "Damn, Anna. What's wrong with you?"

She hit a nerve, oh, she hit a raw, frayed nerve. "The job is not too hard for me, except for in times like this. This is a trying time. As in, I'm trying to hold onto my temper. But I'll take your hamburger back and make sure that it's well-done. Not a scrap of pink."

"I have never had such bad service."

"I've never had such a bad customer." I smiled, tilted my head.

The nonhusband put his head in his hands and said, "I'm glad for that." The other man said, "I can't believe you, Anna."

The woman with the worried expression laughed. Didn't bother to cover it.

"I want to speak to your manager," the priss said.

"I'll get her. I'm sure she'll enjoy the conversation. Don't tick her off, though. She has a bat." I turned away with the offending hamburger. "And she has a gun."

I told Tildy I would be back at the bar in a second. She said, "Okay, Grenady. I see you have Anna Sachs tonight. Better you than me. I always want to smash her with my bat." She cleaned a glass. "Or shoot her. Don't take any crap from her, ya hear? I'm about to kick her out for the rest of her worthless lifetime."

I took the hamburger back to the stove and cooked that sucker myself, flames high. "Fry me a pig and shut up, Anna, you witch," I muttered.

Carlos laughed. "This is gonna be good."

When it was charred and flaming, I took it off, put it back on the bun and, smoke billowing, walked back into the dining room, people's heads turning as they laughed. I put the plate in front of the priss, the meat still smokin'.

"Oh." Anna's face scrunched up even tighter. "You bitch."

I don't like being called that word. It reminds me of a whole lot I need to forget. I was now as hot as that flaming hamburger.

"Now you've done it." I leaned forward across the table. "You've gone and pissed me off."

Her nonhusband said, "I'm out of here." He took out his wallet and gave me a hundred-dollar bill. "I apologize."

"You asked for it well-done, Anna," the other woman said, laughing. "It's well-done." She whispered to me, "This is the best night ever. Thank you!"

"It's on *fire*," the prissy Anna shrieked. "I want to speak to your manager right now." She pointed a manicured finger at me. "Now!"

"Okay," I said. "But first, let me put out the fire on your burger." I picked up her glass and turned it over onto the hamburger. It smoked more. "There. Now it's not on fire, but it is well-done. Eat up, Anna. And don't you ever call me or any other woman in this place a bitch. Do you understand?"

"This is a disgusting, red-necked, white-trash swampland."

"And you are a prissy, vain, silly person who needs to figure out why you're so unhappy so you will stop trying to make the world unhappy with you."

Something flashed in those eyes, and I knew that this time I'd hit a nerve with her. We were nerve for nerve now.

"I'm not unhappy!"

"You are. Now eat your flaming hamburger and shut up." My temper kept rising, high as the sky, then it flew around, unfettered.

I didn't know Tildy was behind me; someone must have told her.

"Who did you call a bitch, Anna?"

Anna's friend with the worried expression pointed at me. "Anna called our waitress a bitch, Tildy. But I didn't. I didn't say it. I didn't think it." The friend pointed at Anna so we could find her at the table. "She did it."

Tildy had the bat. She tapped it on the table. "Get out. I've had it with you. Never come to my restaurant again, Anna. You disrespect my staff every time."

Anna went white.

Anna's friend groaned, "But that doesn't apply to me, does it, Tildy, does it? I didn't say anything mean at all."

"It will if you're with her, Tracy."

The nonhusband started scooting out of the booth. "I'm

sorry, Tildy. Sorry to you, too." He nodded at me. "This is the worst date of my frickin' life. It was a blind date. I didn't know it was her. Somebody should have told me." He turned to the other man. "That would be you, Austin. You should have told me."

"She's a terrible waitress!" Anna's mouth reminded me of a sharp claw. "She almost burned me with that hamburger. She almost caught my hair on fire."

I was so ticked at being called a bitch, I was so ticked at being talked down to, I grabbed the bat from Tildy and smashed it right in the middle of that overcooked hamburger. It made a huge, popping noise, the tomatoes squishing out, the ketchup spurting.

"Get out!" Tildy and I both told Anna.

Anna screamed when the bat bammed and cracked the plate, then started to scramble out.

"No one, especially a dropout *waitress,* talks to me like that! Do you know who I am? Do you know who my father is? You're nothing," Anna said, but her voice wobbled. "You're going to regret this."

"You're going to regret calling me a bitch," I said. I smashed the bat on the table, right where she was. "And I am not nothing." Whoo. My temper was out of control. I hit the table again.

"Worst date ever," the man said to Austin, totally exasperated. "Ever. How could you do this to me? I thought we were friends!"

"We are, buddy. Man, I'm sorry. I'll make it up to you. I'm sorry."

"Is this a joke? Do you hate me?" He turned to me. "I apologize, again."

"Tildy, please," Tracy begged, "I like our waitress. She's fun. Can I stay? Do you have peach pie tonight?"

Anna went to the police to file charges. Thirty minutes later, I was yet again talking with police officers Justin Nguyen, Sergeant Sara Bergstrom, and Lieutenant Mark Lilton.

Tildy told them, the bat safely behind the bar, that she felt threatened by the woman's rage. "I was frightened. I was worried that she would hurt me. Cause harm."

"Yes, harm," I chimed in. "I believed my physical and emotional health was at risk."

I could tell that Lieutenant Lilton, Officer Nguyen, and Sergeant Bergstrom were having a hard time not laughing out loud. Officer Nguyen stared at the ceiling, but the dimples showed in his smile. Sergeant Bergstrom's mouth twitched. Lieutenant Lilton's jaw locked and he fiddled with his glasses.

"She was unpredictable, irrational," Tildy said. "She moved her hand, and I knew she was thinking of stabbing my face with her table knife. My pretty face."

"You do have a pretty face, Tildy," Lieutenant Lilton said.

"No one wants anything to happen to your face," Sergeant Bergstrom said.

"And the worst part," I said, "was that Anna called this a disgusting, red-necked, white trash swampland."

Officer Nguyen actually gasped. "It is not!"

"No way. Especially not with the pies," Lieutenant Lilton said.

"Dang right, it isn't!" Tildy said.

"Do you have any blackberry pie, by the way?" Officer Nguyen asked. "I mean, I would like it when I'm off work tonight, after we finish a complete and thorough investigation here."

The officers asked people at the bar and in the restaurant if they saw anything "suspicious."

Grizz, his gray and white hair rebelling, as normal, said that Anna was like Jekyll and Hyde, only she was always Hyde.

"I'm reading *Dr. Jekyll and Mr. Hyde* right now," Lieutenant Lilton said. "I like it."

Grizz said it was excellent reading material and he did not see me or Tildy swinging a bat. "I did not see Grenady smash a bat flat on Anna's hamburger. That's a flat-out lie. Outrageous! There are no bats in this fine establishment."

Chilton, my snake man friend, said, "Gren was sweetness itself, like a cupcake, and brought Anna her burger perfectly cooked. No, there was no smoke and no fire. Anna's all smoke and fire. Who told you that doggone fictional story? Well, that's Anna for you. Making stuff up like a rattler. Squeezing the life out of everyone like a python."

Another woman said, "Anna's the threat. She's a threat to this town with her gossip. She spread a rumor that I had vaginitis. I do not have vaginitis. I have had it, but I don't now. I was treated. I hate Anna."

A man in his thirties with full sleeve tattoos who had been sitting at a table across from Anna said, "I was in the army for fifteen years. I see three hundred and sixty degrees at all times. I can see a mouse hiding behind a chair leg. If someone had a bat up in the air, I'd be up and defending the victim. There was no bat. All I saw was that high-maintenance woman giving Grenady hell. She called Grenady a bitch, which was untoward and impolite."

"I thought I made her a delicious hamburger," I said. "I made it to her specifications. No pink. Not even a smidgen."

"You cooked it well-done," Tildy said. "As requested."

"I'll take a well-done burger when I'm off shift in an hour," Sergeant Bergstrom said. "That sounds delicious." She turned to me. "But not *flaming* well-done. Well-done. Regular. No fire. No smoke."

"What other pies do you have?" Officer Nguyen asked. "My mother texted me. She heard I was here dealing with Anna. She wants to know if you have chocolate cream?"

There were no charges filed.

"Eudora, can I borrow the camera?" Hendricks' Furniture has a high-quality company camera. The furniture—in particular the most impressive, personal pieces—was photographed and the images uploaded to the website.

"Yes, you may." She handed it to me. "There are better cameras, slim as a pen. Cameras in books, cameras in brooches . . ."

"Do you have a brooch camera?"

She winked. "Used to."

"A lipstick camera?"

"Yep. Some people said those were fictional. They were not. I know."

"Tell me more about your cameras and where you used them."

"Can't. I can simply say that my father was an expert, too."

It was Friday afternoon, so it was quieter than usual, and I went around and took photos of the furniture and, sometimes, the people working on it. It was a nice way to chat with people and get to know them better. Except for Marilyn.

Marilyn said, "And what are you doing with a camera?"

"Smile, Marilyn, as if you're a friendly person."

"I'm sorry, Grenady. I'm not comfortable with you taking my photo."

"Okay." I could tell that twisted her panties up. I took Eudora's photo with her lying on her side on her desk, her beaded necklace suggestively in her mouth, like a "royal courtesan from the nineteenth century who has recently bedded a sheik." I laughed so hard, I had to put the camera down.

Rozlyn opened her shirt, flashed me her chest, crossed her eyes, and stuck out her tongue. We just about died laughing.

When I was done, I knocked on Kade's office door. "Hi. Do you have a minute?"

He looked busy. He had tons of folders and papers spread out over his desk. He stood up and said, "Sure. Come on in."

"I'm going to take your photo." He was wearing a short-sleeved black T-shirt.

"Must you?"

"Yes, I must." I smiled.

He smiled back. "Why?"

"Because you told me I could decorate the lobby and I need your photo."

"No one needs my mug in the lobby."

"I do. Smile pretty for me."

"I don't know how to smile pretty."

"Pretend then, stud man."

He laughed. "Stud man?"

"Yep. Smile."

I told him to pretend he was modeling a suit and tie. He said, "Ties make me feel like I'm being strangled."

I clicked away. "Pretend you're in your favorite place." His eyes darkened, he grew serious, and I took that one, too. I took a few more. "Let's go into the factory."

He let me take five photos of him in front of his furniture. He was a testosterone-driven hunk of a semi dangerous he-man. I did not utter that. As I took the photos his employees joked with him and said, "Aren't you the handsome one, boss?" and "Tilt your head back so we can admire those brown eyes!" and "Doesn't he have an engaging smile?"

Kade threw the teasing right back at them, then said, "Okay. I think I'm photographed out."

"What, the life of a model wouldn't suit you?"

"It would be my hell."

"Thanks for your time."

"Sure. Anytime." He ran a hand through that thick black hair of his. "Anytime, as in, you can come and talk to me anytime but I'm not posing for any more photos."

"Now you've taken all the fun out of my life."

"Poor you. Try fishing."

I laughed; he laughed.

I thought he was going to say something else, but he didn't.

I was not interested in getting involved with any man again for at least a hundred years, but I did have a boss who was plain gorgeous in a wild and sexy Mexican cowboy sort of way. Eye candy.

I felt happy. I was glad I had this job.

For many reasons.

Covey continued to call from different numbers. I continued to delete his messages. He told me I would go to prison for years if I didn't get my "tight little trailer park ass" home.

I thought he could be right.

I would not bring my ass home, though.

*   *   *

I took Cleo shopping for her fabric and pillow form for her own button pillow on Monday. Rozlyn stayed home and took a nap because of another headache. She called it her "menopausal mental pain, associated with having too many thoughts in my head and a true fear that I will never capture Leonard. Did I tell you I saw him yesterday? I waved, twice, but he didn't see me."

Cleo wore an Indian dress with intricate beading that she'd worn at Halloween, pink glitter tights, purple high-tops, and a rainbow-colored hat with a stuffed black cat on top.

She chose fabric with the galaxy on it, and I found a foam pillow.

We went back to my house over the big, red barn. We gave Liddy an apple and Cleo said, "What? You're right, Liddy, I think I am magic! I'm going to cast a spell right now," and she waved her arms around. Liddy bobbed her head up and down, appreciating the magic spell. That connection between horse and kid is amazing.

"I'm fluent in horse language," Cleo said.

"I can tell."

Later we measured and cut the fabric for the pillow and sewed it on the sewing machine. She did almost all the work.

We used white shiny buttons on the stars, a red button on Mars, and tiny glitter buttons around Saturn's rings.

She loved it.

"10, 9, 8, 7, 6, 5, 4, 3, 2, 1. Blast off!" she yelled, then ran around the room, arms out at her side. She was a fast spaceship.

Rozlyn was asleep when I returned Cleo. I made us cheese sandwiches and then put Cleo to bed.

Rozlyn woke up when I was cleaning the kitchen.

"How are you?"

"Fine."

"You've had a lot of headaches."

"I know. Curse them."

She then told me about a girl who used to cast spells on her when they were in high school. That girl is now head of a Wiccan group.

"How magical," I said.

"Indeed. Wonder if her curse extended to thirty years out of high school and that's why I have these headaches?"

"Doubtful. I think spells have a shelf life."

"Let's hope, because she was one mean witch."

We laughed and talked about our favorite movies, politics and social issues, bladders that leaked when we laughed too hard, how coughing while running was a bad idea, how she farted one time with a man in bed, a ripper, and he never called back, and our art—quilts and collages.

She was pale. I was beginning to feel pale with her. I don't like seeing people sick or hurting.

I went home, neighed back at Liddy, put my lily bracelet in my pink, ceramic rose box, and went to bed.

A jail cell flashed in my mind. It took a while to get to sleep after that.

24

FIR GROVE ELEMENTARY SCHOOL
OUR MASCOT, FURRY GROVER SAYS,
"BE KIND TO EVERYONE."

April 6, 1985

Dear Mr. and Mrs. LaMear,

I know that Grenadine is your foster child and
you are working at home with her on conflict
resolution and her temper, as we are. I left you a
voice message last week but you did not respond.
I don't know if you received it, so I will repeat the
story here.

One of the boys in my class whispered,
"Dummido Grenado" at Grenadine on Monday,
and she got up and slammed her book over his
head. His nose hit the desk and bled. I sent her to
the office. That was the third time this year.

When I told her she was going to see Mrs.
Crumps to talk about how to resolve problems
without hitting, she said, "Why?" I told her it
wasn't appropriate to hit other kids and she said,
"If they don't say Dummido Grenado or Stupido
Grenado, then they won't get hit."

She did not want to go to Mrs. Crumps initially,
but then she found out that Mrs. Crumps likes
drawing and she now enjoys her visits. Mrs.
Crumps said that Grenadine has helped her
improve her own drawing skills.

However, there has been no improvement in the
fighting department as only two days ago she was
sent to the office when a boy name Lyle called her
"white trash foster kid." She knocked out two of
his teeth with a stick.

When Lyle's father, a dentist, found out that his
son called Grenadine "white trash foster kid," he
declined to ask the state to pay for his son's
missing teeth and instead has offered to fix
Grenadine's teeth. He apologized for his son's
actions, as did Lyle. Lyle was suspended for two
days, and the principal declined to suspend
Grenadine at all.

I do hope you will take advantage of Dr.
Wellcoll's generous offer.

Mrs. Lynn Ashley

Dear Dr. Wellcoll,

Thanks for the new teefh. I think I look a lot
detter. Not so uggly. I'm glab you pulld out the
gray teefh and gave me knew ones. My smile dont
look scary no more and I dont have to covver my
mouth wif my hand. Also, thannk you for taking
out the two rodden teefh in dack and putting
them in the trach. They

hurt so bab all the time and now I dont hurt none
at all.

Thanks for giving me fifteen new toothbruches
too and tendental flosses. Its good to hve the
extra suplies, for when Im moved agaen to an
other home.

I am sorry I nocked out Lyle's two bady teefh
but Im glad I hit the bady teefh and not teh
purmannent ones. I won't hit again him.
At leest not that hard.

I wish he was nice as you dut maybe he will be
nice when hes a denttist.

Your new freind,
Grenadine Scotch Wild

25

I talked to one of the assistant managers, Tad Kamaka, on Tuesday and told him what I wanted for the lobby.

"Nice idea. Sure, I'll do it."

"Don't tell Kade."

"Don't tell Kade? Why not?" He was a serious and kind man. Wore glasses. Had degrees in chemistry and music. Now he was an expert carpenter.

"It's a surprise."

I could tell he was uncomfortable.

"Kade will like it, I promise."

"I don't keep anything from Kade around here, but I will this once because I like what you're doing."

"Thank you."

"Sure. Hey, my wife, Debbie, and I are going to The Spirited Owl tonight. It's her forty-fifth birthday. Will you be there?"

"I will. I'll come over and say hi."

"That'd be great. We're bringing the kids."

"You have six, right?"

"Yes." He was surprised. "You remember that?"

"Yes, I do. Sabrina, sixteen. Loves chemistry, like you. Matt, fourteen. Hates bacon. Plays the guitar, like his mom. The troublemaker Tina, twelve. Lyden, ten, not so bright, but loves sports, according to you. And the surprise twins, Abbott and Zoe, one year old. Running your wife ragged."

He blinked. "Whoa. That's quite a memory."

"Thank you. What I remember can be a problem for me." I shouldn't have said that; I don't know why I did. Change the subject, Grenady. "What's your wife's favorite dessert?"

"Chocolate cream pie."

"I'll bring it to her. My treat."

"Gee. Thanks, Grenady. That's awfully nice."

"See ya there."

I brought Debbie a chocolate cream pie with forty-five candles that night, my treat. She was so touched, she teared up as we all sang to her.

I had met her a few weeks ago at the bar. "I love my kids, but I'm always so busy. I can't even think. And I used to be sexy. I used to be smart. Now my brain is in my crotch and my crotch is sinking from all these kids and my boobs have sunk, too. I do housework. I'm a chauffeur. A cook. What happened to me? You know, the fun Deb? The smart Deb? The Deb that used to travel and sell computer stuff and drive a Porsche too fast? Now I have a minivan, car seats, and spit up on my shirt all the time. Look. It's right here. I'm leaking, too, from nursing. Yesterday I went to the store in my pajama bottoms and didn't even know until I came home. The day before, my car stalled when I dropped the kids off at school and I had to walk home in my nightgown."

We bonded over her martinis. I called a cab later.

Debbie stood up and hugged me. "Thanks for making my night special, Grenady."

Tad shook my hand. "Thanks, Grenady. You're the best. I'm glad Kade hired you."

"Me too."

Oh, me too.

Saturday morning, I had coffee in my own bed with whipping cream with my French doors open, a cool wind blowing through. The mountains were topped with snow, but the sun was shining.

It was one of those moments in life where you have to stop. You have to put aside all the problems, all the stress, all the worries, and be in that moment. Be happy. Be grateful. Be glad to be alive.

I had my own bed again and a white comforter with pink roses. I had my coffee.

The wind blew through again, cool and gentle.

Peace.

Then my divorce attorney, Cherie called, and said that Covey wanted half my income from my art for the next five years, as he'd launched my career. Cherie cackled and said, "I will smear him into glue for you."

About eleven-thirty I drove to Hendricks' after a stop at the paint store and a light store.

Hendricks' Furniture is a man's place. It's reflective of Kade.

The outside, with the brick, windows, and red barn doors, was architecturally interesting and welcoming, but the lobby needed help. It wasn't Oregon enough, it didn't show off the woods he used, it didn't advertise the furniture, and it wasn't personal to Kade. In addition, it was tripping Alice, My Anxiety, because it was both disorganized and not pretty.

What it did have going for it was that it was a large room with a wall full of windows around the red, double barn doors.

Using a dolly, I moved some ugly file cabinets into a catch-all room with the copy machine. I put the boxes stacked up around my desk into a closet to clear things out. I'd fix the closet and the catch-all room later, but my first goal was the lobby.

I rolled up a rug and had a man named Sugar, who was there working, help me haul it to the trash. It was stained and old. The wood floor was much better. There were some nondescript pictures up, a bulletin board filled with notices and other unnecessary papers, a dead plant, a white board calendar, and other junk. I got rid of all of it.

I whipped out drop cloths, taped the trim up, poured the paint I'd bought earlier in the week on my lunch break, and went to work.

I am a quick painter, as I have been painting walls since I was a teenager. I painted around the trim first with a brush, then used a roller on the walls. I transformed the grayish, depressing walls into a light beige taupe color. Like coffee with a dollop of whipping cream in it. The trim was white, but it needed to be whiter and brighter, so I did that next.

When I was done making that trim pop, I went to pour beer, wine, Cherry Hookers, and Fuzzy Navels at The Spirited Owl.

"Don't mess with Kade, Grenady. None of us do, but he's the best boss."

"What do you mean, don't mess with Kade?" I handed Cory Janes a beer across the bar. It was ten-thirty that night, and The Spirited Owl had finally quieted down.

"I mean"—Cory took a long slurp of beer—"catnip and whales."

"Catnip and whales?"

His friend, Jeeps, next to him said, "Here we go, Idaho. Whenever he drinks too much he pairs opposing words together."

"Yep," Cory said. "Don't know why I said that. Octopus and mirrors. Don't know why I said that, either. Soufflés and turtles."

Cory was a young employee of Kade's. He was smart. I learned that he read two science journals a month, cover to cover. I decided to take advantage of his semidrunkenness to learn something about my boss. "Why do you not mess with him?"

"Because he's one tough mother you-know-what. Bad words and peppermint."

"Cory doesn't like to swear," Jeeps said helpfully. He was twenty-five, like Cory, and on leave from the military for two weeks. He was hoping to find a wife in that two weeks. "His mother taught him not to swear."

"What do you mean, Cory?" I asked while I made a whiskey sour and a mojito for one of the tables.

"I mean that Kade did time," Cory said. "Jail time. He was in a gang in Los Angeles. He was the boss of the gang, I think, by the time he was eighteen or something like that. Spent, like, five years in jail. He showed leadership. Lead. Er. Ship. Gang leadership."

"Kade was in jail?" Jail? Kade?

"He doesn't hide it at all. It's not a secret, and he didn't try to make it one. We all know. Fact, when Arnie Struthers applied for a job he had a rap record. Told Kade he robbed three banks when he was twenty. Now Arnie's thirty, and Kade said he trusted him and he hired him and now Arnie's an assistant manager. Doesn't bother any of us. Same with Tomas and Emiliano."

"I was arrested when I ran naked through town last year after I had too many beers at Gavin's Halloween Party," Jeeps said. "Dumb me. It was cold out so I was shrunk, you know what I mean. This girl named Patty saw me, and now all the girls think I'm small. It's embarrassing. I'm not small. I'm not big, average." He stared into his beer. "Average. But I'm loving. A loving guy."

"Yeah, Kade was in jail," Cory rambled on. "I shouldn't be talking about him. I love the guy. He's been good to me. Day one. Gave me a job. I've been there five years and I'm always learning something new, and he likes to talk about science with me. He knows a lot. We talk about space. We talk about ocean drones, geographic information systems, carbon dating, climate change . . . Pancakes and peaches."

"And?" Tell me what you know before you're too tipsy to talk.

"Learned how to fight in there." Cory stared at the ceiling for a second, as if puzzling something difficult out. "But if he was head of a gang in L.A. he would have learned how to fight there, too. That's how he got those scars on his face, that's what I heard. Knife fights. Gangs and jail."

I swallowed. "Knife fights?"

"He has some scars on his back, too. I've seen them. Reason I know is that about four years ago one of the guys cut his leg open with one of the saws and was bleeding like he had a red river coming out of his leg, and Kade runs up, that man can move, I'm tellin' ya, he's big but he's quick. Quick like a coyote, zip, hide, zip, hide." He raised his beer. "He took off his shirt and pressed it to that waterfall blood and that's when we saw all the scars. There's one from a bullet, one that is about six inches all jagged, and a third one that's raised up. Little ones, too. He has a violent back."

I put a hand to my suddenly sweaty forehead. I did not like thinking about Kade getting knifed and shot.

"I think I could be a romantic, too," Jeeps interjected. "Say pretty things. Write poems. Women like that junk and I could do it, I could!"

"But Kade was in jail once upon a time a long time ago," Cory said, swaying on his barstool. "It was when he was almost a kid kiddy, not like he is now. It's where he learned how to make furniture, though. That was his job. He made furniture in jail."

When he left jail he started a business. Smart man. Who would have hired him? An ex–gang member who had done time. Who looked scary. Handsome, but scary. Like a gang leader who'd been in a gang too long.

"Look at Kade now." Jeeps shook his head in wonder. "Employs a bunch of people here in town. Has a toy drive for a month before Christmas for the poor kids who don't have gifts. Cory and I here, when we were teenagers, we were the kids who got the gifts. Only gifts I got at Christmas. My mom put her name on the gift tags, I don't blame her. She was sad she couldn't afford gifts, single mother, nurse's aide, but later I found out they were from Kade's company."

"Yep. Kade gave me gifts when I was a kid," Cory said. He wiped his eyes. "He was my Santa Claus. Santy Clausy. Reindeer. He gave me clothes so I didn't look like a poor elf, and a football. Still have the football."

I wasn't going to judge Kade on doing time. It was many years ago, starting as a teenager. I might be doing some time in the slammer myself. I wondered though, What had driven Kade into a gang?

As if Cory had heard me, he said. "He grew up in Los Angeles. Tough kid. Poor . . ." Cory shook his head woefully. "Knives and strawberry shortcake."

"I think that my naked run and my shrunken state is part of the reason I can't get a woman," Jeeps mused. "No one wants a man with shrunken manhood. I want a woman to give me a chance. One chance to show her that I'm a loving guy, not a shrunken guy."

"Why was he in jail?"

"Can't remember," Cory said. "He didn't kill anyone, I don't think, maybe he did, maybe not. I think that's a no-no. Yosemite and calamine lotion. Maybe it was dealing drugs? Nah. That's not like Kade. He doesn't want to hurt no peoples. Why did I think of that, though? Robbery? No. He wouldn't steal. I know that because we get bonuses twice a year.

"Hmm. Hmm. Let me thunk about this. What was it?" He tapped his head with two fingers. "Got it. Assault. He and his gang versus the other gang . . . something dumb like that. They locked him up like a gorilla and pecan pie. Love pecan pie. And I need another beer, Grenady."

"Nope. No beer." I turned away and poured grape juice into a wineglass. I had already ascertained that Jeeps was driving. "You can have wine, though."

"Ah, thanks, Grenady. You know, you always make me feel like I'm somethin'." Cory burst into tears. "You're nice to me here, and you're nice to me at Hendricks'. You always say hi to me and now you're givin' me wine like I'm some classy guy or somethin'."

"You are a classy guy, Cory."

Jeeps pounded him on the back. "I'll second that, buddy."

Cory burst into another round of tears.

"It's okay, Cory." Jeeps tapped his glass. "He gets emotional a lot. Isn't afraid to cry. See Cory and I, we're big, six four both of us, so we don't have to worry about our manliness and tears, right, Cory?"

"I'm not afraid to cry." Cory sniffled. "I'm a man schman."

"I'll get you some more wine in a minute, man schman," I told him.

That sent him into another paroxysm of tears. "Shit, Grenady, thanks. Oh no! I said a bad word. I shouldn't say them in front of a lady."

"He's an emotional drunk," Jeeps said. "Been that way since high school. Hardly ever drinks, but when he does, he cries. Sort of a cry baby, but a friendly cry baby."

"Yeah, yeah. I'm a friendly cry baby," Cory said. "Friendly. Like Santy Claus. Like Kade."

I sure learned a lot. I turned to Jeeps. "He must have been drinking before he got here. I didn't serve him enough to get him like this."

"He had a few drinks at the bar across the street with some guys from high school before we got here. Why do you think I can't catch a wife, Grenady? Do you think it's my face?"

"No, a woman will fall in love with that face soon. I'm sure of it."

Cory threw his head back, wiped his tears. "Squids and torpedoes. Oh, golly gosh. Squids and torpedoes."

That night I left the bar with a salad and a baked potato. I thought about what Cory told me about Kade. I was not surprised that this was the first I'd heard of Kade's stint in jail. It's a small town. The people were nice to me, and I felt myself making friends, but that doesn't mean they would open up about the private lives of the people within the town.

Kade was well liked. He ran a company that employed a lot of people. He was fair. He was talented and successful. He was tough. But people respected him and would not like to gossip about him. Cory yammered on only because he was drunk. My guess is that he would regret it later, but I sure wasn't going to repeat what I'd heard.

I drove down Main Street in that faux Wild West town, imagined a gun fight between macho cowboys and headed out into the country. I saw the big, red barn, the outside lights on, glowing through the trees.

I smiled, feeling all weepy.

I used the key to open the first lock outside the red barn, then another key for my door at the top of the stairs. I had left a light on. Home.

Covey and I were married when I was in the "falling in love" part, six months from our first date.

That's a bad move, in my opinion. The falling in love part lasts about a year and a half or two years. You should wait, I have learned, for that love and lust rush to leave. Then, and only then, can you think with your head, and not your hot vagina, about the other person, your relationship, and how your future will fair.

The unbridled lust and passion may still be there, but the brain starts moving again, sorting through issues, problems, personalities, and red flags. You start to be sane in the relationship, and you can ask yourself sane questions about whether it can survive a real-world life with what the real world throws at a couple.

I should have waited until my brain started thinking again. I wanted a happier ending than my beginning. Covey was romantic, attentive, interesting, smart. He made me feel like I was the only woman in the room.

He made me laugh and was thoughtful. As a surprise, he once sent me a huge basket full of art supplies from an expensive store I could never afford.

He bought me six hanging flowerpots when I said that I liked flowers, then hired a handyman to build me a trellis so I could hang them up. When my plumbing went out in my kitchen, he had a plumber there in an hour and paid the bill. When my car broke down, he gave me one of his to drive and paid the mechanic.

He took me on vacations. I had rarely been on a vacation in my whole life. He wanted to "show me some fun. You deserve it, Dina. Where have you always wanted to visit?"

I said I loved the Oregon coast. He rented a house with a view of the ocean. Then he took me to Maui so I could see "another beach, and compare." I was stunned.

It wasn't the money that Covey spent on me, it was the thought behind the gifts. Even now, I can look back and appreciate that part of Covey.

But he had the other side, too, and that side overwhelmed the good like a hurricane over a shack. He was the hurricane, I was the shack.

Covey pushed and pushed to get married. I pushed back, then gave in. He wanted a fancy-pants wedding, I sure didn't. I invited the entire Hutchinson gang, who came in overalls and plaid shirts and played their fiddles, which all our fancy-pants friends loved, even though Covey glared when they played. "That was a white-trash, red-necked concert," he told me later. I almost clocked him. It was a bad start to our honeymoon. I should have left then.

Beatrice Lee came in a formal gown and diamonds, with her husband, Larry, and Daneesha Houston wore blue and hugged me close. I invited six neighbors, but I still didn't know 80 percent of the people there. We had a seven-course dinner, toasts, a band, and a wedding cake that looked like a piece of edible art. It was all for show. All Covey's show, for me and for the friends and potential clients he wanted to impress.

I wore a sleek, lacy white gown that Covey bought for me without my input. He presented it as a gift, but it was more like an order. I thought too much cleavage and too much leg showed. It had a silky train and a veil that shot down my back.

How I looked outside did not match how I felt inside. The whole thing felt rushed. I felt rushed. I felt like I was an imposter. Someone who didn't belong there with Covey and his rich and sleek friends. I had a sordid, difficult past I did not talk about. I hid it. I was a lie.

I should have known. I didn't even have the excuse of being naïve and young when I met him. I was, as often, stupid.

So stupid.

He was a stupid mistake.

Sunday morning I was back at Hendricks' Furniture at eleven o'clock after a stop at the big-box store for curtains and curtain rods.

This would be the fun part.

My hands shook for two reasons. One, I was so excited to be painting on a huge canvas again. In this case, my canvas was a wall. Two, I was worried about what Kade would think. I took off the remaining tape from the trim, pulled up the drop cloths, and cleaned up.

In the left-hand corner, behind my desk, I painted the gnarled trunk of an oak tree, based on the oak tree at my green house, its branches fanning out on both walls and twisting to form a bell canopy. In the opposite corner I painted a maple tree. I put three pines on the center wall right behind where I sat.

The trees were a darker beige than the walls, but not much. I wanted them to look like shadows, their forms outlined but not heavily detailed.

Hours later, I stood in the middle of the room.

Oh, swing me a cat, I liked it.

The mural was simple, but it gave the room a clear focus: This was a furniture making company, these are the woods we use. It somehow seemed to highlight my desk with the pine trees carved into the legs and the buck in front.

I grabbed Tad and Cory, who were working on furniture in the back, to help me move a medium-sized table, the top carved with a polar bear and two polar bear cubs, into the corner. I knew it had not sold yet, because it was not on the website.

Around the table I put three chairs, each with a hawk, a falcon, or an eagle carved into the back. Tad and Cory also helped me move an armoire into the other corner. It was one of my favorite pieces. The doors of the armoire were shaped into howling wolves, heads back.

We dragged in a five-foot-long table and set it against the wall near my desk. The table had raccoons, curious and fun, carved into the thick legs. I took that as a sign of Kade's humor.

When we were done moving things around, they both told me it was "way better than before . . . good job." I hugged them, couldn't help it.

Although there was recessed lighting in the ceiling, the room needed more light for ambience. I had bought four lights shaped like metal lanterns that I had seen in a store in town. That morning Ernie, an electrician I knew from the bar, installed two over my desk and the third and fourth lanterns in the corners.

Ernie has a degree in English from Stanford. He likes owning his own electric company and says he makes "a ton more money than I would as a professor. Plus I don't have to publish ridiculous papers all the time that only your mother and other jealous colleagues read."

I put a light with a base shaped like a steelhead in the corner of my desk and a light with a cowboy boot base on the polar bear table.

"You didn't tell me you were a talented artist," Ernie said. "You remind me of a Shakespearean quote: 'Some are born great, some achieve greatness, and some have greatness thrust upon them.' You are clearly great, Grenady." He whistled. "This is awesome."

"Thank you." I was so pleased. "By shots and by fire, thank you."

He shot me a curious glance at that phrase. "It's from my childhood. I have all sorts of . . . sayings."

When he left, I used a drill to install the wood curtain rods, then hung blue/beige/red plaid curtains on the windows across from my desk, on either side of the barn doors. They would never be closed, but they added color and softness. I briefly thought that a thick rope around the curtain rods would add to the cowboy feel here, but I couldn't do it. No ropes. I swallowed hard, pushed what was in my head aside, and went back to decorating.

Tad Kamaka had done what I'd asked and cut out wood letters, each one a foot tall, with a dark, honey-colored stain, that read, "Hendricks' Furniture." I nailed up the letters behind my desk, over part of the pine trees, so it would be the first thing people would see.

Next to the sign I hung up a photo of Kade. I'd had it blown up to twenty-four by thirty-six, matted it in white, and had Tad stain the frame the same stain as the lettering.

I'd chosen the photo of Kade in his black T-shirt, looking off to the right. Behind him was an armoire that he'd designed, with a carved blue heron in full flight. His black hair, a little long, had a feather to it, probably because he'd just run his hand through it. He filled out his black T-shirt in a sexy way. He was smiling and looked relaxed and happy, a man who owned a company and was proud of what he made, confident of his business.

I'd had eight other photos blown up, too, although not as large. The photos were of the furniture that Hendricks built. I matted them in white and had Tad stain the frames. I hung them on the wall to the right of the offices and to the left of the factory doors. Each piece of furniture was a work of art, and I thought they should be treated like works of art.

I cleaned up and organized.

It was almost nine o'clock at night.

Would Kade like it?

What if he hated it? What if he was embarrassed by it but didn't want to tell me? What if his face froze and I could tell he thought it was as good as rotting deer meat? I massaged my throat. The worry was making it feel tight.

Before I left to go home, I glanced back at the photo of Kade on the wall.

I thought of him in jail. He'd had some tough years.

I'd been in jail. I'd probably be there again. I hoped I would be tough, too.

At least we had one thing in common, though I had come out of my recent stint without any knife fight scars on my face. It would be nice if there were no knife fight scars in my future, although if Neanderthal Woman was still there, it could happen.

Good golly God, Kade was one tough dude.

I hoped he liked the lantern lights.

I hoped he liked the plaid curtains.

I was at Hendricks' by seven-thirty Monday morning, and I was nervous, nervous, nervous. I was desperate to know what Kade thought. Perhaps he would think the trees were strange growths on his walls. Like warts. Or creepy.

Unfortunately, Kade was out of the office. He was with a client who was going to turn an old church into a bed and breakfast and would be buying much of his furniture from Hendricks'.

Two men, Angelo and Petey stopped in the entrance and gaped.

"Oh. My. God," Angelo said. "Fancy me that."

"Blimey. I feel like I'm standing in a painting," Petey said.

"Do you like it?" I wanted a compliment. I know on the inside I'm insecure about a boatload of stuff. I try to hide it because it's victimy and pathetic and weak, but I am what I am.

The men walked around. They studied the painted walls and trees, the polar bear table and wolf armoire, the lantern lighting, the curtains, the photos.

"Grenady . . ." Angelo said. He stopped and put his hands on his hips. He was a college football player and has a nose that has been broken way too many times. "This is quite special. Breathtaking."

Petey, about fifty, weathered, who had a slight Irish brogue said, "It's downright damn beautiful. You gotta come over to my place, lass. I need help. A lot of help."

I kneaded my fingers together. "Thank you. Oh, thank you."

I heard the same reaction from everyone who came in.

Tad said, "Over the weekend? You did this whole room in two days?"

Rozlyn said, hugging me, "It's a gift, Grenady. You have a decorating gift." I teared up and sniffled at that one. Then she whispered, "How come you didn't put the photo up of me flashing the girls with my tongue out? That hurts me."

Marilyn came in and forgot to hide her expression. Her jaw dropped. I could tell she liked it. She said to Cory, "Oh. My. God. Eudora was busy this weekend!"

When Cory said that I had done it, her face closed down. "Oh. Ah. Hmm." She peered around again, eyes narrowed. "Now, why did you choose the paint color you did? And the curtains? Don't you think it looks a little too . . ." I saw her brain pumping away, searching for a put down. "Lower class?"

"I'm going to pretend I didn't see you, Marilyn. Good-bye."
She's an idiot. There's always one petty, jealous person in every group. I wondered why Kade had hired her, and kept her. Everyone else I understood, but not her.

"Don't be so sensitive, Grenady!"

"That's what all controlling, rude people say to other people when they're deliberately making noxious remarks and want to blame their prey. Out you go."

"Don't talk to me like that. You're just the receptionist!"

"And you're just a screwed-up gnome with dead gopher hair." I have no idea why I called her a gnome, but she is short, and she did leave after telling me, "Button up your shirt before you fall out." There was no danger of my falling out.

Between people chatting, I kept myself busy answering the phone; directing people who had come to talk to one employee or another; and organizing furniture that was going to be shipped to Montana, Wyoming, and California that afternoon. I also helped a number of clients who came in to pick up furniture they ordered.

I loved helping the clients, because they were so excited about their purchases. They had been waiting for many months for highly personalized furniture, as we're backlogged, and today was the day. They always loved the presentation. A couple of the employees carried their new furniture into the lobby with a drop cover over it, one pulled it away, and drum roll . . . ta-da!

I watched their expressions. They were delighted, surprised, and thrilled. They put their hands to their mouths, they jumped on their toes, they hugged each other, they laughed. It was better than expected. It was the best! Often they cried. The furniture was expensive, but people bought it to keep forever.

Sometimes they had their name or favorite poem or lines from literature carved into it.

Now and then we had an order for something funny to be carved into the furniture like, *Never fear Grandpa's beer.*

A manly man knows his wife is the boss.

And, recently, in flowing italic, surrounded by roses: *Revenge is sweet. Try it.*

They might have had the family vacation home carved on a table, a beloved pet, or a special view. One woman wanted a penguin because she called her late father Penguin Man. An older gentleman wanted dahlias carved into the front of a woman's desk for his wife, Dahlia.

Kade was often there, too, so he and I would stand and chat with them. They told us they would be back soon, he said we would be happy to work with them again, and they waved as they left. Often they would hug us and hug the carpenters, too. We tried to make it special for them.

That day, though, I was on automatic as I waited for Kade.

Waited.

Waited.

My brain was hyperventilating.

He did not arrive until three o'clock. Which meant my brain had been semideprived of oxygen for hours. I heard his truck, and I made sure for the fiftieth time that all the lantern lights and the cowboy boot and steelhead lights were on and my desk was cleaned off, except for my computer and a vase full of pink freesias.

Kade opened the door, filled the whole doorway with his huge frame, and walked in. His eyes set on mine and I stood up, my hands clenched together in front of me. I tried to smile, but I felt it wobble in a strange and awkward way.

For a second he stood there, looking at me. Then he blinked, smiled, the hit man face softening. "Hi, Grenady."

"Hi, Kade." My smile wobbled again, probably freakishly so. My brain tried to breathe. If he didn't like it, he would think I was incompetent and stupid. *Stupid.*

He didn't seem to notice the change for a second, but he kept on smilin'. Not a huge, pumpkin jack-o'-lantern smile, but . . . quietly pleased.

He took a few steps toward me, as if to chat, then stopped, surprised. His eyes went to the hanging lantern lights, then to the Hendricks' Furniture wood sign on the wall behind my desk and his photo. I could see him taking in the trees. He turned and stared at the eight matted and framed photos of the furniture, the curtains framing the windows, the bird chairs, the wolf armoire, and the polar bear and raccoon leg tables.

When he was done, his eyes found mine again. I waited. I told myself to shut my mouth, as I knew it was open and I was breathing through it, probably like a drowning cow.

He looked stunned. "You did all this?"

"Yes."

"You painted the walls, the trees..."

"Yes. I have a thing for...uh...trees."

"By yourself?"

"I had help moving the furniture, and I hired an electrician. He's an English major. Likes Shakespeare. Quotes Shakespeare. I don't know why I said that, because you don't need to know it."

"It's incredible, Grenady."

I smiled, sagged with relief. "You think so?"

"Yes." He walked toward my desk, still staring at the trees, the photos.

"All this in a weekend?" He shook his head. "Amazing. It's totally different."

"But you like it? It's okay?"

"It's more than okay. It's...it's...perfect. I can't believe this. Nice job."

He smiled. I like when he smiles. It makes me relax. I could not imagine that man mad at me. I think I'd faint, and I am one tough broad.

"I feel like I'm in a different company. Are you sure this is my company?"

"All yours. You have the best furniture line I've ever seen, Kade." I brushed a hand through the air. "Wow. I sounded like an annoying suck-up there. Sorry."

"No, never that." He turned around to study the room again, those muscles straining against his shirt. "This is a hundred times better, Grenady. Thank you."

"You're quite welcome."

"And I heard that you bought Debbie a chocolate cream pie the other night. That was thoughtful and kind."

"She's a nice lady."

"So are you."

"You are, too." I bent my head. Why did I say stuff like that? He laughed. "Thank you. I've always wanted to be a nice lady."

"I meant, a nice guy. Man. Gentleman."

We shared a glance that went on a shade too long.

A shade.

Too long.

I smiled.

Cleo came over that night to practice her artwork. She painted a picture of a blue and pink dog who wore only hats with cats on them. She said her mom "had such a bad hot flash, she was covered in sweat, like someone poured a pail of water over her, but I didn't do it!"

I was not looking forward to menopause. I'd probably be a melting woman, too.

I sketched out a collage on a four-by-six-foot canvas with a pencil.

My plan was to paint a huge magnifying glass. Inside the glass would be a girl with lilies wrapped around her body, like clothes. She would stand all by herself, her hands outstretched to the sides. In her right hand she would hold the Big Dipper, in the other a red, crocheted shawl, blowing in the wind.

Outside the huge circle of the magnifying glass I would paint another lighthouse. I don't like lighthouses, even though I have painted many. They make me feel like doom is coming. They triggered something, but the "something" was hiding in some cavern of my mind and wouldn't come out.

I outlined a dark forest around the glass, too. Towering pine trees, but in shadow, fog lacing the nettles.

I knew I had been found running down a road next to a forest. Daneesha had told me that, which she read in the police report. I didn't remember that part.

I would get a black plastic circle of some sort to form the magnifying glass. I would add white glitter to the Big Dipper stars and paint layer after layer on the lilies, so they would be thick and lifelike. I would put a mirror at the top of the lighthouse. I would make the pine nettles thicker by using a pallet knife to goop on green paint.

I liked the draft. I liked the lilies, the Big Dipper, the shawl.

I hated it. The lighthouse made one of the scars on my head ache. I hated the fog, too, and the dark trees.

Pretty much how I felt about most of my art.

"I think dogs will fly one day, don't you, Grenady?" Cleo asked.

"Yes. But not until they sprout wings first."

She thinks I'm funny.

They kept calling, saying they loved me and that I should hide from that "flaming liberal government, out to get ya, in your business, making you guilty when our raccoon princess daughter isn't guilty at all . . . tell that possum Covey he can come here to hide, and we'll lure him into a weasel trap because that's what he is, a damn cross-eyed weasel. . . . Swing me a cat, I got a hole we could dump him in. He'd be doggone lost forever."

She called, too, offering friendship and tears. "I love you, baby."

I loved them all so much, but I would not drag them into this mess.

They did not deserve it.

There was a check from Kade on my desk when I went to work on Tuesday. I actually said, "Whew," out loud. I knocked on his open door.

"Hey, Grenady, come on in." He stood up, ever the gentleman.

"Thank you for the check, but it's too much." I put it out for him to take. He put his hands up in refusal.

"No, it's not. I would have had to pay one of those decorating people much more than that."

"But I already had the furniture from here. I'm an obsessive bargain shopper, and it didn't cost near this much. It was only frames and matting and paint and supplies, and some lighting. I put the supply bill and the electrician's bill on your desk. You have it, right?"

"I have it, and I have your other receipts. Take the check, Grenady. You deserve it. You spent your weekend doing it, which means you don't get a day off for two weeks. In fact, you can take a few days off here, anytime, full pay."

"I don't want any days off." No way. Then he might get used to me being gone and think he didn't need me. "This is excessive. I can't take it, Kade." I pushed the check toward him again. "It doesn't feel right."

"Keep it, please. Everyone loves the lobby now, and so do I. I've had a whole bunch of people tell me how it's a huge improvement, and it is."

"It's too much . . ."

"Don't argue."

"But—"

"I said I'm not taking it back."

I stared up at him. He was resolute. Decided. I heard that hard tone.

"Fine. But you have to let me buy us a better coffeemaker with this money. The one in the employees' lounge is terrible. I think the machine turns regular coffee beans into high-octane sludge."

He laughed. "Okay, Grenady. But only a coffeemaker. Then we're even."

"A coffeemaker it is, then."

We grinned at each other. I wanted to hug him. I didn't. He was huggable, though. It would be like hugging a bear. Warm and strong, wrapped all up, protected.

I left before I reached out and embarrassed myself by hugging the bear.

I looked forward to lunch every day. Rozlyn, Eudora, and I all have lunch at one o'clock. We're all swamped before that, but around one things start to get less hectic.

"Hey, I'm having a sex toy party at my house next Sunday night," Rozlyn said. "You two are coming. I have to prepare in case I date Leonard. I stalked him yesterday at the grocery store, swung my cart around twice so I could go down the same aisle as him, and I said hello both times, and he smiled back and said hello, then I had a hot flash and had to leave."

"Why couldn't you go to the next aisle, wait till the sweat dried, and then meet up with him again?" I asked.

"Because I think he was triggering the hot flash. I don't want to meet him and sweat, unless we're naked."

"Are you serving wine?" Eudora asked.

"Uh, yeah. Hello?" Rozlyn shook her head, all those black curls flying about. "I said that it's a sex toy party. Did you think I would serve milk? You gotta seize the day and seize the sex toy party."

"Double checking. I don't want to waste my time." Eudora examined her nails. "I like having long nails that are capable of scratching."

"No time will be wasted. And why do you need scratchy nails?"

"You never know when you'll need to defend yourself," Eudora said. She took my hand. She was wearing two diamond bracelets. Gorgeous. Old design. "Grow those nails out, Grenady. Nails can be weaponry."

"I'm familiar with that concept. Thank you."

"What about you, Grenady?" Rozlyn asked.

"Well . . . uh . . . I don't know . . ." I thought of Covey. That killed any thought of sex. Kade strode by the employees' lounge, black cowboy boots on. "I'll be there."

"If I have to hold edible underwear and vibrators and know that no man is on my horizon to help me enjoy them, you're comin' too." Rozlyn leaned over and patted my hand. "And you have to promise me if you get laid you'll tell me all about it."

"Sure. I'll send photos to you at work via e-mail."

"Perfect." She high-fived me, then wiggled her impressive chest. "Come to me, Leonard! Come to me!"

"Make sure it's high-quality wine," Eudora said. "I don't want my palette ruined."

*   *   *

Three days later, Eudora broke two of her toes skydiving. "It was worth it. There is nothing like falling through the sky. Nothing. That was my fifty-sixth jump, although it's been years since jump number fifty-five."

"Your fifty-sixth jump?" I asked, impressed.

"Yes." Eudora arranged her necklace. Turquoise stones, which matched her earrings, which matched her turquoise heels.

"Did you used to skydive with friends?" Rozlyn asked.

"No, for work. Some of them were friends, but mostly we got things done."

"What sort of things?" Rozlyn asked.

"Things." She winked at us. Then she said something in Russian.

"What did you say?" I asked.

"I said that the Cold War was quite cold, but the Russian men knew how to warm a woman up."

Was she serious? I darn well thought she was.

Rozlyn said, "I'll drink to that. I could do with a warm Russian man named Leonard. Is Leonard Russian? I don't think so." We clinked our water glasses.

You never know about people, do you?

Kade was, as everyone always said, a good man.

I felt bad for not being truthful about who I was and the trouble I was in.

I would tell him.

Soon.

I didn't think he knew, but I wasn't sure. The Internet looms like a big brother, even though I was living under my real name, not Dina Hamilton or Dina Wild. Maybe he was waiting for me to say something? But if he knew, why would a smart man like Kade hire me without asking me about it? Who would? Tons of people want jobs, and you hire the flippy gal who's been arrested for fraud and money laundering?

Didn't make sense.

I would have to assume he didn't know.

I smashed down the voice in my head that said he would fire

me if he knew, even if I told him I was innocent. I had lied to him, and to Tildy, by omission. That's reason enough to fire someone.

I had been living in my car when I applied, but that didn't cut it.

I cringed at the thought that he and his company might receive bad publicity from my working here. I don't think I'm interesting enough for the press to track me down and make an issue of it, but they could.

My insane hope was that the charges against me would be dismissed when Covey pulled his head out of his pissed-off butt and admitted my innocence or if Millie could prove it, despite the five papers I signed. I could stay in Pineridge and continue my new, quiet life under Grenady Scotch Wild and no one would know.

If I went to jail, which was certainly a possibility, then I would obviously have to quit. I'd have to tell Kade. Would there be media attention around him or his business as I headed back into the slammer? Probably not.

I groaned. Did I honestly think that? Or was I rationalizing and minimalizing what would happen because it suited me and my need to be employed? Was I being a selfish fool to think that Hendricks' and The Spirited Owl wouldn't get dragged into this? Was I in denial because that's where I wanted to be?

"Ah, shit," I muttered into the night sky. What should I do? Quit now? Work only for Tildy? Quit Tildy's, too? I didn't think that my being a bartender at Tildy's would have any impact on her business, but Kade's, so dependent on an honest and professional reputation?

It could.

I didn't want to quit. I liked the job. I liked seeing Kade all week long, being near him.

But that was all about me. Me, me, me.

I do not like myself sometimes at all.

26

~

Children's Services Division
Child's Name: Grenadine Scotch Wild
Age: 9
Parents' Names: Freedom and Bear Wild (Location unknown)
Date: April 20, 1985
Goal: Adoption
Employee: Daneesha Houston

Although Grenadine's third foster care placement since the Berlinskys did not work out as I had hoped due to Mr. and Mrs. LaMears' divorce, I believe that Grenadine is happy at Mr. Hugh and Mrs. Rose Hutchinson's home.

Their double-wide trailer is out in the country, which means there are many places for Grenadine to run and play. The Hutchinsons have chickens, a goat, and a horse.

Hugh told me that there was a family rumor that his great-great-great-grandmother was a black woman, like me, so maybe we were related down the "ole bloodlines." I told him that I think we're all related, like a big family. Rose and he liked that idea, but we agreed he did not need to call me "sister."

When I went over Grenadine's case file with the Hutchinsons, to explain about her past, Hugh and Rose both said, repeatedly,

"Oh, my shoutin' spittin' Lord" and "Swing me a cat, that is terrible!" Then Hugh started to cry, and we had to take a long break on the porch while Hugh held the cat and had a beer and got control of himself.

Rose told me privately that Hugh could take down a charging bear with one arm, but he had a "sweet, mother-lovin' heart" and did not like seeing people hurt.

The Hutchinsons have bought her many new clothes. Grenadine said, "Finally, I get to be cool."

(I will try to adhere to our department's new policy of directly quoting the kids.)

She wears overalls and plaid flannel shirts and tie-dye T-shirts. She also wears a red feather in her hair that Mrs. Hutchinson gave her and a red bandana around her forehead.

She wears a raccoon hat. Mr. Hutchinson said it was the first raccoon he shot as a boy, and he was proud of it. Mrs. Hutchinson gave her a pink rabbit foot key chain for "fertility and creativity," according to Grenadine. I asked Grenadine what fertility meant and she said that it meant you could pop babies out quicker than an upside-down possum.

Grenadine was also given a pair of pink cowboy boots, two snakeskin belts, and silver chains with good-luck charms. She wears a fake tattoo of a scorpion on her upper arm, which Mr. Hutchinson put on her to match his. I told Mr. Hutchinson I didn't think a young lady should have a scorpion on her arm, and he said he wouldn't do it again.

Mr. Hutchinson's nephew, Timmy Hutchinson, brought her a fishing vest. She has filled the pockets with beads, rocks, and a pet lizard named Smock.

I asked about her dietary habits and Grenadine says she is "hungry as a bull on charge" all the time, and the Hutchinsons are keeping her fed—her words.

She did say that she wanted to throw some "dead possums" at the Berlinskys. The Hutchinsons have been taking her to doctor and dental appointments, and to the counselor, but Grenadine said that Hugh told her whenever she was angry at the Berlinskys to think about shooting them and the pain would go away. I reminded Hugh that she is not allowed to shoot guns, and he said no, ma'am, that wouldn't happen.

As you know, I handpicked this couple, and they truly care about our Grenadine. Although Rose Hutchinson said that she didn't need no government official like me down her throat or telling her what she should do, she said she would be happy to split some moonshine with me any day.

I am so thrilled about this placement. I brought Grenadine a box of art supplies, and she loved it.

Children's Services Division
Child's Name: Grenadine Scotch Wild
Age: 10
Parents' Names: Freedom and Bear Wild (Location unknown)
Date: November 22, 1986
Goal: Adoption
Employee: Daneesha Houston

Grenadine said she and the Hutchinsons have barbeques all the time, go duck hunting, camp in the trailer in the winter, and have target practice. I have told the Hutchinsons that Grenadine may not handle a gun. Hugh Hutchinson agreed and said they won't allow it again.

Grenadine said that Hugh Hutchinson taught her how to wood carve and how to chew tobacco and spit. I talked to the Hutchinsons about it. They denied the tobacco chewing, but I saw Grenadine spit.

Grenadine said Rose taught her how to wring a chicken's neck, pluck the feathers off, and make a delicious Dead Chicken Chili and Butt Beer Fried Chicken. I am unclear on what that is, but I have told the Hutchinsons that Grenadine cannot wring a chicken's neck. They said they won't allow it again.

Grenadine said Rose also taught her how to defend herself against a man who "got too many hands," and Hugh taught her how to smash a beer can against her forehead. Rose taught her how to karate chop a piece of wood.

The Hutchinsons have agreed that the beer smashing is excessive and won't allow it again.

It was Rose's birthday, so Grenadine dried hundreds of flowers between books and hung bunches upside down from hangers. She dried lavender, hydrangea, roses, ferns, and lilies. She then spread them over a canvas that Rose bought her. Grenadine somehow glued the flowers down, then painted stems, leaves, lilies, and a blue sky. It looked like a meadow when she was done. I don't know how she did it. It's remarkable. I could see it in a museum.

Rose framed it and said their daughter, Grenadine, is an artist.

Grenadine says that the kids at school make fun of her and call her "white trash," "stupido Grenado," and "foster kid white trash." Her grades in reading, spelling, and writing are poor. I called her teacher, and she says that Grenadine is struggling in those areas and is getting special help in school. Her grades, though, in art, music, and PE are all As. And when there are art projects in class, she always gets an A.

Grenadine is laughing and talking, although she did tell me that "the program," which means Children's Services Division, "sucks the big one, like a raccoon with rabies," and she is not part of the program anymore. She says she still feels angry sometimes, but when she does Hugh takes her shooting outside.

She also said that she learned a new lesson from Rose: "Don't ya ever get too big for your britches or someone's gonna bust your britches wide open and then they'll find out you got a butt like everybody else. Nothing special about it."

Grenadine said that was something to always remember. And she said it's important that if you feel too small for your britches, you should still keep your chin up anyhow and your shoulders back. That's what Hugh told her.

Grenadine hugged me when I left, as usual. I gave her five new canvases, all large, as she had asked for, and a sketch pad.

Hugh and Rose love Grenadine. They were unable to have their own child, and they treat Grenadine like their daughter.

Rose Hutchinson told me that my skin was the color of her coffee with cream and she loved coffee and cream mixed together. We had some coffee together and had a right nice chat. Hugh offered whiskey with it, but I declined. He said he had a relative back in the 1800s who was the best moonshiner in Oregon. Ever. "The family's damn proud of him, right, Grenadine?" She agreed.

Rose said, "My ass isn't exactly as tight as a whiskey drum, I'm not so young anymore, but I'm plenty young enough to be Grenadine's momma. She's my girl."

Children's Services Division
Child's Name: Grenadine Scotch Wild
Age: 11
Parents' Names: Freedom and Bear Wild (Location unknown)
Date: July 26, 1987
Goal: Adoption
Employee: Daneesha Houston

Grenadine looks great. Healthy and strong.

She has learned how to fish with Mr. Hutchinson, and she built a fort with Mrs. Hutchinson using a drill. They recently took her to a family reunion at a lake where she went inner tubing and toasted marshmallows at the campfire.

She sang me the songs she learned. Some of the words were inappropriate. One song was about a woman trucker who was "wild, wild, like shit-ass wild," and another was about a man who was "lonely for love until I put my hands between my legs and thought about Bonnie Boo." I explained to Grenadine why those songs are inappropriate and talked to the Hutchinsons about it. They said they won't allow it again.

The Hutchinsons said that Hugh's brothers are "red-necked howlers, God-fearing sinners who sin a lot, especially with wine and women," and taught the kids the songs, one about being stuck in a beer bottle. Now Grenadine says she is "stuck in a beer bottle" whenever she feels like things are confusing or she doesn't have an answer to something.

She has also learned how to use a BB gun and how to shoot beer cans off a tree stump. She said she had learned it "by shots and by fire." I have told the Hutchinsons she may not use a BB gun or a real gun. They said they won't allow it again.

She says she rides bareback, no saddle, and I have told the Hutchinsons that that is not allowed. She needs a saddle. They said they won't allow it again.

244   *Cathy Lamb*

Grenadine put together a collage using newspapers and black paint. The painting is about four feet long and three feet high. The collage is of a .38. The Hutchinsons put it on the wall over the fireplace. Hugh told me it was the best art he'd ever seen and said, "Shit. I love it." Then he cried and had to hold the cat and have a beer.

It doesn't sound like much, but it's spectacular. The gun looks like it could come off the wall and be shot.

Grenadine's grades are not high, and the Hutchinsons said they try to work with her, but they don't read or write well—their words, not mine—and the math is too hard. Rose said, "Our Grenadine will be a famous artist. She don't need all this dog-gone reading and writing!"

They invited me to a fiddle party they were having on Saturday night. They said since I am black I would have good rhythm and a strong singing voice and I could teach them a thing or two. They said even though I work for the government, which they curse, they don't think I'm there to spy on them.

They both told me, for the hundredth time, that they love Grenadine more than the whole damn world.

Children's Services Division
Child's Name: Grenadine Scotch Wild
Age: 12
Parents' Names: Freedom and Bear Wild (Location unknown)
Date: February 1, 1988
Goal: Adoption
Employee: Daneesha Houston

Grenadine took a picture of Hugh and Rose in their leathers on their motorcycles, no helmets, and had them blow it up. Then she put the photo in the middle of a canvas and glued the love letters that Hugh wrote Rose all around it. She placed dried rose petals here and there, too, like the wind was blowing through.

Grenadine gave it to them for their anniversary. They loved it. They framed it and hung it up.

"Look at my home!" Rose told me. "It's like a museum! A Grenadine museum. People come over to look at our art! Our daughter is an artist." Rose thinks that Grenadine gets her artistic talent through her line, not Hugh's, who she says can hardly hold a pencil. Hugh agreed that he could hardly hold a pencil and that the talent had to come through Rose's family. He said, though, that Grenadine's skills with a gun are pure Hutchinson and that all his family members can shoot a fly off a fence post.

I told Hugh that Grenadine is not allowed to shoot guns, and he said he won't allow it again. He asked me to sing a gospel song for him, so he can "get completely right" with the Lord and said he knew because I was black that I would know some good ones. We did sing a few gospel songs together, and I reminded him again that he does not need to call me "sister."

I also reassured him that I did not know of any personal plots by the government to get in his business.

Grenadine still aches for her parents, but she is happy with the Hutchinsons. I have grown to like the feathers in her hair, and even the scorpion tattoo, but not the two sets of deer antlers on her wall from their last hunting trips.

27

Eudora and I went to Rozlyn's sex toy party on Sunday night. There were about twenty women there.

I was familiar with a few things, as Covey liked toys, but not with others.

Rozlyn whispered to me, "I want to be prepared for Leonard. Nothing too out of this world, but fun. I saw him yesterday at the coffee shop, and I said hello and pushed my girls out, like this"—she arched her back—"and he said hello and smiled. He wears glasses. I love his glasses. We talked for a few minutes about the pastries, then I had to leave because I could feel my inner temperature boiling up." She sighed. "Do you think my night sweats would alarm him? I mean, I do drench the sheets."

Eudora took a sip of wine and said, "Thank you for not ruining my palette, Rozlyn." Then she picked up one of the sex toys and said, "If you took this apart, it could be used as a weapon."

"That's devious and clever, Eudora," I said. "Why so violent?"

She shrugged, elegant as always. "I'm not. It's training." She coughed.

"Training for what?" I said.

"Training for . . ." She threw a delicate hand in the air. "Self-defense."

I had never thought of using a sex toy as a weapon and was curious as to why she would think of it.

She said something in French, and I said, "What was that, you sex toy weapons expert?"

"I said, 'Love, sex, and murder. It can all be intertwined.'"

Eudora was right. I had loved Covey. We'd had sex. I would like to murder him. I took the sex toy out of her hand and examined it.

There were a lot of single women at the sex toy party.

The woman who was running the party sold a lot of vibrators.

Kade would be an outstanding vibrator.

He's your boss, Grenady, I told myself. Don't think like that.

I picked up a pink vibrator with a bird on it. Ha.

I needed to add pretty to my new home above the horses in the red barn. Without pretty, I am reminded of a few rooms I don't want to think about.

I asked Rozlyn if I could paint the inside when she came over with Cleo for a visit. "Have at it. Paint a rainbow. Paint a woman standing on one foot on a motorcycle in leathers. Paint amoebas. Whatever you want."

Cleo told me, "Paint a picture of a girl who can see her future."

"Now, that's an idea. What would a girl who can see her future look like?"

Cleo jumped up and down. "She would have yellow hair in three ponytails and striped tights and a hat with a dog on it and eyes like blueberries."

"Hmm." I peered into her blueberry eyes. I tapped her hat with a dog on it. Her pink and green tights were fun. "That sounds like someone I know."

"Are you going to do it?"

"No. But thank you for the thought."

"If I could see the future, I would see that we are all going to turn into monkeys," she said. "We were monkeys, we're going to be monkeys again."

"Monkeys are a lot safer than humans."

"Yep. And they like bananas. Mommy made me banana bread. I had two pieces she gave me, and I snuck two more and added whipping cream."

"I have a thing for whipping cream, too."

"I know. You drink it in your coffee. Liddy and I are going to play dress up today."

"She'll enjoy that."

"Yep. I got her a flowered hat."

The three of us chatted some more, then Cleo scampered off to chase a cat and put the flowered hat on Liddy.

"How are you, Rozlyn?"

"Good."

I eyed her. She looked white around the edges and tired. "You sure?"

"Yes, yes." She shrugged her shoulders. "No. My head hurts. Can't shake this headache. It's mild most of the time, sometimes it gets worse, then back to mild."

"You need to go to the doctor." I pushed my hair back and tried not to feel shaky-sick for her.

"For a headache? Nah. It's menopause."

"It's not menopause. Go get it checked out."

She said no, I gently pushed, then we talked about a quilt she'd made years ago of a woman riding a bucking bronco in a ball gown. "When life bucks you," she told me, "get dressed up and buck with it. That's what I'm doing. Bucking. But I would like to be . . ." She let that trail off, and we laughed.

She asked how I felt working two jobs. I told her it was a busy life.

I trusted Rozlyn, I don't know why. I rarely trust anyone, but I did her.

On Saturday morning I slept in until ten o'clock. I hadn't gone to bed until two. I thought about Kade, then made myself stop.

I drank three cups of coffee in bed with whipping cream and sugar, then made scrambled eggs. I thought of Kade again, made myself stop.

I drove to the paint store and stood in awe in front of all the paint colors. It took me an hour, but I eventually bought a yellow the color of sunshine and a banana mixed.

The color was enough to give my family/kitchen area some depth but keep the light. The French doors were white, so the sunshine banana would pop.

I bought a light blue, like central Oregon's sky, for the bathroom and a pastel pink for my bedroom. Yes, pink. I wanted something pretty and feminine as I would soon be wearing blue scrubs stamped with JAIL, and living in a cell with a silver toilet

When I came home, I fed an apple to Liddy, stroked her sleek, brown hair, then went to work painting the family room and kitchen walls yellow. At 5:15 I went off to make Tequila Sunrises and Scarlett O'Haras.

Although I didn't get home from the bar until one o'clock in the morning, I woke up at nine and, in my pajamas, finished the yellow in the kitchen and family room and started in on the light blue bathroom. Cleo knocked on my door after I'd finished. She was wearing all purple. "Today is purple day. In celebration of Pluto." She'd made a purple hat for herself out of construction paper.

We made peanut butter and banana sandwiches. She told me I reminded her of a cowgirl who could shoot a lizard out of the sky. I told her she reminded me of a grape. She likes grapes, so there was no offense.

She put her hands on my hands at one point and turned them over. "Ouch," she said when she saw the scars. "What happened?"

"I had a bad day when I was a kid."

"What happened?"

"Fire."

"Fire hurts. It's so hot." She picked up my hands and kissed them four times. It brought tears to my eyes. "Better now, Grenady?"

"Yes." I sniffled. "I do believe it is."

Later, after we had cookies, I moved the drop cloths from the bathroom, taped the trim up in my bedroom, pulled an old

T-shirt over Cleo's celebratory purple Pluto outfit, and we painted the bedroom pink.

"Do you know how to shoot a gun, Grenady?"

"Yes."

"Can you teach me?"

"No. Why?"

"Because when we're invaded by the bad space aliens, I want to be able to shoot them."

"I'll do it. You get behind me."

She was outraged. "No. I want to fight them! I'm a girl, so duh. I'll be fighting. Me and Liddy. Ta-da!"

I stood back and admired my pink bedroom, my white comforter with the pink roses, the pink-and-white-striped pillows with lace. I had never had a pink bedroom, but I had always wanted one. Now I had one. It matched with the pink ceramic rose box for my lily bracelet.

I loved it.

It was a scene out of a cheesy chick flick that you would watch in your pajamas while slugging down chocolate mint ice cream.

It was 5:14 and I was at Hendricks'. I had to be at The Spirited Owl in sixteen minutes. I darted into the bathroom by Kade's office. He wasn't in the office, and I was desperate.

I *hate* to be late.

I knew that Tildy would be okay with it, but I wouldn't be. I like to be on time. I like my life as ordered and organized as possible.

I whipped off my silky red and pink scarf and my red sweater. Underneath it I wore a red lace bra. I yanked off my black skirt and tights and kicked off my black cowboy boots. I had on black lacy underwear.

I put my bag on top of the sink and pulled out my black jeans and black T-shirt for The Spirited Owl and shoved my other clothes back in. I gaped at my face in the mirror. My hair was a mess. It had been in a neat and controlled ponytail, but it wasn't anymore. I pulled out the rubber band, and brushed my hair quick as I could. I ignored the two scars on my hairline, as always.

The door opened.

I stepped back automatically, brush in hand, so the door wouldn't hit me.

And there I stood.

Hair down.

Red bra pushing up the girls.

Black lacy underwear.

Nothing else.

And there stood Kade, who was not supposed to be here. He was out of the office. At a meeting. Clearly, the meeting had ended.

"Oh, my God," I choked out. I dropped the brush from my hand. It clattered to the floor.

For a brief second, I saw the surprise in his dark eyes. One does not expect to see an almost nude employee.

I put one arm over my boobs, one hand splayed over my crotch.

His eyes, for the tiniest of seconds traveled down, over cleavage, over hip, over leg, before he turned away. His mouth twitched, and his eyes crinkled in the corners. "Might want to use that lock next time, Grenady . . ."

Oh, my shoutin', spittin' Lord.

Almost naked. My boss had seen me almost naked. *Kade* had seen me almost naked, and my ass isn't as tight as a whiskey drum anymore.

Daaaaang but I was glad I wasn't sitting on the toilet doing my business. It could have stunk like a dead possum.

Now that would have been even worse than this.

I tried to breathe. Couldn't.

Cheesy, silly chick flick, but it happened in real life. My life.

I was late to work by five minutes.

I hate being late.

At home that night I grabbed a pint of chocolate chip ice cream.

I thought about Kade.
I thought about the red bra incident.
I wondered what he thought of my cleavage.
I laughed.
I finished the pint.

I tried not to meet Kade's gaze when he came in the next morning after a meeting with a client.

He said, "Hi, Grenady," and I said, "Hello, Kade," and I smiled, but I didn't meet his eye. I went back to my computer and pretended to be extremely busy and focused and professional. I also dressed that morning to appear completely *dressed*. I was in a white turtleneck and gray sweater and jeans tucked into black boots.

About two hours later I received an e-mail from him asking me to come to his office when I had the time.

I felt myself burn, top to bottom. I felt sweaty. I picked up some papers and fanned myself. Was he going to bring up the red bra and black panty incident? No. He wouldn't. He was a gentleman.

Had I done something wrong? I couldn't think of anything . . . oh no.

Did he know about Dina Hamilton? Dina Wild? Covey? I should have told him. I went from hot to cold and back again. I rubbed my neck. "Breathe, Grenady, breathe."

About fifteen minutes later I took a deep breath and headed down to his office. "Hi, Kade. Did you want to see me?"

"Yes, I did. Thanks for coming. Shut the door. Have a seat." He waved a hand toward his table by the window with a view of Brothers, Mt. Laurel, and Ragged Top mountains. It was snowing outside.

This did not sound good. Shut the door, sit.

"How are you, Grenady?"

"Fine." I tried to smile. I think my smile, once again, ended up crooked and creepy. "How are you?"

"Good." He sat across from me and leaned back in his chair,

hands clasped in front of him. He always looked like a man ready to spring if he had to spring.

"It's been a few months. How do you like working here so far?"

I tensed up. This was not going in a positive direction. Was he asking because he thought I had complaints and then he would say something like, "Well, I don't think this is the right place for you, either. Here's two weeks' pay"?

Or was he going to say that in reading my e-mails, he thought that I was *stupid?* Was I making errors? I always triple-checked everything I wrote. I never rushed it.

Or had my nightmare arrived and he was going to say, "You should have told me about being arrested for fraud, theft, money laundering, and embezzlement."

I decided for honest, and I tried not to sound desperate. "I like working here. It's a fun job. I like selling the furniture because I love what you make and design. I like seeing how happy the clients are when they come and get their furniture. I like the people here." I like you, too, Kade.

"Glad to hear it." His eyes did not betray any remembrance of red bras and black panties. "When I walk in and see the lobby, I'm surprised that I own this place."

I did not relax. Was he buttering me up?

"It's so . . ." He stared out the windows while he gathered his thoughts. "Classy. That's the word for it. I like the trees. That was genius."

"Thank you." My heart was thudding and my lips were stuck on my dried teeth. I wanted to peel them off. "Am I getting fired?"

"What?"

"Am I here because you're going to fire me?" I tried to swallow. I was scared. Trembly scared.

"No, not at all. What makes you think you would be fired?" He leaned forward and put his elbows on the table. I thought he was going to laugh. "Is there something I should know?"

"No, not at all." Well. Maybe a tiny something, but I wouldn't bring that up now. "I thought, since you wanted to talk to me, that there was something wrong...maybe a customer complained, or another employee, or I need to change something about how I'm working here. I can do that. Change. Tell me what it is and I'll fix it. I'd be happy to."

He shook his head. "Not at all, Grenady. I asked you in here because I was wondering if you would fix my office."

"Fix your office?"

"Yes, then the employees' lounge."

"You mean, paint and decorate them?"

"Yes. Like you did the lobby."

I sagged with relief. I stared up at the ceiling and tried to pull myself together. My heart was thudding. I exhaled.

"Grenady." His voice was low and soft. Gravel and honey. "I'm sorry. I didn't mean to worry you."

I waved my hand, as in, it's nothing. "It's okay." I ran a hand over my forehead. It had heated up like I had a minibonfire on it. "I feel so much better."

"Grenady, you're one of my best hires ever. You can work here for life as far as I'm concerned."

Life. Work here for life. Work for Kade. For Hendricks' Furniture. I could do that. Then I could surreptitiously watch his gorgeousness five glorious days a week. "Sounds good to me."

We stared at each other for long seconds. "Me too."

I coughed when I started thinking about taking his shirt off and running my hands through the hair on his chest. *Sheesh. What am I doing?* "I'll start in on your office right away."

"Have any ideas for it?"

"Yes."

"You do?" He raised his eyebrows.

"Yes. Sometimes I decorate rooms in my head for fun. I pick out paints, design a mural or a canvas, or both, choose furniture and colors."

"What about the employees' lounge?"

"I've done that, too." I smiled a normal and not creepy smile now that I knew I had a job still. "You spend a lot of time here. It should be a place you like being in."

"I need to spend less time here."

"Why?"

"So I can have a life."

"Don't you have one?"

"Sometimes. I work a ton. I don't have a family, so I can work nights and weekends when I have to, but it doesn't mean I want to."

"No. Fishing is more fun."

"It certainly is." He looked out the window for a second and smiled. "A family would be fun, too."

"A family." I pictured that. I pictured his sweet, skinny blond wife. Lots of teeth in her smile. Stylish clothes. Cool jewelry.

I did not like her at all.

What a cold, dim-witted, busybody she was! How annoying and controlling! I bet she had a dry vagina and wouldn't like sex because it would mess her up and she was a shrew behind it all. She would be one of those helicoptering, arrogant mommies who the other mommies secretly despise because she brags about her children incessantly.

The kids would resemble her or him. Tricycles, bicycles, skiing vacations. The whole image ticked me off. I tried not to let my expression show how irritated I was. "That sounds..." What should I say? That sounds horrible to live with a dim-witted, snotty woman with a dry vagina? I hope you never find her? Let me barf now? "Good."

Mrs. Hendricks was a weasly Kade-snatcher.

"What about you, Grenady? Do you want a family one day? Kids?"

"I don't think that's going to happen for me."

"No?"

"No, I don't." I could not imagine trusting a man enough to marry him. Even Kade. I stared back at him, at that face that seemed so relentlessly tough when I first met him, but now seemed friendly. His size, too, had been intimidating, but now it seemed comforting. His hands had even scared me. I knew they could deliver a punching blow, but I knew they never would, at least against me.

"Why?"

"Because I like to be on my own. If you're in a marriage and have a family, that usually doesn't work. Husbands like to have their wives around."

"Did yours?"

"Constantly." I would never allow myself to get trapped like that again. "Marriage sucks. Don't do it."

He laughed. Why was I so blunt?

"It does, huh?"

"It's unnecessary. It's a bad idea. It's infuriating and painful and can be dangerous." I shut my mouth. I'd said way too much.

"Why dangerous?" He seemed relaxed, but I knew he was listening closely.

"Dangerous in that your spouse can filet you over a fire. I don't want to talk about it." My temper was triggering. I needed to get out of there quick. I stood up. "I'll write down my ideas for your office and send them to you."

He hesitated. "Don't bother. I trust you. Do what you want to do. You're raising this place to a new level, Grenady."

"No, you're already there. I'm simply putting on the finishing touches."

"Thank you, Grenady. I like the finishing touches."

"You're welcome." And if I had met you a long time ago, Kade, when I was a different person, I would have wanted you to be my finishing touch. I turned to leave.

"And, Grenady?"

I turned around.

"I'm sorry about your marriage."

"Don't be. He was suffocating me, and now I can breathe."

28

He ate his chocolate pudding while he wrote his next rhyme.

> Your parents went marching
>   one by one, hurrah, hurrah!
> Your parents went marching
>   one by one, hurrah, hurrah!
> Your parents went marching one by one,
> The mommy cried and sucked her thumb
> The daddy fought, but then I won
> And they both went marching down,
> To the ground,
> Under the rock,
> To their graves,
> By the waves.
> BOOM! BOOM! BOOM!

He had added an extra line, but he thought it was a stupendous idea. Inspired. He stood up and smeared the pudding all over his face. He didn't take it off all day. When he was hungry, he ran a finger down his face and licked it. "I'm a food saver," he said.

He thought of the Getaway Girl. He wanted to lick her, too. Then he wanted to kill her.

"Boom, boom, boom!"

29

I read *Wilton Week,* an online alternative Oregon newspaper, after my shift at The Spirited Owl. I wished I hadn't read it.

"Covey Hamilton is living in his estate in the hills of Portland awaiting trial. He has been charged with embezzlement, fraud, theft, and money laundering. He is on house arrest. His wife, Dina Hamilton, is no longer living at the house and has reportedly filed for divorce via her attorney, Cherie Poitras.

"A neighbor, Felice Donegard, says that Dina has gone to live with her sister on a remote southern Oregon ranch."

I laughed. Felice knew I didn't have a sister. She was trying to cover for me. I loved Felice. Wealthy. Trust-fund baby. Eccentric. She's built like a china doll and is a math professor at a university. She told me that to conquer her insomnia she does math equations at night, each more complicated than the last so her brain will fizzle out. "Thank you, Felice."

I read the rest of the article.

"The list of investors who are suing Covey Hamilton and Hamilton Investments continues to grow.

"Michael Yeable, 55, a dentist who said he gave $100,000 to Covey to invest, stated he has already been interviewed by the authorities. 'They tell me they'll do what they can to get me, and the other victims, our money back, but I'm not holding my breath. There are too many of us out there.'

"Another victim, Vivian Sorley, 82, said she gave Covey $1 million. 'He said there were three start-up tech companies that already had angel investors, including him, and that I would triple my money by the end of the year. He lied. I want to kill him. I may kill him. What? I'll be dead anyhow by the time my trial comes around. What have I got to lose? Plus, I'll be doing all the other people who were ripped off by Covey a favor.'

'Covey and Dina Hamilton will receive a fair trial and justice will be served,' Assistant U.S. Attorney Dale Kotchik said.

"The assistant U.S. attorney would not comment on questions about where the money went, although sources say that Covey Hamilton was into high-stakes gambling in Las Vegas, was involved in heavy betting on sports events, gave lavish parties with his wife, artist Dina Hamilton, had three homes, including one in Mexico, and lived a luxurious lifestyle. He also made poor investments and did not seem to understand the stock market."

I wanted to puke.

I didn't know that Covey was gambling that much. Yes, he'd been to Vegas in the year we'd been married, but he said he was meeting clients. He did say he gambled, too, and once won $1,000 and another time won $1,500. Clearly, he was lying through his teeth.

I didn't know, until the Assistant U.S. Attorney Dale Kotchik told me, about the heavy betting on sports games. I did know about the "lavish" parties, because I gave them. Covey had me hire a caterer, or made me cook for the smaller parties. We had lobster, steak, fancy stuff. He bought expensive liquor and wine. He had me hire a band or some sort of musical entertainment, and he bought "guest gifts," which could cost thousands. Covey invited his happy clients, and people he wanted to become clients.

"It's all about making them feel included," he had told me. "Like I'm their best friend and if they invest with me they'll make more friends, be with the cool people."

What an arrogant son of a gun. I had never been cool in my whole life, and I was smart enough to quit striving for something so inane and shallow when I was a kid.

"My wife and I are innocent of all charges," Covey said in the article. "This is a personal attack by the U.S. Attorney who is trying to make a name for herself so she can run for governor. Dina and I have always had the utmost respect for our clients and are honored that they have trusted us to invest their money wisely through Hamilton Investments.

"We made our clients a ton of money, through careful deliberation and sound, safe investment practices. Now, when the stock market tumbles, when the real estate market takes a plunge, through no fault of our own, we're blamed. Our company, Hamilton Investments, is blamed. I cannot control the economics of the nation and the world, neither can Dina."

I so wanted him dead. "Dina and I" and "we" and "our company"? This was a direct message to me. He was including me in his business, as if I'd had anything to do with it at all.

I was grateful there was no photo of me and my ex-blond hair in the newspaper article.

I am rebuilding my life from scratch because of him. Done it before, will probably have to do it again.

Holy mother of fire and brimstone, I wish an asteroid would hit his house and explode.

I used my sketch pad and charcoal pencil late that night to draw a girl with a gash on her head. I drew her putting out a fire on a man with her hands. I drew her cowering in a corner. I drew her sleeping under a bridge. I drew her alone, alone, alone.

My heart thudded, my tears rolled.

I drew until the memories settled down.

It is the only way I know how to deal with them.

If I don't deal with them, they bring me to my knees, one way or the other.

The past must get back.

When I was released back into the general jail population, after being relegated to solitude for my battle with Neanderthal Woman, most of the women I'd met earlier were still there.

My mind was fried, my emotions a ragged mess. Solitary means solitary. The room is small, tight, claustrophobic. The walls inch in. You don't talk to anyone except a guard who brings you meals three times a day. Your bed is a slab. Your silver toilet is attached to your silver sink. There is no space.

The male guards can check on you through the window whenever they want. They can watch you pee. I did not shower when I was there because there were two creepy guards, Juan Polovov and Brett Masterson, and I did not want to give them the satisfaction of catching a glimpse of me.

No thank you to Juan and Brett.

The first two hours in solitude, I was okay being there, alone, my head in my hands, but by the end of the second day, I started to disintegrate.

I had been arrested.

I was in jail.

I had been in a fight.

I was in solitary.

My past came rushing up, swirled around, and threw me down flat. I had no defenses against all the harsh memories I worked hard to keep at bay.

By the third day in solitary, I was semicomatose and felt that was the best place to be. Depression hit like an elephant dropping from the sky. I was not there, almost completely out of it.

When I came out of solitary, I was allowed to take a shower in my unit, then I joined the same group of women. Although I was supposed to have been released on Monday, via a judge, which usually overrides discipline in jail, I had been charged with assault, so I couldn't leave.

Two days later Neanderthal Woman was released from solitary, too. I learned her name was Pat. Her chin was bruised where I'd pounded back. Her eye was black. I was somewhat of a jail hero for hitting her. I learned that the other ladies hated her because she was a bully. I hate bullies. I hate that they pick on people more vulnerable than themselves. I had been the vulnerable one when I was a kid.

"Hey, Barbie princess, you like solitary?"

I didn't answer. I walked away, but damn, my temper switch flipped on, roaring bonfire style again. *Barbie princess?* Bite me. She followed me, taunting me.

I turned to her. "Look, you ugly, sick freak. I don't want you around me. If I have to go to solitary again for slamming you, I will. I don't care. I liked it there because then I didn't have to hang out with you." Now that was a roaring lie.

She grabbed my ass and put her hand between my cheeks. I was sickened, absolutely sickened. No one is allowed to do that to me again. *No one.*

I hit her so hard, I felt my knuckles crack. She felt straight back and hit her head. We both ended up in solitary. Again.

Three days. Charged with assault. Again.

Three fingers swelled to sausage size. My memories came and lashed me again, harsh and insidious. I peed in my silver toilet attached to my silver sink. I did not shower. The depression elephant came back.

That night, in my dreams, under my comforter in my pink room, I felt the red, crocheted shawl wrapped around me. I felt a kiss on my forehead, a kiss on my cheek. *Look up at the sky, Grenadine. Do you see the Big Dipper? The Little Dipper? Come paint with me ... come draw with me.*

I woke up, clasped the lily bracelet around my wrist, and went back to sleep.

"Hendricks' Furniture," I said into the phone.

"Hi, I need to talk to Marilyn in sales."

"Marilyn won't be in for a few days." Marilyn was in trouble. Marilyn had literally whacked her husband with a frying pan. She was going for his head but hit his shoulder, lucky for both of them.

Marilyn swung a second time and hit his butt, and on the third swing she tripped off her front porch, landed on her face, and broke her collarbone. Good thing because her husband was down for the count, holding his butt.

Marilyn's frying pan debacle took place in front of their house, and a neighbor called police and said that the husband was "being beaten like a dog on the fanny."

Her husband did not want to press charges. He had come home drunk and Marilyn was sick to death of it, but it was out of his hands. She had been charged with assault. I found out why Kade had hired her, too. She had come from Georgia about a month before I arrived, from a company there, and had great recommendations, which he later found were written by the owner of the company, her sister.

"The recommendations were glowing," Eudora said, "because they wanted her out of there. I know Kade was planning on getting rid of her this week."

"Can I take a message?" I asked.

The man on the other end of the phone sighed and said, "Dagnabbit."

"Can I help you?"

"Sure. My name is Sid McNulty and I have a ski lodge I'm opening up in Montana, and we wanted to commission a front check-in desk from you all. We've seen your work, we love it, and I was told to talk to Marilyn."

"Hang on a minute." I walked back to Kade's office, but he was gone, and so was Sam and Rozlyn and Eudora. I remembered they were in a meeting together. "Okay, Kade Hendricks is not available. Can you tell me what you're thinking about and I'll get back to you?"

He did.

"Let me sketch your ideas out while we chat." I asked about the weather in Montana, I told him I liked to fish, he liked to fish, too, so did his wife and kids, I told him I always wanted to go to Montana, he said his wife made a mean steak and I should come and have one and bring Kade with me, he always wanted to meet him . . . chitchat, chitchat . . . then I was done with my drawing.

"Can you Skype me?" I asked. He could.

I held up the drawing I made. "Like this?"

He was bald headed and reminded me of a bull. He beamed. "Hey, hey, hey! Yeah. Like that. Montana-y. That's what we wanted."

I had drawn a ski scene for the check-in desk—one man, one

woman, flying through the air over the slopes, trees in the background. I framed the carving with skis and wrote "Welcome to McNulty's" across the top.

I also sketched a pair of wood skis on top of the check-in desk and drew ski poles on either side.

"You are one smart lady. It's like you got into my head and picked out what I was thinkin' about and made it better."

"Thank you. Kade does excellent work."

"I've seen Kade's work, that's why I called. It's been my dream to order something from him."

"Do you want a table for the front entrance, too?"

"What are you thinkin'?"

I drew a picture of the top of the table, a chair lift, three people in it. The legs of the table were carved with skis and poles. "You put this table in your lobby, use it for a vase of flowers and for a large photo of you, as the owner of the lodge." I played to his vanity; I could tell he had an ego. "This is a classy way to welcome people. Rustic, outdoorsy, but it also says luxurious. Rich. Successful." I pandered to that ego again.

"I want both. Tell Kade."

We had a great conversation. I told him I'd get back to him about pricing, the time line and schedule, etc., and he told me I was "as pretty as my daughters . . . if I had an unmarried son, I'd set you two right on up."

After we hung up I returned the calls I'd let go to voice mail and passed on messages. Two hours later Kade walked back in. I waited for another hour before going to talk to him so he could get settled. I knocked on his door. I was already nervous. I had probably totally overstepped my job. I was presumptuous and pushy. I should have left Kade the message from Sid and hung up.

"Hi. Come on in, Grenady."

"Hello. Kade, a man named Sid McNulty called when you were out. He asked for Marilyn."

"And Marilyn is not currently here . . ." He sighed. "Marilyn has got to learn how to control that temper." He turned his head to the window, distracted. "And control some other things, too, although she will not be doing that learning here. Anyhow, who is he and what does he want?"

I told him about the conversation. "I didn't mean to step on Marilyn's toes. I won't do this again."

"Let me see the designs you drew."

I handed them over.

He said, "Nice," quietly. "We can do this, Artist Lady."

Artist Lady. I liked that. "It's a draft only, that's it, based on what I've seen you do already."

"I like the way you attached carved skis on top of the check-in desk."

"Gets 'em thinking about the slopes."

"And the skis and poles for the legs of the table." He put my drawings on his desk. "I don't think you'll be our receptionist for long, Grenady. I'll forward this to Sam and we'll get together a price sheet and a time line for the finished product. I'll give Sid a call."

I sagged in relief and laughed. "So I still have my job as the receptionist, though?"

He looked puzzled. "At the moment. Sales might be better for you. There's commission in sales, too."

I smiled.

He smiled back. Oh, mobster man, you are delicious.

On Monday evening, as the snow floated down, I found three different, ugly wood lamps with beige shades for about seven dollars each and two seven-foot-tall, ugly, puke green bookcases for ten dollars each at the thrift store. The man at the thrift store said he would have his son deliver the shelves to me in his truck.

We put the bookcases on either side of my gas fireplace. They sure needed a makeover.

I related to that.

I put the magnifying glass canvas aside because I couldn't grasp what I was trying to remember, what I was trying to get the magnifying glass to magnify, but I knew I didn't like it. I started painting the circular glass vase with the lilies, the quaint village, the church steeple, the cobblestone streets and the crack up the side.

Covey called, semihysterical with fury, and left a message for me to call him. Then he swore at me and called me a "white trash bitch."

Millie called. She said, "Prepare for a trial."

Cherie called. Covey was fighting every inch of the divorce for asinine reasons. He would make me go broke. She said, "You married a lunatic. I will slay him."

Marilyn and her husband moved to Coeur d'Alene. Marilyn told me she didn't need "the chicken ladies' tongues wagging" here in Pineridge. I don't know why she called the women "chicken ladies" and didn't ask. She also said, "Tight jeans, Grenady. Are you sure you have the figure for them?"

I said, "If I can't wear tight jeans, you should be in a tent."

She had one more comment, as her eyes dropped to my chest. "Tell me, before I go. Those are fake, aren't they? They look *so* fake."

I lifted my sweater, boobs encased in a purple lace bra. "All mine, Marilyn. Au naturel."

I loved that choking expression on her pinched face.

Her husband came in with her to get her last check. "Her momma's in Coeur d'Alene," he whispered to me when Marilyn was saying good-bye, pretending people would miss her. "Her momma's the only one who could get her to see reason, so we gotta move. I can't get hit in the butt again. She dang near snapped my tailbone. Snapped my ass, that's what she almost did. I can't live with a snapped ass."

I didn't think he should stay with anyone who hit him, but he apparently had made his choice, and they left together after Marilyn shot me one more hate-filled glance. She grabbed her husband's hand as if I'd run out and steal the man. Poor guy.

Kade came out after they left.

"Congratulations, Grenady. You are now head of sales for

Hendricks' Furniture. You get a raise, an office, commission, and more vacation days. Can you find me someone to be the new receptionist?"

I could! I was so happy I wanted to hug him, but he's pretty serious and reserved, so I wrapped my arms around myself and gave myself a hug. "Thank you." I laughed. "Thank you."

His eyes softened, I could see it. "You're welcome. Thank you."

Working at The Spirited Owl that night, making hot buttered rums for a group of women and highballs for a group of men, was easier for me. I had a new job. I was head of sales for Hendricks' Furniture.

I about clicked my darn boots together.

I had a divorce to finance and an attorney to pay. This was on top of, quite possibly, being told to pay back the victims over the course of the rest of my life, post-prison, after all of my savings and retirement money was sucked in to Covey's black hole.

If there was a miracle, however, and I wasn't found guilty, then I could keep this money. I was hoping, like a drunk fool, for that outcome.

My mind was taken off my new position when Rhetta stalked in, grabbed a beer bottle, and charged toward her ex-boyfriend, Wayne, who had broken up with her because of her temper.

I saw her coming, teeth bared, and I climbed over the bar, between Grizz and Chilton, and grabbed the bottle in the nick of time.

Rhetta should have thanked me. She was coming in at an angle that could have killed poor Wayne, who was a dear soul and no match for the volcanic Rhetta.

She didn't thank me. She said, "To hell with you, Grenady! And you!" She pointed at Wayne. "Next time I see you I'm squeezing your balls in salad tongs!"

Wayne paled.

This kind of thing makes me look forward to quitting The Spirited Owl.

30

~~

To: Margo Lipton
From: Daneesha Houston
Date: January 28, 1989
Re: Grenadine Scotch Wild

Dear Margo,

Between you and me, the Hutchinsons had a wonderful
birthday party for Grenadine Scotch Wild and invited my
husband and me. There were about sixty people there,
both sides of the families.

They had a bow and arrow contest and then a shooting
contest with cans lined up on a log. Grenadine was
second place in the shooting contest and fourth in bow
and arrows. I reminded the Hutchinsons that Grenadine
is not allowed to shoot off guns or use bow and arrows.
They both agreed they would not allow it again.

I can now enter my retirement in peace. In my thirty
years as a case worker, Grenadine was my favorite child.
For my retirement she made me a painting of herself and
me sitting together on the Hutchinsons' porch. She
painted matching pink feathers in our hair. We were
wearing cowboy boots and holding bouquets of lilies.

It touched my heart, that it did. I am not ashamed to say
I broke down and had a good cry on their front porch.
Hugh handed me the cat to pet and a beer.

I will keep in contact with Grenadine in the future
through letters and visits. The Hutchinsons said they
had never had a black friend but that I am welcome
anytime for moonshine, along with my husband,
Geoffrey, who can shoot almost as well as Hugh,
I'll add!

Please look out for Grenadine for me in the future.
Please. Keep an eye out for my kid. She's a fighter.
She has overcome one hardship after another and,
remarkably, still finds it in her heart to love others
and bring them joy.

I'll see you at my retirement party. Thank you for the
flowers.

Daneesha

31

HIGHLAND PARK JUNIOR HIGH SCHOOL
HOME OF THE RAIDERS
1988–1989

Report Card
Student: Grenadine Wild
Date: March 19, 1989
Grade: Seventh

English Literature
Grade: C
Grenadine refuses to read out loud in class. The kids made fun of her at the beginning of the year because she stumbled on the words, called her stupid, and now she won't do it. (She has not gotten in a fight in my class for two months, and I am proud of her progress. Between you and me, when Grenadine cut Melissa's skirt up the back for teasing her, I thought Melissa deserved it.)

However, when I read aloud, or other children read aloud, and I ask her what the story is about, she knows exactly, and she will even talk about the theme of the book, the morals, and whether she likes the main characters. She has not liked many of the female characters we've read about, as she says they're "pussies." I have told her not to use that word so she substituted the words "weak" and "boring as a dead chipmunk" and "brainless." Still, her ability to read and comprehend what she has read is poor and is reflected in her homework and tests. I made her flash cards with words on them but, curiously, when she got to the word "rope" she refused to say it aloud. She said, "I never say that word. It's a *bad* word. Next card." Do you know what that's all about?

Math
Grade: C
Still struggling. Does not turn in many assignments. Needs help at home. Will move her to a lower class at the end of the quarter. May be learning disabled in math.

Writing
Grade: C–
Excellent ideas, but I have a hard time reading what she writes and she does not write enough to complete the assignments. Her spelling needs vast improvement. She omits or reverses letters and substitutes the wrong words. She wanted to draw pictures to show the story, I said no. I told her to read more. She said no. I like her bandanas and the pink rabbit foot.

Health
Grade: B
Grenadine built the human body on plywood using popsicle sticks, cement, fabric, cotton, and paint. It was impressive! I have asked if I can keep it for future students. She graciously said yes. She said she did not do the human head because she hates skulls, but it wasn't necessary for the head to be there. She received a B because her written answers are incomplete/unreadable on all tests, but that human body was fantastic!!!

Science
Grade: B

Although Grenadine's answers on our written tests were often left blank, and she spells phonetically, her science project where she painted a mural of the major contributions in science for the last two hundred years was the best project I've ever seen. I hung it in our classroom (although I would like to take it home).

Social Studies
Grade: B+

Much of this term's grade was based on a project. Grenadine received an A+ for her American Indian collage.

The teepees made from leather and sticks looked like true teepees! The leather dresses with the beading, and the feather headdresses were unbelievable! The horses looked like they could gallop off the canvas! That she used her hair, and the hair from several kids in our class, to form the manes was remarkable! We loved the sunset behind the Indians, too. You have an artist for a daughter!

Music
Grade: A+

This is a child who is musically inclined. She has a sweet voice, and I was surprised at how quickly she picked up the piano. She said she has had no lessons. She cannot read the notes well, but she plays what she hears... I am rather struck by this... are there musicians in the family? Grenadine said no, only "crackerjack" hunters and lumbermen and bar fighters, but I bet if you looked...

PE
Grade: A+

Athletic. Fast. Best girl in her grade in all sports. First one in. Beats all boys but one. Not a good sport when her team loses. Likes to win. Aggressive. Tackled two boys last week who made fun of the feathers in her hair.

Art
Grade: A+
I have never had a more talented student. Grenadine's work takes my breath away! For fun the other day, when she came in at her lunch period, I gave her a canvas, feathers, paint, and tinfoil. Over the course of a week, she made tiny chicks following a mother duck using paint and the feathers. The ducklings were walking along a country road, the trees overhanging. She used the foil to create a lake in the background and a tiny silver necklace around the mother duck. We have hung it in the entry of our school.

It was good to see you and your entire family—forty people?—at the school admiring all her artwork at Back to School night. She is lucky to have you and thank you for playing your fiddles for everyone, too. We loved it! (But next year, no songs about beer drinking, please.)

32

I moved into mean Marilyn's old office. The same day I interviewed five people to be the receptionist. I was quick about it. I hired a young woman with a pleasant voice who graduated from college with a degree in English Literature. She was engaged to be married but refused to wear a white wedding dress. A designer at the beach was making her dress. It would reflect her and her fiancé's interest: Motorcycle riding. The dress was black leather.

Tia showed me the design. I liked it. Black leather bustier, black leather short skirt, fishnets.

"I can wear it again, without the train. And I'm wearing a white lace veil when I walk down the aisle, for the traditional touch. For my mother."

"Traditional and fishnets. Perfect."

She would be perfect for the job here, too. Smart. Quick.

I had cleared away most of Marilyn's stuff, including unnecessary paperwork. My office was right by Rozlyn's, close to Kade's, across from Eudora's. It had a wall of windows and a desk with a carving of a cottage near a stream on the front. It suited me.

I had two wood shelving units and a table and chairs.

My own office! I would paint the walls a creamy light blue and fill it with color and pretty, and it would be organized so I could feel safe and years away from what I didn't want to think about.

I did not have time to love it too much, though, because I had calls to make, e-mails to write, and a meeting with the towering, mafia man Kade...

Hee-haw.

I was in sales!

"You're being offered a proffer."

"A what, Millie?" I tightened my grip on the phone to make sure I heard every word my attorney said.

"A proffer. That means you go to a scary meeting that will later give you the runs. Some people call it being queen for the day, but there's no crown or fancy dress, only a possible legal guillotine.

"Anyhow, an assistant U.S. attorney will run the party, but the FBI will be there, the IRS, a postal inspector who's in the mail fraud department, a financial analyst, and a computer analyst, plus assistants and others who will wear suits and glare. You will tell them what you know about this financial fiasco and the lying Covey. I'll be there, too, to keep those suckers in line, don't you worry, but they will ask you questions until you are so tired you can't find your nose on your face. You will be drilled, fried, and dried."

"Don't try to be comforting, Millie."

"They're all smart, perceptive people in there. Pit bulls pretending to be humans. They will ask broad-based questions, then questions of the smallest detail. They will go back and forth. They will accuse and imply and try to trip you up. They will ask questions related to the case and questions that you feel are waaaay too personal, and you will cringe. They will ask about Covey and his travels and his friends and associates and how he ran his business. They will ask all about his finances and accounts, here and abroad.

"They will ask about the homes he owns, including the one in Mexico that they're afraid he'll skip town to. They will be quiet, then they will blast you again. They will be quiet again. Silence makes the guilty and nonguilty talk more. Be ready for their silence."

"You're making it all sound so fun." I was flip, but I swear my stomach had turned inside out.

"It will be the least fun thing you do unless you are in prison or on trial. They will know the answers to many of the questions when they ask."

"Then why are they asking?"

"They're asking to see if you'll tell the truth. If they catch your sorry butt in the minutest of lies, they'll assume you're lying about the whole enchilada and the taco and they may well end the meeting right there, and you'll find yourself at trial facing the human pit bulls again."

"I'm not going to lie."

"I know you're not. They will question you about the papers you admitted you signed—"

"I didn't know they were to help Covey's criminal activities." My stomach flipped once again.

"I know that. The funny thing is, I believe you. Sometimes I know that my clients are lying through their teeth, gums, and molars, but I know you're telling the truth. That's why I'm going to suggest that you take them up on their offer. I don't do this all the time. If I know my client is going to be a lying, swindling son of a gun in there, we skip this part. Picture a wolf, Dina," she said.

I did. "Got it."

"Give him huge teeth, overly large."

"Okay."

"Make him rabid, but make him quietly rabid."

"A wolf that is quietly rabid?"

"Do it."

"Okay, I am thinking of a wolf with overly large teeth that is quietly rabid." My stomach flinched, as if I'd been socked.

"And brilliant. He's a brilliant wolf. Quick and sharp. Knows the law. He has some ego, too. Too much ego. He likes to annihilate and destroy, especially if he is in front of other wolves."

"A brilliant quietly rabid wolf with an ego that likes to annihilate and destroy."

"Add ten more and put them around a conference table."

"I have a pack of egotistical, annihilating wolves around a table."

"That's what you're going to face in the proffer."

That did not sound pleasant at all.

"Dina?"

"Yes." I held my stomach.

"You can do it. Box back."

"I will box back. But I'll need a frickin' rabies shot and a gun before I go into the meeting. I'm a crack shot."

"No guns. Oh, God, no. No guns."

On Saturday morning, after an interesting shift at The Spirited Owl that ended with two men getting into a fistfight over a woman neither one liked—I didn't understand the conflict and didn't try to—I decided to paint the ugly, puke green bookshelves bright white.

I put the bookshelves on layers of newspapers. An article caught my eye, and I turned to read it. Yep. The serial killer was going back to court. It made me nervous. Who likes serial killers? I didn't want that article where I could see it while I painted, so I ripped it up and threw it in the trash.

"Grenady! Are you up there?"

"Come on up, Cleo. Door's unlocked."

I heard Cleo's feet pounding up the stairs. I poured the paint and unwrapped a new paintbrush and roller.

"Hi. Oh! You're painting! White. Can I help you?" Today she was wearing a straw hat. She'd somehow attached a small teddy bear. She was also wearing a blue T-shirt with a teddy bear, green-and-yellow-striped leggings, and pink galoshes.

"You sure can. I need the help." I handed her a brush. "Where's Mom?"

"She's drinking vodka out of a shot glass. Says it'll help her headache."

I grimaced. I wished Rozlyn would go to the doctors and get some pills for her migraines.

"So, Cleo, this is what you do to turn something ugly into something pretty without spending hardly any money."

We primed and painted the bookshelves white, then primed and painted white the three ugly brown lamps, too.

I showed her how to make the lampshades pretty. We used the same material for the shades as for the pillows: blue and yellow pansies, yellow with white tulips, and candy cane red. The flowered lampshades would go in the living area, and the candy cane red lamp would go in my bedroom.

We used a glue gun to add lace around the top and bottom of the yellow tulip shade, red and pink buttons on the rim of the red shade, and on the blue and yellow pansy shade we glued a wide blue ribbon around the top and bottom.

"I like 'em, I like 'em, Grenady!" Cleo jumped up and down, her hat and teddy bear flopping. "Can we do one for my room?"

"We sure can. I'll find a lamp and a shade, and we'll make you a new lamp to go with your new pillow."

We talked about dogs and how Cleo thinks she can interpret not only what her dog, Shimmy, says but what the dog, Raggie, down the street says. The Doberman across the road doesn't speak Dog English, so there are problems understanding him.

She also told me that she thinks the other kids think she's strange. We agreed she still had to be Cleo.

"Liddy took me on a ride yesterday. She likes her hat. We went to Roller Coaster Land."

"Nice. Hope they had good hot dogs."

Rozlyn invited us over for a late lunch of minestrone soup with parmesan and hot bread. When Cleo skipped off, Rozlyn and I talked.

"Look." She pointed at her chin. "Chin hairs. Why do I have chin hairs? Am I a man? Look at this long black one."

I peered at it. "You may be part man or part pirate by the looks of it."

She pulled it out. "And my bladder."

"What about your bladder?"

"It gives out when I laugh unexpectedly or cough sometimes. Like a weak baggie. Squirt, squirt. Whenever I cough I have to cross my legs, like a fat giraffe." She started fanning herself. A bead of sweat lined her forehead. "Dang these hot flashes."

"Laughing pee can happen to me, too, so I cross 'em. Nothing like wet panties to ruin the day."

"In bed I practice Kegels. You know, when you squeeze your privates and hold it as long as you can? Helps, but not enough. I need a bladder lift."

"Squeeze harder."

"I squeeze, I squeeze. Squeeze till my face is red. I went into menopause when I was thirty-seven. Early. Same with my mom and her mom. Lost my period, that was sweet. No more blood and cramps. But menopause has given me courage."

"Courage for what?"

"To spy on Leonard."

"Losing your period made you braver?"

"Definitely. I don't worry what people think anymore. I don't worry in general. I think what I want to think, and I don't hang out with annoying people because life is too short for them anymore."

"I can't wait to lose mine, then."

"You've got some time. You're coming with me to spy on Leonard."

"I'll wear my spy clothes."

She asked about my divorce. I said, "It's a mess. He's a gargoyle."

"I curse him! I wish him bad karma."

She hugged me when I left. We had been laughing for the last half hour about the trouble with gas and embarrassing experiences with it. She tooted in yoga once. Whole room heard, and smelled it. She also tooted once when she was giving a speech when she worked for the social media company. She was miked, and the sound flew across the audience.

Rozlyn was sincere and funny. One day I might even tell her about my past.

I moved my bookshelves, painted white, to either side of my gas fireplace. I filled the shelves with my books on art and artists' studios, colored yarn, fabrics, my gold sewing box, threads, and jars and boxes of paints, colored pencils and pastels. I pulled out a special, heavy book, a seventy-year-old dictionary with a black cover. Inside the pages I had hundreds of dried flowers.

It's odd, it's silly, but it brought me peace.

I am not me, not Grenady, without my art and art supplies.

On Friday, Kade called a company-wide meeting. It lasted about five minutes. He said that our sales were up, production was up, everyone was working way too hard, and we were all to leave and go have some fun.

The stud looked right at me.

We took him seriously.

Rozlyn said, "I'm taking this opportunity to buy some edible panties. I'll need them if Leonard and I get together."

Eudora pushed a diamond bracelet up her arm and said, "I'm going home to research a trip to Antarctica. Now's the time for me to go. Already been all over Asia and Europe, so the cold one is next."

It was three o'clock. I didn't have to be at The Spirited Owl until 5:30. I grabbed my purse.

I went to a coffee shop and bought a huge coffee. The shop was called The Horse and Buggy. I drove home, kept my jacket on, and sketched out a collage on my deck. I wanted to make a collage of a woman in a ball gown from the late eighteen hundreds. I remembered my mother used to draw ladies in ball gowns.

I would make her dress out of charms, buttons, faux plastic jewels, and glitter. She would wear black heels and black stockings. Behind her would be a dark forest. She would be looking over her shoulder, as if someone was following her.

What or who was in the forest?

I would love it.

I would hate it.

My shift was brutal at the bar.

It was Thursday night, so much of the bowling team was there. It was also Girls Night Out for about ten ladies in their forties, which meant that they were being naughty.

Two of the cowboys at the bar were married to the women in the Girls Night Out group. As Russ McConnel said to me, "Grenady, as soon as I see that my Shondra has had enough, I'll peel her off the barstool and head on home. She won't like having a hangover tomorrow, because she has to bake three pies for the kids' school fund-raiser tomorrow night. She told me to keep an eye out, and I will." He sighed. "She gets horny when she drinks too much, so keep me with pop only."

Another man with a naughty forty-plus-year-old wife said, "I'm here to make sure that no men hit on my wife. You see anything, Grenady, you let me know and I will take that somofabitch out."

I assured him I would.

And then there were the other cowboys sitting at the bar.

"Grenady? Like grenadine? That's your name?" one of them said to me. He was about fifty. Huge gut. Balding.

"Yes."

He smirked and deliberately ran his eyes over me, head to foot, so I could see it. Yuck. Do men think that we're so brainless our vaginas will heat up to a boiling point when they do that? "I think I want some of your grenadine, Grenadine. It would go down nice, if you know what I mean."

Oh, I knew what he meant. I leaned forward in my black T-shirt and my stylin' red apron with the owl on it. "Is that all ya got, tiny dick?"

He seemed a bit taken aback.

"What do you mean?"

"I mean, it's uncreative. It's boring. I've heard that line a hundred times. It's disgusting." I rapped my knuckles on the bar. "What impresses me in a man is intellect. You want to discuss Van Gogh or Matisse or Monet, then I'm up for it. You want to say something vulgar, I might spit in your beer before I give it to you. Want to start over, Tiny Dick, or do you still want to treat me with disrespect?"

"You're feisty." He winked. "I like that. Fight me, baby. You got the face of an angel and an ass like the devil. Makes me think of sexy things. Like stickin' it to your devil's ass."

I stalked around the bar, well and truly into my flaming temper. I knew my regulars were watching what was going on. I didn't care. Tildy didn't care. In fact, she drawled, "No broken bones. I don't need the lawsuit, Grenady."

I came up behind the delusional one on the stool. "Look in the mirror." I pointed above the bar. He grinned at our reflections, my smiling face close to his overstuffed red one. I put both my arms under his armpits and yanked him clean off that stool. He landed with a thud on his stomach, then flipped over. I grabbed the neck of a beer bottle.

Grizz and Chilton and two men who were in a motorcycle gang with only mild arrest records leaped off their stools and held him down when he said, "What the fuck you doing?"

"Don't you ever talk to me like that again." I bent down and shoved the bottom half of the bottle right close to his face. "I am not your eye candy that you can abuse with your obnoxious, sexual, and low-class behavior. Leave. You go home and think about how disgusting you are." I tapped his nose with the bottle, sort of hard. "Don't make me break that next time."

"Yes, ma'am." He shuffled out, head down after handing me a twenty for his beer. I went back to the bar and a flurry of orders from suddenly extremely well-behaved and polite men.

Grizz said to me later, when my temper had simmered down like cooling soup, "Grenady, this place is so much more exciting to visit now that you've arrived. I tell all my buddies. We got a show going on here, and it's only the price of a couple of beers and a Grenady tip."

"Thank you, Grizz."

He left me a twenty-dollar tip. He always does. And he's always polite.

I sure like Grizz.

That night I collapsed on my deck chair and stared at the stars.

The truth was that my seventy-five-plus-hour weeks were killing me.

Even my bones were tired. My brain was sludge by Friday night.

I couldn't go on like this much longer without a couple of days off. I would ask Tildy if I could get a Friday and Saturday night shift off soon, then I could have a weekend off.

But what would I do? Time alone gave me time to think of my future, and my past.

The future made my heart shake with fear, and the past about ripped it out.

I located the Big Dipper and the Little Dipper. I thought of the canvas with the magnifying glass that offered no clarity, the girl dressed in lilies, the dark woods, and the lighthouse that illuminated nothing. I hadn't worked on it again. It bothered me too much. There was something about it. . . .

I pushed both hands through my hair and massaged my head.

If I could only remember more. Two minutes more even. Then I might know. It was the not knowing that had thrown me for much of my life. The mystery. The tragic mystery.

Who was I? Who were my parents? Where did I come from?

Run, Grenadine, run!

I remembered that part.

"Okay, let's go over the orders," Kade said.

It had been a busy week. I helped clients personalize the furniture they wanted. A dining room table carved with the family's boat in the San Juan Islands. A willow tree carved on a bride's hope chest because as a child she loved reading under the tree. Bedposts carved with honeysuckle because a man's beloved wife loved the honeysuckle vine he'd given her ten years ago when he'd asked her to marry him.

Kade and I went through one order after another. I had also reached out to hotels and lodges, sent information, drew sketches, and took orders, and we discussed where we were with each one. We were efficient.

When we were done, I gathered up all the folders, smiled professionally at him, not in a Can-You-Get-Naked-So-I-Can-See-What's-Under-Your-Blue-Shirt sort of way, and said, "That's it."

"Good job, Grenady."

"Thank you."

"I'm thinking of expanding into new lines. I need a woman's perspective. Any furniture you would like to see?"

Yes! There was! "How about oversized rocking chairs?"

"Oversized?"

"Yes. Huge. You can sell them to lodges, hotels, even personal buyers. The old-fashioned type. I could even see libraries buying them for the children's reading corner. Or you could advertise rocking chairs for families. You know a Goldilocks type of thing—one huge one for poppa bear, a medium-sized one for momma bear, on down the line."

He nodded, and I could tell he liked the idea.

"Can you sketch it out for me? I like your sketches."

"Sure. I'll draw a woman in a rocking chair holding a bottle of wine and a glass."

He smiled. It transformed his face. Gentled it. Softened it. "Wine sounds good about now, doesn't it?"

"I'm afraid I pour too much of it to appreciate it anymore."

"It must be tiring to work two jobs."

The question came as a surprise, and I stumbled with my answer. "I . . . I . . . like working."

I could tell he didn't buy that.

"Is the salary not high enough here with commission?"

"It's high enough." My checks had been much higher, and I was darn grateful. I could tell that Kade was offended that I had a second job. It made him feel as if he wasn't paying me fairly. "It's more than high enough. I'm saving for . . ." I swallowed. "A house."

"I think you'll be able to get one soon. You work hard. You're making me a lot of money, but you look tired, Grenady."

"I hate when people tell me I look tired. It's another way of telling me I look like crap." I sucked in my breath. "I'm sorry, I didn't mean to snap."

"I didn't mean that." His voice gentled again, and he leaned forward. "Not at all. You do not look like crap. You're . . ." He stopped, glanced away, then back. "Sometimes you seem worried."

"I'm not worried." Oh, hell, yeah, I am.

"If you ever want to talk—"

"No, I'm fine. Everything's fine."

"Working two jobs is exhausting. I've done it. I know."

I felt tearful for a second around that sweet concern, but I bucked up. "Hopefully I won't have to haul anyone out tonight. It does, however, add excitement to my life." I used my old tool: Change the subject, be amusing. "On Thursday, three women from Los Angeles decided to have a wet T-shirt contest on the bar."

"Heard about it." He didn't smile. He's a man, so I was surprised he didn't find that amusing.

"You missed out," I said.

"No, I didn't."

"Tildy made them get down after a few minutes. She thought they were going to fall and get hurt, then sue her." I tilted my head. "You don't come in often."

"I like the food at The Spirited Owl, but I don't like the bar scene."

"Me either."

"That's too bad, since you work there."

"If I didn't work there, I would come in for the hamburgers. I love their hamburgers. Gerard puts all this crumbled blue cheese on my hamburgers, and these crunchy onion rings and mustard. I feel like I'm eating my own heart attack, but I love 'em."

"Me too. My favorite is the Blue Stallion Crunch." He looked off into space. Men are so easily entertained by food and beer, I almost laughed.

I tapped the folders. "I better go. I know you're busy."

"Not too busy," he said. He smiled again. Friendly, those eyes watchful. He had huge shoulders. I wished he'd been in the car with me when those two masked creeps tried to break in. He would have smashed their heads together like two pineapples. "Any time you want to chat, come on in."

"I'll do that. Thanks. See you tomorrow."

"Bye, Grenady. Have a good night."

A good night. I was trying to enjoy each day of freedom. I would, therefore, try to enjoy tonight, though I had to serve a hundred beers.

That night, about two in the morning, I thought about Kade. I worked for him. I needed the job. I knew him well enough to know he would not date an employee even if he wanted to, and I wasn't saying he wanted to date me—he had not given me that indication at all.

But if he did . . .

Hell.

He'd be a lot to handle, but I could gather myself up and rise to the occasion.

I leaned back in bed and smiled, wondering what he would look like naked.

Hot.

Wide chest. Black hair on it. Muscled arms to hold onto in the throes of multiple orgasms. Solid hips. Solid ass. Enough to wrap my legs around. Long legs. Those lips could do wonders. I imagined lying on top of him naked. I imagined kissing him. I imagined moving against him, with him, under him. I imagined my mouth on his . . .

I reminded myself not to look at him with unbridled lust and passion while at work.

No panting, Grenady! I laughed.

33

He had always liked the nursery rhyme about the old woman in the shoe. He liked the part about the whipping best.

There was an old woman who lived in a shoe.
She had so many children she didn't know what to do.
So she gave them some broth without any bread;
And she whipped them all soundly and sent them to bed!

He decided he could not improve the poem. It was perfect as it was.
Danny came in and screamed at him, told him what to do.
"Get out of here, Danny," he yelled. "Out. I'm working."
Danny wouldn't leave, so he hit him in the face, again and again, he hit him, until he was bleeding.
Then he pulled out a hair and sucked on it.

34

Eudora, Rozlyn, and I continued to have lunch together most days.

Rozlyn was upset because she did not know how to approach Leonard for a date. "And, see this? I weigh more than he does. I would squish him. But look at my boobs. They're my best asset." She lifted up her shirt. Luckily there were no men in the employees' lounge.

"You're right, Rozlyn," I said, in slight awe. "Your boobs are porn star boobs."

"I know, right? I could do a peekaboo movie with these girls."

"You should be proud of those two," Eudora said, leaning back in her chair. She resembled a seventy-year-old model, sleek and stylish, white hair pulled back. "Those are boobs to behold."

Rozlyn put her shirt down, then rubbed her temple. "I could go to his front door and ask him out, but I can't get up my woman's nerve yet. My female power."

"Do it," Eudora said. "If he says no, he says no. You'll live. You don't want to look back on your life and say, 'What if I wasn't a wimp? What would have happened? What could have happened?'"

Eudora had made reservations to go to Antarctica. "I must go. I have to wear one of those red coats and watch whales. Last time I was in a red coat like that, I was in Siberia," she mused.

"Why Siberia?" I asked.

She blinked a couple of times. "Vacation."

"In Siberia?" Rozlyn said.

I laughed.

We watched Dell park his car outside of Hendricks'. Kade drove up at the same moment in his truck. He talked to Dell, gently, then thumped him on the back and walked him back to his car.

"Poor Dell," I said.

"I wish I could feel sorry for him," Eudora said, "but I can't. He wants someone to take care of him. Cook. Listen to him. Stroke his ego. Be there when he gets sick and starts to die. I don't want to play that role. He sees me based on what I can do for him, not who I am. He has an image of me and he doesn't want to see beneath the image. You can't be with a man who is unwilling or unable to see the real you."

"That never works out for the woman," I said. "She can't live happily with a man who doesn't want to know who she is, how she thinks. He wants a smiling robot. Playing the role of a robot is incredibly lonely and isolating. Better to be alone."

"I think that Leonard would want to know how I think if I could get him on a date," Rozlyn moaned. "What I want to know is if he has a girlfriend. If he does I'll ... I'll ... give her a one way ticket to Siberia!"

After my second stint in Hotel Isolation Hell, I was released again into the general population. I had a new roommate. Her name was L'Andi Howe. She seemed sane and friendly to me. She actually shook my hand when I walked into our suite. We talked about politics and social issues and both agreed that the world would be a better place if there were no guns.

I found her friendly and engaging. When the guards weren't looking, she imitated them. She was brilliant, totally hilarious; her impersonations dead on, down to the sound of their voice, posture, the way their head and hands moved, how they walked.

L'Andi was arrested because she had assaulted a woman in the street who had backed into her car and didn't apologize and didn't give her the insurance information until L'Andi had her on the ground. "Don't you hate rude people?"

I assured her I did, although, I said, "Sometimes I'm rude."

"I'll remember that, Dina. It is not in my nature to be rude. Serenity is in my nature. Peace. Tranquility. Meditation. Yoga. Sharing my love."

Sure, sure. L'Andi was an angel. This was only her third assault charge.

We showered at the same time, one after the other. We talked, we laughed. When the other inmates called us the Lesbian Couple, we ignored them.

I met a number of prostitutes in there. After talking to them, I wondered why they were in jail. Two of the women had tattoos of their pimp's name. He *owned* them. If they didn't make enough money on the streets, he beat them up. If they worked the streets, they were arrested.

They couldn't win. And we were arresting the women?

Some of the prostitutes were teenagers. Why was a teenager in jail? Why weren't the men who were buying sex with a minor arrested? They were too young to give consent. That made it rape, even if those SOBs pretended they didn't know the age of the prostitute.

What about the pimps? They're selling people. That's sexual slavery. They ruled by beatings and an occasional murder. Were they in jail?

It made no sense to me.

My being in jail made no sense to me, either, as I had not committed a crime, though L'Andi, the serene assaulter, did make me laugh.

I found Cleo an old lamp at a thrift store.

The next Sunday we painted it pink and put some of my extra pink-striped material over a shade. She added sparkly buttons.

"It's not a princess lamp," she said.

"No?"

"No. My mother says that princesses are silly. She said that when parents tell their girls that they're princesses, it's ridiculous. No one is a princess, and if you tell your girl she's a princess she'll grow up to be a spoiled brat."

"Could be."

"I'm not a spoiled brat, am I, Grenady?"

"Nope. You're smart. And funny."

"Yeah. And I like hamsters, but I think they should be bigger. Like the size of a seal. What do you think?"

On a rainy afternoon, I made sketches of rocking chairs. Poppa Bear, Momma Bear, Kid Bear Chairs. I drew an oversized one with a pillow on it for a library. I sketched a huge one, maybe for a lodge, with spindles that went up eight feet. Three people could sit on it. I sketched a rocking chair that looked like it might have come from *Alice in Wonderland,* with a back that curved. Another one had a seat four feet off the ground.

I put the sketches on Kade's desk.

He e-mailed me to come by when I had a chance. I saw him after lunch. He had the rocking chair designs in front of them. "I love 'em."

"You do?"

"Yes. I talked to Sam, and we're going to fast-track these, get them on the website, and see what happens."

"I'll cross my fingers. Could be that I gave you a lousy idea."

"You didn't. I'm sure of it." Kade leaned back in his chair. "Ever been to Ashton?"

"No."

"Want to go?"

"Uh . . ." I paused, confused. Did I want to go to Ashton *with him?* For the day? Overnight? For work? For a weekend of carnal pleasure before I was locked behind bars for years and could not experience carnal pleasures? Yes and yes!

"I'm sorry, Grenady." Kade put his palms up. "I should have explained this better first before asking that question and putting you on the spot like that. I apologize. Legacy Hotels is building a lodge down there. They want us to make a bid for two sixteen-foot-tall wood hearths with carvings, a long bar for a saloon, sideboards, tables, a couple of wine racks, the check-in desk, etc. Upscale, expensive, and comfortable."

"Super." Whew. It was for work. *Of course* it was for work. Kade would not make a pass at me, at any time, or toward any of his employees. I wanted to bash myself in the chin with my fist. Duh.

"I need you to work your magic with the sales. Come up with ideas with me, and we'll present them to Legacy." He leaned forward, tapping his pen. "I've been told, quietly, that they haven't asked anyone else for a bid. We're it."

I was thrilled for him, for us. For Hendricks. "Yes, I'll go. . . ." I thought about that. I would have to clear it with my pretrial release gal, but I think I'm allowed to leave if I stay within Oregon. "I'll arrange it with Tildy and switch my schedule. When and for how long will we be gone?"

"I'll get you the exact dates and have Rozlyn make the reservations. It'll be for two nights, at least. The planning for it is tight, but we can do it and it'll open a lot of other business for the company."

"I'm sure it will." I was suddenly nervous and jumpy. I smiled. It was a tight, nervous, jumpy smile.

"I'll pay you, Grenady, for your time on the trip and whatever you would have made at The Spirited Owl."

"Oh, no, that's okay. I need a night off, anyhow."

"I insist."

"It's totally fine. You don't have to."

"No arguing. You argue too much. I'll pay you. We'll have a lot of work to do to get ready for this."

We had ourselves a business meeting. I did some sketching, and he did, too. I looked up the Legacy Hotels company and tried to figure out how to incorporate something from their company into the furniture.

All the while I thought, two nights, three days with Kade. Two nights, three days.

Tough man, Kade.

Reserved, observant, private, kind, and incredibly smart, Kade.

Two nights.

Whew again.

Four months into my marriage I told Covey I needed more space. He wanted to know where I was and who I talked to constantly. His anger flared if he thought I was omitting anything, and when I refused to submit to his possessive grilling, he would follow me around the house, relentless, that handsome face of his tight. The man I married was—poof—gone.

"Why do you want space?" he asked, his face flushed.

"Because, you call and text me all day long and it's tiresome."

He slammed a hand down on the kitchen counter. "You're my wife, so we talk throughout the day."

"Not this much. You get upset when I don't call or text you right back, but I don't have time. I have work to do in my studio, I have client calls, clients come here, I go to their offices or homes—"

"You don't have time for your own damn husband?"

"That's not what I said."

"It is, don't deny it. Don't lie."

"Covey, we both work a lot. I will call and text you back when I have time, but you have to stop pestering me when I don't immediately respond."

His tone was condescending. "Fine, Dina. I'll leave you alone during the day."

For a week he left me alone during the day, and when he came home at night he would be seething and refuse to talk to me.

Finally, late on a Sunday night, the seventh day of the silent treatment, when I started to wonder if I should pack up and leave because what was the point of staying with someone who wouldn't talk to me, he said, "Who's the other guy?"

I was stunned. "There is no other guy."

"Yes, there is." He stalked over to me, stopped three inches away, and shouted, "Who is it? Who the fuck is it, Dina? I want a name, and I want it right now!"

It went from there, a trajectory down to marital hell. Jealousy. Suspicion. Demands. I learned later that he was checking my cell phone and my e-mail to see who I was contacting.

It was creepy. It was smothering.

Covey put a tracking device on my car, which my mechanic, Britz, who is also a whiz at computers, discovered about six months into my marriage. I had no idea when Covey put it there; it could have been when we were dating. For revenge I had Britz put the tracking device on his own car. He was leaving for Disneyland that afternoon with his wife and four teenagers.

The calls and texts from Covey flew in—What's going on? Where are you? Damn it, Dina, call me!—I didn't answer. Covey drove after my mechanic, who was two hours ahead of him, for five hours.

When I finally picked up my phone and told him I was home, he was livid. He paid a guy to drive his Hummer back to Oregon, and flew home.

At first he stormed in, raving that I had wasted his time, how dare I put my tracking device on Britz's car, he was a busy man, he didn't have time for this shit, why didn't I answer his god damn phone calls?

This went on, like he was a human tornado, until I said, "Shut up, Covey," nice and quiet. I told him I would not put up with his possessiveness any longer. He could not put a tracker on my car. He was to stop being so sickeningly possessive, or I would leave.

First he had another fit, then he gradually turned white as he saw how resolute I was. "No, no no. Please, Dina. Don't leave. We'll work this out. I'm . . ." I could see his brain ticking away, trying to find a way out of this, to soothe and cajole me. "I'll change. I love you so much. You're my whole life. I won't put a tracker on your car again. I did it for you. For you, Dina. I wanted to know that you're safe. If something went wrong, I could come and save you."

"Not true, Covey, and you know it. You're paranoid about me. You think I'm having an affair. That you are actually spying on me like this, following me, watching me—"

"Honey, it was *for* you. I want to protect and defend you at all times. That's my job. I'm your husband."

"Give me a break you odd, obsessed man. You will stop tracking me, you will stop smothering me, e-mailing, and texting me all the time. You can call once during the day to say hello, that's it."

"What?" He was flabbergasted, pissed, the cajoling tone gone.

"Once, Covey."

"That isn't going to work."

"It will work. Or I'm leaving."

That about lit him on fire. He flipped. When he calmed down, at my insistence or I would leave that night, he said, "I love you, Dina. If that's the way you want it, then fine. It's not something a loving wife would do, and I'm sorry you can't show more love for me—"

"Covey, if you need me to show love for you by allowing you to call me all day long and to keep a tracking device on my car, get someone else."

"No, I don't want anyone else. I only want you." He pushed and tried to manipulate me, and I pushed back and he backed down.

I knew it was only temporary. He tried to make love to me that night, but I rolled over. Covey was technically excellent in bed. That was one of the things that I loved about him when we were dating. He took time to make love to me. Foreplay, romance, music, candles, dinner.

He always waited until I had several orgasms before he did. He liked watching me orgasm. I thought it was sexy at first. Loving. Passionate and lusty and generous.

After we were married, I knew it was all about utter and complete control.

He had me all to himself, in bed, or on the couch or in the hot tub or in the pool. I was focused on him, physically and emotionally. He could play with my sexual reactions, make me wait when I was on the border of having an orgasm, then pull out at that crucial moment until I begged him to come back in again.

He would wait for me to recover from an orgasm, then make me come again, even when I said, "I can't come anymore."

"You'll be too exhausted from sex with me to even think about having it with anyone else," he whispered into my ear one night.

That was what all the orgasms were about. They weren't about my pleasure, or loving pleasing me, or enjoying the sex we shared as a gift to each other. It was about exhausting my sex drive.

I used to think his postsex comments were romantic, too. "You and I will always be together. . . . I will always love you. . . . Don't ever leave me, Dina. . . . I can't live without you. I won't be able to live without you."

I would reassure him that I wouldn't leave, but as I grew to know him better after the wedding, I heard it for the threat that it was. I heard his insecurity, his clinginess. His possessiveness was strangling me.

Was true love mixed up within the caverns of Covey's obsessive, grainy mind? Or was I simply a new human possession he couldn't part with? I think he loved me somewhere in that, but it was an unhealthy love, wrought with tar and sludge and deception and lies.

And that is no kind of love.

About a month after finding out that Covey had put a tracking device on my car, he gave me a new "updated" phone. I was no fool this time around. I took it to a phone whiz I knew. Covey had put a GPS on it.

I bought a new phone, new account.

Stalked.

Spied on.

Sick.

I finished the canvas with the lilies in the vase with the miniature bucolic village. I drew the crack in the vase straight down. I liked the peace of the village.

I saw the crack as a representation of life. Life cracks some-times.

I liked it.

I hated it.

I hung it up.

"Grenady, thank you."

"Why thank me?" Kade and I were on the deck of our bed and breakfast in Ashton late Monday night. Ashton's a southern Oregon town with outstanding live theatre, a downtown filled with funky shops and restaurants, and an unbelievably beautiful public park that follows a river. "It's your furniture they loved. I simply filled in a few details."

"You did more than that. Bringing in the wood as you did was so smart. They loved the scrapbook, too, of our furniture."

"Aw, gee shucks." Sounds silly, but it worked. It was a scrapbook of eight-by-ten photos. I put a photo of Kade in front, then photos of the outside of Hendricks', the red barn doors with the sign over it, a kaleidoscope sunset, the deer that visit, the lobby, and the production area with his employees working with the saws and tools. I included photos of the most spectacular furniture Hendricks' had made in the past.

It gave the Legacy Hotels people more information about the furniture we made, but it also made it personal. Here's Kade Hendricks, the owner, and here's Tim, Petey, Cory, Rozlyn, Angelo, Eudora, etc. This is who works at Hendricks'! See—nice, normal people who love wood, and this is how they'll make *your* furniture in their rustic yet modern shop surrounded by mountains, fresh air, and deer.

"And the way you attached the sketches to the wood was another smart Grenady idea."

"And gee shucks again." I had Cory cut wood in twelve-by-twelve squares, then glued the sketches of the furniture down on top so the Legacy people could feel the wood while analyzing the sketch.

"Plus, you know how to talk with people and make them

laugh. They liked you, and that's huge. If clients don't like us, they won't buy from us. They found you personable and funny. I think the story you told about Cleo and how Liddy follows her around like a dog, and the things she says and the clothes she wears, hooked them completely."

I laughed. "She's a funny kid, but it's you, Kade. It's you they bought. You and your art furniture. That's what I call it in my head—'art furniture.' "

"I like it."

I held up my beer and clinked it with his. "To Hendricks'."

"To Hendricks' and the best damn sales director I've ever had."

Our presentation was in front of six people from Legacy. In typical Oregon fashion, most people were in jeans, including Kade and me.

I also wore black heels, a black sweater, and gold jewelry. I had my hair down, my smile on. Kade wore his cowboy boots and a light green button-down shirt, sleeves rolled up.

Kade was sure, confident, and personable as he spoke.

I could tell that the three men and three women, although not the owner, were a tad overwhelmed by him. He's six feet five inches of solid gold tough with scars on his face, but he smiled, he shook their hands, and away we went. They ate him right up. They ate his furniture right up.

They did not even bother to hide their enthusiasm after the first few minutes.

They loved it.

"We love it," the head honcho-ette and owner Bettina Rhodes said. "Love it." She winked at Kade. She had wavy white hair and wore loud, expensive jewelry. "I envision myself enjoying my Manhattan at the bar after a long day of busting heads together. Being the boss, you gotta bust heads sometimes, right, Kade?"

Kade laughed.

"Now, I don't waste no time, and you don't either, do you? How much money am I going to shoot through my nose for all this?"

We were ready with that, too.

Kade told her the prices she would have to shoot through her nose, handed her a price list. We had worked on them together along with Rozlyn.

Bettina didn't haggle much. Kade met her mild haggling with humor. He re-sold her on the quality of the furniture, the wood, and how he would carve a peacock into the pieces she bought, as the peacock is their symbol—not surprising after meeting Bettina.

"What do you think, Grenady?" Bettina asked me, her diamond bracelets running partway down her arm.

I told her. I told her how furniture affects a home, then related it to a hotel and how people needed to feel at home in a hotel. I told her how the right furniture held the theme of the hotel together, how if the furniture and décor was somewhat uniform in a chain, people felt more comfortable. They knew what to expect whether they were in Colorado or Carmel. I appealed to her inner snob and how our furniture would appeal to people who were used to the finer things in life.

"Sold, sweetie," Bettina boomed. "I been lovin' your furniture for years, Kade, and now that we met, I love you, too, and this here Grenady, too. We have ourselves a lovin' deal. "

"Happy to work with you, Bettina," Kade said.

"Baby, I am, too." She shook Kade's hand, then mine, with vigor. "If I had looks like yours and a smile with all those teeth and that hair, I would be able to snag me a fourth husband. As it was, with this old figure"—she indicated her curves—"I could only find three. You married, Grenady? No? Maybe you'll meet a husband in my hotels one day, sugar."

I felt Kade shift beside me, and he drummed his fingers.

"I want a husband about as much as I want a hole in my head," I said, the words leaping out of my mouth before I could stop them.

Bettina's laugh ricocheted off the walls. "I think you're right. What do I need a husband for? Money? Don't need that. Sex? Believe it or not, this ole girl still has it. Now let's go and have some ribs and potatoes and celebrate with some women's booze that can sear the skin off a cow. I have a hankering to get some meat on my bones."

"I'll take some meat on my bones, too," I said. "And a beer."

"But no hole in your head!" She cackled.

"No hole."

I could see Kade studying me, thinking, but I ignored it.

We all went to a local restaurant and had a blast. A band played in the corner, and we got some meat on our bones and drank some beer. The deal done, we all relaxed, laughed, and chatted, Kade beside me. I tried not to think about how natural it felt to be sitting by Kade, in a restaurant, with people who were surprisingly fun and funny.

Bettina said, "I do business quick as a lick. We shake on this, and I know you'll hold up your end." She had her accountant give us a check. "I right like you two. I look forward to more business and beer in the future. Y'all get started now, ya hear?"

There were a lot of zeros on the check.

We left about midnight, and Kade winked at me.

"Cheers, Grenady." We clinked our glasses together on the deck of the bed and breakfast. We were both having wine. "It's a huge sale. Excellent for the company. We have work for months."

I grinned. I was delighted. That would be the word for it. It wasn't even my company, but I was delighted.

I would miss Kade and Hendricks' when I was in jail. I thought of those bars closing in on me, tighter and tighter. So tight. They reminded me of another time.

Not a happy time.

That night in my dreams I saw a red, crocheted shawl. It was on the clouds, floating, then it formed into a heart and disappeared.

"Let's go walking in the park."

"What?" My eyes flew to Kade's over breakfast the next morning. It was ten o'clock Tuesday. I figured we would head back to Pineridge.

"You told me once that you like to hike and walk. We have the afternoon open, so let's go."

"I'd love that." I missed walking. I missed nature.

"You need a break, and so do I."

"My boss has a whip and a chain," I quipped.

"Then we'll exchange the whip and chain for a trail. It's cold, but not that cold. Grab a jacket."

We stopped at a sandwich shop for lunch, then went to a grocery store for snacks. Kade, I learned, has a thing for barbeque potato chips, and I like licorice. We bought both.

"I spent six years in prison starting when I was nineteen."

"I'm sorry, Kade." I knew he wasn't surprised that I knew. Pineridge is a small town.

I took another bite of a chocolate chip cookie and handed the other half to Kade. He ate it.

The hike we were on started in the city park. It followed a river. There was a rose garden that would be beautiful in the summer, a pond, an outdoor amphitheatre, and towering trees. There was a light dusting of snow, the silence complete except for the river, as we wound past a Japanese garden. It felt like we were walking through a snow collage.

"I did not enjoy it at all."

"I'm sure you didn't. What was the worst part?"

"Being trapped and angry. I was behind bars, like an animal. It was dangerous. I got into fights, some with homemade weapons. At first I lost a couple of fights, which is how I got one of these scars." He pointed to his cheek. "I had the one next to it coming into jail. Anyhow, I got tougher, I worked out all I could, even in my jail cell, and I started winning. And I kept winning. I was not going to lose."

We crossed a bridge, the stream rushing below. He had been nineteen. A kid. In jail with killers and pedophiles. "What did you do?" I had a vague idea, but I wanted to hear it from him.

"I was running around with a gang in L.A. Tough neighborhood. Join or be beat to shit. I was an angry, messed-up kid from a messed-up background. We got into fights with other gangs all the time. Knives and other weapons. That's how I came to a few of the scars on my back. We were a bunch of angry young men, few with fathers, living poor. Petty crimes. I was tough and getting tougher, which meant I had an attitude problem. During one fight, the fight that sent all of us to jail, both sides, guns were shot off. I shot mine off, too, once, after I was down on the ground, with a bullet through my shoulder blade from one of the opposing gang members. Luckily I didn't hit anyone. To this day I am grateful for that."

I handed him another cookie. I pictured shredded muscles, chipped bones, and ripped skin, and closed my eyes. I do not like to think of people, especially not Kade, getting hurt. "What was your home life like?"

"Home life would probably not be the word for it." He stared up at the snow-crusted branches forming an intricate arc above us. "My father was more out of my life than in. He and my mother never married. He was a successful businessman. It's unfortunate that his product was drugs. More unfortunate that I ended up in jail, too, like my old man." He laughed; it was bitter. "Can't call him my old man, though. He and my mother had me when they were eighteen. She was pregnant in high school."

"What is your mother like?"

"Was. She's dead. She struggled. She tried." He smiled, soft, gentle. "And she loved me. I did know that."

"So you had her in your corner." I sniffled. A mom in your corner.

"I did. But I also had a lot of rage, too. My father did not live with us. Once when I was seven he went to jail for three years. Another time he was jailed when I was thirteen. Everyone knew my father. I was the son of a drug dealer. He was the leader of one of the largest drug rings in Los Angeles. Nothing to be proud of, in a normal life, but in my life, in that neighborhood, with the poverty and drugs all around me, in a twisted way I was proud of it. I didn't know anything else."

"And then you joined a gang."

He nodded. "I joined a gang, then ran it. Apparently leadership skills for criminal conduct runs in the family. Perhaps it's hereditary. In my genes."

"Outstanding. You showed leadership skills as a teen." I was flip because I was feeling emotional. "You just needed a different place to lead 'em."

"That's true. Sometimes I led guys into fights. But the guys in my gang were like family, too. We offered each other protection and friendship. There were about fifteen of us. Three are in jail today. Three are dead. Two you met at The Spirited Owl, Ricki Lopez and Danny Vetti."

"Oh, yes, of course." They had seemed tough under the friendly smiles.

"Ricki ended up working in private practice for another man who contracts with the government, and Danny owns five auto shops in Los Angeles. We're still friends with five other ex–gang bangers. We're older, wiser. No one wants to go to jail again." He winked at me. "The food is terrible."

Yes, it was. "Tell me about your mother."

"My mother worked full time as a nurse's aide and another twenty hours a week at a 7-Eleven if my dad was in jail. If he wasn't in jail, she only had to work as a nurse's aide, as he would give her money. I was alone a lot."

"I bet she missed being with you."

"I hope so." He smiled wryly. "I was not an easy kid, but we got along well when she was sober. Laughed all the time. We spoke Spanish only. She wanted me to be fluent and not to forget where my ancestors came from."

"Sober?"

"She had problems with alcohol. Every three or four days she'd drink until she passed out. I grew up watching her conked out on a couch hoping she would breathe. She would retch over the toilet. She would stumble and fall, she would cry and cry, I'd have to put her to bed. She entered rehab, straightened out, fell back in to addiction, went back to rehab, and got cleaned up again."

"I'm sorry, Kade." I pictured that scene. I knew what it was like to live with an alcoholic. Unpredictable. Often abusive. Neglectful. People tiptoeing around, managing the situation, hating what the alcoholic was doing.

"I am, too. She'd had a horrible home life herself. She came from Mexico. Her family had been poor, way poorer than we were in L.A. She lived in a hut, no running water or electricity. Her father used to beat her and her sister. Her mother died when she was five. She was shot in the middle of a drug fight. My mother and her sister came to America when they were children, and by the time she was fifteen, they were out on their own. Better to be out on their own than living with their father, that's what she told me.

"I'm sure she was an alcoholic by the time she was twenty, based on the stories she told me. I used to be furious with her for drinking, but now, as an adult, and understanding where she came from, I don't judge her as harshly. My dad was gone a lot, she worked all the time, and she could never shed her past. Her system was shot. She'd been beat down too hard by life and had a tough time getting back up. She died of liver cancer years ago."

"Were you out of prison then?" We stopped and stood in the middle of a bridge and watched the stream bubbling and churning.

"Yes. I took care of her the last six months up here in Oregon. I flew her up." I saw a film of tears in his eyes. "She was a different person by then. Hadn't had a drink in five years. She could not apologize enough to me. Every day she told me she was sorry. Sorry for not being a better mother. Sorry for not being there for me. Sorry for the addiction, and the men she drunkenly ran in and out of our house when my dad was in jail until I bashed one of them up at fourteen because he hit her. That was it for the men. She didn't bring any more home."

"I'm glad you had that time, Kade." My throat tightened. I felt for his mother. Who knows? Maybe I would have been an alcoholic with her life, too. Always easy to judge someone else.

"Me too. It helped a lot." He ran a hand over his eyes.

I wanted to hug him tight, but I didn't. "What was your father like?"

"He was running drugs. No one who is a good person does that. He was dealing death to a whole bunch of people. Destroying them, their lives, their families. Teenagers, mothers, fathers, friends. I dabbled in drugs myself when I was in my teens. Nothing serious, and for some odd, inexplicable reason, I didn't become hooked. But he was the person out there dealing the drugs. I was probably taking the drugs that my dad was bringing up from Mexico."

"Straight up the highway," I said.

"Yes."

"Did he not get that? That he was possibly dealing death to his own son?"

"He always told me not to get into drugs, never to try them."

"How do you think he justified that to himself?" I tried not to be pissed, but I had known kids on drugs when I was younger, two who overdosed. It was tragic. A waste. It never needed to happen.

"I don't think he even tried. A drug dealer tells his own kid to stay away from drugs but actively deals them to other fathers' sons, other fathers' daughters. It burns me up whenever I think about it. I hate that part of him. Hate that greed and selfishness."

He started walking, his pace quick, and I walked beside him. A branch heavy with snow cracked and fell to the ground in the distance.

"Was he Mexican like your mom?" It started to snow, light flakes. They landed on Kade's black hair.

"No. American. Blond hair, blue eyed. My height, my build. He came from a solid family, too. His father was in the aerospace industry, and his mother was a teacher. He had an older brother who ended up owning a successful technology business. Who knows why my father turned out as he did. I think he liked the danger of being in the drug trade, the excitement, breaking the law, being a rebel..."

"And the money." Money for the lives of children. What a sick deal.

"Without a doubt. He would come and see us when he wasn't in prison. I remember he read me stories, I rode on his back, he taught me how to ride a bike, he talked to me the whole time, and when he left he always gave my mother an envelope full of money."

"He was kind to you when he was around?"

"Yes, he was. And to my mother. She hugged him when he came in, hugged him when he left. He often spent the night. She cried when he left. I think they loved each other. They were soul mates, but my father was a lousy husband because of the drug running. I remember a few times I ended up in the emergency room. Needed an appendectomy once, football concussion, my first knife fight where I had some cuts on my chest, and he came in, hugged me, hugged my mom. Stayed around for a few days, then took off again, that pile of cash in the envelope in her purse."

"Sounds like he had two sides to him." I was crushed. Sad for Kade. A father who was more out than in. A father who would rather sell drugs than be a dad. How hurtful to Kade.

"Without a doubt. I'd heard he would off people who challenged him or threatened his business. But then he would come to our house and beg my mom to bake him her chocolate cake. She'd smile and laugh, he'd kiss her, hug her, and she'd make the cake. Then we'd all sit down and eat chocolate cake together." He laughed, but it was filled with pain.

"I remember eating dinner with him, too. He would tell my mom he loved the burritos or the enchiladas, tell her that no one cooked like her, then he'd get up and use the phone, swear like you wouldn't believe, in both Spanish and English, threaten to put someone in the ocean. He'd tell someone else to get the delivery in or start running, something like that, then he'd slam down the phone, sit down with us, reach for my mother's hand and say, 'Yours is the best steak I've ever had, Consuelo. The best. What'd you put on it? I tell everyone, you are the best cook in the world.'

"And he and my mother would then launch into a discussion about steak, spices, burritos, enchiladas, her Chinese food—she made outstanding Chinese food—and that would be that. My father also liked talking to my mother about her garden. In spring she would show him her plans for the garden. He always made sure that she planted string beans, zucchini, three types of lettuce, three types of tomatoes, carrots and corn. When that garden grew in, he would come over, at night, and she'd send him back out with his bag full of vegetables.

"I laugh now when I think about it. Mighty drug kingpin leaving his girlfriend's house with a basket full of vegetables, but that's what he did."

"Who did he live with?" I asked, but what I was thinking was, "How dare you hurt Kade, hurt your son, by not being a dad to him."

"He lived on his own. He told me a couple of times that he would never live with us because people were trying to kill him and he didn't want us in the crossfire. From anyone else, that would have sounded like pure bull, but from him, it was the truth. My father had enemies, no question."

"And he's still in jail?"

"Yes. This last sentence was his longest. Almost out."

"Have you seen him?"

"Yes. I fly down twice a year. He's a changed man. Humble. Broken. His whole life, wasted. He could have done something, built something, helped others. He had the American dream in terms of opportunity—a well-off and caring family, a college education, and he blew it. This last stint did him in. His mother died of cancer when he was there and he couldn't be with her, take care of her."

I didn't say, but thought, what an irresponsible and selfish person.

"I've had to do a lot of thinking about my dad. He hurt people. He hurt his family, he hurt us, he hurt others. I used to go and visit him when I was a kid in Los Angeles before I went to prison, too. We weren't at the same prison. We joked, rather blackly, that the jail mixed up our hotel reservations.

"He wrote me a letter and told me to leave L.A. when I was released from jail, to stay out of gangs and not become him. I wrote him back and said I had already decided to go. Later I realized he was also probably afraid that I would be the victim of a crime, a deliberate hit on him. Jail changed me. Who I was when I went in and who I was when I came out were different people."

I wondered how different I would be when I walked away

from those bars. Would my hatred for Covey and what he did to me turn me into some bitter woman I didn't want to be? Would I have a mental breakdown in there? Would I be bashed up by Neanderthal Woman, or would I turn into a basher? I have been hit enough in my life, and I would not put up with that again.

"Who were you when you went in and who were you when you came out?"

"I was an angry, rebellious kid, run by my emotions, when I went in, and I was a more reflective, calmer, grown man when I left. I learned how to make furniture in prison. I took a whole bunch of college classes, earned two degrees, actually, in accounting and business, and I studied how to run a business. I worked out, stayed tough, did not take any shit, and planned a life for myself that did not involve gangs, knives, fighting or, most especially, jail."

"And your life turned out so well." What a story. Drug dealer for a father. Alcoholic mother. Running in a gang. Arrested. Jail time. I pictured him in the degrading, dangerous pit of jail, with its barbed wires, strip searches, confinement . . . *as a teenager.* I was all choked up but tried to hide it.

"Grenady, what's wrong?"

"Nothing." I turned my face away and watched an osprey. Two tears fell. "Damn," I muttered.

He stopped me on the trail and made me face him. "What is it?"

I made a gaspy noise and put my hands over my face when more tears spouted out without my permission.

"Why are you crying?"

"I'm not crying." My heart hurt.

"Yes, you are."

"Not much."

"Why? Did I say something that upset you?"

I wiped my cheeks, then another round fell. "I was thinking of you as a kid with your mom, and dad, and being in that neighborhood, being in a gang, getting stabbed and shot, going to prison, and it made me sad."

He was stunned, I could tell. "You're crying because of my childhood?"

"Well, yeah. It wasn't like you were at Disneyland the whole time." My tone was snappy. I impatiently brushed away a snowflake that landed on my eyelashes. "You have a problem with that?"

He was silent for a minute. "No, Grenady, I don't have a problem with that."

"So quit asking if I'm crying."

"I'll do that."

"I don't like being pestered when I cry."

"I understand. I won't pester you."

I sniffled, then handed him the bag of chocolate chip cookies. "Don't let me have any more."

He held another one out. I took it. Couldn't help it. I love chocolate chip cookies.

That night, on my own deck, Liddy neighing below in the barn, I was again killed by guilt.

Kade had been honest about his past, and I had not. He'd asked a few questions about my childhood and my marriage, over the three days, and I had danced around the answers, then said, "I don't want to talk about that, so quit asking." He respected it, and we moved on. But I had not taken the opening to be truthful. There was so much to hide.

I tapped my fist against my head, then opened my hands. Those light, tiny scars stared up at me, as if asking me to be honest.

It was all about me. Me, me, me. I wanted a job. I liked the people. I liked Kade.

What I wanted.

What *Grenady* wants.

I don't like myself sometimes.

Not at all.

I've got a moose up my butt and I've got to get it out and get moving in a better direction.

I stared at the forest on the mountain, a few wisps of fog clinging to the tops of the trees. I would not go in there at night for anything. Never. You can get lost in a place like that.

Like you can get lost in life.

The first models of the oversized rocking chairs were done. We had an All Hendricks Meeting, as Kade called them, for the unveiling. Tim had put drop cloths over them, three over the largest ones.

Drum roll . . . Ta-da!

They were fantastic. The seats were wide, the backs extra tall—one back six feet tall—the scrolling intricate. The rocking chair that looked like it came from *Alice in Wonderland* with the curving back was super fun. There was a poppa bear, momma bear, and baby bear chair, too.

We clapped and cheered, and Kade yelled, over the noise, "Nice idea, Grenady."

Eudora took photos and put them up on the website the next day. They sold immediately.

Kade opened a new section on the website for them. The page was titled "Wild Rocking Chairs."

I was pretty darn pleased he used my last name.

Eudora said, "I once sat in a rocking chair at a sheik's home overlooking the gulf. It didn't look anything like these. His had gold handles. There was gold all over, in fact. And no kidding, a harem. Teenage girls. Appalling. He wore too much aftershave and thought he was suave. He was so arrogant, he didn't know how ignorant he was."

What? "Why were you there?"

She shrugged her shoulders. "Making new friends."

"You needed new friends in a harem?"

She rolled her eyes. "I would never be in a harem."

Rozlyn said, "I bet I could put Leonard on that Papa Bear rocking chair, climb on top, and rock him all the way to heaven."

"I'm going to hope you get that chance, Rozlyn," I said.

"Me too," Eudora said. "Although the rocking sensation might make you dizzy. It did me."

What? With the sheik?

"Put him to sleep, though, then I did what I needed to do."
Eudora pointed to a brooch on her jacket.

"Are you going to tell me what you're hinting at someday?"
Was she telling the truth? I looked at those high cheekbones, the
elegant beauty, the sleekness and smarts. Swing me a cat, I bet
she was.

"Maybe over tequila."

Kade winked at me when I raced out of there to start my shift
at Tildy's.

On Monday I asked around about doctors. The name Camille Johnson came up several times. I made an appointment for
Rozlyn. I wrote down the appointment and gave Rozlyn the information.

She burst into tears at her desk. She had an ice pack sitting on
her head like a hat.

I gave her a hug. "You have to go. Your headaches are making me feel ill."

She nodded. "Okay. I think I will. It's probably hormones."

"Yep."

"Or stress."

"Absolutely."

"Or I'm dehydrated."

"Sure. Drink up."

Alice, My Anxiety, skipped up another raggedy notch.

That night I started working on the collage with the woman
in a ball gown from the late eighteen hundreds. I painted part of
the background first, the dark forest and trees, then sketched
and painted her. I laid out the trinkets I would use on her dress.
The charms, the shiny buttons, the sequins . . .

I must art, or I don't exist.

35

~

Children's Services Division
Child's Name: Grenadine Scotch Wild
Age: 13
Parents' Names: Freedom and Bear Wild (Location unknown)
Date: January 18, 1990
Goal: Adoption
Employee: Angel Hollis

Grenadine has been removed from Hugh and Rose Hutchinson's home as the police raided their compound and arrested them for a large marijuana-growing operation last night.

Grenadine is inconsolable and says she will "run away" and go back to the Hutchinsons. She said she has not been a part of the Children's Services Division for five years because we "suck the big one" because of what happened to her at the Berlinskys and that Daneesha Houston only came to see her as "a friend." She said that Hugh called Daneesha "sister," and they were all part of a big family.

Grenadine said she is the Hutchinsons' daughter.

Children's Services Division
Child's Name: Grenadine Scotch Wild
Age: 14
Parents' Names: Freedom and Bear Wild (Location unknown)
Date: March 5, 1990
Goal: Adoption
Employee: Angel Hollis

Grenadine was picked up by the police after her foster parents, Aaron and Shelley Corrinder, reported her missing. This is the fifth time. She was trying to hitchhike to Silverton City to be with Mr. and Mrs. Hutchinson, who are out on bail.

We have returned her to the Corrinders. I explained to Grenadine that she will not be able to live with the Hutchinsons again and that they are going to jail for selling drugs.

She said, "But they didn't sell them to me, and they don't do drugs, and it's just mowi wowi, so why can't I live with them?"

She vows to run away again. She said, "You got a moose up your butt? Get it out and get moving."

I told her I didn't understand what that meant, and she said Rose taught it to her and it means that I need to get the moose out of my butt and help her.

I am crushed for Grenadine, and I have arranged counseling at her school and privately, but she refuses to go. She is losing what she considers to be her family after five years. I will go and see her in a few days and see how she is doing.

Children's Services Division
Child's Name: Grenadine Scotch Wild
Age: 14
Parents' Names: Freedom and Bear Wild (Location unknown)

Date: March 6, 1990
Goal: Adoption
Employee: Angel Hollis

The Hutchinsons have asked that Rose Hutchinson's mother, Margaret DeSalle, be allowed to take care of Grenadine. That is not going to be possible, as Margaret's second husband is an ex-felon, arrested for robbing multiple banks years ago.

They then asked if Hugh's mother, Clara Hutchinson, could take custody, but Clara was arrested for assault last year when she pistol-whipped her husband because he was "flirting with a slut."

The Hutchinsons then asked if Rose's sister, Tulip Tenley, could take Grenadine, but Tulip was released from jail only three months ago for running a prostitution ring. You may have seen Tulip's quote in *The Oregon Journal*: "I didn't have any girls working for me, only women over twenty-one and they wanted to do it. Hell, they make $95 an hour, set their own schedules, and can quit anytime. Plus I paid their health insurance. Where's the abuse?"

Many other relatives have stepped up to care for Grenadine, but for various reasons—including criminal records, probation, out on bail—they are not suitable. (It should be noted that none of Rose or Hugh's relatives have records for any crimes against children or women. It's bar fights; a war with one of the neighbors, which reminds me of the Hatfield and McCoy feud; assaults against other antigovernment, gun-toting hotheads, etc.)

The Hutchinsons say they are going to sue like a (expletive) tornado to get Grenadine back, and they have told me that I am (expletive) colder than a cow's tit in December. How they believe they can sue us from jail they could not explain. They are both livid and swear up a blue moon when I talk to them, and say it's all been a governmental plot. Then they cry and I can't get off the phone.

Grenadine is near hysterical, furious, and says she feels like her second set of parents has died. She told me she feels like "a rabbit flattened under a steamroller." She also told me she hates CSD, hates me, and that she hadn't been in the program for years so what was I doing there?

I have applied for personal counseling myself, as this situation has been tremendously upsetting, with everyone crying, but I have not heard back from the counselor. Who do I talk to?

Children's Services Division
Child's Name: Grenadine Scotch Wild
Age: 14
Parents' Names: Freedom and Bear Wild (Location unknown)
Date: March 13, 1990
Goal: Adoption
Employee: Angel Hollis

Hugh and Rose Hutchinson were arrested today for disorderly conduct and harassment when they came here to talk to me and a supervisor about Grenadine. They were accompanied by Rose's mother and stepfather, Hugh's parents, Rose's sister, Tulip, and about ten other assorted relatives whose names I can't remember.

Two of them were wearing hunting clothes and three were in camouflage—that's something I remember clearly. I am not embarrassed to say that I was concerned about guns.

The Hutchinson family, and company, insisted on getting Grenadine back. We told them that was not possible. Our discussion went on for a long time. They said that they knew the government had been spying on them and they were going to start a revolution.

Hugh, Rose, Tulip, and their parents cried and became highly emotional and said something about swinging a cat, then Hugh kicked a desk and yelled "by shots and by fire," which made me nervous. Rose threw a chair. The police were called. Hugh and Rose were shouting and said that we were keeping their daughter hostage and it was all a government plan.

Hugh said because he was out on bail, he should be able to parent his "princess," and Rose said that Grenadine was her soul daughter and without her she was missing her soul.

They were, again, told that they could not parent Grenadine. Hugh protested with a liberal use of the f word while Rose told a police officer to shove it. When the police officer told her to leave, Rose said she wasn't leaving until she got her daughter back. When a police officer grabbed her elbow, she swung and hit him. The police officer restrained her, Hugh swung at him and told him to get his (f word) hands off his wife, and that was when chaos started.

All of the relatives engaged the police with verbal threats, arguing, slugging, or pushing. All of the Hutchinsons resisted arrest, and more police officers were called.

Hugh and Rose were crying. Hugh kept yelling, "I love you, Rose, we'll get her back from these (f word)!"

Grenadine is in her new placement. She will not be allowed contact with the Hutchinsons. Her new foster parents, Bill and Sal Golden, say that she was, at first, almost hysterical, then she cried silently, and now she won't speak at all and has a dead look in her eyes.

It is my personal opinion that Grenadine should go back with the Hutchinsons while they are out on bail. She was safe and happy there, there is no indication that she was on drugs or even that the Hutchinsons smoked much marijuana, and never in front of Grenadine. (That's what they told me.)

Is shipping her from foster home to foster home for the next four years the best idea? I don't think so. I would like to request a meeting to discuss this situation . . .

36

"What's your favorite color, Kade?"

He leaned back in his chair and stretched his arms. He was packed. *Muscle* packed.

"Hmm."

He looked right at me across the table in his office. Outside it was beginning to snow. Light, fluffy flakes, swirling around.

"I think my favorite color is about the color of your hair."

"Funny." We laughed. I was trying to get him to choose a paint color for his walls. "So a burned orange with some brown thrown in?"

"I'd call it fire. That's my favorite color."

I thought of orange walls. "No can do. Orange won't work. What other colors?"

He smiled. "Blue."

"Blue? I can work with blue. Okay, here's what I'm thinking for your office."

I had brought paint chips with me. I pulled all the blues. He looked at them, moved them around with his hand for half a minute while I thought carnal and lusty thoughts, and said, "I'm a guy and I'm confused already. I don't decorate. This is your gig, Grenady."

"How about this one?" I held up a light blue-gray. "I call it steel blue. It's manly, hint of gray."

"A manly paint color. I like it."

"I was thinking that, in terms of the décor of your office, we could consider the history of your company. What do you think?"

"I don't really know where you're going with this, but I think that's another good idea."

"Tell me about your business. How did you start it? How did it become what it is today?"

"You might regret asking that question, but I'll keep it short so as not to bore you to death. I came up here after I was released from prison and got a job in a mill. Nights and weekends, I made furniture. I rented out a back room of Grizz's house. I know you know Grizz."

"Yes, I love that man."

"Me too. He's generous. Helpful. Anyhow, he rented me a room and let me use his garage to make furniture. I even told him about my background, and he said, 'I'm not here to judge you, son,' and that was it. I've always been grateful for that."

"He told me you built him a desk, dresser, and bed."

"I did. My gift to him for helping me. The rent he charged was nominal. He deserved it. Anyhow, at first I sold the furniture through a man in town who owned a shop, but he took twenty percent commission, and that didn't make sense to me to lose that much. I sold three tables in three days through him, then dropped him.

"I took out ads in the newspaper with photos of my furniture, and the orders started coming in. I was selling tables, chairs, desks, you name it, out of Grizz's garage and out of the back of my truck. I also bought an old, beat-up trailer and took the furniture to shows.

"I'd be in and out in three hours. Every piece I made I sold immediately. Soon I had enough money to rent out a heated pole barn. I worked in half of it and lived in the other half. When I had enough customers, savings, the saws and equipment I needed, and I was sick of working seventy-five hours a week, I quit my mill job and made furniture full time."

"That must have been one of the best days of your life."

"It was. I could never go back to working for anyone else."

"You hired people pretty quick, didn't you?"

"Within a month of moving into the pole barn. I had done the math and knew that I could make more money if I could hand off part of the construction, then I would do most of the carving. I hired Sam and Angelo first, then Petey. I was selling the furniture to private parties, but I knew I had to expand to businesses, so I did.

"I cold-called hotels, lodges, other businesses. Sent them my information, photos, met with them, took orders. I hired Eudora to organize everything. She had just arrived in Oregon. I didn't know much about her when I hired her. She said she worked in D.C. for the government but wouldn't say much about what she did. All I knew was that she was supersmart and quick. Anyhow, it went from there."

"And your pole barn?"

"I kept having to hire. I knew I couldn't live there much longer—too many people, equipment, saws—so I rented a house nearby. I run a tight ship and I saved money, so when we outgrew the pole barn, I was ready with cash in hand to build this, with little debt, which has since been paid off."

"Do you happen to have photos of the pole barn and Grizz's garage with your saws? Maybe your pickup truck that you used to haul the furniture around?"

He thought about it. "Maybe. I have a box of photographs somewhere at home. I'll look."

"Thanks."

"What are you going to do with them?"

"It's a secret, cowboy."

"A secret?" He chuckled. "I don't like secrets."

"You'll live. Buck up."

He tapped a pen. "In addition to my office, I want to hire you to make me a painting, too, when you have time. I know you're busy right now, so no stress." He held up both hands. "Whenever you can."

I sucked in my breath. Art. For Kade. Oh boy.

"What would you like me to paint?" This would be nerve-racking. What if he hated what I made? "Have any ideas, Smart One?"

"Nope. Again, I'm a guy, Grenady. G.U.Y."

I thought quickly. "How about if I make a painting, a collage of Hendricks' Furniture? Of the building itself?"

"I already can't wait to see it."

"It's a neat building, all the brick, the red barn doors, the trees, the deer. I'll paint the sign and put some of the furniture out front."

"Go for it."

"What season do you want the background to be in the collage? Fall is always pretty with all the leaves changing colors, but maybe you like the snow?"

"Let's do fall. You started working for me in fall, too, and it's my favorite season."

"It'll be fall, then. I don't want to mess with your favorite season."

"Good."

Kade was the exact opposite of Covey. Kade could knock the snot out of Covey.

"Good," I said, not able to look away. "And good."

He smiled. I liked his teeth.

I worked until seven that night. On Tuesday, I worked until three o'clock, then Kade, Cory, Petey, Angelo, and I painted Kade's office. It was fun. We joked and laughed. It was done quickly. At five o'clock I headed for The Spirited Owl. It took me a little longer to get there because the town was reenacting a cowboy-to-cowboy, 1850s shoot-out and there were people lined up and cheering them on.

I was wound up after my shift at The Spirited Owl, because two women launched into a fight over a man. When their voices pitched, I walked around the bar, put my arms around both of them, and gazed at the man in question, who had a smirk on his face. I knew he was enjoying the ruckus and the attention, because I knew him, and said, "Lorene, McKayla, do you think that Eric's worth all this? Take a hard look. I mean, would either one of you want to spend the rest of your life with him? Are you kidding me?"

They stopped catfighting.

Lorene's shoulders slumped. "He's like a game. I wanted to beat McKayla. We always compete over everything. Have since we were ten."

McKayla humphed, then said, "I don't want Eric for my whole life. Yuck. I only want him for the weekend to get my libido under control."

"Don't ever ruin a friendship over a man," I said. "They're never worth it."

"Hey!" Eric, who is not that bright, said, "I'm worth it."

"No, buddy," I said. "You're not."

I brought home pasta primavera and a slice of raspberry pie, then took a bath for an hour.

Lights off. Candles on. Bubble bath.

Bliss.

On Sunday I woke at six o'clock in the morning to turn the heat on higher. There was snow on the ground and fog stuck on the mountains. I closed the drapes to keep the fog out and went back to sleep until eleven. My body was breaking down, I could feel it. Too much work.

I grabbed coffee and went back to bed until Cleo came up. She was wearing a Superman outfit, a green tutu that hung to her knees, and pink high-tops.

"I'm lovin' that outfit," I said.

"Thanks. I'm a superhero who can dance ballet. Want to watch me?"

"Sure."

She jumped and pirouetted, then turned around and pretended she was fighting a zombie with a big gun.

She said, "If I came back as a piece of art supplies, I'd come back as a paintbrush. What about you?"

I told her I'd come back as paints because then we could make a painting together.

She said, "I wish I had three ears" and "Why is dirt brown?" and "There are billions of stars, billions of aliens with one eye. Cyclops City!"

"You sure think a lot."

"I know. It's like my brain"—she made spinning motions with her fingers by her ears—"it doesn't stop thinking of weird stuff. Do you think I'm weird?"

"Sort of."

"Yeah. Me too."

"I'm weird, too, Cleo. Be proud of it."

"Okay, weirdo."

"Nerd."

"Nerd rhinoceros."

I called Rozlyn. Rozlyn was weepy. Her head was hurting again. I told her we should go to the ER or, for sure, the doctor's tomorrow. She insisted we wait until she had her appointment. I walked over and argued with her. She wouldn't move. Her headache made me feel sick.

Cleo and I watched a Disney movie while Rozlyn took a nap, then we made brownies out of a mix and added extra chocolate chips. We ate two brownies each, then got Liddy, and she followed us around the property like a dog.

Later, I studied the quilt Rozlyn was working on. Three women, about Rozlyn's size, in black bikinis, doing the cancan onstage.

"That's Mommy saying she can do what she damn well pleases," Cleo said. "And this quilt"—she unfolded one on a shelf—"is Mommy saying that women need to get out and see the world and the tigers and lions." It was a woman in a Jeep on a safari, animals all around. The woman was wearing a silvery cape.

I fell asleep on the couch. I woke up with Cleo curled up next to me. I checked on Rozlyn and gave her an ice pack for her head, which was pounding.

Something was wrong. We both knew it.

"Found them." Kade dropped an envelope on my desk.

"The photograph of your truck with your furniture in the back?"

He nodded. "Grizz took it."

"And maybe a photo of Grizz's garage and your saws and equipment inside when you first started?"

"Got it."

"And the pole barn?"

"Yes, ma'am."

"Perfect." I about wriggled with joy.

"Now what are you going to do with them?"

"That's a secret for me to know and for you to find out."

He had such a sexy smile. "I told you, I don't like secrets."

"And I told you to buck up and too bad."

He laughed. What a sexy laugh.

"Okay. Keep the secret. And why don't you take Tuesday, Wednesday, and Thursday off, too. Don't come in here. Stay home. Paint my picture."

"I don't need to—"

"I asked it as a question, but I didn't mean it as one. Your schedule makes me tired. Stay home. Paint the picture. I'll see you on Friday." He held up a hand. "No arguing."

I was wiped out. I was frazzled inside and outside. I thought about painting in my apartment, padding around in my slippers and pajamas all day, making a collage. It was like my old life, before Covey. I missed that life.

"But what about—"

"Friday. Besides, Grenady, I have more work than I can handle, and I don't need any more, thanks to you."

A vision of drinking coffee while I worked came to mind. Being alone. Sleeping in a tad. I would still have to be at The Spirited Owl at five-thirty, but... "Thanks, Kade." My eyes burned.

"You're welcome."

I sagged with relief.

"Sleep, Grenady, please."

His softened-up eyes about undid me.

I stayed home.

I loved it. I slept in. I outlined Kade's mural on my sketch pad in bed, drinking coffee. I dropped off the photos he gave me at a photo shop and told them what I needed. I bought frames and mats. I put together a six-by-three-foot canvas, then started outlining my collage on it. I ate chocolate cake and a lemon cookie. More coffee.

I went to The Spirited Owl, had a good night in tips, and was home by eleven. I slept in until eight on Wednesday and Thursday, and worked on Kade's collage, humming, lost in my art, the world gone, until my bartending shifts.

On Friday I went back to Hendricks' and was buried. E-mails. Calls. Clients. A meeting with Kade about sales, Rozlyn about pricing for pieces, and Eudora about logistical stuff with the company, but I felt better. Not quite as exhausted. Those days at home reminded me of how much I love working at home. I'm a homebody at heart, that's for sure.

I slept in Saturday, then worked on Kade's collage until my shift at The Spirited Owl. I was nervous. I wanted Kade to like it. How humiliating if he didn't. Plus, he would feel compelled to hang it in his office so it wouldn't hurt my feelings.

Cleo came up to visit while I worked. She was wearing a red, blue, and yellow hat with one of those twirly, spinny things on top of her head. She was also wearing one red tennis shoe and a tap dance shoe because today was "mismatch shoe day."

"Can I paint with you? I want to paint a picture of a monster with black teeth and a red cape."

I laid out newspapers for her on the table, then realized that the front page story was about that serial killer again. Ugh. I didn't know why the story was bothering me so much, other than the usual reasons, but I didn't want to look at it. I snatched it up quick and put the comics down for her. I gave her a small canvas. She painted the monster while I worked.

I didn't know that Cleo was watching me until she said, "Grenady, you are the best artist on the planet and on Pluto." She fist-bumped me. "But do you know how to make friends? I'm having problems with that. Except for Liddy. We're best friends."

*   *   *

On Tuesday night Moose came in. We chatted. He asked me out, I said no, he said you're breaking my heart, and I said I'm sorry, and he said, "But don't worry, Grenady, I won't sing you a song. Have you met my mother? Mom, this is Grenady . . ."

I did, indeed, like Monica very much.

But I was not in love with her son.

I received a message from Covey on Wednesday. He was raving, barely in control.

"Look, Trailer Trash Lady, no one's going to jail here except for you. *I'm* innocent. You want to plead out, go ahead, it's your time behind bars, and as I remember it, you have claustrophobia, anxiety, and a certain aversion to being locked in or locked out of anywhere. I don't think jail's going to work for you. Call me right now."

I did not call back. Alice, My Anxiety, was curled up under a table.

"You outdid yourself."

"Pardon?" At least Kade was smiling.

Of all the freakin' mornings to be late. I'd set up Kade's office on Sunday, went to bed early, and woke up at eight-thirty on Monday. I'm always at Hendricks' working away by then.

I had flown out of bed, taken a three-minute shower, brushed my hair out, and dove into my clothes. I brushed my teeth, shoved makeup into my purse to put on later, and took off.

I sprinted into Hendricks' and tried to sneak into my office, but Kade saw me coming.

"Thank you, Grenady."

"Do you like it?" I tried to catch my breath from running in.

"Yes, I do." He put his hands on his hips and shook his head. I could tell he was happy. "Grenady, I hardly know what to say."

I peeked into his office, where about twenty employees were gathered. I heard the excited chitchat.

"It's like looking at one of those before-and-after pictures of a house," Kade said. "Only it's my office and I barely recognize it."

"But you still want to work in there?"

"It'll be hard. Distracting." He winked.

On the steel blue wall to the left of his desk I hung five matted and framed photos. I'd had the photos enlarged and placed in twenty-four-by-thirty-six-inch frames. One was of Kade standing in front of his pickup truck years ago, his hand-carved furniture piled into it, when he first started Hendricks' Furniture.

Another photo was of Grizz's garage filled with Kade's saws and workbenches and Kade working in a white tank top. (Seeexxxy!)

The third was of the outside of the pole barn; the fourth was a sign that said HENDRICKS' FURNITURE, the first sign Kade made for the pole barn. The fifth was Kade's building now, with the modern brick exterior, the multitude of windows, and the red barn doors.

To the direct right of the office door I hung the old Hendricks' sign that I'd found in storage. On the other side I hung his work gloves.

I'd found the gloves in the storage room and asked Kade whose they were. He said they were his: he'd used them when he started the company, and they'd lasted ten years. Sounds silly, but I framed them. They were in bad shape and had a couple of holes, but to me they spelled out hard work and determination. I put a lamp with a wood base and a white shade on the grizzly bear table in front of the wall of windows, and I moved the armoire with the leaping salmon at an angle in the corner.

Behind his massive desk with the fly fisherman in the stream I'd hung the collage.

When I walked into the office with Kade, Rozlyn turned around and said, "I don't think I can work today, my friend. I have to stand and stare at this work of art and have my hot flashes."

"It's sooo good, Grenady," Sam said. "So good. Wish I had a better vocabulary to talk about this.... I mean, it's very, very good."

"I am, once again, stunned speechless," said Angelo the ex–football player with the broken nose, spreading his muscled arms wide. "More breathtaking artwork from Grenady. Breath-taking."

Petey said, his Irish brogue so musical, "I need one of these, lass. This is not a want. I need one like I need my Irish whiskey."

I smiled and felt myself tearing up.

"Oh no! She's crying!" Rozlyn yelled, and pulled me into a hug. "It's okay if you cry, baby, we all do. Maybe you're pre-menopausal. How are your mood swings? That's an indicator."

Kade's collage of the Hendricks' Furniture building was huge, a six-by-three-foot canvas. I'd painted the background with several shades of blue, the sunset spreading across the horizon, with slivers of pink, purple, and red, like liquid silk. I set it in fall, as Kade asked, so the trees' leaves were orange, gold, brown, green, and yellow.

Then I added the collage elements. I made a copy of the photograph of Kade's old pickup truck and glued it to the canvas under a pine tree. I'd had Sam cut out thin wood rectangles and I painted them red and attached them to the building as the barn doors. I painted HENDRICKS' FURNITURE in block letters above the door, and I painted sandpaper a reddish color to give the brick texture.

I glued dried chrysanthemums across the front of the building. I used tiny slivers of wood on the trees surrounding the building.

"She put the squirrels in," Petey said. "Smart lass."

"She even put in the mailbox," Rozlyn exclaimed. "And the little red flag is up. It says Hendricks'!"

"And she put the squirrels in!"

I'd painted two squirrels in a tree, then used fur to make their fluffy tails. I painted the three deer that came by Hendricks' and used painted toothpicks to form their antlers.

"And that rocking chair," Angelo said. "Charming!"

I'd painted an oversized rocking chair and put it under the pine tree, and I wrote Kade's name on the top of the chair. I used a piece of red-and-white-striped fabric to form the pillow on the chair. I painted the armoire with the howling wolf doors out on the front porch of the building, next to Kade's desk with the fly fisherman and the table with the raccoon legs. On the table I painted a vase, then put a dried chrysanthemum in it. I painted Kade's old gloves on the table, too.

"It's outstanding, Grenady," he said, quietly, as the others talked, and more people came in to see what the commotion was about. "I don't know what I was expecting, but not that. I don't want you to quit, but you need to quit, quit both your jobs, do exactly what I did, and go back to your art full time. But don't quit here. Forget I said that."

I would love that. But I'd miss Kade. "Maybe someday. But how could I leave this place? I'd miss out on lunch with Rozlyn and wouldn't be able to hear about her hot flashes or her love for Leonard." I was not breaking a confidence; Rozlyn openly discussed these issues with Kade.

Kade laughed. "She's blunt, isn't she?"

"And I'd miss out on Eudora's wise words, and wondering what in heck she did in D.C. and Russia and the Middle East, and I'd miss talking to Dell once a week. And pouring beer and wine for hours every night at The Spirited Owl to people who do and say strange things? Now that's special. How could I leave that heaven?"

"Okay, you can quit The Spirited Owl."

"I'll tell Tildy you said that. She probably won't make you your special hamburger anymore, though."

"I would miss that hamburger, but you need to have time for your art. You have to go back to this, Grenady." He studied the collage. "Right away."

"Soon. Maybe. We'll see." Change would be forced on me one way or the other. Probably 'the other.' Hello, blue, jail-stamped clothes and silver toilet!

"It's going to be hard for me to work in here now, Grenady. You've made it so much more . . . relaxing."

"Good, you work too hard, Mr. Type-A Workaholic."

"Me? You're calling me a workaholic? You who has two jobs?"

I put my hand under my chin and pretended to think about that. "That was slightly hypocritical, wasn't it?"

"I believe so."

He turned me on. He did. I could not control my body, and my body wanted that man.

Eudora walked in, stared at the collage, and said, "My God. And she was answering the phone for months?"

Kade put a check in an envelope on my desk that afternoon. I opened it up, saw the amount, and walked straight back to his office. I take pride in my artwork and I want to be fairly paid, but this was too much.

Way too much. I held it out to him. "No."

"Yes. Don't argue or you're fired."

"Ohhhhh!" I feigned fear, waving my hands. "Now that's scary!"

Eudora was there and drawled, "I feel scared myself."

"You're fired."

"Okay." I put the check on his desk and walked out.

Eudora said, "If you're fired, can I hire you to make me a painting?"

The check was back on my desk in twenty minutes when I stepped out to talk to Rozlyn, who was planning a spying adventure for me, Eudora, and herself. The target: Leonard.

There was a note attached to the check. "You're still fired, Artist Lady. See you tomorrow."

I was constantly worried about the upcoming meeting with the assistant U.S. attorney, the FBI, the IRS, and any financial or computer whizzes who were there to take me apart and eat me.

I was even afraid of the postal service guy from the fraud department. I never would have imagined myself being afraid of the postal service.

Alice, My Anxiety, was up and shakin', and it felt like I was stuck in a beer bottle without the relief of a beer.

I had hoped that eventually Covey would cave and tell the truth about me. This hope had no basis in reality, as his ranting phone calls indicated. He had lost it when he was told I'd be talking to The Scary Gang at a meeting, Millie told me. His lawyer screamed at Millie, telling her not to let me talk to them, and Millie screamed back, louder, and threatened to box him in the face if he ever talked like that to her again.

Covey had had a lousy childhood. His mother took off when he was four and he didn't see her again until he was sixteen. His father had one girlfriend after another. One woman stayed from the time he was five until the time he was ten. When she left, she never contacted him again. He had called her Mom. There were a couple more substitute moms. He would get attached, love 'em, then they would leave when they'd had it with his irresponsible, selfish father, and never contact Covey again.

I cried when he told me that story, and he did, too. He said when his mother left him, he cried for a week. When his next mother left, same thing. His father never made much money, and was stingy with what he had. Covey had paper routes starting when he was ten and worked at least twenty hours a week when he was going to school. He gave half his check to his cheap, neglectful, cold father.

He eventually had a huge falling-out with his father, punches were thrown, and his dad had literally thrown him out of the house. Covey was sixteen. His father died in a car accident five years later when they were still estranged. Covey had been born poor, and that fueled his greed later on. He had had nothing, so he had to have material positions—house, cars, stuff—to make him feel equal or, hopefully, better than others.

He'd had loss after loss after loss as a child, so he tried to control any future personal losses in a twisted, narcissistic, semipsychopathic way.

I didn't know how severe his abandonment issues were until we were married. He did not want me to leave him. I was his. His forever. He and I.

And now we were done. I was one more woman who had left him. That could not happen, in his mind. It absolutely, positively could not, and I had to be punished.

I didn't think he would tell the truth about me and my total lack of involvement in his schemes, as it gave him power over my destiny, and me. If he couldn't have me, it would be better if

I was locked up where no one could have me, like in a jail cell. Especially if he was locked up, too.

Sick.

"I have a tumor in my head."

"You have a what?" Eudora and I leaned forward across the table in the employees' lounge.

"A tumor." Rozlyn tapped her head, left side. "Right there. It's what's causing my headaches, my vision problems. Think of it as a plum that's rotting and shooting out minifireworks."

Eudora and I leaned back in our seats, stunned into silence.

"It's not good," Rozlyn said.

"Precisely what does 'not good' mean?" Eudora asked, reaching for Rozlyn's hand.

"I mean . . ." Rozlyn hesitated.

I put my hands to my head as a wave of nausea hit me like a brick.

"I went to Dr. Camille Johnson, who you found, Grenady. She had tests run that day." Rozlyn waved her hand, as in, I don't want to pause on the details. "They're going to use radiation, then chemo. It's a tricky tumor, I'm told, based on where it is. There's an experimental procedure, a clinical trial. I might qualify, I might not. It's still new, risky, probably won't be covered by insurance anyhow, and it's in New York." She took a deep breath. "I have about two years."

"What?" My voice came out stricken. "What are you talking about?"

"I have about two years to live."

The room spun, then settled. I grabbed Rozlyn's other hand.

"How do the doctors know that?" Eudora said, throwing a hand in the air, a diamond ring glittering. "They think they're geniuses or something? Those blowhards."

"They know based on how fast it's grown, where it is, and the life spans of other people who have had the same thing."

We sat in silence for long minutes, shocked. Utterly shocked. What to say?

"I'm sorry, Rozlyn," I said. "I am so sorry."

"At first I thought," Rozlyn said, " 'Why me?' But then I thought, 'Why not me?' Why should it be someone else? Unless they're ninety. Or a criminal. A bad criminal. I'm not special. I'm Rozlyn, mother of the cutest kid on the planet, a woman with perfect boobs, although a large and packed butt, a woman who sews women's power–truth quilts, wants to spy on a man who hardly knows she's alive, and is fanatic about making numbers work, but I'm not special. "

"You are to me," Eudora and I said at the same time.

Rozlyn squeezed our hands. "My friends."

We talked more. We were silent again.

I thought of Cleo. I knew Rozlyn was thinking of Cleo, too.

"Have you told her?" I asked.

"Not yet. Only you two. I'll tell her when I have to. Soon."

"She'll sense something is off."

"She already does."

"That kid is too damn smart," Eudora said. "She could be a spy."

"That is the truth," I said.

It wasn't a fun lunch. Eudora and I cried into our salads.

Rozlyn didn't cry.

I crawled into bed that night feeling like an old, old woman, weighed down hard by too much life. I pulled my white comforter with the pink roses tight around me, as if I were in a cocoon in a pink room.

I've never felt young. People talk about a carefree youth, and I have no idea what they're talking about. I was never carefree, I never felt . . . youthful. My goal was to survive.

Now, with Rozlyn's news, I felt old. Worn down and out.

I thought of Cleo. I thought of her having no mother, like me, same age.

I put my hands on my face and let the tears slip through my fingers.

*   *   *

"How are you at planning parties, Artist Lady?" Kade asked me, leaning in the doorway of my office.

"Where and when?"

"We're having a State of the State of Hendricks' Furniture in two weeks," Kade said. "Sunday night, six o'clock, at my house."

"That soon?" I could feel the old, resentful, pissed-off feelings well to the surface. Covey roped me into planning his parties and dinners almost immediately after we started dating, which were all designed to promote him and his company and to get more clients to bring money into his scheme. They were a ton of work.

I later realized that not only was he trying to make money via his parties, he was trying to get my attention off my art and completely onto him and his work, so that he would be my whole world. When he knew that my mind was distracted by a multitude of paintings, collages, clients, or an upcoming show, that's when he *had* to have me plan an urgent dinner or celebration of something.

He once called my art a "charming hobby." Oh, that fight was rip-roaring.

"Not enough time?" Kade looked so apologetic.

I took a deep breath. This was *Kade*. This was my boss. I was his employee. He paid me well. There were no other manipulations involved, no mind games, no obsessions. "It's plenty of time. Dinner and dessert, beer and wine?"

He nodded, so relieved. I could see it on his face: Planning parties is not my thing, Grenady. Please help me.

"I'll take care of it. You remember to show up."

"It'll be a Sunday night, Grenady. I'll be there even if I forget."

"And I will be calling you that day to remind you."

"Thank you. If you can't reach me, I'll be winter fishing."

"Winter fishing? And where would I find you then?"

"Somewhere on a river in a drift boat."

"Now that sounds fun."

"It is." He opened his mouth to say more, but then closed it. "Thanks, Grenady."

"No problem, boss."
I would miss him when I was in prison.
I thought of Rozlyn, Cleo, Eudora, and Tildy.
I would miss everyone.

After my Spirited Owl shift, my nerves all rattled for some unknown reason, I grabbed my sketch pad and charcoal pencil. I sat on my bed and drew a girl whose toes were being pulled by pliers. I drew her walking up, alone, to another home, the door shut, dragging a black trash bag. I drew her being teased by other kids. I drew her hiding food. I drew her in clothes that didn't fit.

I drew her lifting up another girl hanging by the neck from a rope.

I hung my head on that one.

I kept drawing with my charcoal pencil until I'd beaten the past back and my nerves smoothed out.

"I want to ask you something," Rozlyn said. She sat down, gingerly, on her porch swing, and I sat down next to her. She had put Cleo to bed and brought a quilt out for our legs. I held it up. It was a woman, black haired and about Rozlyn's size, dancing in a meadow, arms up, smile bright, pink dress swirling around her. It spoke of Rozlyn's love of life.

"Anything, Rozlyn."

"I don't want you to answer yet. I want you to think about it, and please know that I'll understand if you say no."

"I'll say yes." The rain pitter-pattered on the roof, so peaceful, so at odds with a tumor in the head.

"Grenady, you may not."

"I will say yes, Rozlyn."

"Cleo loves you." She started to rock the swing, back and forth. "That kid thinks you're her personal ice-cream sundae. She loved you from the start when you saved her on the horse. She calls you her 'Grenady Angel.' She talks about you. Feels comfortable around you, likes your sarcasm and humor. She has not yet seen the temper, but I'm sure she'd be impressed."

"Tell her to come to the bar."

"Sure thing. I'll do that. She can order a beer."

"I adore that odd child."

Rozlyn wiped tears off her cheeks.

"Oh no. Rozlyn, what is it? More bad news?"

"When I die, do you think, could you, I would like you to . . ." She took a ragged breath. "I would like you to be Cleo's second mom."

"I'm sorry. What?"

"I would like you to be Cleo's mom when I'm not here anymore." Her voice shook.

"You want me to be her mother? *Me?*"

"Yes."

I was shocked.

Rozlyn trusted me, liked me well enough, to be her daughter's mother? Cleo's mother.

When Rozlyn was gone. When she was dead. When my new friend was dead. My eyes burned, hot as fire. Me. A mother. "I'll do it."

"Grenady, don't answer yet." Rozlyn wrapped her arms around herself, her whole body trembling. I put my arm around her. "You have to think about it. You would be her mother forever."

"I don't have to think about it. I'll take her. I'm happy to take her. We have two bizarre personalities that will blend well. I don't know how I'll be as a mother, but I'll give it my best shot and stick with it till I've got her grown up, healthy, and safe, and then I'll look after your grandchildren, too."

She sniffled and rocked the swing under the pitter-patter of the peaceful rain. "Are you sure? I understand if you're not sure. I'll still think you're an awesome friend. Being a parent will change your whole life."

"I want it to change." I so did. "I'll be her mom if something happens to you, but it won't. You'll get better, we'll get this tumor shrunk and blasted, and we'll spy on Leonard."

"And I'll say hello to him without hot flashing. That's my goal!" She pointed a finger in the air.

We laughed the type of laugh you laugh when you want to cry and fear has its claws in you and is pulling you down but you're keeping your chin up and holding it together because if you don't, you'll be flat wiped-out.

I tried to put myself in her position. Her parents were dead. She didn't know who Cleo's father was. She was told she was dying. She had a young daughter who needed a home. "I will be Cleo's second mom, and I'm so glad you asked me."

"Truly, Grenady?" Her voice pitched upward, hope and gratefulness mixed.

"Yes. I'm positive. Never more so in my life." And that was the truth.

"I'm so relieved. I trust you. I knew it when I met you. It was karma, I know it." She exhaled. "Thank you, Grenady. You know you'll have to take Liddy, too, right?"

"Yes, I do, and don't thank me yet. We're going to kick some tumor ass first." I put my hand on her head, where the tumor was. I wanted to reach inside her head and pull that mass out. "I'm so sorry, Rozlyn. I truly am."

"Yeah, me too. It is what it is, so I have to plan. I have to provide for and protect Cleo, and that's what I'm doing, and I'm trying not to cry my way through it."

She cried anyhow. I held her as she sobbed and we rocked, back and forth, the rain pitter-pattering on down, so peaceful, when nothing on the porch swing was peaceful. A mother was giving away her daughter. There is nothing peaceful about that, ever.

In bed that night, the rain pounding down in a torrential downpour, I did the calculations. The doctors thought that Rozlyn had two years. Could be longer, could be shorter. I hoped it would be much, much longer, but being brutally and necessarily practical . . .

I put my hands over my face and rubbed it. I was getting a sympathy headache. Rozlyn's tumor was hurting my head. "Holy shit."

If I was found guilty by a jury, I'd spend five years in jail, Millie predicted. I could not parent Cleo if I was in jail.

If I pleaded out, she told me, admitted to being guilty, even though I wasn't, the U.S. attorney's office would agree to eighteen months and all my assets and money, including everything I had before I even met Covey.

Eighteen months in jail. Suffocating, dangerous, locked-in, nightmarish, jail. I tilted my head up to the skylight and the rain. Pound, pound, pound.

If I took the eighteen months, I would be here for Rozlyn during the last six months when she would need me most and I could spend time with Cleo. We were in for a lot of trauma, and tragedy, but their world in their light green farmhouse would be better if I were here.

Our conversation had been so surprising and had moved so fast tonight that I hadn't had time to process it and figure out how to address my secret situation with Rozlyn. Would she even want me to be her daughter's mother if she knew the truth?

My first answer was no. I'm officially a criminal.

But I would tell Rozlyn the truth. I think she would believe me. I would be humiliated and mortified, but I would tell her immediately so she could choose someone else if she felt it right.

Rozlyn. Tumor. Dying. Cleo.

I wrapped my arms around myself and shook and shook and shook. "Good God," I breathed. *"Good God."*

I wouldn't even have to worry about this if it weren't for Covey. Oh, my shoutin' spittin' Lord, I wanted that man dead.

The rain continued to pound the skylight of the big, red barn. Pound. Pound. Pound.

37

Ring around the rosie
A pocket full of posies
Ashes, ashes,
We all fall down!

If there was a nursery rhyme he liked the best, it was this one. It was about the bubonic plague in England. The ring was what grew on people's skin when they were infected with the plague via rats. Rats! He loved rats. Dirty and dangerous, sharp teeth. The ashes referenced all the bodies being burned.

He would change it to make it his. To reflect on a personal memory. His lips puckered, and he twitched. He knew what to do. He was a poet. He giggled.

Ring around the rock
A pocket full of cock
Fog in, fog out
They're all bones now!

He put his rhyme book over his head and blew into it. It was perfect. Sensual. Rock and cock. Brilliant!

He thought of the Getaway Girl and her red hair. He bit down on the book and groaned. He had wanted to taste her! He remembered her mother. She tasted delicious.

38

Children's Services Division
Child's Name: Grenadine Scotch Wild
Age: 14
Parents' Names: Freedom and Bear Wild (Location unknown)
Date: September 28, 1990
Goal: Adoption
Employee: Angel Hollis

Grenadine has been placed in Jill and Havel Preston's home. There are ten total children there. This is not an optimal situation. There are five bunk beds in one room for the girls, who range in age from twelve to sixteen.

There are five boys, ranging in age from ten to seventeen. The home is about 3,600 square feet on three levels. We will be moving Grenadine as soon as we can find a new placement.

She is a pretty girl, especially with those bright green eyes and red hair, although she continues to struggle academically in school with reading and writing. She says the kids tease her about being "stupid" and for not having cute clothes (which I have addressed with the Prestons. She has outgrown many of her clothes) but she won the schoolwide art contest, and I am so excited for her!

Children's Services Division
Child's Name: Grenadine Scotch Wild
Age: 14
Parents' Names: Freedom and Bear Wild (Location unknown)
Date: October 4, 1990
Goal: Adoption
Employee: Angel Hollis

Grenadine says that living with Jill and Havel Preston is okay, but there is one boy living with them (Taryn Walters) who has a raving monster in his head. She says that he talks to voices, wrestles with chairs, and likes to stab scissors into the walls. The only thing that makes him calm down is when she lets him watch her draw, so she draws for him every day for almost two hours. She's a giver!

One of the teenagers, Dev Matteson, tried to hang herself in her bedroom with a rope. Grenadine found her, stood on a chair, and used scissors to cut the rope. Dev survived. It appears that Grenadine caught her in the nick of time. Grenadine insisted on visiting Dev at the hospital, and skipped school to do it. Grenadine said Dev was upset because of "loneliness that didn't go away."

Grenadine also said she would never touch a rope again.

When she talked to me about what happened to Dev, she fainted. She says she feels sick when people are hurting.

She has a job as a waitress and says she likes it because the owners are nice to her and she gets a free meal a day.

This is a poor placement, and I will be requesting a switch immediately . . .

Children's Services Division
Child's Name: Grenadine Scotch Wild
Age: 15
Parents' Names: Freedom and Bear Wild (Location unknown)
Date: February 13, 1991
Goal: Adoption
Employee: Angel Hollis

Havel Preston says Grenadine is "a little stupid" because she can't read or write well and her teacher has called and asked for extra help at home, but Havel says he works all day and can't help the kids at night, too, plus his wife is sick so he has to cook dinner and do laundry and cleaning so his wife can go to bed.

Jill Preston looks tired. She can hardly stand up. She said she is suffering from migraines, ovarian cysts, which she says are causing her pain, and diverticulitis. She could not initially remember which child was Grenadine, but when I mentioned the one who liked drawing, she knew exactly who I was talking about. She says Grenadine can draw anything. She has put up the pictures that Grenadine has drawn on their bulletin board.

One picture is of a bird alone in a nest holding a tiny, red kite and crying. Another picture is of a girl wearing a red, crocheted shawl. She is standing alone in front of a forest with fog. The third picture is of three people dancing around a bonfire wearing lilies.

I've never seen artwork like this. There's something eerie about them. Haunting, but beautiful. Grenadine says she hates all the pictures.

Jill apologized profusely but said that with her health issues, she is unable to care for all of the children anymore. She said she had already contacted Bruce about this, but he hadn't gotten back to her. She would like us to take seven of them, but she said that Grenadine can stay, as she is the best behaved child and helps out around the house.

Grenadine told me that Havel and Jill fight and Havel yells. I talked to Havel about this, and at first he denied any yelling, but then he cried and said that he did yell, that the family is overwhelmed and can't do foster care anymore, except for Grenadine, who is their favorite.

I assured Jill and Havel that we would move the kids out of their home immediately. Henry Chao is handling that.

I will begin my two-week vacation tomorrow. My 35 kids will be checked on by other case workers, as planned.

39

⌒

Multnomah County Police
Incident Report

Case No. 91-9473

Reported Date/Time: March 8, 1991 20:30
Location of Occurrence: 8221 Deauville Dr., Portland, Oregon
Reporting Officer: Maria Jefferson
Incident: Girl living alone in home

On Friday, March 8, we were called to a home in the Benson-
ville neighborhood. The home had been abandoned by its previous owners the month before, according to the neighbors. The
lights were on in the house, the curtains were closed, and they
could hear music.

When we arrived we knocked on the door and the girl inside
asked who it was. She did not open the door. We told her it was
the police, and she told us that her parents were on vacation and
to come back in two weeks. We told her that we wanted to talk
to her, and she said she did not like talking to police officers on
Fridays.

I asked her if she could make an exception this one time. She
said no, no exceptions. I asked her why she didn't talk to police

officers on Fridays. She said it wasn't a good day to talk. We asked her to open the door, and again she refused.

We told her that if she didn't open the door we would have to break it down. She said, please don't, she needed the door, as it would soon be snowy out and cold.

We told her one more time to open it, and she finally complied. She opened the door, and we stepped in. It was clean and neat inside, although there were only a few pieces of furniture. An old couch, a table, and chairs. There was no one else in the home.

She had made chili and politely offered us some. We declined, and she sat down and continued to eat. We asked her her name, and she said it was Flower Child.

I asked her where her parents were, and she said that she wasn't sure, but they were somewhere in the galaxy. I asked when they were returning, and she said, "Now, that's a mystery. It's a bad and sad mystery."

I asked how long she had been living in the house. She said she had been living there long enough to have some peace and quiet. She said it was "damn hard" to find peace and quiet, and did I think the same thing? I said I did.

We asked her a few more questions, but she kept changing the subject. She talked to us about Van Gogh, the artist—Had we seen his paintings? What did we think? What about Monet?

While I was talking, Officer Micah tried to find out who she was. She finally told us her parents names' were Freedom and Bear Wild and asked if we could look them up for her. Obviously those were not their real names, and when we asked what their real names were, she said she didn't know and that she called them Mom and Dad.

I noticed some drawings at the table and asked to see her artwork, and she handed them over. I wanted to see if she'd written her name down, but I was distracted by a drawing. It was of a girl sitting on a lily pad on a pond, only the pond was a mirror with handles. Deep in the pond was a snake wrapped around a knife.

It's hard to explain, but it was a neat picture. She'd torn construction paper into tiny pieces and added it to the picture.

I saw her name, called it in, then we got CSD on the phone.

While they were looking her up, I asked the girl if her name was Grenadine Scotch Wild. She said, "Not today."

Grenadine had been assigned to a foster home run by Jill and Havel Preston. She had not been reported missing.

When we told Grenadine she had to come with us, she said, "No, thank you, I'm fine here," and continued to eat her chili. She said she had a job as a waitress and has this house and didn't want to leave. She asked if we were sure we didn't want some chili and said that she felt bad eating in front of us when we weren't eating, but she was as hungry as a bull on charge.

We told her we weren't hungry and again told her she had to come with us, and she said that she didn't mean to argue with us and she hoped we didn't think she was being rude, but she was happier here and did not want to live in foster care anymore. She called it "a fucking zoo. But animals could do a better job of running it than they do." She also said she'd rather throw a dead possum than go back.

We finally insisted she come with us. We thought she was going to cry, but she didn't. She cleaned up after herself in the kitchen, wiped down the counters, put the dishes in the dishwasher, and swept the floor. She said she had to go diarrhea because foster care gives her diarrhea and left the room.

Within a few minutes we realized she was gone. We caught Grenadine running down the street with her backpack. She is fast. I've hardly ever seen a kid run that fast. She was not happy to go back to foster care and said, "Swing me a cat, I hate fucking foster care."

We will be contacting CSD immediately about this placement . . .

40

To: Staff
From: Margo Lipton
Date: March 9, 1991
Re: Jill and Havel Preston's home

Jill and Havel Preston's foster home has been shut down,
as they did not know that Grenadine Scotch Wild had
been missing from their home for three weeks. Remember to refer all questions from the press to Wilson
Deveneaux.

41

"Rozlyn."

"Yep, darlin'?"

"I need to talk to you."

"Sure, sure." I saw the worry in her eyes. We took a short walk, following the pathway into the woods from Hendricks'. The mountains loomed, blue and purple in this light, like a postcard, a dusting of snow on the ground.

I told her about Covey, his arrest and mine, my stint in jail, upcoming jail time, my predicted future. I told her that Covey would not tell the prosecutors I was innocent because he was pissed off I was divorcing him. "And, I don't think you want someone like..." I choked, held the tears in. "Like *me* to raise Cleo."

Rozlyn, without hesitation, hugged me. "I want you to raise Cleo, Grenady."

"But what about the charges? Going to jail?"

"The charges are false. I know it. I believe you. You would never steal from anyone. Your ex-husband should be neutered. This doesn't change things for me except I need to stay alive long enough for you to get out of jail if you're headed that way."

I was so mad. One more thing that Rozlyn had to worry about now. Damn Covey. "When I'm out, I will come back and be the best second mother to Cleo that she could ever have. I promise you, but please, Rozlyn, don't give up."

"I will never give up. Never. I will fight like hell. But sometimes fighting like hell does not change the outcome of things. That's why I have you, you potential jailbird, you."

"And you're sure?"

"Positive. I wish I'd met you the day I was born, Grenady."

"Me too." I thought of my life from the day I was born. Specifically after I turned six. My life, with Rozlyn in it, would have been unimaginably better.

"You're like my soul sister, Grenady."

"And you're mine. It's the oddest thing."

"If I were gay, Grenady, I want you to know that I'd marry you."

I laughed. "I'd say yes, Rozlyn. Unfortunately, I do not want to see you naked or touch your boobs, even though they are spectacular and perfect, but if I did . . ." We let that one fly on our laughter, up through the trees to the tops of the blue and purple postcard mountains.

"But I would want to marry you only if Leonard said no."

"I understand."

"You're not offended that he's my first choice?"

"Not at all. He sounds quite handsome."

"He's smokin'. He needs my 225 pounds of eternal love and passion. I want to mount that man like a horse."

"You betcha."

We held hands, my scarred hand in hers, back to Hendricks'. I had a feeling we'd be holding hands often in the future.

And I would hold Cleo's hand when Rozlyn was not here to do it herself. I would reinvent myself, once again, and become a mom. A darn good mom, too.

On Sunday I finished the collage of the woman in the ball gown. Her dress was filled with trinkets and color. I even added tiny beads to her white gloves and plastic purple jewels to her shoes. It was a blast of creativity and motion, the dress filled with a hundred things to marvel at.

The dark forest loomed behind her.

I loved it.

I hated it.

I hung it on the wall next to the cracking vase village.

"Good to see you, Grenady."

"Hello, Kade." I smiled and shut the door to my car. "Perfect weather for a party."

We both tilted our heads up to the blue sky. Freezing cold, as cold as a cow's tit in December, but blue as blue can get. Like blue cotton candy.

"I think we'll do okay."

"Me too," I said. "It'll be fun."

Kade was standing on the front deck of his home. He was in jeans, a black thermal, and cowboy boots. Deadly, sexy, dangerous to my Big V. If I was a woman who wanted a man in her pants again, I'd choose him. I was wearing jeans, black boots, and a pink silky shirt and tank top underneath my jacket.

"How are you?"

"Not bad at all." I was faking good cheer behind a bright smile. Rozlyn, Cleo, and I had made a collage together of three bluebirds on a bird bath early Saturday afternoon. Early this morning I'd had a dream of two bluebirds crying over a coffin.

"Yeah?"

"Yep. Doing well." I ignored the concern in those dark eyes. "How are you?"

"I'm ready for the State of the State of Hendricks' Furniture."

I laughed as I reached the deck and stood in front of him. "No, you're not. You're not ready at all."

"You're right. That's why you're here. Come on in."

"Already love your home."

"Thanks, Artist Lady."

Kade's home was right down the street from where I parked my car and went to sleep one night when I did not yet have a home that was not on wheels. It was up on a hill, lots of wood and rock, tons of windows, and a deck around the whole thing.

It was private and quiet because of the forty acres he owned surrounding it.

"Unbelievable." I stopped in the entryway. It was like walking into indoor nature. There was a spacious great room, kitchen, and dining area with a two-story rock fireplace, wood floors, and leather furniture. It was a home for a stud. But what struck me was the view of the mountains through the two-story windows. Right in front of me. The window frames framed the mountains like they were a picture. "Wow."

"Like it?"

"Geez, Kade. That view. And the house looks like it's from a magazine. Did you design it?"

"I did, with an architect in town. Her husband built it."

Kade built the kitchen cabinets and the island. The island had two pillars on either side that rose to the ceiling, and two raccoons were carved into the pillars, as if they were climbing up it. "You definitely have a sense of humor."

"I try," Kade said. "Despite what people may think. I do."

I ran my hand over his kitchen table. He had carved a huge nest in the center of it. The back of each chair had a different bird carved into it—a blue heron, a hawk, an osprey, an owl, a chickadee . . . and a penguin.

"The penguin would be the humor," Kade said.

"I love it. That's the seat I'm going to sit in."

"It's yours."

There were carved wood pillars in the entry and living space. On two of the wood pillars he had attached bald eagles, as if they had landed there that second. The corners of the window frames had been carved with animals, too: elk, deer, grizzly bear, raccoon, wolf, falcon, cougars . . . and a giraffe. "And I'll take the giraffe."

"The giraffe is now yours, too. Behold your giraffe."

"I behold my giraffe."

He was a master carpenter. Extremely talented. "Kade, I hardly know what to say. It's beautiful. It's home art."

He seemed pleased, truly pleased. "It's a good place to drink a beer."

"That's it?"

He shrugged. "And steak. Steaks taste good up here, too."

"I would think anything would taste good up here."

"Want to see the rest?"

"You bet I do." Could I move in? I was glad I didn't say that.

Besides the great room and kitchen, Kade had an office downstairs, manly, with a huge desk, much like the one at his office. Upstairs were four bedrooms. One of the bedrooms had workout equipment. The other two were bare.

Clearly, when he had designed the home, he had planned for kids. I tried not to let that ridiculous, controlling, blond bomb of a future wife with a dry vagina irritate me too much.

"That is one enormous bed." I said when I saw his master bedroom. "Built for a giant. Hmmm. Who's the giant?"

Kade laughed. "It's a king. It seems bigger because of the way I built the frame."

"You almost need a ladder to get into it. Or one of those springboards that gymnasts use before they hit the vault. Do you have a springboard?"

"Got rid of it. I tried it and almost broke my neck."

"I would have liked to see that flip and jump, Kade."

"It was somethin' special." He winked at me. I could feel myself blushing.

"You should sell beds like this. Overly large and high. Fun." There were two bald eagles carved on the headboard. "I love those bald eagles. I'm not trying to butter you up, because then I would annoy myself, but I feel like I could touch those eagles and feel their feathers."

"Then don't touch it. You'll be disappointed. It feels like wood. "

It felt oddly intimate to be that close to Kade's bed. He slept here. Under the moon. When it was summer and winter. Naked? Half naked? Boxers? This was a bed you could bounce and cuddle in. "Why bald eagles?"

"I love the bird. And they mate for life. They do this incredible dance in the air. They lock claws, spin and tumble, then break away, do it again."

"For life?"

"Yes."

"Life is a long time," I muttered, then shut my trap.

"Life is a long time. Right person, good life."

I thought of Covey. If we were bald eagles I would take my talons and I would scrape him from his head, through his eagle dick, and down his wings. I would rip off his feathers, then stick my longest talon in his heart and turn it. I exhaled. Whew! *Way too violent, Grenady,* I told myself.

"You don't agree?" Kade asked.

"I think it takes an enormous amount of luck to meet someone you can be in love with for your entire life."

"Me too. But I believe in luck. Don't you?"

"I believe in good luck and bad luck, but mostly I believe that when the good luck arrives we should be grateful and when the bad luck arrives we should beat the crap out of it."

"You always say things that make me think, Grenady."

I could tell he was amused. I turned back toward the bed and the in-love bald eagles. I wondered how many women Kade had had in this room. He was tall, rough, raw, incredibly masculine, and manly. It was a small town and I hadn't heard anything, but a man like that certainly wouldn't have to live an abstinent life. Still. Dating someone in a town like this would be awkward, too. When you broke up, the whole town would know it. Ugh. No privacy.

I decided that I did not like any of the women who had been in Kade's bald eagle bed. All were undoubtedly weird with odd compulsions. They probably liked eating drywall or hoarding Barbie dolls and earwax.

I turned away from the bed on which one could bounce and cuddle before I grabbed him and pulled him down. He was my boss, problem number one. Problem number two, I was still married. Problem three, he would not want me to grab him and might be disgusted. Four, I do not need a man in my life to screw with my head again.

I left the bedroom but kept stopping to enjoy his home, the peaked ceiling, the chandelier made from antlers . . . and the staircase. Honestly, it was the neatest staircase I'd ever seen. The banister was built to resemble entwined branches.

I stopped to touch it. "You did it, of course?"

"Yes."

"I think I'm going to steal your idea and paint a background of these branches, then make a collage on top of it, okay?"

"It's yours. You now have the penguin chair, the giraffe, and the branches on the stairwell. Anything else?"

"I think I'll take the rock fireplace, too."

"Hard to carry out the door."

"I'll manage. I brought my muscles with me."

The pirate eyed my muscles and I eyed his. I let my gaze flutter away before I made an awkward lunge.

"So tell me about the house. Did you draw pictures for years? Go to sleep dreaming about it?"

"Both. I was young when I went to prison, but I was old enough to know I never wanted to go back. I used to lay on my bed in that damn cell and envision a new future, my own home. Not a small, cramped apartment. Not a dangerous neighborhood. No crime, no drugs, no guns. Pretty soon I was thinking about a home in the country, with a view of the mountains. That sounded better than the ghetto and gang fights.

"I'd heard about Oregon, had never been, so I started studying towns and I settled on central Oregon. There was fishing and hunting and skiing, all things I wanted to try. I wanted land, outside of a small town, and I knew I'd find it here."

"And here you are." I spread out my arms. "I love it. I've never seen a home like this."

"Come outside. You'll like the view."

On the deck, the cool wind puffed by, the blue sky endless, the town of Pineridge spread out below. The view at night, with the twinkling lights, would be magical, especially if you were sitting in Kade's hot tub. "How do you ever manage to leave your home and go to work? Leave the view?"

"It can be hard."

"I bet. You work all the time and you're away from this? Now that's a problem."

"I miss it sometimes. I'll be sitting in the office and thinking about being up here." He grinned, so sweet, and leaned against the railing. It made him a little shorter. Maybe down to six two.

"You can watch the weather change, the seasons change. Animals?"

He nodded. "I see deer, squirrels, coyotes, raccoon, rabbits, bald eagles, golden eagles, peregrine falcons, and skunk, which I avoid."

"Have you named them?"

"Named the animals?"

"Yes."

"No. Not that friendly with them yet. Maybe when they come up and have a pizza with me I'll start naming them."

"You have to name the animals. They're your neighbors, only they're furry and speak in their native animal tongue."

"Better than neighbors. They mind their own business and don't gossip."

"Animals are not known for gossiping or minding others' business unless they want to eat them."

Was his smile a tad flirty? Was I delusional?

We were standing rather close. I could see that his dark eyes had flecks of green. I imagined him totally naked and in that hot tub with me on top of him, my breasts in his hands. I was burning hot in seconds. "It's cold out here. Shall we go in?"

"Thank you for coming to our semiannual State of the State of Hendricks' Furniture," Kade said to all of us, smiling in front of that towering, two-story stone fireplace.

We clapped, and a few people whistled and hooted. I smiled. Rozlyn winked at me. She was wearing a low-cut blue dress to show off the spectacular girls. She'd said to me, "I decided to dare to be daring tonight." She tapped her head. "I think it's time to try everything now."

Eudora was cool and elegant, as usual. She had been rock climbing in a gym that day. "I rock climbed when I was younger— outside, not inside—and found it much more challenging than what I did today by far. And back then, I was wearing a heavy backpack full of gear, too."

Gear?

"First off," Kade said, "I want to thank Grenady for planning our party."

The applause and hooting was deafening.

"I think we've moved up about ten levels in terms of class," Kade joked, and everyone laughed. "Six months ago we were out on the deck in lounge chairs, slamming beers that I'd packed in coolers and eating pizza. This time we have a catered event with lasagna and calzones and wine poured for us by waiters in black with red aprons."

"Fancy!" someone called out.

"And we have candles and flowers, glasses not paper cups, silverware that isn't plastic, and napkins wrapped up in some strawlike stuff. Now we're livin' the high life."

People pounded the tables and clinked their wineglasses as the fire crackled in the fireplace behind him.

"But, seriously, Grenady, this is real nice. Thank you."

One person called out, "Bravo," and others followed suit. "Speech! Speech!"

I laughed, but good golly God, inside I felt all choked up and dang emotional. I liked these people. It had been a long time since I'd been around a group, not counting the kids in my art class, who I liked as much. In fact, it had never happened before.

Most of the employees at Hendricks' are men. This is not sexist on Kade's part; it's simply that most of them are carpenters, which is a male-dominated field, and he has a furniture-building company.

Although they would be bringing wives and girlfriends, the overall atmosphere I wanted was masculine, no frills and fluff— that was not Kade, that was not the company, but Hendricks' was first class. So I needed a classy, Oregonian, natural, organic style.

Over the tops of the crisp white tablecloths, I used burlap as a table runner. In the center of each table I put wildflowers, heavy in red, in three Ball jars on top of a stack of wood that represented the furniture we made.

I bought wood chargers at a dollar store and used those under the pure white plates. I bought red napkins and tied raffia around them. I put out tea lights in wood candleholders on the tables, which I knew would sparkle off the crystal water and wineglasses. I also placed them on the hearth, the serving tables, and in the kitchen. I turned the lights down and the rock music up.

"So let's talk about the company," Kade said. And he talked. Not too long, but enough to give us a clear picture of where we were. The finances were, in his words, "reflective of all of us working our asses off together," which made everyone laugh.

He talked about what type of furniture he wanted to build in the future, and how he was going to expand the markets.

"I want Hendricks' to grow, but to be honest, I don't want the company to grow so much that I'm working eighty hours a week, or that you're constantly working overtime. I know you have family and friends, and Phil and Glenna need time to get out for their annual hunting trip and come home without, yet again, any deer."

Oh, funny. Phil and Glenna stood up and bowed to loud applause. Phil yelled, "Hunting season isn't only for the hunting. We drink beer, too!"

"And we want to make sure that Harry has time for his fake motorcycle gang," Kade said.

Harry stood up, white hair still thick despite the fact that he's seventy. "We're not fake, Kade. We're bonified! Certified! We're dangerous. We're lawbreakers! Don't mess with us, son, don't mess with us."

"And," Kade said when the laughter died down, "we have to have enough time off so that Cory and Lan can, hopefully, get out there and find a date one of these years."

Cory stood up and protested, stabbing his fork in the air three times, "I had a date! Six months ago today. I had one,

Kade! And I'm hopin' for another one! Anyone got a sister? A cousin? A friend? A *woman* friend."

Kade thanked all of us for our hard work and then, "So let's get to the fun part. Your semiannual bonus checks." He rapidly called out people's names, including mine.

"Thank you, Kade."

"You're more than welcome, Grenady."

I heard the happy chatter, the laughter. I opened my check.

Oh, my shoutin' spittin' Lord. It sure was profitable to work for Kade. There was a note: "Party Planning," and then the amount he paid me, over and above my bonus.

I caught his eye. He smiled. I smiled back.

Soon someone turned the music back up, the tables were pushed aside, and people started to dance. I have hardly ever danced in my life. I ended up dancing with Rozlyn and Eudora, Cory, Petey, and Angelo. It was a lot of fun. Rozlyn kicked off her heels and taught us a new dance that involved a lot of hip twisting and arm waving. She told me later, "I've always wanted to do that. Gotta boogie when you can."

I didn't dance with Kade, but I wanted to.

For these reasons I didn't: One, he is my boss. Two, I might try to take off his clothes. Three, he might not want to dance with me.

Ugh.

Still, it was fun, and a couple of times I saw Kade watching me, that hard-ass face smilin'.

I stayed afterward to help clean up along with about ten other people. The people who stayed to clean took home the wildflowers in the Ball jars. Kade insisted I take home one of the large bouquets. I would give it to Rozlyn. He would bring the other in for the lobby.

Tildy's waiters and waitresses said good-bye to Kade and me and left with their gear, the table and chair people came and grabbed their stuff, and before I knew it, everyone was gone, the last of the candles flickering, the fire burning down.

"Sit down and have some of Tildy's chocolate cheesecake with me," Kade said. "I was too busy talking to eat."

"Me too. She told me to tell you she outdid herself again."

"She always does."

He cut me a slice and we sat on his couch in front of the fire. It was like we were an old married couple. We talked about the food, then we talked about the people there, the funny things that were said, the social dynamics.

He asked how I became so adept at planning parties, and I said, "By force and by curse. That would be in my other life."

"If you want to talk about your marriage, I'd like to hear about it."

"If I talk about my marriage, I'll start plotting evil ways to have my soon-to-be-ex husband beheaded."

"Don't. That would be a crime."

"Might be worth it."

"That bad?"

"Worse. Stupendously worse." I realized I was clenching my jaw and forced myself to unclench it. "It was a poor decision on my part. Lost my brain on that one. Suckered in."

"We all make poor decisions."

"This was a doozer of a poor decision." I rubbed my face. "Calamitous."

"How's the divorce going?"

"Also poorly."

"Will it be over soon?"

"Probably not. He doesn't want the divorce and he's making things hard. His strategy is to crush and annihilate unless he gets his way." I waved my hand. "Let's not talk about this. If I do, I'll turn into a raving mad woman."

"Do you have a good attorney, Grenady?"

"I do."

"Do you need money to pay for the divorce?"

"No, I'm fine." I don't take handouts.

"Are you sure? I can give you the money if you need it—"

"No." My tone was snappish. I am sensitive to people offering to help me. There was always a catch, an emotional string, something that I would then owe to someone else and be beholden to, as if now they owned a piece of me and I had to pay it back in blood money. That was a scraggly mess I didn't need in my life. "I can do it on my own."

"I'm sure you can, Grenady, but I'm happy to help if you change your mind."

"I got it. But no. I do not need *help*." Now I was irritated.

"Now you're being irritating."

He chuckled. "Dang. Don't want to irritate you."

"I don't want you to irritate me, either." I crossed my arms. I hated Covey.

After a second Kade said, "So what's the next collage you're going to make?" and I took a breath, reined in my prickliness. We talked on, and soon it was natural and easy.

About an hour later he got a call, picked up his phone, saw who was calling, and said, "I'm sorry, Grenady. I have to take this. It's from that hotel in San Francisco—you got this business, remember? The man who owns the hotel has a vacation home in Carmel. You sold him a desk and two chairs. Anyhow, I told him to call tonight."

I nodded. "Go for it. I want to be alone with another slice of cheesecake, anyhow." I felt silly being there still. It was late. I would leave as soon as Kade was off the phone.

It was warm in front of the fire and most of the lights were off. A few candles still burned on the mantle where I'd placed them.

I leaned my head back on his leather couch for only a minute. For *one minute* I would close my eyes, then I'd be back up. I would say good-bye to Kade when he was off the phone and head to my house. . . .

One minute.

I woke up snuggled under two thick, white blankets with a pillow under my head. I sat straight up, totally confused. My hair was half over my face, and I pushed it aside.

I was in front of a rock fireplace.

My apartment does not have a rock fireplace.

I was on a leather couch.

I don't have a leather couch.

Someone was making bacon.

I don't have bacon.

"Oh, my shoutin' spittin' Lord." I peered over the couch and saw Kade in a blue tank top and jeans making coffee, early morning sunlight streaking through those two-story windows. "This is bad," I choked out.

"Good morning, Grenady. And it's not bad."

"Bad, bad, bad." I tried to stand up, quick as I could, but my feet were caught in the blankets and I landed on the floor. I said a bad word, untangled myself, and popped up like a jack-in-the-box. I had spent the night at Kade's house. *His house!* He was my boss! "I'm so sorry, Kade, I'm leaving. I'm so sorry."

"It's no problem, Grenady. Want some coffee? I made bacon and eggs for us."

"Uh-oh. No." I whipped around the couch, aiming for a fast exit, hit a carved wood chest and went straight down, *again*. I said yet another bad word and scrambled up.

Kade was right there. "Are you okay?"

"Yes. Yes, I'm fine. I have to go. What time is it?"

"Seven thirty."

"I can't believe this." Then I heard myself mutter, "Shoot me a possum."

"Why can't you believe it? And what did you say about a possum? Come have some of my coffee. You're not late. Plus, the boss will give you a pass. He's a reasonable guy, and I said last night that no one needed to be in today until ten o'clock."

"I know, I know. But I'm still here and they're not and I can't believe that I'm here still. Oh, my God. Where is my purse?" I put my hands to my head. "I can't remember . . ."

"It's in my office. But come and sit down and have breakfast with me. I never have company in the morning."

Never? I thought. Never? No women in the bouncy, cuddly bed?

"Kade . . ." I turned to him. "Are you kidding me? I can't stay and have coffee with you."

"Why not?"

He was barefoot. Casual, strong, that body hard and muscled out. He made it hard to think.

"I can't have coffee with you. I need to leave. This is a small town, Kade. I don't need people talking about me, about us. I spent the night at your house. This is so bad."

He shrugged. "No one knows. I don't care if they do. I stopped caring about what people think of me many years ago."

"Well, I care." I grabbed my purse. I wondered if I stunk. I danced last night. I sweated. I probably stunk like sweat. "How do I get out of here with the least number of your neighbors seeing?"

He laughed. "None of my coffee before you make your escape?"

I sighed at him and rolled my eyes.

"Okay, Grenady, you can take the back roads. There are no neighbors here to see, anyhow. I'll drive my car and you can follow so you don't get lost—"

"No. I do not want to be seen this early in the morning with you, Kade. Come on. Think."

"I always think." He saw my expression and sighed. "Take a right at the end of my driveway . . ."

I took the back roads home, over a hill, behind a meadow, then I followed the river. I didn't see anyone I knew, the streets pretty deserted.

I did see a long rope looped over a fence. I rubbed my neck as it automatically tightened.

I pulled into my driveway. Liddy neighed at me and I neighed back, then I darted up the stairs. I wasn't worried about Rozlyn seeing anything. She would think it was fantastic that I "got some action." She wouldn't gossip about it, either.

I scrambled up the stairs, past the saddles, and shut my door, as if by moving speedily I could out run any rumors. On one hand I don't care what people think of me, either. On the other, I don't need people thinking I'm sleeping with Kade Hendricks. He's too well known, I'm too new, and I don't want any crap at work.

I exhaled and leaned against my door.

I didn't have to go in until ten. It was eight. I hopped in the shower, washed and cream-rinsed my hair, then pulled on a robe and a jacket and sat out on my deck drinking coffee. I watched the earth painting move, the soft colors blending over the horizon, while I thought about Kade and my possible upcoming stint in the slammer.

If I went to jail, it would be nice to have sex beforehand.

But Kade was my boss and he would never date or sleep with an employee. He was honest and had integrity. Even with me, he was friendly, and professional, but there was a distance there, and sex would be totally against his company rules and against his values. I knew that.

My mind raced.

Aha! I could quit working for him *before* my trial and ask him to pop into his bouncy, cuddly bed with me and bounce and cuddle about.

But daaaaang. It would be wrong to have sex with him and not tell him that I had been arrested for fraud, embezzlement, and other beastly charges and simply wanted him for prejail sex. I could not do that. He would feel used. It was already wrong that I hid my unfortunate arrest record from him when I applied for a job.

He would not want to sleep with someone who was going to jail for stealing from other people anyhow—no, he would not. He would have no respect for someone like that. He would not want me around him, especially not naked.

Finally, even if I didn't work for him, even if I didn't have a dandy arrest record, there was a high probability he wouldn't want to sleep with me in the first place. One must not forget that part.

Well, now, shoot.

I tipped my head back to the winter sun. I would have liked to have coffee with Kade. He's a private, reserved, calm, thoughtful, introspective, kind man. He was laid-back but in a serious, I-Have-Seen-a-Lot-of-Life sort of way.

* * *

I wondered what Kade was doing. What did he think of my darting out like a fool?

On my way to work I reminded myself to be friendly to Kade, like normal, but not too friendly. Say hello. Don't stare at his chest. Don't smile too long. Keep your nose down and do your job. Don't think about him as anything other than your boss, not a well-hung stud. Be professional. Be respectful. Be efficient. No envisioning the cuddly bed.

I would do that.

I could do that.

Ho-ho-ho. Sure ya can, Grenady.

Ho-ho.

" 'Morning, Grenady," Kade called out as he walked past my office with Sam discussing something 'er other. Sam waved at me. "Hey, Grenady. Great party."

" 'Morning." I thought of Kade naked in his bouncy bed, with the married bald eagles, his third leg swinging.

That was not a professional image, Grenady! Shut it down! I blushed, head to foot. I thought of his buttocks. That wasn't respectful! I thought of those strong, creative hands. That was not efficient!

42

The tracking devices in my car and on my phone that Covey had installed were bad enough. The only reason I didn't leave was because we'd been married for only six months. A divorce already? Had I failed that quickly? Covey, sensing my running instinct on high, turned on the charm again, too. Thoughtful. Caring. Listening.

But about six months after that, I found out he'd strategically placed *cameras* in the house. One was facing our bed, the other faced our shower and tub area, and a third had a view of the family room and kitchen. The fourth was pointed at the front door, probably to detect my multitude of lovers sneaking in and out of the house.

The cleaning lady accidentally found the first camera. She was dusting and knocked a vase over on a high shelf in our bedroom, and the camera came tumbling down with it. She thought it was some funky thing Covey and I were doing—recording ourselves in bed. She thought she'd damaged the camera. "I so sorry, señora. So sorry."

I have zero problem with couples recording themselves having sex. But both people should know about it and feel comfortable with it. It should not end up on YouTube.

For me, that camera was it. I called a client who ran a security firm. Tommy came right over. He put the tape in, and there I was. Naked on top of Covey, him on top of me. Rolling. Having sex. *It was our bed.*

I was livid. I felt so violated. I didn't even feel embarrassed in front of Tommy. He was in his sixties, former Marine, and was not even remotely shocked. He leaned towards me. "Dina, there are other cameras here. We need to find them. We also need to find the other tapes. Guy like this, if you leave him, he'll hang these tapes over your head, threaten to put them on Facebook or YouTube, anything to get you back. I know this kind of man. He's dangerous. Probably a personality disorder under it all."

While Tommy went to find the other cameras, I went to a corner in the garage. I'd seen Covey in that same corner, on a ladder, several times. I found the box. Tommy found the other cameras.

"Lady, you need to get out of this marriage."

"No kidding."

When Covey came home that night I had the cameras, which I'd smashed with a sledgehammer, on the kitchen table. I had also smashed the CDs and cut all the tapes.

I told Covey I was leaving and I no longer loved him. I told him he disgusted me.

Covey flipped out. He had come home stressed, even I could see that, and he cried, he clung, he dropped to his knees and begged. That handsome face that I had fallen in love with was now the face of a clingy, obsessive, sneaky man. It was pathetic. His reaction made me more sure that I was doing the right thing. I knew what unhealthy looked like, and we were swimmin' in it. We were rotten because of his diseased mind.

I had loved living on my own in my green house with my upstairs attic studio. I loved teaching the kids art. I loved the independence, the peace, the quiet, the control over my own home and mind.

I had given it all up for Covey. I had sold my house because he'd insisted, and now I wanted it back. I wanted that life back. I wanted this life to disappear, as I'd wanted so much of another life to disappear, too.

I locked myself in the guest bedroom, then locked myself in the guest bathroom and turned on the bath. I climbed in to get away from his pleading, the way he was trying to twist this into being my fault, that I was overreacting, overly sensitive. I had pushed him into spying on me because of my evasiveness, my secretiveness, not letting him call me all the time. He kicked both doors in, wood splintering.

I lay in that tub, covered in bubbles, and watched him lean over the bath, crying, still crying, begging me to stay.

I was weary beyond weary. I was exhausted from the last months, the last weeks, the last days, the last hours. I had had my doubts about marrying Covey, but I had smashed them down in favor of hope and love.

To get him back under control, I told him, okay, I had changed my mind. I would forgive him. We would work it out.

He went limp with relief and left the bathroom to take some antidepressants. When I climbed out of the bath, I deliberately turned toward the mirror to see the scars on my back. By shots and by fire, those scars gave me courage. I would not be with someone who treated me badly. I had made that promise to myself long ago.

I stayed up and planned. Divinity Star and her past lives were coming tomorrow for the carousel collage, then I would leave. What would I pack? What would I leave? Should I rent a truck? Where would I go until I could buy myself another little green home or persuade the new owners to sell it back to me?

Covey kissed my cheek in the morning, game face back on, three thousand dollar gray suit all buttoned up, and went to work. "We need a vacation, Dina. Name a place, I'll plan it." Which meant his secretary would plan it. He was the tough guy again, in control. It was two people in one.

That morning it all went straight to hell.

At lunch on Wednesday Rozlyn told us she had seen Leonard in town the other day. "After menopause some studies say that the female libido goes down. Others say it goes up. Mine is up. I'm in the up group."

"Mine has never dipped," Eudora said, breaking apart a roll. "I'm not that type of woman."

"Any man on the horizon for you and your non-dipping libido?" I asked.

"Not yet. I'm looking." She leaned toward me and whispered, "You should look at Kade."

I whispered back, "I already have."

She nodded with approval. "He's a gentleman. I've known him for years. Honest. Fair. Kind. He's a man who wants a wife, if you ask me."

"I will never be a wife again."

"Then you can role-play being a wife in bed," she said. "And Kade can play the role of passionate husband."

I could do that!

"I think women's sex drives dip in menopause because the man they're sleeping with doesn't turn them on, the lazy oaf, the inconsiderate dragon, the mean mongoose," Rozlyn said. "Leonard turns me on."

"Where did you see Leonard?" I asked.

She squirmed. "At the Cassidy and Butch Café."

"And?"

"I had a hot flash and had to leave before I ordered my nut berry muffin and could talk to him."

"That's unfortunate," Eudora drawled. "Next time, fan yourself, then get back in there. Don't hide unless it's life threatening."

Life threatening?

"If it is life threatening, do not return to your home. Change your appearance. Assume someone is tailing you. Avoid airports, trains, and bus stations. Get a private party to drive you out." She stopped. "That's all."

I furrowed my brow and studied Eudora.

She shrugged her shoulders, that elegant profile giving nothing away. "It's proper advice."

"I want Leonard to tail me. Next time I see him, I'm going to ask him out," Rozlyn said. "I don't have the time not to anymore."

"Go for it," I said, though I felt a piercing pain in my chest.

"Smile. Show him the cleavage of your porn star boobs," Eudora said. "And I think you'll get your yes."

"Yep," Rozlyn said, wriggling her chest. "That's the plan."

That night I studied my unfinished collage of the girl in the magnifying glass dressed in lilies, the looming lighthouse in the distance.

I set it on my table and painted some of the lilies. I used thick paint. I thought of it as butter paint. It made the lilies seem alive. I painted the red, crocheted shawl in her left hand and used an old toothbrush to get the texture I wanted. I added glitter to form the Big Dipper rising from her right hand. I painted her hair auburn, like mine, then I made tiny daisies from scrapbook paper and put them in her hair.

I could not finish the lighthouse.

Or the trees.

What was there? What memory was trying to plow its way through? Why had I never been able to retrieve it? Was my subconscious holding tight to it? Would it ever let go? Was it too traumatic to handle? Did my six-year-old brain lock it out forever?

Run, Grenadine, run!

On the day I was released from the slammer on an unsuspecting public, I shed the blue scrubs stamped with JAIL, the squishy sandals and the jail-issued pink bra, worn underwear, and socks in the bathroom. How many other bottoms—with what sorts of problems—had been in my underwear? Yuck.

I had been arrested on a Friday, in the afternoon. Gee. No judges available to talk to me, so the assistant U.S. attorney got his wish and had me in jail for the weekend. The timing was done to crush me. I get it.

I was supposed to be in front of a judge on Monday, but because of my unfortunate encounter with the Neanderthal Woman, and the pending assault charge, I spent three days in isolation. Then another three days because of the next fight. The charges were dropped when it was determined it was self-defense.

Ten days in jail.

I was processed back out, paperwork signed. They handed me my clothes in the dark blue bag with the black zipper; my envelope with my silver bangles, wedding ring and diamond studs; and, to my relief, my lily bracelet.

In the bathroom, I stood naked in front of the small mirror above the sink. My face was sad and defeated, as if I'd aged ten years. My eyes were tired, with purplish circles underneath them, and my face had a grayish cast to it. I'd lost weight, and my cheeks were sunken. My bruises from my fights were purple, green, and blue. The scars near my hairline seemed to glow against my paleness.

I leaned against the sink, head bent, my hair half covering my ghastly face. My heart fluttered, my stomach churned.

I was bad. I was stupid. Stupido Grenado. Less than. Poor. White trash. Nothing. Doesn't fit in.

And yet, this time, I raised my eyes to the mirror again. I wasn't bad. I wasn't any of that.

Covey was. This was all him. Not me. I was not at fault. I had signed papers because I trusted him.

Maybe I should have found a hit man, or, more accurately, a hit woman, when I was in jail. That would have made the last ten days of hell worth it.

I brushed my blond hair and put it in a loose bun on top of my head, the first step in making myself look like Dina, *artist*, not con artist. I pulled on my skinny jeans and belt with the silver buckle, my knee-high black boots, a white tank, and the white lace top without the white ribbon that the officers had taken in case I wanted to use it to hang myself.

I slipped in my diamond studs and put my silver bangles back on my wrist. I kissed the lily bracelet because no one could see me doing it, so therefore wouldn't think I was insane. I pocketed my wedding ring.

Better.

Better, at least, for a battered jailbird who was going to flap her torn wings and fly out of town as soon as she was allowed.

* * *

After I was dressed, Millie and her assistant, Glory, met me in the jail lobby and we walked up the stairs to the third floor. I had told her to tell Covey and his attorneys he was not to be there or I would attack him.

There were four courtrooms. We went into the second one. It all blurred together because I was shaking, but I was soon in front of a U.S. magistrate judge for a detention hearing and an arraignment. The judge told me what I had been charged with, I pled not guilty, and he set the trial date for ninety days down the road.

Millie whispered to me, "That'll never happen. Don't worry. I'll get it changed. We have at least nine months, count on waaaaay longer."

It was determined that I was to be free until my trial. I was not a looming danger to the public, had no record, and I said I would not skip town to Mexico, although Millie told me later that was exactly what they were worried about with Covey. He had a home there, and money in foreign accounts. I agreed to give up my passport.

A pretrial release person named Lavinia Slade had already met with the judge about me and said I was not a flight risk. I met with her, too.

Lavinia had blond hair and was about five feet tall. She told me I could travel within the state of Oregon. I had to check in with her regularly, which I agreed to do. She told me the rules and regulations and the consequences if I didn't follow the rules and regulations. I heard about legalities and received warnings. She said a whole bunch of other things, but they faded and blurred.

I nodded, but all I could think about was that I never, ever wanted to return to jail.

Millie and Glory each took my elbow as we left the Justice Center jail. We were greeted by both a reporter and a photographer. "Look this way, Mrs. Hamilton . . ." the photographer told me. I turned my head in the opposite direction.

The sun was shining. People were walking around, cars driving by. Teenagers were laughing on the corner, a mother was pushing twins in a stroller, a group of preschoolers were being led down the sidewalk. All normal. I had lost out on all of this. I had lost out on life. I had lost out on the weather. I had lost out on roses, daisies, lilies, coffee with whipping cream, paints and canvases.

More time in my life, lost. Gone.

The reporter started pestering me as we made our way to Millie's car. "You've been charged with theft, fraud, embezzlement, and money laundering . . . are you guilty, Mrs. Hamilton . . . what do you have to say to your victims . . . your husband was released seven days ago from jail, why weren't you . . . your husband said he's innocent . . . is it true that you were in two fights during your stay in jail and had to go to solitary . . . is that where all your bruises are from . . . who hit you?"

I turned to tell the reporter that I knew nothing about what Covey had done, nothing about his illegal activities.

Millie yanked at me on one side, Glory on the other.

"Mrs. Hamilton has no comment," Millie said. She glared at me, pinching my arm hard.

I couldn't keep my big pie hole shut. I was shell-shocked from jail but not shell-shocked enough to keep quiet. "I have been arrested, yet I did nothing wrong. I had no part, at all, in Covey's business, ever. I had no idea that his clients' money wasn't where it should be. I would never steal from anyone, and I apologize to everyone my soon-to-be ex husband has stolen from." Millie yanked on me again, her fingers hurting so much I thought they would pierce my skin, blood spurting out. That would cause quite a sensation. I had a parting remark. "Covey is a dick."

"Why do you say that, Mrs. Hamilton?"

"First off, my name is not Mrs. Hamilton, it's Ms. Wild. Second, I said that Covey was a dick because he is one. A small dick."

The reporter laughed.

Millie hissed to me, "Close your mouth. Now, Dina. Close it. Don't make me do it."

"And if he's any sort of man, he will tell the authorities that I'm innocent. We'll see if he's got a big enough dick to do that."

"He's told us that you and he own Hamilton Investments together," the reporter said, "that you are equal partners."

"That is a lie. I can't even balance my own checkbook." That was the truth. The numbers flipped and shifted.

Millie and Glory shoved me into the backseat of an SUV, and Glory sped us off. Millie turned around, huffing and puffing. "Listen to me, Dina. I can't help you if you don't do what I say. We have to let the process work . . ."

"We have to let the process work?" I sputtered, my anger so red hot I was surprised I didn't turn into a flame. "I was arrested by the FBI, had my rights read to me, and handcuffed. I was strip searched and had a jailer look in my butt for anything I might have shoved up it. I've spent ten days in jail. I smell like a jail cell. I've been in two fights. I've been in isolation. I had a roommate who stroked an imaginary cat and an imaginary pig. I was sexually harassed by a woman the size of a rhino.

"My photo and my name have been in the paper. My reputation has been sliced and diced, and I'm sure I've lost all my clients. I may well get my butt slung right back into jail for a crime I didn't commit." I took a deep, hugely pissed-off breath. "The *process* is not working for me."

"It will. Pipe down. I will work the process. You will be found innocent if you let me do the talking and rein in that temper of yours."

"I *am* innocent." I put my hands to my face and groaned. "Where is Covey?"

"He's at a meeting with his attorneys. I know this because a little bird told me."

"When he gets home, I will kill him in the dining room. No, the family room. No, I'll drown him in the pool. No, I will electrocute him when he's taking a bath by throwing my plugged-in dryer in. No, I will poison him. How else could I kill him?"

"You could take a boat out into the ocean and push him off," Glory said. Glory went to an Ivy League law school. She's a trust-fund baby. She races cars. She loves the courtroom and loves defending criminals. It's odd. I learned this when I saw them in jail.

"I mean, it's so cliché," she went on. "It's been done before, but it is effective. Say that he was drinking heavily before bed, you went to sleep, and you woke up and he wasn't there. Darn it all, anyhow."

"That's a splendid idea. One of his boats. He has three . . ."

"Hello? Do we need to feed our client's murderous intents?" Millie asked.

"No, we don't. But"—Glory wiggled her fingers—"you could slowly poison him. I do believe that arsenic still works. Maybe there's a drug you could give him to cover up the arsenic?"

"Isn't that enough?" Millie snapped.

"One more," Glory said. "There are certain herbs that can—"

"That's it," Millie said.

Glory closed her mouth, then opened it again. "I was trying to be helpful."

"Help in a different way," Millie snapped.

I was smashed, dashed, and scared to death.

I went with Rozlyn to her next doctor's appointment. It was in another city, a larger city than ours. We left work at three o'clock on Monday.

Rozlyn hadn't told Kade about the tumor yet, simply asked if we could have the afternoon off for a medical issue she was having. He was quick to agree. He probably didn't want to hear the words "pap smear" or "breast check" or "women's troubles."

"Take notes when the doctor talks, Grenady," Rozlyn said. "I freeze up when I see a white coat. Makes me feel anxious. My anxiety might bring on the jitters."

"I'll take notes." White coats yanked me back to places I didn't want to be, either, and things that were done to me I didn't want to think about.

"I'm worried about Cleo," Rozlyn said, rubbing her face. "So worried."

"Does she know?"

"Not yet. But soon. I'm getting many calls, and making many calls, and she senses something is wrong. For a kid, for any of us, it's better to know. I don't think I'll tell her how long the doctor thinks I have yet. It's too much. I'll be honest about the tumor, though. I'll tell her I have a block in my head that shouldn't be there."

I tried not to cry. I was driving, after all. I felt sick, though— my heart sick, my head sick, because Rozlyn was sick.

"Life never stops twisting, does it?" she asked.

"No."

"Sometimes the twists are like orgasms and ice cream. Delicious. Sometimes they're harsh. Like lava being poured down your throat."

"True."

"The question is, How will I deal with this lava?"

I was quiet for a minute. "I think you'll deal with the lava like you deal with everything else in your life, with courage and humor."

"I'm trying. I want to be an example to Cleo. I've always wanted her to embrace the beauty of life, but I want to show her how to die, too, if that's my road. I want her to look back on me, when she's older, and respect me for how I acted right now."

I swallowed hard. I am not a mother, but that had to be the worst part of this disaster, by far. To think of your young, beloved child out in this world without a mother . . . terrifying.

"I want to be brave in front of her, and not freaked out, but real, and comforting. I want to show her that my tumor isn't stopping me from living, from being with her or cooking or quilting, and working with numbers at Kade's like I love doing. That I might cry, but then we'll go swimming, or ride Liddy, or watch the sunset."

"You're the wisest person I know, Rozlyn. So strong."

"I'm being forced to be realistic." She put up a finger and wagged it around. "One thing I'm definitely not going to quit doing is trying to get a date with Leonard."

I sniffled. "You can never give up on that. Never ever, ever give up!"

"Heck, no. He's my eye candy. I want to eat him." She wiped the tears off her face. I saw her put her chin up. "On the way home, let's get ice-cream sundaes."

"My treat." I reached for her hand, and she held it.

I had been that young child without a mother. I knew what it felt like.

It would not happen to Cleo. I would be Mom Number 2 if the wisest mother in the world, Rozlyn DiMarco, didn't make it.

The doctor's appointment did not go well, but not because Rozlyn and I get anxious around white coats.

There was hope for a miracle.

It was tiny. Rozlyn would need her insurance to approve it, as it was a clinical trial, experimental, new, and only at one hospital, in New York. If the insurance didn't approve it, it would cost a fortune and she could not pay for it. She would go through radiation and a specialized sort of chemo for her tumor.

We held on to the thought of a miracle as we left, and we held hands on the way to an ice-cream parlor. We had ice-cream sundaes, chocolate and caramel sauce, bananas, and whip cream.

"Ya only live once," Rozlyn said. She had a hot flash in the middle of eating the sundae. It didn't stop her. She held a glass of ice water to her head.

"Unless you believe in multiple lives." I told her about Divinity, the fantasy queen. "Can I have some of your extra chocolate sauce?"

That night I had a dream I was crying into the red, crocheted shawl. They were there, stroking my hair, hugging me close. *Stand tall. Chin up. Shoulders back. Be brave, Grenadine. You can be scared, but you must be brave.*

I'm trying. Trying to be brave.

"See you tomorrow at the meeting, Dina. Remember: Rabid wolves with egos."

"Thank you for the peaceful vision, Millie." I tapped the phone with my finger, then rubbed my hand over my face, sure it was aging by the minute. It was Sunday evening and the snow was coming down. It would be a frightening drive to Portland tomorrow over the curving Santiam Pass. That road had cliffs you could drive off and never be found again except by mountain lion and deer. "My head will be on a platter by the end of the day, Millie. Make sure you carry it out and don't drop it."

"As your attorney, I'll make sure I carefully walk your detached head out to the car. I'll drag the rest of your body out later when I have time. Remember, be honest. They can sniff out dishonesty like hounds after a raccoon. I've told you what they know. I know what I know. The proffer will work for you only if you're upfront and honest. If not, you're a burnt enchilada. You'll go up in flames. Prepare for trial and, we hope not, jail."

"Aren't you supposed to be my cheerleader or something like that?"

"I am your cheerleader. But I'm painting you your boxing ring and who your opponents are." She paused. "Dina, I want to tell you something."

"What?" I stared out my French doors into the dark. Beyond the dark was the forest. Towering trees, a harsh wind, maybe fog. What a fright.

"I like you."

I paused, waiting for the next line. The "but," or the joke or the funny put down.

"I like you," Millie went on. "I hope this works out for you. I've done all I can and I do believe you, Dina, that you knew nothing of what was going on with Covey's schemes."

"Thank you." I was surprised at her words. "I like you, too, Millie. You've been a shark for me during this whole fiasco, and I appreciate all you've done."

"My pleasure. When this over, we'll go to lunch and act like proper ladies instead of planning strategies to keep your skinny ass out of jail."

"Do you know how to act like a proper lady?"

"No. Do you?"

"That's a negative."

"We'll try, anyhow," Millie said. "We can order proper salads and tea and talk about the weather."

"Yes, and other inane things like fashion."

"How dreary. Good night. Try to sleep. Remember I'll be with you the whole time. Me and you against the wolves. I have sharper teeth than them."

I knew this was not going to work out well for me. I could feel it in my bones. Covey had still not fessed up. He kept harping that he was innocent, though the facts against him in the newspaper alone were overwhelming.

Fry me a pig, I wanted that man to rot, *after* he admitted what I had not done.

43

Children's Services Division
Child's Name: Grenadine Scotch Wild
Age: 15
Parents' Names: Freedom and Bear Wild (Location unknown)
Date: July 22, 1991
Goal: Adoption
Employee: Aleta Cohlo

I talked with Grenadine today and she hates "fucking foster care" and wants out.

Grenadine says she has a job waitressing and the regulars give her generous tips, and she wants us to give her the money that we give the foster parents so she can get her own apartment.

I told her it wasn't possible because she is only fifteen and we could not guarantee her safety if she was out of our care. She said to me, "Look at my case file. Fuck the safety that you all offer me. I'd be safer on my own."

She is, of course, still furious that she had to go to the juvenile detention center for three weeks, and I cannot blame her for that at all. She felt like she was being jailed, yet had done nothing wrong.

I told her, again, that there had been no room in any of our foster homes for a teenager, so she'd had to go there until a group home opened up.

She said the alcoholic stepfather with a temper at her last foster home was awful and scary, and she says that she is sick of hauling her things around in a black trash bag, because it makes her feel like her stuff is trash and she is trash.

She is wearing layers of clothes to school in case she is moved to another home before she can get back to the first one. She has a backpack and she keeps all of her art supplies in it, and takes it everywhere with her.

She says that the little kids in the foster homes are always crying for their parents or for brothers and sisters from whom they're separated, and she tries to comfort them but she says it only works for a while and the teenagers are all "messed up." She has done drugs now and then, and drinks now and then, because it slows down the pain for her and she can forget about being alone.

Grenadine says she tries to save and hide food for herself and the other kids because they're all afraid of being hungry and she's sick of needing to hide food.

She doesn't feel wanted in the foster care homes and she hates how things aren't organized or always clean. She has trouble sleeping, it's noisy, she hates trying to figure out how to get to school when she's in a new home, and how to get home.

She's nervous and anxious all the time. She does not look well. I know she's been depressed for a long time.

The long and the short of it is that she wants out.

I told her I would arrange counseling, and she says she is never with the same counselor long enough to trust her and that it's pointless.

Children's Services Division
Child's Name: Grenadine Scotch Wild
Age: 15
Parents' Names: Freedom and Bear Wild (Location unknown)
Date: October 22, 1991
Goal: Adoption
Employee: Aleta Cohlo

Unfortunately, we still cannot locate Grenadine. Rumor has it she is living in the car of a friend, Izzy Olletti, who goes by the name Leather, who is in our program. Izzy overdosed on drugs and is still in rehab. I have been out looking for Grenadine every day for weeks. My husband and I have been out at night many times, too. I've talked to the foster kids she knows. They won't tell me anything.

Grenadine has dropped out of school to avoid being pulled back into the foster care system and the group home she was in. We need to locate her so we can put her in a new foster care or group home and get her back in school. I am concerned about Grenadine's health and safety. I am also concerned about her not being in school, where she has close relationships with the principal and several teachers and where she painted a mural of the school in the entryway, which is an excellent example of the talent our kids have if they're given a chance.

I am worried to death about this child.

Children's Services Division
Child's Name: Grenadine Scotch Wild
Age: 15
Parents' Names: Freedom and Bear Wild (Location unknown)
Date: October 28, 1991
Goal: Adoption
Employee: Aleta Cohlo

The police found Grenadine sleeping in a long, black Ford she called Clunker and brought her to the hospital because she was so thin and sick. Apparently, two other homeless teens called for an ambulance. They thought she was dying. She was hospitalized for a week for acute pneumonia, and I did see her every day and brought her art supplies, as she requested. She went back out on the run the day I came to get her to take her to a new home. I've heard through the grapevine that she's living with a friend in a white van.

I drove around looking for her most of the day yesterday, and my husband and I and his mother and brother also drove around, but none of us could locate a white van. I'm extremely concerned about the pneumonia, and it's getting so cold out. I will continue to search for her each evening. I am worried sick.

The principal of her school and her teachers have all called me (repeatedly) to check on Grenadine.

Children's Services Division
Child's Name: Grenadine Scotch Wild
Age: 15
Parents' Names: Freedom and Bear Wild (Location unknown)
Date: November 10, 1991
Goal: Adoption
Employee: Aleta Cohlo

Grenadine was burned on Sunday night when a veteran having some sort of hallucination accidentally set himself on fire. Grenadine was sleeping under the Booker Bridge with other home-less teens, and she tackled him, then put out the fire with her coat and hands. He was fighting her and she somehow hit her head and split it open.

Grenadine and two other teens took the homeless man to the hos-pital. He thought that he had been set on fire by the Viet Cong.

She had eleven stitches on her head near her hairline, which the doctors say will scar. They treated her hands. Second-degree burns. They kept her overnight because they weren't sure if she had a concussion, too.

I went to pick her up the next afternoon for a new placement with Callie and Joseph Niemeyer, but she had run off again.

I spent several hours looking for her, phoning people, and I went downtown, but I could not find Grenadine. I am extremely worried about her—especially because that head wound and the burns on her hands could become infected.

Children's Services Division
Child's Name: Grenadine Scotch Wild
Age: 15
Parents' Names: Freedom and Bear Wild (Location unknown)
Date: December 8, 1991
Goal: Adoption
Employee: Aleta Cohlo

Grenadine went back to school in the middle of November. The school neglected to tell me that. I believe it is because she has a close friendship with the principal, Damon Greene, who has had many arguments with this office about Grenadine's care.

I went to the restaurant where Grenadine was waitressing, to talk with her, but the manager said she'd quit. I don't believe him, and I will swing by tomorrow and look for her. The manager said that as case workers we all "suck the big one." He told me that Grenadine had been living in a car and we obviously didn't "know shit" about how to treat a child.

I told him I worked for the state and it was my job to protect Grenadine, so she would need to contact me, and he said that I obviously should be fired as I hadn't protected her at all and he told me he would call the police if I didn't get off his property. His wife told me to stay away from Grenadine because I was a threat to her safety and health. She pulled the spray thing out of the sink and sprayed me.

In another issue, I need to talk to you about my case load. I have 37 kids. My health is shot. This is impossible. I am requesting a medical leave due to stress and exhaustion.

44

"Mrs. Hamilton, thank you for coming."

"Thank you for having me. I appreciate it."

Dale Kotchik, an assistant U.S. attorney, looked slightly surprised. Perhaps he was thinking I would walk in combative? Swinging a sword around? Juggling knives?

I had nothing to fight out. I was completely at his mercy and the mercy of all the other serious and anal and formidable-looking people at that long table in an intimidating building in an expensive office in downtown Portland. Ironically, the furniture, I was told by Millie, had been made by prisoners. I thought of Kade.

The list of people from various organizations was frightening. Dale Kotchik was from the U.S. attorney's office, as were his assistants. There was a woman from the IRS; two special agents from the FBI; a man and a woman, one of whom was a computer specialist, the other a financial fraud specialist; a man from the postal service; a woman from a finance and corporate securities division; and other suits whose titles I forgot.

I tried not to be scared down to my gut, but it didn't work. I knew they were here to beat the heck out of me, legally speaking. I exchanged a glance with Millie. She nodded at me, as in, you can do this.

"Let's start from the beginning, Mrs. Hamilton," Dale said. I guessed him to be about fifty. He reminded me of an overbearing owl. "You and Mr. Hamilton were married for about a year. Correct?"

"Yes. Covey and I are separated and will be getting a divorce as soon as he stops being an asshole and cooperates. Which could be a long time. Also, please don't call me Mrs. Hamilton. The name makes me nauseated. You can call me Dina, or Ms. Wild." But not Grenady. That name is for my new life, not this one.

"All right, Ms. Wild." Dale had a calm and cool demeanor. "When did you leave Mr. Hamilton?"

"I know it's hard to believe, but I planned on leaving Covey the day I was arrested. I'm an artist, and I had one client coming in that morning to pick up a collage, then I was going to pack up and leave. I was arrested before I could get out of there."

"Why were you leaving him?"

"Let me count a few of the most creepy reasons." I put my hands up and started pointing at my fingers, ignoring the scars. "He was obsessive and possessive. He called and texted me all day to see what I was doing and who I was with. He accused me of seeing other men. He had anger and jealousy issues. He liked money and his toys too much. He did not support my career as an artist. In fact, he did what he could to sabotage it. Without telling me, he put a tracking device on my car. He put a tracking device on my phone. Finally, I found cameras set up in our house, including our bedroom, so he could watch me. I didn't know they were there. That's some of why I left."

There was a loud silence for long seconds.

Dale studied me through his glasses. "Tell me about your investment business."

"It was not my client's investment business," Millie said.

"That's right," I said. "It wasn't mine. Covey founded it, he worked at it. I knew next to nothing about it. I did not work with Covey."

"But you were an officer. It's on the letterhead."

"I was a figurehead only. He said he needed another person, someone he trusted"—I put my fingers up in the air to make quote marks—"to be an officer in his investment business. He said that he wanted his business to be our business, that as a married couple we should share it. I thought that was romantic and sweet at first, but now I know it was like signing a warrant for my arrest and committing myself to time with Boob-Swinging Bertha in a jail cell."

Dale coughed.

"When he wanted me to become an officer, I told him no several times. I know little about investments or real estate or playing the stock market. To me, the stock market sounds like gambling—buy and sell, buy and sell, hope the dice rolls your way." I leaned on my elbows. "But Mr. Kotchik, hell, I'll admit it. You are looking at one of the most naive wives in the country."

Dale blinked. "Why do you say that?"

"Because I am." I could feel myself flush. "It's embarrassing. I'm embarrassing to myself."

"Your signature allowed him to move money, open accounts for two shell companies, and make withdrawals that eventually lost a massive amount of money for your clients, among other things."

"Covey's clients, not mine. Covey always had a reason for needing my signature, and it sounded plausible. For example, the account in New York. He said he needed it for tax purposes because of his clients there and he said we both needed to sign. He always had the same excuse—we were a company, and as a couple, the bank had to have two signatures, the government had a bunch of rules we had to follow, there was investment protocol, tax reasons. I didn't know what he meant. It sounded complicated, but he sounded confident. I'd sign, and out he'd go."

"Did he put pressure on you?"

"He was always in a rush. He'd come in when I was at work in my studio or a client was there. I'd tell him I'd look things over, but I couldn't at that point because I was busy and he'd get angry, be pushy, tell me that I wasn't trusting him. If a client was there it was especially demeaning for me, so I'd sign it to get him out of there. Now I know it was all part of his plan. I had no reason not to believe him. I didn't know he was cheating anyone. It never occurred to me that he was."

"Why not?"

"Because I loved him. I thought he was an honest man. I thought he was an honest businessman. I had never heard otherwise." I took a quick look around the table. They were all staring right at me, judging me. "Now I hate him and wish he would be kidnapped by a Mexican drug cartel and buried in a desert."

They asked questions I couldn't answer about Covey's business, his accounts, and shell companies called, ironically, Scotch Electric, GrenWald, and Wild Construction.

"Ms. Wild, Mr. Hamilton is adamant that this is a company run by both of you. If you're innocent, why would he implicate you? Why wouldn't he say, 'Hey, I'm innocent, and so is my wife, but she wasn't involved in my business at all'?"

"My leaving has enraged him. He threatened me and said if I didn't move back in with him, if I testified against him, if I divorced him, he would bring me down with him. He told me he would fry my 'tight little ass in jail,' and that's a direct quote.

"He also told me that he would tell you that I was the mastermind behind it all. I don't know how to mastermind any of this. I can't even balance my own books for my art, so I had to hire a bookkeeper and an accountant."

"And if you moved back in with him?"

"If I moved back in, Covey said he would get us out of this, that he and his attorneys would fix it, get the case thrown out on technicalities, they would shred your evidence, say it was false arrest, *something*, and that neither one of us would go to jail."

"Ms. Wild, this is your life. In all likelihood, you will go to jail. If Mr. Hamilton said that all you had to do was move back in with him and then he wouldn't bring you down, too, why risk the situation you're in now?"

"Because I am not going to let him control me anymore. I won't. I didn't do anything wrong. Nothing. And I cannot stand—" I paused and tried to get myself together. "I cannot stand . . ." I rolled my lips in, trying not to let a single cry out. "I cannot stand to live with him. I don't want to be around him. I don't want to talk to him. I don't want him to . . . to . . . touch me. I am hoping you all will believe me, that I didn't know about any of this, and that I won't go to jail, but . . ." My voice cracked.

"But?"

"Even if I do go to jail for this, I would rather be there than live with Covey. I will not let him tell me what to do or force me to do what he wants." I'd had enough of that when I was younger. I would not put myself under someone else's power again, ever.

Mille patted me. I stared down at the scars on my hands for a few seconds. It was easy to do. This meeting was taking me back to a time years ago when it was hard for me to look anyone in the eye at all.

"Ms. Wild, do you remember signing this paper?" the woman from the FBI asked. She had brown hair, brown suit, brown heels. My eyes flicked down to the signature. I studied it, caught my breath. Oh, that was bad. I wiped the tears off my cheeks. Damning bad. *That was not my signature.* The room tilted, as if we were on a sinking ship. "No, I don't remember signing it because that's not my signature."

"What do you mean that's not your signature?"

I had signed my legal name to the documents Covey had given me: Grenadine Scotch Wild. "I didn't write it. See? The way the G is for Grenadine? I don't write my G's like that. And that W, it looks pretty close to mine, but it isn't. I don't do a loopy doop there . . ." I pointed to the W and moved the paper back to her.

"What about this one?"

She handed me another paper. Fine print. Legalese. Grenadine Scotch Wild, written at the bottom. Getting worse. So worse. "That's not my signature, either."

Again and again. Forged signatures.

"What about this one?"

"That's my signature." I flipped through the paperwork. I remembered that Millie had shown me the back page. It was my nightmare. On closer inspection of the six previous pages with all the fine print, I had signed to transfer money from our company to another company with a name I didn't recognize. "Shit."

"Not shit. It's fraud."

I met Dale Kotchik's owl gaze. "I didn't know I was doing anything fraudulent. See, this back page? That's what Covey handed me. It has the name of the bank, his signature, and mine. I don't remember these other pages attached to it at all. He gave me this one sheet and said he was opening up an account for us for retirement. We were investing in minerals, or something like that. I think he even said gold, that prick."

Dale studied me for a minute, as did the other serious, uptight people in there.

"What about this?" Dale pushed another paper across the table toward me.

Millie had shown me this one, too. I leafed through the pages before it. I felt as if the floor beneath me had cracked and I was teetering on the crack. "That's my signature. Same thing. I don't remember all these attached papers . . ." The words and letters were moving on the page, but I understood the main points. Covey invested money for this company. I thought I would pass out. "Williams and Sons went out of business."

"Yes, they did. The investment losses they suffered with Hamilton Investments sank them. A hundred-year-old company. Gone. Al Semore's went out of business, too. Liberty Trucking. Red Tail Plumbing. Hundreds of people lost their life savings."

"I never saw all these pages when I signed. You can even tell here." I pointed to the left hand corner. "See? It's been stapled twice. Do you see that? Covey took them off before he gave them to me."

"I do. So you're innocent, Ms. Wild?"

"I'm guilty because I signed those papers, but I believed Covey when he told me what they were for. I never wanted to steal money from anyone. I have never done that. I would never do that." I knew why I hadn't read the papers more carefully, but that was a poor excuse. On the other hand, should I not have questioned Covey's money? The easy flow of it, all the cash? The house and cars and vacation homes? Yes. I should have. I thought he was a successful investor. Period.

Dumb.

"There is one thing that is not fitting here at all with me." The financial man from the FBI tapped his pen. He was a human calculator, I could tell. "You're a smart woman. Articulate. Quick. I understand that Covey may not have included all the paperwork when he asked for your signature, but on a couple he did. Why did you not read any of the papers you signed? They are somewhat complicated, but the gist of them is quite clear. Why didn't you ask questions?"

My deepest, deepest shame. I stared down at my hands. *You are stupid. Stupido Grenado. She's retarded. She can't read. Dirty Grenadine.*

"Ms. Wild?"

I felt myself go red. I was suddenly hot. I felt like I was in grade school again. Everyone staring at me. Everyone thinking I'm stupid. Ready to leap and make fun of me.

"Because . . ." I ran a hand through my hair. I thought about saying something like, "It was too boring" or "too complicated" or "It was written in legalese." But that would sound flip. It would make me sound shallow and silly. It would make me appear guilty, like I was being evasive and vague.

"I didn't read all of it because . . ." I about choked. All these smart people. So smart. Brilliant. Lots of degrees. I *barely* got out of high school.

"Because you didn't want to know," Dale said, quite calmly. He thought I was trying to get out of being prosecuted. "Because you wanted Mr. Hamilton to continue to bring home the money he did for your expensive cars, the boats, the clothes, the jewelry, the vacations."

"Don't attack my client," Millie said.

"I didn't care about any of that," I said.

"You liked the wealth and all that went with it. You didn't really care where he got the money, as long as he got it."

"No." The word wobbled out, as a rush of ragged emotions hit.

"Don't be obnoxious, Dale," Millie said.

"You signed the papers. You aided and abetted him with his criminal activity. You were a part of it. A willing participant. You brought in clients, Mr. Hamilton told us. You smiled and gave dinner parties. Lavish parties on his boat. A Christmas party. Hundreds of people."

"I did not try to help Covey cheat people. I didn't even know he was cheating people. I didn't read the five papers I signed...."

"Why?"

"Because..." I wanted to disappear.

"Yes?" Dale prodded.

"I didn't read the papers Covey gave me because..." I wanted to dive into the ground and stay there.

"No lies, Ms. Wild. We don't have time."

"I can't read ... well."

"What?"

"I have..." I felt tears spring to my eyes. A lifetime of shame and humiliation came flowing up.

"Yes?"

"I have dyslexia."

"You do?" Millie said, semi outraged. "Why didn't you tell me that? I'm your attorney. Hello? I should have known that."

"I'm ashamed of it. I shouldn't be. It's not my fault, but I can't read quickly, or well, sometimes."

No one said anything for a long minute.

"I found out in high school." I heard my own ragged breath. "I thought I was stupid. Unbelievably dumb. That's why I couldn't read in school. I was in special classes, sometimes, and other times I wasn't. The teachers let it slide."

"I don't understand," one of Dale's assistants said. "You're saying that your teachers let it slide, they didn't notice you couldn't read, that this problem wasn't addressed until high school?"

"Right."

"That's not believable." She narrowed her eyes at me.

"Sure, it is," Millie said. "Kids slip through the cracks all the time."

"I moved around ... frequently."

"What about your parents?" She leaned forward. "They usually notice when their kids can't read."

I felt like I'd been slugged in the stomach. The air rushed out of me, though I'm sure I didn't make a sound. "My parents didn't notice it—"

Millie interrupted. "Why the drilling about her parents? We're off topic. You're bullying her."

"It's okay, Millie," I said. "My parents didn't notice it because they weren't around."

"What do you mean they weren't around?" the human calculator asked.

I put my hand over my lily bracelet. I remembered a woman with long red hair and a daisy chain crown and a red, crocheted shawl she let me wear and a flowered skirt. I remembered a father with a tickly beard and a tie-dyed T-shirt in the same colors as mine. I remembered an orange tent and a yellow VW bus. "I was in the foster care system starting when I was six."

"Foster care? At six?" Dale leaned back in his chair.

"Yes."

There was a surprised silence in that room. I would have thought they'd known.

"What happened to your parents?" the human calculator asked.

"I . . ." I stumbled again. "I don't know. I remember them. I remember camping. I remember roasting marshmallows. I remember finding the Big Dipper and Little Dipper with them, and how my dad taught me how to make a rocket. I remember fishing in rivers, going to festivals. We used to paint and draw and do crafts, all the time. I remember being on my father's shoulders. I remember dancing by lakes. Then, nothing."

"Nothing?" This was from the man from the postal inspector's office.

"No. They were there, then gone. I was picked up on the side of the road by a trucker, my head bleeding. I had a concussion. He didn't know where I came from. Apparently I was running down a road near a forest, screaming. He called the police. No one knew who I was. I remember waking up in the hospital,

WHAT I REMEMBER MOST   395

screaming for my parents, but I couldn't remember what happened. I knew my name."

"Your birth name of Grenadine Scotch Wild," Dale said.

"Yes. I could write my name, although I flipped a few letters,
so they didn't get it at first."

"And they couldn't trace your parents?"

"No. I remembered that people called my mother Freedom
and my father Bear, but I called them Mommy and Daddy, and
of course those nicknames, with the last name of Wild, weren't
their real names, so they couldn't be traced. I was, officially, an
abandoned child."

"But your grandparents, your parents' siblings . . ."

"No other family member came for me. No one asked for
me." That still hurt. Still. I did not know where I came from. I
didn't know anything about my family.

Dead, dead silence.

Millie patted me. "You're breaking my damn heart."

I put my shoulders back. I didn't want to look pathetic or like
I was using my past as an excuse. "One of the families I lived
with for five years, they were wonderful to me, they still are, but
to put it kindly, they weren't . . . academically inclined. Neither
one of them read well, either." But they loved me, I wanted to
say. They taught me how to hunt, how to shoot, how to fish.
They taught me how to love and how to be in a family again,
which was far more important than reading

"I did try to read, and even with the dyslexia, that probably
boosted me up enough so teachers didn't feel the need to act on
it or analyze it. In the summer before my junior year, after my
new foster parents got me straightened out, because I had been
making some poor choices with my life, they realized I had
dyslexia and I had a tutor for two years. She taught me all sorts
of strategies and techniques to read and write and caught me up
academically.

"I can read now, to myself, not out loud, if I read slowly, and
if I'm not pressured or nervous, and I can write." I blinked
rapidly. "So, when Covey came in and was in a rush . . ."

"Didn't he know you had dyslexia?" The postal inspector man again.

"Yes, he did. He took advantage of that, too, took advantage of my being embarrassed about it, took advantage of my trusting him."

"What about at work? How do you function?" the human calculator asked.

"I'm in sales now. A lot of my work is talking to people over the phone, talking to people about the orders we've received, meeting people, drawing and sketching out plans. I spell-check all my e-mails and I read and reread them. I remember what I was taught by my tutor, and try to relax. I didn't need to know how to write and read to become an artist."

I actually saw Dale nod. He stopped mid-nod, as if he hadn't meant to give that away.

I could hardly meet their eyes. I wanted to hunch my shoulders, disappear, but the tone in the room had changed. It wasn't so . . . bloodthirsty anymore.

I didn't know if they believed me or not.

The woman from the FBI put one of the legal papers in front of me that I'd signed. "Read this."

Millie objected. "What? Is that necessary?"

I felt like I'd been slapped back into grade school. They were all staring. Waiting to pounce. I wanted to slink into my seat, but over Millie's protestations I read it as best I could. I became more and more nervous, more agitated. I felt my eyes tearing up. I felt myself get hot. I read slowly to keep myself calm. I know I pronounced many of the words correctly, but not all. I must have skipped some and flipped letters in others, because I couldn't understand the unfamiliar words altogether. I stumbled. I said words out loud that didn't make sense next to each other. The words moved. I felt dizzy.

Two minutes later, when I burst into tears like a damn fool, my attorney stood up and yelled, something about boxing the crap out of Dale, and Dale yelled back and I said, "I'll do it, I'll do it."

I kept reading, or trying to read, stuttering through the docu-

WHAT I REMEMBER MOST 397

ment, while other Scary People jumped into the fray. One said that was enough, I shouldn't have to read more, and another said shut up. The FBI man said she could be faking it, the FBI woman said she's not faking it, she sounds exactly like my son and he has dyslexia, too. My attorney kept yelling, and I kept reading.

I stopped when Dale the owl leaned across the table and said, "Ms. Wild, let's take a break."

I walked out.

Squished. So low.

I was Nothing. White trash. Trailer trash. Foster kid. Dirty Grenadine. Stupido Grenado.

Again.

The meeting went on until eight that night. They asked many questions about Covey, his friends and associates, where he traveled, who visited the house, how many times he'd been to Vegas, our parties, what people from which foreign countries had been in our home, where he stashed cash, did we have a safe and where was it, and on and on. I knew the answers to some questions but not too many. By the end of it, I was looking out the window and wondering if I should jump.

"How much money did you take with you when you left Covey?" Dale asked.

"I had $520.46."

Dale raised his eyebrows. He seemed surprised. "$520.46? That's it?"

"Yes."

"No, Dina," Millie said, "they're asking about how much money you took with you that the court allowed you to take from yours and Covey's joint household account for living and legal expenses."

"I didn't take anything. I didn't know I could. My own personal and business accounts were frozen. I had $500 in my jewelry box, twenty dollars in my wallet, and I found change in my car under the seat."

"What?" Mille was absolutely baffled. "What are you talking about?"

"Where did you live in Pineridge when you first moved there?" Dale asked. "A hotel? An apartment? With a friend?"

I did not want to say I had lived in my car. It was hard enough to admit as a teenager. As an adult, it's a whole new level of degradation. "I had two jobs."

"When did you get those jobs?"

"Fairly soon after I arrived in Pineridge."

"When?"

"What does it matter?"

"It matters because something is not making sense here. You're being evasive. You're hiding something. Please answer the question."

"I lived with myself."

"One more time." Dale didn't hide his impatience. "*Where* did you live?"

"I live in an apartment above a barn."

He leaned forward, arms crossed. "Where did you live *initially,* Ms. Wild, when you arrived in Pineridge, with who, and how did you afford it?"

Homeless. She's homeless. No family. I heard those lonely words ping-ponging in my head. Poor-o Grenado. White trash foster kid.

I could stare down again, avoid their eyes. They knew I'd been in foster care. They knew I had dyslexia. They knew I was married to a criminal and believed me to be one, too. But suddenly I was tired of bending my head. I put my chin up. "I lived in my car."

"Your car?"

"Yes. An Acura MDX. I had it before I married Covey."

Millie groaned and slapped the table. "Homeless. Damn it. Why didn't you tell me? How did we miss this step? You had legal access to your joint account—"

"For how long?" Dale asked.

"Weeks. Many weeks." Miserable weeks, but I did it.

"You lived in your car," FBI lady said, appalled.

I nodded.

Postal service man shook his head. "Cold out."

The human calculator said, "That's rough."

Millie sighed and patted my arm. "You're my worst client, but you're the toughest."

Dale leaned back and steepled his hands.

Millie hugged me when we left and said I had "kicked some attorney ass."

I didn't believe that at all. I didn't think they believed me.

I had messages on my phone from Kade asking a couple of questions about a client. It was nothing important, though, and I knew he was calling to see how I was. He even said, "Grenady, I want you to know that you can always talk to me. You've seemed worried lately." I had asked him for a day off through e-mail, and he'd said, "Sure, but remember to come back."

Rozlyn's message said that she and Eudora had talked and the spying night on Leonard was on.

Cleo's message said she thinks it would be better if humans had glue on their hands so they could climb up buildings and trees. She said that Liddy missed me.

Rozlyn's "damned insurance" had denied the experimental procedure for her tumor. I was so upset I had to pull over. Cold, gut-wrenching fear and grief for Rozlyn followed me all through the night as I drove back home.

Covey called from another mysterious number, trying to avoid the recording device he believed was on his phone. I was a bitch and a traitor, but he still loved me and we could make this work, come by the house after the meeting. He didn't want to do what he'd been doing to me, but he could fix it, fix us.

The Santiam pass was frozen, snow fell, my car slipped several times, twice into the other lane. I did not go over the edge. It took more than four and a half white-knuckled hours to get home.

I thought about my last stint in jail. The light green paint on the walls, the fingerprinting and photos, the humiliation of the strip search and the get-naked-and-spread-your-butt-cheeks part.

I thought about the cells, the slits of windows, the slabs we slept on with the thin mattresses, the silver toilets attached to the silver sinks, being locked in, locked out, stuck. I thought about isolation. I thought about Cleo.

It was a long drive.

I arrived at one in the morning. I checked on Liddy, she neighed at me, I neighed at her, I gave her apple slices, then I headed upstairs to bed.

I lay awake all night, Alice, My Anxiety, running around unleashed, screeching, and watched the sun come up.

I prepared my mind for the tight walls of jail hell.

I was standing on a stepladder in the employees' lounge at seven o'clock on a Monday night with a paintbrush in my hand and one in my mouth when Kade walked in.

A bunch of the guys had helped me paint the employees' lounge a light yellow on Saturday. It hadn't taken long. Kade paid them extra, and I brought in pizza. There was a wall full of windows, so the room was now bright and cheerful.

I had taken photos of all the employees and framed them with rough wood frames, in keeping with the woods we used. Rozlyn and Eudora helped me, and we hung them together on the wall. Around all the frames, I painted another huge, rustic-looking frame with room, top and bottom and to the sides, for new employees. I liked the photos. They weren't formal. Some of the guys angled their faces close to the teeth of a huge saw, or sharp tool, as a joke. A few pulled on cowboy hats. One put on a bow tie.

Rozlyn wore a pink, feathered boa and Eudora wore a wide-rimmed, black hat, pulled partially down to hide half her face, those gorgeous cheekbones an elegant slash. Kade was Kade . . . sexy, smiling.

I bought a huge light, built from a wagon wheel, and hired Ernie to hang it from the ceiling. He muttered Shakespearean quotes as he worked.

I bought yellow and white picnic tablecloths and put them over each table, and I stuck daisies into vases I bought for a dollar apiece at Goodwill and placed them in the center.

On Sunday, and today, in between sales calls and e-mails, I painted Mt. Laurel, Brothers, and Ragged Top Mountain on the wall opposite the windows.

Kade was at a meeting out of town all day, but I knew he would be in tomorrow. I was, once again, nervous about what he would think of my work. Everyone seemed to like it, and I hoped he would, too.

When Kade walked in I about swallowed my paintbrush.

"Good job, Artist Lady."

I said, "You like it?" around my paintbrush.

He shook his head, admiringly. "Transformed again. From boring to perfect." He looked up at the employee wall and laughed. "Gotta love Martin's flamingo hat and Cory's T-shirt that says, 'I'm single.' "

"Hoping for a wife."

"And Petey's tuxedo jacket? That's hilarious. And Angelo holding up two wooden spoons."

"I didn't know he liked to cook."

"He's good at it, too."

He turned and stared at the mountain mural. I was painting a sunrise behind the peaks.

"Damn, Grenady. That's . . . that's . . . I don't even know what to say. I've never seen a painting of mountains that looked so . . . real. It's exactly what I stare out at every day."

"Now when you're eating in here, you can still stare at 'em." I grinned at him. He was pleased, so I was pleased. I climbed off the ladder. I knew I had blue and purple paint on my face, but I hadn't expected him back.

"I should make furniture that you can paint on," he said.

I laughed. But painting furniture had appeal. I loved the idea.

"I don't mean it as a joke, I'm serious. We could have a whole other line. The guys can build it, I'll carve it to your design, and you paint it."

Not from a jail cell, I couldn't. "Oh no."

"Oh yes. We could. We should." He put his hands on his hips, smiling. "Want to?"

Yes. But it wasn't going to work. I would soon be locked up like a rat. "You're serious?"

"Absolutely. We'll draw up a contract, split profits . . ."

"I'll think about it." I was touched. Fighting back emotion. "And thanks for asking, Kade."

"I think you should think yes. Quit The Spirited Owl and let's do it. Your oversized rocking chairs are selling faster than we can make them."

For a moment, I let myself dream. "If I did paint furniture, I think we should use bright colors. Fun designs. Whimsy, magical, even."

We both became more excited about the project as we talked.

"I'm ordering Chinese food," he said after a half hour.

I was starving. "I could use a fortune cookie."

"I could use a dozen. And shrimp, noodles, chicken . . ." He wandered off. Never get between a man and his food.

Maybe Kade and I would share one of those fortune cookies. We could chomp on the same one together until our lips touched and I leaped across the table like a horny banshee and tackled the poor man to the floor.

I was prejail horny. That's what it was. I went back to work. I had fifteen more minutes on the mural and it was done.

I was done, too.

"You've never talked about your family, Grenady. When I ask you, you sidestep, you dodge. Want to talk about them?"

I don't know why I opened up in Kade's office that night over white boxes of Chinese food and fortune cookies. Maybe it was because I felt old with worry. Worried about Rozlyn and Cleo, worried about jail. Maybe it was because I liked him so well. Maybe it was because I needed to talk to someone who cared.

I kept it brief, as brief as I could, but I told him. Gave him the bare outline. Lost parents, probably dead. Foster care. The abuse with the Berlinskys, which I skimmed over, but he still became upset. Lots of foster homes. Living in cars. Running away. Homeless. Hospital trips. Scary and sad group homes. Dabbling in drugs, alcohol, and sex as a lost, lonely teenager. I told him about the love of the Hutchinsons and the Lees, my last foster care parents.

"Let's talk about something else," I said. "What are you working on?"

"No. Please. Go on." He was shaken, I could tell.

I stumbled, I mumbled. He prodded and held my hand. He wiped his eyes again.

"I remember happy times with my parents. I had a memory of flying a red kite with my dad and mom, someone else was there, too, I can't remember who, then I woke up in a hospital. My screaming woke me up." I told him about the trucker, the police, the deep cut on my hairline that was bleeding profusely when I was found, my concussion, the search for my parents. "I don't know where I'm from, Kade. I don't know who I am, I don't know my parents' real names or if they had families. I don't know what happened. I think they were probably killed. I felt their love, so I think it's highly improbable that they abandoned me."

By the end he was holding his head in his hands. I tried to comfort the tough guy with the soft heart.

It didn't do much good, so I cried, too. I don't like seeing people cry. "I'm sorry, Kade. I didn't mean to make you cry. I'm so sorry."

"Grenady." He stood up, walked around the table, pulled me up, and hugged me. I sank right into him, my scarred hands around his back, my scarred forehead against his shoulder. It was as if I'd hugged him a thousand times, as if we fit, as if we had our hugs down pat.

That night I was too preoccupied with sweet Kade and his tears to sleep.

He was upset about my childhood, and I had only told him about a tenth of it.

Afterward, because it was so late and he wanted to make sure I arrived home safely, he insisted on following me to my apartment above the red barn, then he went home. I liked the feeling of being protected.

I turned off the lights, lit a vanilla scented candle, and took a bubble bath. When I was done, I wiped the steam off the mirror and turned around, studying the scars on my back. The ones on my hands were light, hardly noticeable. The two on my fore-head—one from that night, one from the veteran who was lost in his own war nightmare—were covered by my hair for the most part. Kade had scars, too. He understood mine. They would not be a turnoff. They might make him cry, though. . . .

I later stared across the room at my unfinished collage with the magnifying glass, the girl dressed in lilies, the dark forest, and the outline of the lighthouse. It reminded me of something or someone I didn't want to think about, but I didn't know what. It felt like the memory was getting closer, clearer. I needed my own mental magnifying glass to see it.

I took a sketch pad out from a nightstand I'd bought at Goodwill for ten dollars, then drew a snake wrapped around a knife. I held it up and stared at it, then stared at the lighthouse again. What was their tie? Was there a tie?

I shredded it into tiny pieces, then drew lilies with pastel pencils.

One lily, after another, after another.

I heard their voices. *Do you want to paint with me? Do you want to draw with me? Let's draw lilies.*

Light pink with burgundy and yellow centers.

Deep purple with a golden strike.

A bearded lily with dark and light blue mixed.

A field of lilies, mountains in the distance.

A jail.

I dropped the pencils.

The next morning Cleo popped up before I left for work. I heard her banging up the stairs singing a song about a chicken and a horse, a chicken and a horse, "cluck cluck, neigh neigh, oink oink."

She was wearing a white nightgown with lace, her flowered rainboots, and a hat with a pink pig.

"I brought you cookies, Grenady. Pinwheels. Me and Mommy made them."

"Thank you. My day is now delicious."

"Ya. Cookies make it delicious. I have some in my lunch. I can't wait until lunch. On Saturday are we going to paint together again?"

"We sure are."

"Good." She jumped up and down, the pig snout flopping. "Saturdays are my favorite days now because you don't have to work until the night."

She clomped back down the stairs.

"Bye, Grenady, I love you!"

"Love you, too, baby."

I let my whole body droop against the kitchen counter, as if I were wilting. Alice, My Anxiety, roared on in . . . and then, about five minutes later, she left. Like that. Gone.

It was a clear, cold winter day. Blue and white. Snowy and crisp. I had another cup of coffee with whipped cream and I enjoyed the heck out of it.

I made my decision.

45

He loved spiders, so it was one of his favorite nursery rhymes.

The itsy bitsy spider went up the water spout.
Down came the rain and washed the spider out.
Out came the sun and dried up all the rain
And the itsy bitsy spider went up the spout again.

He thought he'd change that poem. It was too cheerful. He'd make it about Danny. Danny would like that.

The scary, furry spider went up the water spout.
Down came the people when the blood spurted out.
Out came the devil and dried up all the blood
And the scary, furry spider went out to kill again.

Oh, that was *genius*. He thought of a furry spider. He drew a furry spider with his pencil, then reached down his pants and pulled out pubic hair and laid it over the paper to make the spider hairy.

Danny started yelling at him again, telling him what to do. He didn't like Danny. He never had.

He cried all over his rhyme book and the pubic hair spider.

46

"Sunday night's the night," Rozlyn said, handing me a pink pin-wheel cookie across the table in the employees' lounge. "Cleo's spending the night at a friend's because there's no school the next day, and Grenady doesn't work."

"The night for what?" I asked. I loved Rozlyn's pinwheel cookies.

"For Spying On Leonard Night," Eudora said. "I'll get all critical supplies and inform you of our strategy."

Rozlyn nodded. "Fab. I don't want to get caught."

"Get caught?" Eudora scoffed, seeming offended. "We will never get caught. I know what I'm doing."

At one o'clock in the morning, after my shift at The Spirited Owl, I put on my coat, grabbed my sketch pad and charcoal pencil, and sat outside on my deck. I breathed in the cold mountain air and tried to settle myself and Alice, My Anxiety, back down. Alice was giving me a hard time lately.

I drew a picture of a girl in front of a mud pie birthday cake she'd made for herself using sticks for candles. I drew a picture of her in juvenile detention, angry and scared. I drew a picture of her running away into the night, alone, a bag over her shoulder.

When I was able to breathe normally, my mind not so frazzled, I put my sketch pad away.

Past in back.

For now.

Again.

We met at Rozlyn's house at eight o'clock Sunday night. We were all wearing black. Eudora had even brought us black ski masks. The ski masks reminded me of the creeps who broke into my car months ago, but I slipped mine on, anyhow. I wouldn't let them control me.

Eudora opened up a bag and dumped its contents on the kitchen table. I could not believe what I was seeing.

Night vision goggles.

An old-fashioned pen with a recording device. ("If he's talking, we'll record it and listen for clues later," Eudora said.)

A small drill. ("In case we choose to hide the listening device inside his home.")

An antique-looking hollow lipstick. ("So we can pass messages to each other.")

A compact that when turned towards the light had numbers reflected in the mirror. ("We don't need any code work yet. But still.")

She gave us detailed instructions about how to be a competent spy. Be aware. Listen. Multitask. Eye on the target. Know your escape route.

Eudora announced that she would drive the car there and back, headlights off, and could drive backward at a high speed in case we're chased. (She included this gem: "Do not give in to torture for as long as possible if you're caught. We will come back for you.")

"I'll give you a short lesson on how to use the devices, and how to survey the target without detection, then we will proceed on our mission," Eudora said. "Listen closely."

We listened closely. She sounded like a drill sergeant, so now and then Rozlyn and I leaped to our feet, saluted, and shouted, "Yes, ma'am!"

A half hour later, we were crawling on our bellies through the wet, cold, icy grass of Leonard's property. We wore all black. We wore our black ski masks and black gloves. Rozlyn and I had binoculars. Eudora had the night vision goggles.

Rozlyn and I could not help laughing as we slithered, even though Eudora glared at us.

"I'm a spy snake!" Rozlyn hissed.

"I'm 008," I hissed back. "Spy Woman. One moment, please. I have to call for my flying car."

"I want more spy gadgets," she whined. "I want a spy gadget between my bosoms."

"Oh boy! Now I have a vision, Roz!" I couldn't stop laughing. I could not believe I was on a spying adventure, butt in the air.

"Nice ass," Rozlyn whispered, straddling my bod.

"Thank you."

We laughed so hard when we crawled through an icy mud puddle, Rozlyn said, "Stop . . . stop making me laugh . . . oh no . . . I wet my pantaloons!"

This made me laugh and I squirted, too, covered in mud, and told Rozlyn about my wee-wee accident, and that made her wet her panties again. "I hate my menopause bladder!" she gasped.

"What's my excuse?"

"Do a Kegel!"

"Here I go! Kegeling!" I squeezed. It didn't help at all.

It started to rain halfway through our mud crawl to Leonard's house, which made Rozlyn and me laugh even harder.

"I'm a soaked and horny hormonally off-balanced rat," she whispered to me.

"I'm a sexy snake," I whispered back. She moved in front of me, and I told her, "It's a pleasure to be this close to your butt."

She stopped, head down, then crossed her knees, her whole body shaking as she laughed.

"Don't pee now, Rozlyn. You'll hit me." Her butt moved up and down as she laughed, which about did me in. I made high-pitched gaspy sounds and said, "Hold, bladder, hold!"

Eudora snapped, "Control yourselves! Anything can happen on a mission, and you have to be ready to react."

"Yes, like bladder loss," Rozlyn said. "I bet that happens to special agents all the time."

"Or you could become a slinky mud snake." I picked up my binoculars and looked through them at Rozlyn's butt. She saw what I was doing and howled. Then she picked up her binoculars and pointed them right at me. Then we put our binoculars together, and Eudora took off her night vision goggles and declared, "You're being unprofessional."

"Quit staring at me!" I whisper-shouted.

"No! You quit staring at me!" Rozlyn said, giving me a shove. I shoved her back, she shoved again, and we both ended up in the cold, wet mud. I took my hand and put mud on her black mask. She did the same to me. Then she rolled on top of me, and I pushed her off and rolled on her, with Eudora insisting that we "stop that mud wrestling this instant! Focus! Focus!"

When we finally creepy-crawled to Leonard's house and poked our muddy heads above the window, black masks on, panties wet with pee, what did we see?

Leonard, watching a TV show, hands on his knees!

Alone. Yes, he was alone. No girlfriend in sight.

We surveyed the target for a while, and Rozlyn said, "I could straddle him on his easy chair and ride him like a bucking bull" and "I'm imagining him and me on that couch together. As one" and "Do you think he's turned on by muddy girls?"

I said, "You can tell by the way that he's watching TV that he's full of testosterone and lust."

"You betcha," Rozlyn said. "Streaming out of him."

We shimmied back through the grass, smothering laughter, butts up.

When I was only a foot behind Rozlyn she accidentally farted, a true ripper, and we laughed so hard we had to lay down. Then she farted again, a medium snooker, then a giggly fart that came out like a small machine gun. "Oh, stop, bottom, stop!" she demanded.

"Yes, do stop!" I buried my hands in my face.

"Bottom!" Rozlyn reprimanded her back end. "Get control! Squeeze!"

Eudora said, "You're both fired. You're going home. I'll get you desk jobs."

When we had finally slunk like mud wrestlers to the end of the property and "reconvened" at the car, Rozlyn was euphoric. "I knew it. He's single." She dripped water and mud. "Now I have to hike my nerve up to ask him out."

I didn't even bother flicking the mud off. "After all this, you'd better. It's not every day I have to follow your laughing, farting bottom through mud and water."

Eudora said, "Mission complete. You two were terrible, though. A disgrace to this country. It's a wonder we got out alive."

Rozlyn and I cracked up again and peeled off our black ski masks after we took photos with our cell phones of the three of us for immortalization. We each tried on the night vision goggles and took more photos. We posed as if we were holding guns, pointer fingers in the air.

"I'm afraid I might be suffering from vaginal dryness," Rozlyn said. "Let's complete this critical spy journey by going to the pharmacy."

We went to the pharmacy because of vaginal dryness. It was late, and the store was empty, which was a good thing since we were wet, muddy, and probably smelled like pee, which made us laugh even harder, and Rozlyn and I had to cross our legs in the middle of the aisle and do our Kegels while making attractive choking-snorting sounds.

"You're hopeless," Eudora said. "I'm very disappointed in your spying abilities and your inability to competently execute a mission."

Rozlyn bought another tube of anti-dry vagina cream. "Bring it on, Leonard. I'm gonna give you 225 pounds of loving you won't forget. I will shake you down and turn you around and spin you up." She shook her bosoms. "Everything in my imagination will become my reality."

"Well done, ladies," I said when we returned to Eudora's car. I pulled my black ski mask on and crossed my eyes at both of them. "We should have worked for the CIA."

Eudora raised her eyebrows at me.

"Okay." I corrected myself, putting the binoculars up and pointing them right at Eudora's face. "Maybe only you, Eudora, you spy queen, you."

I called Millie.

"I'm changing my plea."

"You're what?" She sounded like she was panting.

"What are you doing, Millie?"

"I'm boxing. Hang on. Okay, what did you say?"

"I'm changing my plea."

She panted harder, like a bull. "What the hell are you talking about?"

"I'm pleading guilty. I'm taking the eighteen months."

I actually heard her pounding the bag, swear words streaming from her mouth.

I thought about Kade. Strong, smart, calm Kade.

I was dreading telling him the truth. Dreading seeing the disappointment in his eyes, the anger, the betrayal.

I had not been honest with him about my arrest and flight out of Portland because it benefitted me.

It was all about me.

I had hoped, unrealistically, for a fairy tale miracle from Covey, that this would all go away, but I knew there was none coming. I had always known it. And yet I still did what I wanted in terms of my employment with Kade, even though it could backfire on him and the reputation of his company.

I picked up my phone.

"Kade? Hi. It's me, Grenady. Do you have a minute?"

We sat out on his deck, in jackets, the sky clear and silky blue, his backyard endless. I felt like I was sitting in artwork, a nature collage that moved, invisible brushes changing the scenery in front of us. A hawk dove, the trees swayed, the weather rolled through. Layers of colors and textures, all framed by the snowcapped blue and purple mountains. There was a tiny patch of fog in the distance, but it didn't bother me so much since I was sitting with Kade.

I would try to forget this view when I was in jail, or it would kill me.

I brought deli sandwiches and praline ice cream with me. He smiled sweetly when I walked in.

"Hi, Kade. Sorry to barge in on you like this. I brought lunch."

"Barge in anytime, Grenady. Oh, hey, you didn't need to bring lunch, but I'll eat it. That was kind of you." He grabbed a couple of beers. "Want to eat outside?"

"Sure."

We chatted while I handed him a sandwich, then we settled in.

"How are you?"

His smile was gonna kill me. I would have to forget that smile, too. I put my hands in my lap to control all the shaking they were doing. "Not well."

His eyes flickered. He put his sandwich down and leaned forward. "What's wrong?"

"First, I want to apologize to you. I have loved working for you, and I'm so grateful for the job."

"Thanks. But what's going on?"

"I lied to you."

He did not seem surprised.

"You don't seem surprised."

"I know you did."

"How do you know?"

"I looked you up on the Internet."

"But . . . But, I'm going by my real Grenadine Scotch Wild, not . . ." I paused.

"Dina Hamilton? Dina Wild?"

"Right."

"It doesn't take much anymore to find things out about a person, does it?" He smiled. "Especially when one of your best friends from childhood is a private detective."

"Oh, groan. Which one?"

"You remember Ricki Lopez?"

"Yes. I do. But I thought you said he worked for a man who worked for the government..." Ah. It clicked. "He was a private contractor. As in, a private detective. What made you ask him about me?"

"I could tell you were lying."

"Bad liar, I am. I know it. I don't have enough practice."

"And you were scared to death. That was a clue for me." His eyes were so gentle.

"What do you mean?"

"In the interview. And at lunch at Bernie's. In the bar when you worked and you knew I was watching you, you were nervous. I could smell the fear on you. I knew something was up. You were less than forthcoming. You dodged my questions, you changed the subject, your eyes would skitter away from mine. About a hundred other clues."

"And you didn't hire me at first."

"No. I had to figure out what was going on."

"And you did."

"Yes."

"Why go to all the trouble? Why didn't you toss my application and hire someone else? And if you knew what was going on, why did you hire me?"

"Because I liked you. You're smart. You wanted the job. I knew you'd work hard, because I saw you working at The Spirited Owl. I knew you'd represent the company well when people came in and when they called because you're articulate and friendly. You listen. You're an artist, so I knew you'd have an eye for what I was trying to do. Plus, you knew my furniture. You knew it well. You even knew which woods we used, and we had a great conversation about it. You had opinions on the pieces. And you're charming. And kind."

"I don't feel charming or kind. I feel awful. I can't tell you how awful. I am so sorry I lied. A hundred times over, Kade, I am so sorry. This could backlash on you and your company."

"It won't, I'm not worried, and I understand. You were desperate. I was desperate for much of my childhood. I was desper-

WHAT I REMEMBER MOST 415

ate in jail and desperate when I was first released, until I could make money. And . . ."

"And what?"

He shifted in his seat, set his eyes on Broken Top, then back to me. "And I knew you were sleeping in your car."

"You did?" Oh, let this deck open so I could drop through and disappear. "How?"

"I was driving home the night you and I talked at the bar and I saw your car parked alongside the road. I saw you in it. So, I knew if what you were accused of was true, you wouldn't be dead broke. You wouldn't be living in your car. If you had embezzled funds, you would have had money stashed somewhere."

"I didn't have any money stashed anywhere. I had $520.46 when I left Covey, in cash. My personal and business accounts were frozen."

"I also knew that if you were the type of person who cared about comfort, you would not have left your home. You would have stayed where there was a roof, a bed, a kitchen, but you didn't. You would rather live in your car than stay with Covey. That told me a lot about you, your courage, determination, and strength, your noninvolvement in Covey's business and, frankly, your level of hatred for your husband."

"I am trying not to hate him," I said. "It's hard. I want to kill him most days."

"I can imagine. I want to kill him, too."

"First for what he did to other people who entrusted their money to him. It wasn't all wealthy people who could lose a few hundred thousand, even though that's so wrong, too. It was regular people, with normal incomes. He convinced them he could make them a fortune. They will now get pennies on the dollar back. For sure many will never retire. They will never be able to put their kids through college. Their savings are gone. And, for what he did to me . . ." I waved my hands. "You know I've been charged with theft, fraud, embezzlement, money laundering?"

"Yes."

"I had no idea what Covey was doing, Kade." I bit my lip, tried not to cry. "None. I was married to him for a year, and I knew I'd made a mistake a few months into it." I told him about Covey's possessiveness, the tracking devices, the cameras, Covey's anger. I told him how Covey had implicated me and told me I had to move back in with him or he would cook me like a dead possum on a grill in trial and how I'd refused. I told him about my stint in jail.

Kade stood up and stalked across his deck, a hand pushing his black hair back. He was furious. He swore, swore again. I wanted to hug him, but I didn't. I stood up and walked over to him.

"I wanted to talk to you about this, Grenady, but you were so closed. So private. So defensive when I offered to help you. It was clear that you didn't want to talk. I was waiting—"

"Waiting for what?"

"I was waiting for you to trust me and tell me yourself."

"I hardly trust anyone, Kade."

"I wish you would trust me."

I took a deep breath. I could trust Kade, I knew I could. I wish I had sooner. "I have to tell you something else."

"Something else? What is it?"

"I'm pleading guilty."

He was shocked. I still felt shocked.

"What do you mean? I thought you had an upcoming trial?"

"I'm going back in to talk to the assistant U.S. attorney on my case. I told him I was innocent, but I'm changing my plea."

"Why in God's name would you do that? You do have an attorney? Is she asleep?"

"No, she's a kick-butt kind of lady. I recently told her I was pleading guilty. She advised against it. She yelled and threw a fit and threatened to box me. But the thought of spending five years in jail . . ." I clenched my jaw so I wouldn't cry.

"Damn. You don't want to risk it, do you? But you have to, Grenady. You have to fight this."

"I can't." I paused. I told him what Covey had sworn to do, about the signed documents, the unpredictability of a jury. And, because I could not stand to have anything between Kade and me again, I told him about Rozlyn and sweet Cleo.

He hung his head.

We talked, round and round, his free-ranging anger at Covey impressive, his worry for me touching. When there was nothing more to say, when I would not relent on my plea, he held me close, my forehead in his neck, my arms linked over his shoulders, his arms around my waist.

He cried. I could feel his tears on my cheeks. Warm, gentle teddy bear.

I don't know who moved first, but our lips caught and held and fire ripped through my body, the sexy kind of fire, the intoxicating yum of fire. For a second I thought I should pull back, stop, but I didn't want to, not one iota of me wanted to stop, plus he was holding me tight, his lips moving on mine.

My head tilted back as he kissed me in a manly and take-charge sort of way, and I let go of my entrenched anxiety, my past chaos, my future jail cell, and I kissed him back with all I had, riding lust up into that nature collage that moved.

Kade picked me up and carried me up the stairs to his bedroom, like out of some romance movie, and laid me down, our lips hardly leaving each other's.

"I want you to know, Grenady," he said, as I hurriedly unzipped his jacket and pushed it off those broad shoulders, "I have never dated, or even flirted, with any of my employees, not that there has ever been anyone working for me I ever wanted to date, but I'm going to have to temporarily fire you."

I pulled away for a second as our clothes went flying off— shirt, bra, panties, his jeans. "Don't fire me. I quit."

"Got it," he said, his chest heaving, his arms around naked me. My, was he well hung! We fell back onto the pillows. "I temporarily accept your resignation."

We tumbled around that bouncy, cuddly bed with the bald eagles who mated for life, and I wrapped my legs around those tight and manly thrusting hips and that hard butt as I had thought and dreamed and obsessed of doing a thousand times.

*   *   *

Kade was a gifted and delicious lover. Gifted from the skies, the moon, butterflies, the galaxy, and all things hot and sexy.

He was awesome.

I lost myself in that man and that man's hands and mouth. I did not worry about the scars on my hands or the scars on my back or the scars near my hairline. I have never let go with any man like I did Kade. I have always held back, always held *myself* back, but not so with him. I fell in deep, free, and I cherished it all.

It was heated and steaming the first time, slower and gentler and explosive the next time. In the darkness he kissed every scar, on my forehead, my back, my hands, and I kissed his.

We had a lot of scars to kiss.

"I couldn't hire you at first for the reasons I already told you, but Ricki got the info I needed back to me pretty quick. I still didn't hire you. Want to know why?" Kade asked, the moon shining through his windows, like white magic.

"Yes, why?" I was curled up next to him, his arm around my shoulders.

"Because I wanted to date you."

"You did?" I leaned over him, safe and warm, my boobs on his chest.

"Yes. I saw you in McDonald's."

"Now, that's not what I wanted to hear." I remembered that morning. Living in my car. Sicker than a dog. Exhausted. Asleep in the booth, probably with my tongue hanging out. I put my hand over my face. He removed my hand and kissed me. "I am so embarrassed."

"Don't be embarrassed, honey. Please. I see this woman with all this dark red hair in the booth." He picked up my hair, ran it through his fingers. "I knew you didn't live in town, that you were visiting, or new here and, I don't know, Grenady, what it was, I don't. But when I saw you, I actually stopped walking, stopped moving."

"I could hardly breathe. It was this instant . . . lust. Instant attraction."

"For me too." He grinned. Not such a tough guy anymore. "Then you arrived at Hendricks' for the interview and I liked you so much, I could hardly talk, hardly focus, but I had to hide the attraction and see what was behind the secrets and the fear. It was a tough day on my brain."

"Poor you." I kissed him, and he kissed me back and rolled on top of me, his elbows propping him up.

"I was going to ask you out after we had lunch at Bernie's, but I had cold feet."

"You. Kade Hendricks? You had cold feet?"

"Hell, yeah. And when Moose sang to you, even though I could tell you wanted to escape, I was pissed. Here I was, wanting to ask you out and that lunatic gets up and starts in on his opera."

"You could have sung, too, Kade."

"You do not want to hear me sing, honey."

"Yes, I do. It would be music to my ears." Like the word *honey* is.

"But the wanting to date you and not hiring you because of it changed when I found out you were living in your car. Then it was more important to me that you had a job and a home than I had you. So I called the next day. It was my intent to get you into an apartment or a rental house immediately. In fact, I had about five calls in to people I knew who rented their homes out, but then I heard you were living above Rozlyn's barn in the apartment."

"Thank you for looking for a place for me to live, Kade, and thank you for hiring me." What an awesome man he was.

"My pleasure, darlin'. You're the best."

I drew a finger down his cheek. I kissed him, long and slow, and we both teared up, messy and snuffly.

"I love you, Grenady."

"I love you, too, Kade." I became even weepier. "I fought off my feelings as hard as I could because my life was such a mess and I have trust issues and I have anxiety and you're sexy and huge."

"I didn't fight off my feelings at all. I tried to hide them from you, but they were always there. It feels like I've been waiting for you to arrive my whole life." He sniffled.

"I feel the same. I've wanted you for forever." I hugged him close and wrapped my legs around him. The man looks like the gang leader he used to be, but his heart, ah, that heart, so beautiful, so loving.

"And now you're finally here." He kissed me again . . . and we kissed the other's tears away.

Kade cried in my arms Sunday night. He tried not to let me see it, but I did, and I insisted the gentle bear let me see it.

The next morning, after we made love, I hugged him like I was never going to let him go. My bones felt cold. My body felt cold.

"Let me go with you."

"No." We had already been over this, many times.

"Let me drive you, please. I'm begging you, Grenady."

"No. I'm driving myself."

He argued; I put my hand on his mouth, then kissed him. When I was dressed, he walked me to my car and hugged me close.

"Grenady, I'll see you when you get back."

When I returned to Pineridge, my life would be shaken, stirred, and upside down again. The cold was spreading, head to foot. Alice, My Anxiety, was unhinged, her hysteria barely smothered.

Kade kissed me hard and held me to his chest. Our tears mixed and blended and dropped, then I yanked myself away and drove off.

I did not look back.

Freezing.

Frozen.

Dying of cold.

Hello, Alice!

WHAT I REMEMBER MOST   421

*   *   *

I went back home and talked to Rozlyn. She was on the couch with an ice pack on her head. She told me her head was banging like a "drum being played by a teenager who doesn't know what he's doing." I gave her her medication and called Eudora to come and sit with her so she could run her to the hospital if necessary.

Then I told her what I was going to do. She deserved to know.

"Are you pleading guilty and taking eighteen months because of me?" She gripped my hand, tears streaming. "Be honest."

"No. I'm taking the eighteen months because I'll be burned at the stake at the trial. Think about it, Rozlyn. Even my own husband is prepared to say, in endless detail, how he and I ran his business together and how I was an active participant in gaining new clients. He has even used the word *mastermind* to explain my role. Can't beat that."

"Grenady, I am so sorry." She waved her hands in front of her face, then flushed, then burst into another round of tears.

The truth was, I wanted to be out of jail as soon as possible for Cleo and Rozlyn. But I am realistic, too. There was a chilling chance I would go to jail for five years. Would I have gone to trial without Rozlyn's tumor? Yes. I'm ticked off. I don't want to do time for something I didn't do. But eighteen months was the better and more rational decision now and, probably, the better option no matter what.

If Rozlyn knew what role she played in my decision, she would feel guilty, overwhelmed, and blame herself. The stress of my being in prison, and not taking a chance at a trial, would make her health worse. I think somewhere deep inside she knew, but her head was hurting too much, her panic too high, her death hanging too close, to think as she normally would. And she is a mother. Her first priority was, is, and always will be Cleo. I got it.

"I'm so sorry, Grenady, soul sister." She patted her heart. "I am so sorry. I love you."

"Love you, too, Rozlyn, soul sister." Our tears ran together when I bent to hug her.

My eyes fell on my lily bracelet. It still sparkled after all these years. I would have thought the sprayed-on gold would have faded, but it hadn't. I would leave it with Rozlyn, my friend, while I was in jail. For luck. In friendship. A promise to her I would be back to be with her and Cleo.

Cleo hopped in a minute later wearing foil wrapped around her from neck to knee. "Hi, Grenady! I'm a Uranus zombie."

On my drive to Portland, through the snowy, icy, curving Santiam Pass, I replayed my delicious time with Kade, every caress, stroke, moan, sigh and pant, my heart racing, his keeping pace with mine. I thought of kissing his mouth, his face, his neck, his chest, lower. I have never been a huge fan of blow jobs, but for him, and seeing how much pleasure he got out of it, how it made him lose control in a sexy way, well, I've now changed my mind.

Blow jobs for Kade, and Kade only.

I thought of how I'd run my hands over the scars on his back, the bullet hole, the knife swipes. I thought of how strong and solid he felt in my arms, how I felt in his as he held me close. I thought of his voice, what he said, his love, his strength, his courage, and how he had the strength and courage to cry.

I missed him.

"Ms. Wild," Dale Kotchik, stern and solemn assistant U.S. attorney, said to me, "I understand you want to talk to us about your plea."

"I do. I am changing my plea."

He blinked a couple of times, then steepled his hands together like last time. The whole Scary Gang from the first meeting was there: the IRS, the FBI special agents, including the human calculator, the postal service mail fraud man, the woman from the finance and corporate services division, assistants, and other suits.

They all stared back at me at that long table in the intimidating building in the expensive office in downtown Portland, with the furniture made by prisoners.

"Why?" Dale asked.

"Because I'm guilty." My hands were clasped, tight and white. I was wearing my black skinny slacks, knee-high black boots, and a thick burgundy sweater with a clasp in front over a black turtleneck. I was freezing cold.

"I'm going to tell you one more time, Dina," Millie said, so mad she leaned all the way into my arm, inches from my nose and spit out, "Do not say another word. Let's leave now."

"No, Millie."

"This is a mistake."

"Guilty of what?" Dale said.

Millie made a loud, guttural groaning sound. "Think, Dina. Think. I want it on the record that I have advised my client against this. She is not guilty."

"I'm guilty of signing those documents," I said, "and I knew what I was doing."

Millie threw her head back and swore at the ceiling. "You've lost your head. Where is your brain? Are you not capable of rational thought?" She gave Dale one of her piercing glares. "She's innocent. You know the lying, arrogant, narcissistic, possessive husband. She's doing this because of him."

There was a tense silence in the room . . . and something else. I saw those seriously anal people exchange glances with each other. One coughed. A couple wiggled in their chairs.

"Which papers in particular, Ms. Wild?" Dale asked.

"All of them that I said I signed and all of them I said I didn't sign." Damn but I hated that butthole Covey. "The ones where I said my signature was forged, I signed."

"And you're signing away your life," Millie sputtered. She grabbed my arm and squeezed it. She is quite strong. "You should not be doing this. Please shut your mouth."

I didn't blame Millie for her electric fury. It's her job to defend me to the best of her ability, and she could not do it with a client like me. I was grateful to her. She had worked hard for me. She'd been honest, and tough, from the get-go. Now I was messing things up.

"Dina," she snapped. "We all saw those signatures. They're not yours."

"Yes, they are."

"No, they're not."

"Sometimes I . . . I write differently."

"No, you don't." Millie shook her head so vehemently her black curls whipped her face.

"Yes, I do."

Dale leaned forward in his seat. I saw the FBI lady raise her eyebrows at the FBI human calculator. The IRS people stared hard at me.

"I don't understand," Dale said. "You said you signed five of the documents last time we met. Now you've requested this meeting and you're saying you signed all of them."

"What is there not to understand? I'm pleading guilty." I felt myself leaving me. I felt myself shutting down and shutting out. I felt myself, the myself I'd gained in the last months in Pineridge, working for Kade and Tildy, making friends with Rozyln and Eudora, painting with Cleo and starting my art again, fading, smearing away, getting lost in the fog.

"To which charges are you pleading guilty to?"

"All of them that I was charged with."

"All of them?"

"Yes."

"Can you list those charges for us?"

"Fraud. Embezzlement. Theft . . ." There was another one. "Money laundering."

Millie cut in. "My client had no idea what her maniacal husband was doing. She's having a mental breakdown of some sort." She put her face too close to mine again. "You are not guilty."

"Then why is she pleading guilty?" Dale asked.

"Because her creepola of a husband is threatening to bring her down with him. Because she doesn't want to risk a trial. You people have scared the crap out of her. She's pleading guilty to get the eighteen months you already offered and not risk five years. This is not justice, this is a woman who has been badgered and threatened into pleading guilty."

I had not told Millie that the other reason I was pleading guilty was because I needed to be out in eighteen months for Rozlyn and Cleo. If I had, she would have told all these scary people, because she's my attorney and has been charged with aiding in my defense, and that information would have ended the meeting. Intimidating Assistant U.S. Attorney Dale Kotchik would not allow me to plead guilty at that point knowing why I was doing it.

Then I would have to go to trial and risk five years.

Dale thrummed his fingers on the table. "Tell us why you're guilty, Ms. Wild."

"You already know, Dale." I was a little irritated. I could tell he was surprised that I'd used his first name.

"Tell us anyhow. Give us the details so we're all clear."

"I will. But I want your word that my jail sentence will be eighteen months if I tell you what I know."

"We've already discussed that."

"Say it."

"If you cooperate and you're guilty, your sentence will be eighteen months."

I studied him and his owl features. He was relentless. Smart. Dedicated. Like an owl pit bull. But he was honest, and he had authority. Though he'd been my nightmare, I actually trusted him.

He suddenly leaned forward, as if he'd made a decision. "Ms. Wild, did you help Covey Hamilton, your husband, move money from one investment account to another to hide it?"

No. I wouldn't even know how to do that, but this was it. I felt myself sinking into an iceberg. "Yes."

"For God's sakes. For all hell's sakes," Millie sputtered. "She did not do that. She wouldn't even know how."

"Yes, I would." I was slightly offended that Millie thought I couldn't do that, even though I couldn't.

"No, you wouldn't."

"Yes."

"No!"

"How did you move the money around?" FBI lady asked with her brown hair and, again, a brown suit.

How? I had no idea. Over the phone? Do you call banks for that stuff? Aha! I remembered. "By signing the papers. That gave Covey the ability to move the money. It gave my permission. My signed permission."

"You knew he was moving around the money, then?"

Hell, no. "Yes."

"She did not!" Millie interjected.

"To banks?"

No. "Yes."

"To offshore accounts?"

No. "Yes."

"She's a lying client!" Millie said.

"To shell companies?"

No. "Yes."

For a moment, no one spoke in that room with the furniture built by people in prison.

Dale adjusted his glasses. He clasped his hands. He bent his head then, after a few seconds, lifted it again. "Ms. Wild, did you know that Mr. Hamilton was moving money to shell companies in Thailand?"

Thailand? What the heck? "Yes."

"Thailand?" Millie semishrieked.

"And to the stock markets in France and Russia?"

France and Russia? Had they talked about that earlier? "Uh . . .yes."

"What in tarnation are you talking about?" Millie said, pounding a fist. "When did France come into this?"

"So you knew," Dale said, owl eyes never leaving mine. "That Covey had created an artificial tech company in Kansas to launder money?"

That shithead. "Yes."

"And a metal scrap business in North Carolina to launder money?"

I wished I could put Covey under one of those scrap metal smashing machines. "Yes."

"And you knew about the fake ball bearings factory in Utah?"

Ball bearings? Covey needed *balls*. "Uh. Yes."

"What the hell is going on here?" Millie demanded. "I didn't know about any of this. What happened to disclosure?"

There was a dead silence in that room. I felt the intensity, the judgment. I tilted my chin up and wrapped my arms around my waist. Colder and colder.

Dale rubbed his chin. IRS man rolled his shoulders. FBI brown woman tilted her head and studied me like a bug.

More silence. A couple of the seriously anal people shuffled papers. They exchanged glances with each other, then back to me. I didn't know what was going on.

"You're pleading guilty, but you could go to trial," Dale said. "You could be found not guilty."

"And I could be found guilty. You said you would ask for five years, at least, of jail time." My voice wobbled. I teared up. I thought of Rozlyn. I thought of Cleo.

I thought of Kade.

I thought of myself. Five years. I would lose my mind. I know I would. I would shut down so hard I wouldn't come out of myself.

Eighteen months, though, and I would be out in time to help Rozlyn at the end and be a mom to Cleo. I would be a wreck when I came out, but I could put myself back together. I could.

I wiped the tears off my cold cheeks with cold fingers.

They waited.

Tears filled my eyes again. I wiped them off again. My fingers were freezing, and so was my face. Millie patted my shoulder a bit too hard. "We're done," she snapped. "We've got broken rules all over the place here. No one informed me about France or Russia or Thailand or any ball bearings factory. Let's go, Dina."

I felt that familiar depression settling on my shoulders. Black and heavy. I felt an unbearable sadness. I started to feel claustrophobic thinking about being trapped in a cell. I wondered if I would see Neanderthal Woman again. Alice, My Anxiety, buried her head. I saw a red kite. And fog. Dark trees. I don't know why.

"Ms. Wild," Dale said.

"Yes?"

"We have a problem here."

"Yes, I know." I swear there was ice around my heart.

"I don't think you do." He leaned back in his chair. "Covey did not set up a shell company in Thailand. He did not move money into the stock markets in France and Russia. There is no artificial tech company, no metal scrap business, and no fake ball bearings factory."

"There isn't?" I asked

"No," Dale said.

"Oh."

"And now we have to ask you why you just lied to us about your involvement with Covey's business when you're clearly not involved at all."

"And," the human calculator said, "why you're pleading guilty when you're not."

47

To Margo,

What in the world is going on with my kid, Grenadine Scotch Wild? I returned from a trip to Italy and found a note from her on my door asking me to help her. I talked to Scotty and Mel, and they filled me in on her case. I am requesting to be hired, immediately, half time, and I want Grenadine. Six homes in two years? I will find her another adoptive placement.

I cannot sleep at night until that child is safe and well.

Daneesha Houston

To: All Staff
From: Margo Lipton
Date: February 12, 1992
Re: Daneesha Houston

Please welcome Daneesha Houston back! As you know, she retired in 1989 but has decided that traveling the world is not exciting enough for her.

She will be working half time.

Daneesha, we're glad to have you back!

Children's Services Division

Child's Name: Grenadine Scotch Wild
Age: 16
Parents' Names: Freedom and Bear Wild (Location unknown)
Date: March 28, 1992
Goal: Adoption
Employee: Daneesha Houston

I am delighted to write that Grenadine's placement with Mr. Sean Lee and his sister Ms. Beatrice Lee is going well, as I knew it would. I have known the Lees for fifteen years. They live in an expansive, modern home over-looking the city on the west side, and they have plenty of room.

Grenadine is in counseling for some drug and alcohol abuse, although the abuse was not serious. There was some promiscuity, but that behavior, I am confident, has stopped. She had a physical and was diagnosed with chlamydia, but she has the medication and it will be cleared up soon.

The Lees have taken excellent care of her.

There have been outbursts, swearing, tears, and throwing things at the Lees', and Grenadine has already been in one fight at school, but they seem steadfast in their devotion to her, perhaps because of Mr. and Ms. Lee's own placement in foster care fifty years ago when they were children.

Ms. Lee is an artist, and she and Grenadine work on their art together for hours. Ms. Lee has encouraged Grenadine to "art out" her feelings. Grenadine is working with paints and learning more about collage.

As an interior decorator, Mr. Lee has shown Grenadine the art of decorating, and she is working with him in his business in the evenings. She says she loves it.

Mr. Lee says that she is a natural decorator. He and Grenadine painted her bedroom yellow, then painted birds across the wall. A few have lilies in their mouths. Mr. Lee bought Grenadine her own sewing machine, showed her how to use it, and she made curtains for her room and a bedspread and a bed skirt.

Mr. and Ms. Lee sent Grenadine to an educational specialist, and they say that Grenadine has dyslexia. They have hired a tutor to come and work with her after school.

The tutoring does not interfere with her Wednesday night art class at the university, or her Saturday art class at Portland Craft, which lasts all day. They wanted Grenadine to quit her waitress job; she adamantly refused, but they did manage to convince her to work only ten hours a week.

The three of them enjoy going to the Lee family beach house.

Children's Services Division

Child's Name: Grenadine Scotch Wild
Age: 16
Parents' Names: Freedom and Bear Wild (Location unknown)
Date: September 16, 1992
Goal: Adoption
Employee: Daneesha Houston

I am extremely happy to announce that the Lees would like to adopt Grenadine. Grenadine has agreed. We will begin the paperwork, home visits, interviews, etc., immediately.

Grenadine says she wants to be called Dina Wild from now on. She and the Lees thought it would be a new beginning for her, plus Grenadine says she doesn't like having the name of a syrup used in drinks. I don't blame her.

In even more wonderful news, Grenadine entered her work in several local art competitions and won first prize in one and third prize in two others. She painted the backdrop for the school play, which, the drama teacher told me, was the finest backdrop he's ever seen. It was for *Les Mis*, and she painted a French city. . . . She is unbelievably talented.

Children's Services Division

Child's Name: Grenadine Scotch Wild
Age: 18
Parents' Names: Freedom and Bear Wild (Location unknown)
Date: June 14, 1994
Goal: Adopted
Employee: Daneesha Houston

On Tuesday Sean Lee died of AIDS. Grenadine was with him, as was his sister, Beatrice Lee. There was a tearful memorial attended by hundreds of people, including my husband and me.

Grenadine gave a eulogy. She spoke about Mr. Lee being a father to her and how he was kind and loving when she arrived in his home, even though she was angry, difficult, hurting, threw things, and swore like a "horse thief."

She talked about how Mr. Lee taught her to decorate a home and why having beauty and color around you was so important. She talked about the tutoring he and his sister provided, the art classes, the trips to the beach.

Mostly she talked about how Mr. Lee made her feel special, and wanted, and loved, even when he himself wasn't feeling well.

She said, "Mr. Lee and Beatrice probably saved my life. How do you thank someone for that?"

She cried. By the time Grenadine was done, I swear there was not a dry eye in the whole place. I cried a hundred tears. Even my husband cried, and that man never cries.

Heartbreaking.

Grenadine/Dina will continue to live with Beatrice. Beatrice told me if she didn't have Grenadine, she didn't know what she'd do.

48

WILL OF SEAN BAKER LEE

October 16, 1992

I, Sean Baker Lee, of Multnomah County, Oregon, declare that this is my will. I revoke all prior wills and codicils . . .

To my adopted daughter, the daughter of my heart, Grenadine Scotch Wild, $100,000 to be used only to buy a home so you will never be homeless again.

Plant some roses to remember me by, decorate wherever you live with beauty and harmony, and continue creating your art.

My favorite artists: Van Gogh, Picasso, Grenadine Scotch Wild.

With all my love, eternally,

Mr. Lee

49

When Dale asked why I lied to them about my involvement in Covey's crimes and the human calculator asked why I pleaded guilty when I wasn't, I told them I was petrified of a long prison term and then I broke down and told them about Rozlyn and Cleo.

"Ms. Wild," Dale said. "We are dismissing all charges against you."

"What?" I heard a roaring in my ears, like the ocean mixed with, for the oddest reason, a French horn. Millie's triumphant cry, "Ha. I've won again," penetrated, too.

"We believe you."

"You do?" My body sagged. A sliver of warmth started to pierce the ice around my heart.

"We believe you're innocent." Dale smiled, a tiny smile, probably hard for such an analytical, precise, serious man. "Covey's a piece of work, isn't he?"

I decided to stop by my old home, the faux mansion, the dwelling of dishonesty and mental torture, as I now thought of it, on my way out of town.

I knew that Covey was out of the house because Dale told me they had a meeting with him right after mine.

I had a message from Covey from another mystery number. He was crying. He was deflated, broken, and defeated. Told me he loved me. Told me he was sorry. Told me he had done what he had to provide me with a home, and car, and all of the expensive things I had never had. He had wanted to please me. It was all for me.

What a crock. Covey was obsessed with money, with proving himself through material possessions. That was just like him, to put his crimes on me and to present it as an altruistic and romantic gesture.

He told me he loved me again but said he'd done something else to me and he was sorry about it. Told me if I went to the house I'd see what it was. He would meet me there tonight, he couldn't wait to see me, and talk face-to-face. Sorry, sorry.

I had no pity. Anyone who allows their wife to go to jail for something she didn't do is not deserving of pity.

I deleted the message.

He would soon be completely deleted from my life.

I took the freeway and drove up into the hills, the homes old and graceful. At the top I turned into the winding, oak-lined driveway of our house and stopped. I stared at the two-story, sprawling brick home, the white columns, the white stairs up to the impressive entrance, and the black doors with gold handles.

I parked my car and the breaks squeaked. It rumbled when I turned the key. I remembered the sleek, slick car I used to drive that Covey bought me. Expensive moving machine used for show, to impress a whole bunch of people that I didn't care about but Covey did, not that he liked them.

I patted the seat of my car. "Good car," I said out loud. It made a grumbling noise.

I climbed out and stopped in front of the fountain, which was now turned off. It was a statue of Zeus. It was a penis thing with Covey and I knew it. I hated it.

The green grass was too long. Covey probably had to give up the lawn service, and he sure as heck wasn't going to mow it himself. That would remind him of his poor years.

I used my key to unlock the door and stepped inside, feeling slightly nauseated at being back. I wondered what Covey meant when he said he had done something else to me here.

When he lost at trial, the home would be sold immediately, as would Covey's other homes in various places, including Mexico. They would sell his fancy cars, all lined up in the six-car garage next door, three boats, five motorcycles, a small plane, a motor home we never used, and my jewelry. He would then sit in a jail cell and have tons of time to think and be a dick.

I walked through each room. I had never felt like I fit into this life, or this home—Covey's home. It felt foreign to me, ostentatious, and loud. Covey had hired an interior decorator before I met him, and she had done her thing and charged him a fortune. It was snobby and obnoxious. It screamed of wealth and a man who had low self-esteem and needed to brag.

Why hadn't I seen that before I married him?

I headed to the immense kitchen with its own brick fireplace, an island long enough to land his plane on, and a massive amount of white cabinets with gold handles. I thought of the endless dinner parties we'd had here.

I felt the exhaustion I'd felt then. The frustration. Tears. A breaking marriage. After a dinner party, Covey would have to "make a call," and I'd clean up. He was sound asleep when I climbed into bed, but he'd wake up and want me to work on him, too. He was enraged when I eventually told him, after months of that crap, that after working all day, making dinner and cleaning up, or hosting a hundred people at a catered event, I didn't want to have to make, bake, and clean him up, too.

I ran my hands over my face. Why had I taken that? Why had I allowed myself to be in that relationship for as long as I had?

Covey's den was covered in wood paneling. As I now knew much more about wood, I realized that even in a home like this, the quality was nowhere near what Kade worked with. Not even on the same planet.

Covey's computer and the contents of his desk had been confiscated, but his books were still there—which he had ordered online so he could stack them behind his desk and pretend that he had read all those literary works.

I opened the door to our bedroom, with its view of the city. We had a fireplace, a thick rug in front of it, a couch in white, and two padded white chairs with gold pillows. The bedroom was much larger than my whole home over the barn. The bathroom had a tub big enough for four, a shower for two, and granite counters.

I felt a rush of anger so hot I could hardly breathe when I finally brought my gaze around to the king-sized, four-poster bed and the white lace draped over it. Mind games, emotional games, sex games. Burned onto a DVD. It all culminated right there, in an act that should have had love in it.

I turned away and opened my closet doors. Those clothes weren't me anymore. The heels, the silk, the lace, the designer outfits. The handbags. They weren't me from the start. Covey bought them for me, pouted if I didn't wear them, his ego hurt, and I gave in.

Why did I do that? Why did I wear something I wasn't comfortable in?

My fury rose to the ceiling. Fury at him, but fury with myself. I allowed my brain, my life, and myself to be hijacked.

He had indulged in criminal activities and had me sign papers to not only implicate me in his schemes but to hold over my head. He told the authorities I was the "mastermind" of his business because I left him. He threatened me. When he could have saved me, he didn't, even when I was locked up in jail. He was willing to let me make a plea deal and go to jail again.

I picked up a wedding photo and hurtled it across the room, a raw scream breaking free. The frame made a hole in the wall and shattered.

I threw the rest of the photos of us against the wall, the glass splintering, then I started in on the expensive stuff in the room—vases and artwork, curtains I ripped down, and lamps from around the world I knew he was proud of. I threw. I smashed. I put more holes in the wall. My temper triggered and storming, I stomped down the hall to my art studio.

How could I pack all of the supplies I'd left behind—my collections of colorful rocks, my stamps from all over the world, old photos of a circus I'd found in an antique shop, game pieces, mosaic tiles, colorful glass—plus my red chair, which I loved. Would it fit in the car if I shoved hard?

I opened my studio door, still steaming, and there was . . . *nothing*. It was all gone. Cardboard boxes littered the floor, along with newspapers and tin cans I'd stored brushes in. My jars and boxes filled with beads, yarn, dice, dollhouse furniture, sparkly jewelry, feathers, Scrabble letters, rocks and shells, gone. My fabrics and lace, gone.

The rest of my art books, the colorful dressers and shelves I'd had from my little green home, my canvases, my plants and precious bonsai trees, even my red chair . . . gone.

There was nothing.

This was what Covey was talking about. He'd destroyed my art studio.

He hadn't taken the clothes and purses and heels. He knew I didn't care about those things.

But I cared about this.

So he trashed it.

I leaned against the wall, tears of frustration, of loss, streaming down my face. I hated him so much.

On my way out I stopped at the home of the principal of the elementary school where I used to teach art. Keesha James was surprised to see me but gave me an exuberant hug. "Dina Wild! I am so glad to see you. The kids miss your art class like you would not believe."

She invited me in for coffee, and we chatted. I told her briefly what had happened, including that all charges had been dropped against me. It was important to me that she knew that, as I liked her and we'd worked together for years.

"I knew you were innocent! I met your husband that one time and I thought to myself, Now that is sleeze in a suit. No offense."

"None taken."

I gave her three collages I'd packed into my car. They were in a closet next to the studio. Obviously Covey had forgotten about them. "For you to sell, or auction off, at your Back to School Night, for art supplies for the kids."

She was thrilled. She was teary. She begged me to come back.

"I can't. I'm sorry." I felt the weight on my shoulders, so heavy, begin to lift, like a thousand feathers were lifting the rocks off my shoulders. "I have a new life."

I dropped off Divinity Star's mural of the carousel. When I arrived at her house, she was having a meeting with her fellow friends and time travelers who believed that they all had past lives. They were each dressed in costumes that reflected who they had been before: Joan of Arc, a cave woman, a nun, a 1920s flapper girl, a pioneer woman, a fairy. The fairy didn't fit, but whatever.

When Divinity Star saw her collage, she screamed. "Dina! I love it. This is where all my past lives started!"

I know, Divinity, I know. I hugged her.

I rolled down the windows as soon as I was outside of the city, pulled out my ponytail, and let the wind whip my hair around. I was crushed about my art studio. It had taken years to amass what I had. My art supplies had been so personal, from the bottle caps, to the clothespins I'd painted in rainbow colors, to the blue and green sea glass.

What was done was done. I decided not to stay in my anger for one more minute because that would mean Covey had control over my emotions. I would go to Goodwill, I would go to thrift and antique shops, I would go to art stores and restock my art supplies.

I felt like I was shedding Covey and his evilness as I drove farther and farther away from town. Shedding his muck and manipulations, his suffocating personality, his mercilessness.

Shedding jail.

Shedding the FBI, the assistant U.S. attorney, the IRS, the human calculator.

Shedding my life as Dina Hamilton, wife of Covey Hamilton, investor, possessive and dangerous husband, criminal. Shedding

Dina Wild, too. The woman I had become during high school because I didn't want to be named after a syrup for a drink and because I was trying to start over.

I was Grenadine Scotch Wild again. Grenady for short. The name given to me when I was a baby by my mom and dad, Freedom and Bear Wild. The name I would not give up again. That girl/teenager/woman had been through many hard things, but she was now a free woman, an artist, a friend, and totally in love with Kade Hendricks.

I smiled, then I laughed. I thought of that man without his jeans and T-shirts and thermals and cowboy boots. Plain naked.

My, oh my. He was delicious. Lots of steely muscle and hard buttocks and a broad back to stroke and caress. What hung between those two legs like a bull stallion was heaven itself.

I turned on the radio to cheerful, powerful hard-core... country music.

I sang aloud—not well, not on tune, but loud.

50

He loved being a poet.

He tore off a small corner of his poem book and chewed on it. He liked pigs, too.

He wrote a new nursery rhyme.

This little piggy went up the hill.
This little piggy fought back.
This little piggy hit him.
This little piggy had a nice rack.
And this little piggy went wee wee wee all through the forest
Until she was gone.
All gone.
This little piggy was under a rock.
This little piggy was, too.
They had company there,
Though none had to go to the loo.

He'd lost the littlest piggy. He screamed, as loud as he could, head back. She had ruined it! Ruined it all! He crumbled up the poem and put it in his mouth. "Now you're stuck in there, Danny. You're stuck, you can't get out!"

He put both hands on his hair and pulled.

51

~

It was midnight when I drove through the quiet Wild West town, by the cowboy on the bucking horse, and headed up my driveway.

I said hello to Liddy. She neighed, and I neighed back and gave her an apple.

Then I skipped up the stairs of the big, red barn. On my door was a detailed picture, drawn with colored pencils, of a quilt. It was of three women, their butts way in the air, slinking through the grass wearing night goggles, miniskirts, and bikini tops over well-endowed bosoms. Rozlyn wrote at the top, "I will call it the Spy Girls quilt. Love you, Roz."

I turned on all the lights, threw my arms out, and spun like a kid. I lit candles and sunk into my bath and washed my hair. I added too much strawberry scented bubble bath

Dale had told me that my checking, savings, and retirement accounts for me and my business would be released to me immediately. I would not have to give up the money I had now, either. I could pay off Cherie.

I was not broke. In fact, I had money. I felt better. Not because I wanted anything fancy, but because I needed financial security. I needed to feel safe. I needed to know I could handle tomorrow and all the bullets life shot at me.

I would stay in this apartment over the red barn to be with Cleo and to help Rozlyn. If Rozlyn died, I would move into her house to keep Cleo's surroundings the same, and raise Cleo.

When she was raised, I would move out, and Cleo would have her mother's home, as it should be.

Later that night, tucked into bed, covered in my white comforter with the pretty pink roses, I hugged myself. I loved my bed. I didn't love it quite as much as I loved Kade's bouncy, cuddly bed with the married-for-life bald eagles, but I still loved it.

I held my pink ceramic rose box and placed my lily bracelet inside of it.

Home.

That night I dreamed that I heard my parents' laughter. I saw my father's fingers strumming the guitar. I saw my mother's red, crocheted shawl.

I felt a kiss on my cheek.

All will be well.

At six o'clock in the morning, I turned on my computer and looked up *The Oregon Journal*. I was so hopeful, and so scared. I didn't want any more attention—except the type of attention that cleared my name.

The article was on the front page of the metro section, at the top. My heart thudded. The headline, "All charges dropped against Dina Hamilton, wife of disgraced investor Covey Hamilton."

The article detailed the charges against us, Hamilton Investments, the investigation, the amount of client money lost, and that I worked as a painter and collage artist and had been married to Covey for one year before starting divorce proceedings.

The highlights . . .

"The case against Dina Hamilton was complicated by several factors, mostly by Covey Hamilton, who was furious that Dina left him and was threatening to take her down with him unless she came home. He lied repeatedly about her and her involvement in his company. Dina had nothing to do with Hamilton Investments. It's a typical controlling husband type of case. . . .

"Covey Hamilton is still declaring his innocence, although sources have told *The Oregon Journal* that his attorneys are talking with the U.S. attorney's office and trying to negotiate his prison sentence.

"Asked why Dina Hamilton initially plead not guilty, then changed her plea to guilty, assistant U.S. attorney, Dale Kotchik said, 'Dina Hamilton has a friend who has two years to live. The friend is suffering from a brain tumor and Dina is the guardian of the friend's child. Had a jury found Dina guilty, she would have received at least a five-year prison term. By pleading guilty without a trial she would have received eighteen months in prison, which guaranteed that she would be out in time to tend to her friend and to care for the friend's young daughter. She decided not to risk it. When she told us she would be pleading guilty, we were already well aware of her innocence—from numerous sources—and never would have allowed her to go to trial, much less jail.'"

I had mixed emotions. I was thrilled to be publicly declared innocent, but my stomach sank. I slapped my hands to my cheeks and bent my head. This was also terrible. Pineridge is a small town, and now Rozlyn's secret was out. I never expected it to land in the paper. I would need to beg forgiveness.

I hoped that Covey would be beaten in prison, attacked by bats, stung by fleas, infested by lice, and stabbed with homemade prison weapons.

But for me it was all over.

I made coffee and put whipping cream in it, then went outside and watched the sunrise.

Peace.

Kade called me at seven.

"I saw the newspaper." I heard the hope in his deep voice, the gravelly intensity. "Where are you?"

"Home. I came in late last night."

I heard a long pause. I thought he might be crying. When he spoke, I knew he was, that gentle bear. "I'm inviting myself over, honey. I'll be there in five minutes."

"Really?" My voice was embarrassingly breathless.

"Yep."

I knew it would be more than five minutes, but I still flew to my shower, brushed my hair, ignored the scars on my hairline, as usual, put hair goop in, let it wave down, brushed my teeth, and put on makeup.

I pulled on jeans and a white, lacy negligee and a white blouse. I put on dangly earrings with red stones and a red stone necklace.

The doorbell rang.

A second later, I was holding onto Kade, my legs wrapped around his hips, like I would never let go.

A few seconds later, I was up in his arms and he was dumping me on my bed with the white comforter and pink roses.

"I missed you," I panted between heated, tingly, long kisses.

"I missed you, too, Grenady. I love you, Artist Lady."

"Love you, too."

We stopped talking. Action speaks so much louder than words and our action was lusty . . . and loving.

Tender and loving.

Love and lust. Your best friend and your passionate lover. In one.

The best combination.

Afterward, Kade wrapped me up in a hug on top of his chest. I felt his heart beating right beneath my cheek.

I tried not to cry, but I did. Right there. On top of Kade. So many, many tears. He held me close and made soft murmuring sounds. He kissed my cheeks and my forehead while I choked on my sobs and snuffled and sniffled. He cried, too, that sexy hit man with a soft heart.

I pulled back, still crying, and said, "I'm making you all wet," and he chuckled and said, "You can make me all wet anytime," and hugged me close. "I'm so glad you're home."

"Me too, stud, me too."

I apologized to Rozlyn up one side and down another that I had not kept her secret, told her I never thought it would end up in the paper, that I thought it was confidential, and she was gracious and kind.

"Grenady, my partner in spying, I understand and I don't mind at all. I have to tell people right away anyhow because of the last-ditch chemo they're trying, and I'm losing my crowning glory hair soon, so it doesn't matter. I love you, girlfriend."

"Me too, Rozlyn."

"And I have a confession." Her face scrunched up and she burst into tears.

"Oh no. We don't need any more of those." I wrapped my arms around her, aching for her pain.

"I have to apologize to you. I know that in my heart, or back in my busted brain, that you were taking the eighteen months for Cleo and me."

"It was the better bet."

"A bet for us." She held my hand, still crying, hiccupping.

"That, too."

"And I didn't urge you to fight more. I didn't insist you go to trial because I wanted you out in eighteen months for Cleo." She had a hot flash, sweat pouring, like the elf was back with his hose. I wiped her forehead with my fingers. I don't think I'm going to like menopause.

"It was all about me and my daughter." She wiped her tears away with both hands, then fanned herself. "Us. Me. I'm so sorry, Grenady."

"Nothing to apologize for." And there wasn't. "I'm sure I would have done the same thing."

"Please forgive me, Grenady. I'm begging you."

"Done. Forgiven. How about we eat some chocolate?"

"Excellent." She sniffled. "It's an aphrodisiac, and I'm going to get the guts to ask out Leonard before I lose my hair, so I need it." Rozlyn ran a hand over her curves. "Two hundred twenty-five pounds of chocolate lust. Right here. Ready and waiting for Leonard."

Rozlyn decided to "take drastic dating action," track down Leonard, and ask him out.

Eudora, Rozlyn, and I engaged in high-level surveillance. Okay, we sat in Eudora's car and watched Leonard leave work while we ate a box of chocolates, then we followed him in the car and watched him go into a grocery store.

Eudora said, "Don't even attempt a spying maneuver in there, Rozlyn. You are a poor spy."

"Go get 'em." I turned her toward me, fluffed out her hair, handed her a lipstick, and undid a button on her shirt. She yanked her bra straps up so the girls were higher, said, "This is it. Porno boobs don't fail me now," and out she went.

Rozlyn came out a half an hour later and proudly announced that she had spoken with Leonard, had not had a hot flash, and had asked him out to dinner.

"What was the target's response?" Eudora asked. "Affirmative?"

"He said yes."

We cheered and clapped.

"I'm going to get one more tube of that anti-dry vagina cream, in case I get lucky beyond lucky."

"That's three tubes, Roz," I said.

"It's best to always be prepared," Eudora said, waving a finger. "For all contingencies."

"To the pharmacy we go!" Rozlyn said. "I'm living life, every second of it, and I want it smooth and orgasmic."

Cherie Poitras rammed through my divorce.

Covey caved.

She sent me flowers with this card: "Another dirt-eating husband bites the dust."

Covey's lawyers, Skiller and Goldman, who let me go to jail knowing that I had done nothing wrong, who never told Dale that I was innocent, or told Covey to do so, were disbarred for a previous case they worked on for Covey for misconduct and misrepresentation and other legalese I didn't understand but it all spelled one thing: Ya can't practice law anymore, suckers! Say good-bye to the fancy houses!

*   *   *

Millie called me. Covey pled guilty. He was headed to jail for eighty-four months. I wondered if he would meet up with a Neanderthal Man. When he was released from jail he would pay back the victims for the rest of his life.

That made me laugh.

I decided not to think about him again, ever.

Deleted.

I worked on a collage in one of Kade's empty upstairs bedrooms, on a cool Sunday morning, when Kade was fishing with Ricki Lopez and Danny Vetti. Kade had helped me bring over a few canvases, paints, and my trinkets. It felt . . . sweet.

That was the word for it—sweet. Kade wanted me at his house, wanted me doing my art, even if he wasn't there. "I like thinking of you here, Grenady," he said, hugging me close, bearlike. "If I'm at work, if I'm skiing or fishing, I like knowing you're here. It makes me happy. You fit here."

It was a pretty romantic setup. I would be painting or collaging in "Wild Woman's studio," as Kade dubbed it, and he would be sitting at one of the long wood tables he brought in for me, working. We would talk now and then, or listen to country music, sometimes we'd stop and have fun in a naked sort of way, then I'd get back to painting, and try to ignore him kissing my neck or exploring my curves and saying, "Let's take a nap, Artist Lady."

That day I was working on a five-by-three-foot canvas. I had turned it vertically and painted a tree using my favorite sculpted butter-type paint. I painted the trunk brown, and twisty, like a tree candy cane, then let the purple and red flowers burst above. The thick paint lifted the flowers up, like butterfly wings.

I would put a glass bead in the center of the flowers and spray the edges of the painting with a light dusting of gold. At the base of the tree I would paint Cleo, with her pink cowboy hat, striped tights, and her favorite outfit: a yellow dress with a tree on it with purple and red flowers and a twisty trunk.

I would paint Rozlyn beside her, in her long Mexican-styled skirt and red shirt and cowboy boots, Liddy in the background with her flowered hat. I would add one of Rozlyn's women-power quilts hanging from a tree branch, using scraps of fabric.

Rozlyn and Cleo would love it. I felt teary thinking of Rozlyn, but I made myself concentrate on making the best collage for her I possibly could.

Rozlyn's dinner date with Leonard had gone well. So had the second one. She told him about her health issues. He was not scared off by them. He was a tall, gangly, smart man who knew how to brave life.

Hours later I went downstairs to make coffee. Two weeks after all the charges were dropped against me, I quit working at Tildy's. I couldn't work both jobs anymore. It was killing me, plus I had my money back. I felt bad about it, though, I truly did. She had hired me when I was desperate and treated me well. Tildy hugged me. "You're the best bartender I've ever had."

Kade and I broke his rules about his never, ever dating an employee. I kept working for him in sales. I also sketched out more plans for rocking chairs, and we worked together on a line of painted furniture. He made me sign a contract where we would split profits for the rocking chairs and furniture. I told him it was unnecessary, this could be part of my job description, but he refused to make the furniture unless I signed it. I signed it, then we made love on his leather couch in front of the fireplace.

He built the dresser or table or sideboard or armoire, then I showed him the plan for the carvings—blue-haired mermaids or zebras dancing or moose playing poker in the woods—he carved it, I painted it. The furniture was called Grenadine's Designs.

At work we were as professional as we could be, but it was hard to hide that love.

We knew the gig was up when someone cut a huge heart out of wood, painted it red, wrote "Kade 'n Grenady," and hung it in the employee room next to my mural of the mountains.

Kade laughed and kissed me.

I blushed.

Everyone clapped.

As the coffee machine hummed, and those blue and purple

mountains glowed in the distance, I picked up the newspaper Kade left on the table. When my coffee was made, my whipping cream sin poured in, I sat down at the kitchen table.

I read the headline about the man on death row. I had shied away from it, but this time I read it. The article covered a two-page spread, as his time to be executed was near. His crimes were so hideous, I had to put my coffee down and close my eyes for a second. He had killed this couple, that man, that lady, another couple, two female teenagers, and had been caught only in the last few years. He hid the bodies.

I turned to the second page where pictures of him from previous years—personal photos it turned out, no mug shots—were printed in a line. He had led a "normal" life, with a wife and kid and a job and a bike before it was found that he was a serial killer.

I studied his face and curly brown hair in the first photo, then the second . . . and the third.

I felt chilled suddenly, from the inside out, and shaky, as if someone had wrapped me up in their iceberg arms and was squeezing the life out of me.

I knew that face. *I knew it.* The room tilted, and I couldn't breathe. I saw towering, dark trees and fog. I saw a lighthouse.

Alice, My Anxiety, came roaring to the surface.

I focused on his name. Terrence "Bucky" Lancaster.

Bucky.

Two tattoos were mentioned: A woman's face with the word "Mom," and a hatchet. In my mind I saw another tattoo, a knife with a snake wrapped around it. I saw three miniature skulls on a necklace, too.

I looked in his black, hollow eyes.

I saw a red kite.

I looked at the scar on his chin, jagged like a snake.

I saw a dark forest enshrouded in fog.

I looked at that demented smile.

I saw a guitar, a tie-dye shirt.

I looked at his mouth, twisted.

I saw a red, crocheted shawl and a flowered skirt.

I looked at that huge forehead.
I saw a knife whip through the air.
I heard a scream, a guttural shout.
The knife made contact.
I saw blood.
Run, Grenadine, run!
The floor came rushing up to meet my poor face, and I closed my eyes.
Run, Grenadine, run!

52

I did not want to be standing in front of the penitentiary, but I knew I had to be there.

My visit had been arranged by many people. I had initially called assistant U.S. attorney Dale Kotchik, not knowing who else to call, and he had taken it from there, involving those who needed to be involved, including the police and the FBI and a special task force that had been investigating Bucky.

I told them I remembered a tattoo of a knife with a snake around it. They had been surprised, as the description of that tattoo on Bucky's right arm had not been released to the public. I told them about my red kite. They knew nothing about a red kite. I told them about the three skull necklaces he was wearing. They were surprised at this, too. That fact had not been released to the public, either, but each of Bucky's victims had been buried with a skull necklace. He'd been wearing three when I saw him that night. Obviously he'd hoped I would be the third victim of the evening.

To see a prisoner on death row, you have to make an appointment. You have to be checked out and approved by the prison. You have to give them your social security number, your driver's license, address, date of birth, etc. The prison has to approve the visit. The inmate has to approve the visit.

I could not wear suggestive clothing. No short skirts, no see-through clothing, no spaghetti straps, no bikini tops. It would have been funny if the whole thing wasn't about murder. No denim. No gang clothing or camouflage. Gee. That wasn't going to be a problem, either. No underwire bras, as that could set off the metal detector. No belts with metal.

I had to have ID, as did Kade.

The entrance to the death row visiting area is a beige–yellow cinder block outbuilding with brown trim. We went through a heavy metal door into a room with lockers for our personal items, a wood desk, and a bathroom, which I used and threw up in. There was a guard and our escorting, uniformed officers.

We signed in, showed our ID, and went through the metal detector before walking through a tiger run, a barred corridor that's open to the outside, to the visiting area. There was another metal door and four visiting cubicles.

I had recognized Bucky, the younger Bucky, in the photographs in the newspaper. Maybe my mind had finally relaxed because I had Kade and felt safe. Maybe the trauma had finally worked itself out enough to open the door into my past. Maybe my collages finally helped me to answer the questions. Maybe there was enough detail in the article to trigger long-dead, violent, unspeakable memories.

But I remembered that we had met him at a festival. He sat with us when my dad was playing the guitar one afternoon. My mom and I danced as he played and sang. I remembered we went for a drive with Bucky because we decided to go to the beach to fly my red kite.

We started climbing up a hill as the sun started going down. I heard the waves. I smelled the salt. I saw two fishing boats out in the water. I remembered tall, dark trees, a swatch of fog, and a lighthouse. Bucky said we were going to fly my red kite in the dark; he knew a good place.

The rest is fuzzy, except I remembered angry words. I remembered my father swearing, shouting, my mother screaming. I remembered a fight, my father's fists swinging, my mother leaping onto Bucky, and I remembered that knife.

That knife.

Slash, slash.

More screaming. My father falling backward, then getting

back up. My mother sprawled on the ground, and struggling. Blood. Blood, blood.

My parents yelling at me, *"Run, Grenadine, run!"* And I did. I was six.

I had to talk to Bucky.

I wanted to know what happened to my family. Where they were buried. If he had known their real names. I wanted to know who I was, where I came from. That I was hoping a convicted serial killer would help me was like hoping I could catch a ride on a comet and drop myself onto Maui.

He had slashed away their lives. He had consigned me to being an orphan and the resulting disaster. He was soulless and cold.

He was a psychopath.

He was the only one who might know something.

I had to try.

I sat in front of Bucky, Kade beside me, the corded phone in my hand, a glass partition separating us, armed guards standing at attention.

Bucky was wearing a navy blue T-shirt and denim blue jeans stamped with OREGON DEPARTMENT OF CORRECTIONS INMATE. His hair was in odd tufts, and he was bald in some places. The years had been harsh. He was wrinkled, stick thin, sagging. I still recognized him.

"I'm delighted you're finally here, Grenadine Scotch Wild. Welcome! I knew you'd come." He whistled an odd tune. "I've been writing nursery rhymes for you for years. I remember you. A poet never forgets."

He grinned at me. A lopsided, twisted grin. His eyes rested on my breasts for long seconds, then back up to my eyes, back down to my breasts.

It was a power move. I knew it, he knew it. I felt Kade shift angrily beside me. Bucky's eyes never once strayed to Kade. They stayed locked on mine.

"I remember you." I felt Bucky's evil like a black, curling force, pulling me toward him. There was nothing behind his eyes that was human. There was no warmth, no kindness. He was hollow, except for his evil.

"I wish I could shake your hand and give you a hug. Mmmm mmmm." He moaned, then shook his head back and forth, as if in ecstasy. "You were a delectable child back then. Like your momma." He smacked his lips. "Pat-a-cake, pat-a-cake, baker's man, they're in an earth oven."

And there it was. The confirmation. He had done it. I wanted to kill him. Kade made a sound deep in his throat.

"Your momma was delicious." Bucky pulled on his hair, and a few strands came out in his fingers. He grimaced, put them in his pocket, then giggled. "I tasted her before she was gone, up up up into the ethereal heavens with Him. You were three blind mice. See how you ran. I cut off their tails with a carving knife because I'm the farmer's wife."

My stomach churned like someone had put a stick in there and twirled it around. I thought of what he meant, and I wanted to cry for my poor mother. She was so young, so kind, so loving. And this monster . . .

Kade said, "Go to hell."

Bucky ignored him.

"She looked like you, Grenadine Scotch Wild. You were, you are, your momma. The red hair, those bright green eyes, those lush lips, those high cheekbones. Sexy!" His eyes lingered on my breasts again. I wanted to cross my arms. It was like being attacked through glass. "She was little, too, short and curvy like you. I remember how heavy her breasts felt in my hands. It would be the same as how yours would feel."

"You're disgusting," Kade said, jumping up and swearing.

I put my shaking hand on Kade's thigh to make him sit down. I needed him to control himself so I could get what I needed.

Bucky laughed as if what Kade said was so funny he could barely control himself. He still did not look at Kade. "So I've been told, darling."

"I want you to tell me what happened to my parents."

"No can do. One, two, three, I'll keep it all to me."

"Why?"

"Because I didn't have the time I wanted with you, Grenadine, and I'm mad about that. Mad!" His laughter abruptly stopped as his face tightened and flushed. "I like things wrapped up neat and tidy, tidy, tidy, and you ruined that for me. You were scared, so sweet, Little Miss Muffet. You were in a pink dress that day. Purple pants. Your mother had made you a crown of daisies. You were both wearing your crowns. Daisy people. Daisy girls. Daisies, daisies. I loved my daisies."

I suddenly heard those soft, loving voices in my head.

Start from the beginning, walk him through it.

It was them.

Be brave, Grenadine. You can do this.

I stuck my chin up, but I was scared, the hysterical fear he had brought to me as a child bubbling up. "We were in our bus with you."

"Yes. Your parents' bus. A hippie VW bus. Your dad bought it in Wyoming, he told me. For five hundred dollars cash. From a cowboy. Hee-haw. Cowboy! We took the bus to the ocean to frolic and skip and fly your red kite at night." He made motions with his hands of frolicking. "It would be a pleasant day for all of us. My idea. Mine."

"It wasn't pleasant for any of us."

He winked at me. "It almost was for me, but I didn't get my gift. You ran away. I saw you fall, like Humpty-Dumpty, but your daddy hit me and I had to punch back with my knife. Did you hit your head that night? Did it crack like Humpty-Dumpty?"

Yes, it had. I'd had a concussion and I still had the scar. "Your gift?"

"You. You were my gift, Grenadine. You were a sexy child, mmm mmm!" He moaned again, as if he were eating a tasty steak. His tongue poked out and licked his lips. "Sexy. Like your momma. Your dad, he was a pain in the ass. Broke my nose. That's why it's busted, broken, cracked up. See?"

"Why did he break your nose?" I would keep calm until I had my answers. I would.

"He was trying to protect you and your mommy. Your momma.

Mom. Mother. Mommy. I stuck my knife into him and he kept coming at me, again and again. He kept punching me."

"And you killed him."

"Yes, I did. Blood here and there." He threw his hands in the air and grinned maniacally. "Everywhere! Like a fountain!"

"And my mother?" A whimper escaped my lips. I shut them tight.

He sang, "Twinkle, twinkle, little star . . ."

"And my mother?" But I knew. I needed his confession. Out loud.

"Your daddy would have killed me with his bare hands for what I did later to your mom. Mother. Mommy. Ya la la la. Your mommy."

"What did you do?"

"She died, died, died, too. Knife, knife, knife."

"You killed them both." Tears burned my eyes.

"I didn't. Someone else did."

I was confused now. "Who?"

"The man inside me." He twisted his hair, pulling hard. He giggled, high-pitched.

He was so sick. "The man inside you killed them?"

"We exist peaceably together. As one. There's the two of us in here. The other one killed your mommy. His name is Danny. He is not a poet, like me."

I swayed.

"Awwww. Grenadine. I've upset the Miss Muffet girl. The girl with her daisy crown and her pink dress and her purple pants. I see you still have the lily bracelet. Interesting."

"What about my lily bracelet?"

"I get it. Silly me, silly you. I know all about it. It's in my brain." Bucky's face twisted into anger. "Your mommy's mommy made one for herself and one for her daughter. Your momma with the nice, heavy breasts gave you hers. They told me that by the campfire."

"What were their real names?"

"What were your mommy and daddy's real names?"

"Yes."

"What were Bear and Freedom's names?"

"Yes."

"What were Mr. and Mrs. Wild's real names?"

"Yes."

He giggled. High and pitchy. "I won't tell you."

"Why?"

"Why would I?"

"Because I want to know the truth about my parents. I could track their parents, their brothers and sisters. My family." I choked up. I had family out there. I belonged to a family. Bad or good, I had two families, my mother's family, my father's family.

"Ah, family. You know what my daddy did to me? You don't, do you, because you weren't there. My daddy whipped me. He raped me up my yin yang with his sword. I hate him. When I was a teenager I killed him, too, with a hatchet." He pointed to his tattoo. "With a hatchet!

"My mother told the neighbors that Daddy took off for Oklahoma with a floozy whore. A floozy whore!" He stared into space, then wiggled his fingers together like worms. "She was a wonderful storyteller. I have a tattoo of her, too! See?

"I killed him one night when he told me to go down to the basement for my punishment with his sword. My mother swears she didn't know he was ding-donging me, and that could be the truth." He drew circles in the air with his fingers. "She was a nurse and worked nights. That's when it happened. Night. Black. Cold. He was a bad, bad man."

"Where are my parents' bodies?"

"I cannot tell you, rock-a-bye baby, in the treetops, when the wind blows the cradle will rock, and down came your parents and died."

"Why not? You're going to die in jail. Tell me so I can find them, give them a proper burial, maybe find out who the rest of my family is."

"Family. Schamaily. I don't have a family, and neither do you. I put your parents in a hole."

"Where? Where are they?"

"It's getting crowded up there now. My own personal cemetery. But it isn't an animal cemetery." He shook his head back and forth, back and forth. "Hey diddle diddle, the cat and the fiddle, the cow jumped over the moon, the little dog laughed. There are no cats or dogs or cows up there. People only. I put a necklace around them. A skull necklace."

"I remember the skull necklaces." I waited. My fists clenched tight. Kade grunted next to me. He wanted to take Bucky out, I could feel it.

"The third one was for you, Little Bo Peep who lost her two sheep. You don't feel well, Grenadine." He smoothed his hair down, preening. "Or is it my beauty that is making you dizzy?"

Crazy, so crazy. "Where did you bury them?"

"I'll give you a riddle." He clapped his hands. "You could go to Japan from there. You could go to Australia. You could see a whale shredding a shark. Blood. You could see white froth."

"I don't know what you're saying or hinting at."

"Forest. Tall trees." He smiled at me. "Fog! Fog!"

Forest. Tall trees. Fog. They'd followed me all my life. His expression was joyful, excited. I wanted to pitch myself through the glass and strangle him.

"The ocean waves roll. The tall trees grow. Above the tide pools there's a cliff. On the cliff there's a sign. A sign about a lighthouse. A sign about a woman. Seagulls playing." He clapped again. "Go fifty long paces east, by a rock that's tall. Dig you may, dig you might, you may find a body, you may find a red kite."

"And that's where my parents are?"

"Yes. Decaying flesh. Eyeballs popping. Fingernails dirty. Bugs. Worms in their eyeballs. Bugs in their ears. Maggots eating their intestines. Bones only, though. Bones only. Others there, too. Mother Goose in her shoe, that whore. Mother Goose had a red, crocheted shawl! She let you wear it, one of her blind mice!"

A red, crocheted shawl. I swallowed down bile. "Where is this place?"

"I'll give you another clue for the haiku. A hint for a mint. A sentence for your parents who were sentenced by me. Their judge. I judged them to be in my way. They were in the way of you!" He opened his fingers wide and tapped them together. "A beach in the sun, a beach in the rain, high on a cliff, that's where I caused pain."

"Why? Why did you cause them pain?" I felt the tears burn. I blinked. I would not cry though my entire body was racked with pain. He would see his power over me then.

"Because I wanted you." He smiled at me. Sexual. Predatory. "I wanted you, sweet Grenadine. Daughter of my new friends. Small. Tight body. Little girl. Yummy girl. But then"—he smashed his hands on the table in front of him—"your father fought me. He fought, he wouldn't die, and your mother, she fought, too, tried to protect her daisy girl. Her man. Your daddy. Da da. Dad." He smashed the table again. "But I won. I was the one out for fun."

I couldn't even speak.

"They told you, run Grenadine, run! Run!" He whistled, a haunted, jagged tune.

I closed my eyes, totally overwhelmed. Sickened. It was true. The words I'd heard ringing in my head for so long. My parents had tried to save me. They had fought for each other, they had fought for me.

"Run, Grenadine, run!" He imitated a woman's voice, my mother's. "Run, Grenadine, run!" He imitated my father's voice, deep and low. "Run, Grenadine!" he shrieked. "Run!"

I shivered, felt faint. Kade put his arm around me. He swore at Bucky again, but Bucky didn't even pause.

"I had to hit her, smash her, to get her down and keep her down. Run, Grenadine, run! Like your daddy, dad, father, your mother, mommy, mom, they wouldn't die! Wouldn't die! They fought so I couldn't get you! You! They ruined it. You ruined it!"

He was frustrated, angry.

"You got away, sugar and spice and all things nice. You ran through the forest. At night. Down a hill. To a trucker. But no one ever wanted you. Your parents dead. Alone. Lost. They put signs up. Your face on the news, but no one ever came for you. No one wanted you. I took their hippie bus, do you know that? Drive, drive, drive, I took myself for a ride."

I heard myself crying inside. For my parents. For the grief
that was still within me. It would never leave, I knew that now.
I would have to grieve for them all over again, now that I knew
what happened. I would find their bodies and bury them. I
would do that for them. For us. For the family we were.

"Where are they, Bucky? Tell me."

"I did tell you. One, two, three, I have a riddle for thee."

"I need more information."

"The devil, that's Danny, he buried them near a rock, by a
lighthouse, over the sea." He pulled on his hair, both hands,
above his ears, as if trying to pull the insanity out. Then he tilted
his head back and giggled.

My emotions boiled over. "I hope you're never executed.
Then you can stay here and rot."

He laughed. "I am already rotten, you pretty girl, all grown
up to a pretty woman with heavy breasts like your momma's.
Jack and Jill went up the hill, Jack and Jill were killed, but the
baby black sheep, black sheep, have you any wool, she got
away."

He bent his head and started sobbing. "It's the bad devil in
me. It's Danny. He makes me do these things, but I will tell
you." He whipped his head up, and it was as if I was seeing a
different man, his eyes filled with tears, his face slack. "Grenadine Scotch Wild, I would have killed you so you could have
been with your parents with Him. I would have. But you dashed
away and ruined it all.

"I knew your parents for a week before I killed them. All they
wanted to do was play with you. Sing. Dance. Love you, love
you, love you." His face changed again into one of unleashed,
uncontrolled fury. "My daddy didn't love me, he didn't! And
when I'm out of here, Grenadine Scotch Wild, I am going to kill
you! No love is allowed! No love is allowed!"

He was utterly insane. Vicious and cruel.

"A sign about a lighthouse, a sign about a woman," he sang,
then whistled. "Seagulls playing with Mary had a little lamb.
Dig you may, dig you might, you may find the bodies, you may

WHAT I REMEMBER MOST 463

find a kite." He whistled again. "You may find your parents killed by my might!"

And that was it. He lost it.

"I am going to kill you, Grenadine Scotch Wild!" He stood up and started pounding on the glass with his fists, his face contorted and red, the veins in his neck popping. "You didn't play right, you ran away, you little cunt! One, two, buckle my shoe, three, four, shut the door, five, six, I'll kill you with sticks! Run, Grenadine, run!"

The guards were there. They grabbed him and yanked him back, but he kicked at the table, kicked at the chair, struggled and screamed.

"Run, Grenadine, run!" he screeched.

Dizziness swamped me, and I slumped against Kade, as Kade sent a volley of swear words and threats through the glass to Bucky that Bucky didn't even hear.

"Run, Grenadine, run!"

"We got all of it, Dina," Dale said to me when I could breathe normally again and stand up on my own outside the prison. "We have to figure out what Bucky's talking about. Where it is."

The whole conversation had been recorded. Dale was there with the FBI agents, police, and other officials in and out of uniform. They were all talking. One of the agents had her computer opened. "I can find this place."

Dale nodded, then reached over and hugged me. I hugged him back. Kade shook his hand. "We're on it, Dina. Try to rest. I'll call you as soon as we know anything."

Dale called at two in the morning. Kade and I were still up. We'd had some mind-blowing sex, my legs wrapped around his hips, my back against the wall.

Afterward I'd cried in his arms in bed. Cried and cried as he smoothed my hair, held me close, kissed my forehead, my chin, my lips. I assured him I would not always cry after sex. He told me I could cry whenever I wanted.

"Dina?" Dale said.

"Yes." Kade and I sat up in bed.

"We think we know where your parents' bodies might be."

We were soon on the road, driving through the night. We sat on the sand as the sun came up behind us, waking up the sea. We didn't talk. Kade held me.

The ocean sparkled behind us, sunlight caressing every wave, the white foam frothing, like soap, while seagulls squawked. It was crisp and cold and lovely, a direct contrast to the grim, harsh scene in front of us.

The police had shut down the road to the red-and-white lighthouse so no one could come up. Kade and I stood back from the rock that Bucky had talked about, along with local and state police, the FBI, the task force, and other official-looking people with badges and uniforms.

In my head I heard Bucky say, "The ocean waves roll. The tall trees grow. Above the tide pools there's a cliff. On the cliff there's a sign. A sign about a lighthouse. A sign about a woman. Seagulls playing. Go fifty long paces east, by a rock that's tall. Dig you may, dig you might, you may find a body, you may find a red kite."

We were there. There was a sign about a lighthouse. There was a sign about a woman who had lived in the lighthouse in the 1900s named Eleanor Sherwood. The rock was almost hidden by trees. A perfect place for Bucky's graveyard.

The lighthouse keeper and his wife stood beside us. They were in their early thirties. When they heard why we were there, they served coffee and cinnamon rolls. I couldn't eat or drink, and neither could Kade.

As the area around the rock was dug up, the wife, Amelia, held my hand. Her husband patted my shoulder a couple times. Kade's arm never left me. In the middle of such evil, kindness and care. I blinked back tears, then let them roll down. I put my hand over my lily bracelet.

The ocean sparkled behind us, sunlight caressing every wave, the white foam frothing, like soap, while seagulls squawked. It was crisp and cold and lovely, and the digging went on and on and I closed my eyes.

I remembered my parents . . . how huggable my dad was. I remembered his beard, his smile. Riding on his back. Drawing pictures with him. Singing along with him on the guitar, finding the Big Dipper. . . . My mother holding me, teaching me how to paint, reading to me, the lines all squiggles on the page, laughing, dancing . . . daisy crowns . . . lilies . . . camping . . . rivers . . . sunsets . . . Freedom. Bear. Grenadine. Wild.

"Got something," a woman from the FBI called out.

Kade's arms tightened around me. Amelia squeezed my hand.

I wanted to know.

I didn't want to know.

I wanted to find my parents.

But not like this.

What Bucky had said was so horrific, I could barely wrap my mind around it without it exploding.

They had dug a trench around the whole rock, several feet out. As I was told, bodies can, and do, shift over time.

Six other men and women started digging, same place.

I felt dizzy, sick-dizzy, when a woman in an FBI jacket pulled out a tattered, holey red kite.

"Oh, my God."

The ocean sparkled behind us, sunlight caressing every wave, the white foam frothing, like soap, while seagulls squawked. It was crisp and cold and lovely, and there was my red kite.

Dale turned toward me, his face wreathed in sorrow.

"That's . . . that's my red kite." The edges of my vision became black, blurry, and I shook my head.

"Sit down, Grenady, sit down," Kade said.

"No, no, I can't."

They kept digging.

Dale walked toward me. "It looks like they're here."

"Both of them?"

"Yes." He nodded, his face grim, tight. "Both of them. I'm very sorry, Dina."

I was sorry, too. Beyond sorry.

We stayed the whole time. I couldn't leave.

I watched when my parents' skeletal remains were lifted up and out and bagged.

I saw my mother's red hair, my father's brown hair, covered in dirt. I saw a glimpse of my father's tie-dye shirt. I saw a scrap of my mother's red, crocheted shawl, her flowered skirt.

I couldn't look away, though at one point Kade asked if I wanted to go and sit by the lighthouse and watch the waves. No, I couldn't. I would see them. I would witness this. I would make sure their bodies were treated with care and respect from this point on, though I knew that the people there would do so.

I was my parents' daughter, the daughter of Freedom and Bear Wild, Mommy and Daddy, and I would be with them now, as I was before, when it was the three of us. A family.

When my parents were bagged and driven down the road, the red, crotched shawl disappearing, the tie-dye shirt disappearing, their souls long gone, I walked to the edge of the cliff, the lighthouse in back of me. Kade put his arms around me.

My parents had been found.

I was still alone, but they had been found.

I felt the tiniest bit of peace creeping in around the rage I felt for Bucky and my overwhelming sorrow.

My parents had not deserted me.

They had been murdered.

They had died trying to protect me and each other.

I had heard them, their soft voices in my mind, for years. I had had their love with me my whole life.

Sometimes, in the dark depths of my despair, I had wondered if my parents had left me as I could not remember their end. They were there, happy, laughing, dancing, then they were gone. But inside my heart, I had always known: My parents would never have willingly left me.

I would mourn them forever, but now I had an answer. A tragic answer, but an answer.

It's hard to move forward when you don't know where you've come from, who you are, but now I knew.

I came from the most important place a person can come from.

I came from love.

There were four other bodies buried beside the rock near my parents. The dental records were processed quickly. Bucky was on death row, and the detectives wanted all the loose ends and details tied up. Plus, they wanted to share the information with all of the victims' long-suffering families. The families deserved it.

There were other loved ones out there besides me who had never had peace, who had grieved forever through black, wrenching nights and cold, lonely days, who had been hysterical, wondering what happened to their family members, their friends. It was the unknown that would have kept them crying, worrying, feeling like they were dying.

At least the families would now know. They would have an idea of when their loved one died, and how, and by whom. It would not settle their hearts, their loss, but at least they would know something. They could move forward a little bit. They could remember the person, relive the happy memories, and know they were gone and not still suffering.

All of the victims wore a necklace with a skull. I could never stand skulls. Now I knew why.

For me, my parents had finally been found.

Mommy and Daddy . . .

Who called themselves Freedom and Bear Wild . . .

Who called their daughter Grenadine Scotch Wild . . .

I was given their birth names by Dale: Lilly Maybelle Whitney and Liam Marcus O'Malley.

Lilly. Liam. And I had a lily bracelet and have painted lilies my whole life. I must have heard her name.

Lilly and Liam's families were notified.

My grandparents, Lilly's parents, arrived on a private plane with their two private nurses. They did not bother to call.

He was wearing a dapper blue suit. He was on oxygen and moved slowly. She was wearing a tailored pink suit, bone-colored heels, a diamond necklace, and a bracelet with lilies. The lily bracelet was exactly like mine.

When my grandma saw me, she passed out.

Kade caught her.

My grandpa attended to his wife, then hugged me close, crying and crying . . . and crying.

My grandparents' names are Elizabeth Maybelle and Peter Whitney. They own department stores. I have shopped in their stores many times, but only for a sale and with coupons, as they are rather spendy.

I can see my own face in my grandma's.

I have, however, my grandpa's nose and his bright green eyes.

My lily bracelet was not from a dime store. The green stones are emeralds. The purple ones are amethysts. The stones I thought were fake crystals are diamonds. The pinks are pink topazes. The reds are rubies. The gold is gold. That's why it never faded. "One for Elizabeth, one for Lilly," my grandpa cried. "And now, for Grenady." He kissed my hand, regal gentleman.

They brought photos of my mother, at all ages, and five photos of my father, which we pored over. They often cried. I heard about my mother as a baby, as a curious toddler, as a girl, a teenager. I could not hear enough. I wanted to know it all. Not surprisingly, my mother loved art.

"She had the wandering, curious, adventurous soul of an artist," my grandpa said. "She was immensely talented. You inherited that, dear."

They told me the story of my parents, and both took the blame, the guilt. My grandpa spoke first, but then became so upset, the nurse had to adjust his oxygen and give him a pill.

The basic story is so old, so familiar, it's a cliché. Only this time, two people lost their lives because of it.

My parents met in Central Park in New York City. My grandparents did not like my father. He was poor. He had only a high school degree. He worked on the docks. He played guitar in a band. He lived with his father, a tough, hard-drinking man who worked on the docks, too. My father's mother had died of leukemia when he was seven.

My mother, however, had been accepted to a private women's college. She was a daughter of privilege, wealth, and excellent schooling. My father was not good enough for my mother. My grandma cried when she said this. "I was so wrong, Grenady. Wrong, wrong, wrong."

My grandpa said, "I am the man. This was my mistake. My responsibility. The pain I have caused! The pain!" He burst into tears. Kade comforted him, man to man. "This tragedy. Inexcusable."

My grandparents forbid my mother from seeing him. My mother snuck away from school and parties to meet my father. When my mother was eighteen, they took off together. She called my grandma and told her what she was doing.

My grandparents sent out the bloodhounds, so to speak, but no one could find their daughter or Liam. It sounds like they travelled with the wind. They had me when my mother was nineteen. They changed their names, unofficially, so there was no record of Lilly Maybelle Whitney and Liam Marcus O'Malley. There is no record of a marriage, and there is no record of my being born in a hospital, so who knows where the grand event took place.

"Your grandpa and I became close to your dad's father when your parents disappeared," my grandma said, her hands clenched tight over a tissue. "Liam had been estranged from his father because he drank all the time. As soon as Liam left, Gene stopped drinking. Said he needed to be sober to find his son. Missing the children, not knowing what happened, has almost killed all of us. All these years I didn't know what happened to my daughter, to Liam. Had I been more loving, more open, they never would have left, never would have been killed. This is all my fault."

"It is mine!" my grandpa called out through his oxygen. "Mine."

Ironically, neither my grandpa nor my grandma had come

from money, they told me. They started the stores after they were married. My grandma was the fourth of eight children born to poor farmers in Arkansas, who came to America from Wales. As a child she spent hours in her mother's kitchen, in a farmhouse, wringing chickens' necks for dinner, slaughtering hogs, feeding pigs, shooting deer so the family wouldn't starve, and sewing and darning. She became a secretary.

My grandpa worked in the salt mines, then ended up in the Korean War. He was one of nine kids. His ancestors hailed from England. They worked as servants in the kitchen for the king.

The two met and married and started a used clothing store, which morphed into the Whitney department stores.

"We came from nothing, Grenady," she said. "Nothing. All we knew how to do was work. When you grow up poor, you never forget it, and it guides your life."

"I know," I said.

When they found out I had been in foster care, both nurses were called in to help. I thought we were going to have to take my grandparents to the hospital, they were so upset.

"We will thank the Hutchinsons, the Lees, and Daneesha Houston," my grandpa announced.

Their apologies were heartfelt, endless.

Later, with my grandparents in the Wild West Bed and Breakfast in town, their nurses in an adjoining room, Kade took my hand.

"Looks like you have a grandma and two grandpas who love you more than the Earth."

"It does look like that." It was heartbreaking.

Would my parents, as they aged and matured, have gone back to see their families?

Of course. Absolutely. They were only twenty-five when they died. They would have forgiven, forgotten. A grandchild would have brought the families together again.

They never made it, their lives destroyed. So young, so much younger than me now.

Many lives were ruined.

But here we were. We had now.

* * *

My grandparents met Rozlyn and Cleo.

We all made my great-grandmother's recipe for apple pie together. "It was your mother's favorite, Grenady."

My grandpa asked Rozlyn about her health, as Rozlyn was wearing a head scarf.

Rozlyn told them. "I've got a tumor in my head that was not invited, and if I could I'd shoot it out myself."

My grandpa made one call.

They flew Rozlyn out the next day on their private plane to the hospital in New York that was doing the experimental surgery that Rozlyn's insurance company had denied paying for. Leonard went with her. As her boyfriend (who did not mind an occasional hot flash during sex, and also thought she looked like a "seductive Buddha" with her bald head) he was proving to be outstanding.

They did the experimental surgery on Rozlyn.

My grandparents paid for it.

I hoped. I hoped for life. Rozlyn's life.

My grandparents and their two nurses stayed in Rozlyn's house and took care of Cleo while Rozlyn was gone. They adored her and her blue fairy wings, her hats with antennae, and her spaceship helmet. They loved how Liddy followed her around like a dog.

They watched me finish the canvas with the magnifying glass. I used black plastic that Kade found for me to form the magnifying glass, then I took out the outlines of the dark trees and the leaning lighthouse. They didn't belong anymore.

Studying the photos of my mother as a girl, I made the girl look exactly like her, with a cheeky grin on her face, the daisy crown on her head. The red, crocheted shawl rising from her left hand and the Big Dipper from her right were done, but I put a sunrise in the background, pinks, oranges, yellows.

I painted lilies flying off my mother's dress, as if by magic, the lilies spinning through the air and landing around the edges of the magnifying glass, as if caught on a wind stream.

My grandparents loved it. It was my grandma who gave my mother the red, crocheted shawl; she had made it herself. I gave the collage to them. They were overcome.

Leonard called us. The experimental surgery had not worked.

That night I wrapped myself in Rozlyn's quilt with the woman in a skimpy blue dress sitting in a huge martini glass, her legs spilling over the side. I leaned against the red barn and cried my eyes out for her, for Cleo, for me.

Liddy neighed.

Three days after my grandparents arrived, my granddad Gene and my great-aunts came to visit us, too.

I cannot even imagine his grief. He and my dad fought all the time because of his drunken rages, then my dad ran off. Gene feared that his son had been killed, but he had never known. He blamed himself.

He's a broken, gentle, humble man, and he is dear to me, kind and loving, as if to make up for what he did to my dad.

My great-aunts, Margaret and Jenny, cried all over me the first time we met. They are loud, emotional, and outspoken. They like blue eye shadow, purses as big as suitcases, and dresses with birds.

They told me that losing Liam "damn near killed Gene, slammed his heart against his rib cage again and again. We cannot believe he's still alive, no, we cannot! Damn near killed us, too! We're so happy we could sing, so we will. You sing with us!"

Margaret and Jenny later sang Broadway show tunes at The Spirited Owl to multiple standing ovations. They were former nightclub singers and still had it, by God, they did. My great-aunts told me that blue eye shadow would bring out the green of my eyes.

I had a photo of my father when he was about seventeen. I painted it on a canvas and gave it to Gene. He cried and cried, old and shaky, and held the canvas on his lap, rocking back and forth. His sisters, surprisingly, grew quiet, their devastation heavy.

Then they sang, "Hallelujah." It was, without a doubt, one of the most emotional moments of my whole life.

Poor Kade. "Hallelujah" did his soft heart in, and he cried with Gene.

Gene met Eudora. I think he likes her. I think she may like him. She said, "As long as he doesn't cramp my travels, I might consider him." She had loved her trip to Antarctica. Thailand was up next. I asked Gene what he thought of Thailand. "If Eudora invites me, it's a yes."

He found her stories of being a spy for the United States fascinating, as I did. She even showed us some special "mementos," from her spy days, and letters from the CIA. Who would have guessed a spy during the Cold War would end up in Pineridge, Oregon?

My grandma has become the mother I never had. She started nagging at me, over the phone one day, about how she felt I worked too much, didn't sleep enough, and inquired about what I'd eaten that day. When she found out I had a pop and chocolate chip cookies for lunch, she told me exactly what she thought of that.

I felt a rush of emotions all at once. You don't know how much you need a mother nagging over you until you don't have it.

The next day, a basket of "natural, organic" foods arrived in a crate.

She's like that.

I love my name now. My mother loved Shirley Temples, my grandma told me, which has to be why they named me Grenadine. My granddad Gene told me that he drank Scotch. That has to be why my middle name is Scotch. My parents were living wild and free, hence our last name, and my mother's name, Freedom. And Bear, for my father? He looked like a cuddly bear. Grenadine Scotch Wild. I get it.

The Hutchinsons came to visit me. The whole huge family, about sixty of them. Noisy. Feisty. Opinionated. They arrived in their pickups and shot off their guns to announce their arrival. They set up their tents and trailers on Kade's property.

"Fry me a pig, there's our Grenadine!"

"Well, now, shoot, Grenadine!" Rose's stepbrother Zeke said. "It's so good to see you, it done make my heart leap."

My grandparents had given me a gift card for Hugh and Rose Hutchinson to the Whitney department stores. They were touched by the gesture and said no gift was needed, as I was their "pink rabbit foot princess . . . their shooter . . . their raccoon-wearing daughter."

They did express some concern that if they used it, the government would know exactly what they bought and could use it against them, but I told them not to worry about that.

I insisted they take it, and after some arguing they asked if Whitneys sold guns. No? Not even huntin' guns? Ammo? No? Tractors? What about ATVs? They would like an ATV!

We had a loud, noisy, feisty time. Hugh and Rose told me they had not sold pot in years. "Good golly God, at least not much. Only to hunting buddies," Hugh told me. "Or fishing buddies."

"Not much at all," Rose agreed. "Only to my sisters and half sisters and cousins, but not Hilly. I still can't stand that prissy peacock."

She hugged me. "We still feel bad about that, down to our souls. When you left, we felt like rabbits flattened under a steamroller. We cried every day like sad, swinging cats. You're my soul daughter. By shots and by fire, when you turned eighteen, that was the best day in our lives! The damn tootin' best! Isn't that right, Hugh?"

Hugh shot off his gun in reply and declared, "Hell, yeah. Got my raccoon daughter back then."

It had been one of the best days for me, too, as they were out of jail and came back into my life and stayed there. I visited them, they visited me. We called and e-mailed, after the Hutchinsons finally agreed to get e-mail and did not believe it was a government attempt to spy on them and their guns.

"We always knew you were innocent, sweet daughter, mine," Hugh said. "Damn government. Can't trust 'em. And I wish

Covey was down in a swamp. I know a good swamp for that son of a bitch."

"Let's shoot some cans and see what Grenadine's got in her back pocket nowadays," Rose's half brother Squirrel told me. I grabbed my .38 special and shot five out of six cans right off a log.

"Daaaang, girl. You still got it."

We spit tobacco. We put a pig on a spit. Hugh's cousin twice removed, Shirley Girl, said, "I'm hungry as a bull on charge. You hungry, too, Grenadine?"

We practiced shooting with bows and arrows. Hugh's nephew, Timmy Hutchinson, an ex-con who had given me my .38 many years ago and who had found Christ the last ten years declared, "Oh, my shoutin' spittin' Lord, Grenadine, you can still shoot. Hallelujah and praise the Lord!"

We smashed beer cans against our foreheads, and Hugh's sister, Dallas, said, "There. Now I'm not stuck in a beer bottle," and she later told me that my ass was "still as tight as a whiskey drum," and I thanked her. She handed me some chew.

When it grew colder that night, Rose said, "Why, it's colder than a cow's tit in December."

And when Rose's nephew Charlie Jr. didn't get up quick enough to get her another helping of potato salad, she hollered at him, "You got a moose up your butt? Get it out and get moving, Charlie!"

Kade won at poker. Rose's brother Tinker was miffed at that and told Kade, "Don't ya ever get too big for your britches or someone's gonna bust your britches wide open and then they'll find out you got a butt like everybody else. Nothing special about it." But he came back later and apologized for what he said.

Kade made Rose and Hugh an oversized rocking chair. He carved *To The Hutchinsons, Love, Grenadine* on the headrest. Those two gun-totin', pot-growin', bad-mouth-swearin', government-hating, loving and kind people cried their eyes out and so did the rest of the loud and feisty Hutchinsons. Then they took turns rocking in it by themselves, with another person, with two other people, and with me.

People talk about "white trash." I was called "white trash," and "white trash foster kid," more times than I can count. I had heard others call the Hutchinsons white trash.

I hate that term. Always have. Being poor and white does not make you white trash. Trash comes from the heart. Covey was trash. Bucky was trash. Many of our rich "friends" were trash.

The Hutchinsons are not white trash. They were, and are, pure, shiny gold, the kind that never dims. I love them. When I arrived at their double-wide trailer, beaten down and defeated, they put me up right again and, as Rose said, "Loved you silly." They saved me.

Beatrice and her husband, Larry, came to visit, too, after the Hutchinsons. She rolled up in her new Mercedes, her diamond bracelets shining. She did not let go of me for five minutes.

Beatrice had wanted me to live with her forever. I moved out when I was twenty-one, when she married Larry. I bought my little green house for $120,000, $100,000 of which was Mr. Lee's money. I had been waitressing full time, working at the same restaurant I had in high school, but also selling my art at Saturday Market, at art shows, and to more and more private clients.

Beatrice's husband, Larry Schneider, was also an artist, but he understood the business side of selling art, too. He was gentle and sweet, like Beatrice, and he helped launch my career.

I kept waitressing until I was twenty-five because I was tremendously insecure about money, and saving money, and never being poor again, but I finally quit when Beatrice and Larry pointed out I was working about seventy hours a week and made far more money on my art than waitressing. My health at that point was unraveling, too. It was time to become a full-time artist.

While Larry went fishing with Kade one day, Beatrice and I painted a picture of Mr. Lee in my apartment. We used fabric to make his bow tie, added a line of rocks around the frame because he loved nature, and put a gold hoop earring in his left ear. "I miss him every day," Beatrice said.

"Me too."

Kade made Beatrice and Larry an oversized rocking chair, too. He carved *Beatrice, Mr. Lee, Larry, Grenadine* across the top. When Beatrice cries hard she snorts and snuffles, poor woman. Larry hugged me tight and whimpered, "Our girl, our girl!"

I know that the reason I didn't come out of foster care addicted to drugs, pregnant, prostituted, or incarcerated was because of love. The love of my parents for my first six formative years and the love of the Hutchinsons and the Lees. The care and steadiness of my case worker, Daneesha Houston, and how she came out of retirement to help me when I had sunk into foster care hell may well have saved my life. The interest and kindness of teachers and principals made all the difference.

I will always miss my parents. But what I've learned is that nostalgia, the "if onlys" can be dangerous. It can bring on heavy sadness and sharp despair and it does not change the past.

So I am here, in the present.

Rozlyn DiMarco died in the fall when the leaves were on fire. Bright golds, scarlet reds, pumpkin orange, the mountains blue and purple at dusk, the sunrises full of streaks of pink. Nature was a layered, colorful collage, a last gift, it seemed, to Rozlyn.

Before she died, she told Eudora and me she would "Live like crazy," and so she did. She and Cleo went to Disney World for a week. They went to the beach and splashed in the waves. They made a Thanksgiving dinner in August together and invited everyone. They baked an eight-layer chocolate cake and a pizza in the shape of a smile.

They sewed a special, queen-sized quilt. They cut up their favorite old clothes into squares and made a double border around the edge. In the center, they cut out a huge red heart.

They rode Liddy and took long walks. They took photos of everything they did together. Rozlyn gave me the photos, and

Eudora and I put them into photograph books. Who knew that ex-spy Eudora would know how to cut out papers and stickers and make those fancy album pages?

Rozlyn wrote Cleo a letter and gave it to me. I put it in the back of the last photograph book, the finality sobering.

Rozlyn danced outside one night naked to the song "Greased Lightning" and made Eudora and me dance naked with her. We went skinny-dipping in the river and got drunk off margaritas. We took Cleo roller-skating, rafting, and camping.

She lived like crazy until the disease beat her down and she couldn't live anymore, her head aching.

Rozlyn died as she wanted. She had a special date with Leonard three nights before and said good-bye to him. She said he "blubbered like a baby, but I told him to quit it because I wanted to ride him like a bucking bronco one more time." She knew it was over. She hugged me and Eudora, then closed the door to her home on a Saturday morning to spend time with Cleo only.

There are, sometimes in life, gracious moments, as I call them, and Rozlyn had one. Cleo left for school on Monday. I took a day off work to be with Rozlyn, and she came upstairs to visit. We sat out on my porch, the sun shining on her face, the billowy white clouds moving right along, the trees singing a whispery song.

Rozlyn didn't look well. She was pale, shaky. She'd lost weight. Her time had been less than expected. She was supposed to have two years, but her doctor had told her recently it could happen anytime, the tumor in her head instantly sucking the life out of her. I felt angry about that, cheated, defeated.

She reached out her hand and I held it. "I love you, soul sister," she told me.

"I love you, too, soul sister." I choked up.

She closed her eyes, sighed, and her whole body jerked twice, as if it had been shot, then her head fell to the side.

I felt her life drain out in my hand, her grasp loosening. "I love you, Rozlyn," I cried out, wanting her to hear those words as she left. "I love you."

I did not call 911. I did not try to save my soul sister. She was not savable. She would not want to be revived only to die again anyhow. She had died as she wished. She had not wanted it to happen in front of Cleo, and she had kept her promise to herself to live like crazy.

I put my cheek to hers and cried for my friend, my tears dripping off both our faces.

I cried and cried for Rozlyn, then I cried for Cleo. Then I cried for all of us.

It is inexplicable how some of the very best people die way too young.

It knocks you flat, that it does, and you wonder how you will ever, ever get up again.

Rozlyn's funeral was held outside, on her property, the Christmas tree farm and the meadow in the distance, the mountains towering behind. It was attended by two hundred fifty people, including everyone at Hendricks'.

We had a potluck dinner afterward, as Rozlyn wanted. "Cleo needs this to happen in a familiar, loving place. Make sure Liddy is nearby. That horse is her best friend."

We set up white tents and long tables. Kade brought the wine and beer, as Rozlyn had requested, so that people could have a drink on her, and "rock and roll on."

Liddy was tied to a nearby tree wearing her flowered hat. Cleo went and hugged her often. In the middle of the potluck, after the service, Cleo untied her and Liddy followed her on a walk through the meadow, one of Rozlyn's "women-power" quilts around her shoulders.

Cleo had, at first, been quiet when I went to school and picked her up the morning Rozlyn died. The funeral home had been by for Rozlyn already. She had not wanted Cleo to see her dead. "Her last memory of me should be of my wicked awesome smile and my love, not a stiff, scary corpse."

Cleo and I went on a walk, past the big, red barn, and I held her hand and told her, as gently as I could, that her mom had died. She didn't say anything for long, painful moments, but I felt her hand quiver.

She had known it would happen, but children, as adults, often don't understand the finality of death until they're in its irrefutable black depths.

"She's not dead! She's not!" She ripped her hand out of mine. "Do you hear me, Grenady? She's not dead! I know it! I want my mommy! I want my mom!"

I felt my whole chest constrict. I was Cleo and Cleo was me. I had thought those same words a thousand times as a child . . . *I want my mom! I want my dad!*

I dropped to my knees and hugged her, my tears streaming. "I'm sorry, honey, so sorry."

"No! No! Get her, Grenady, get her!" She cupped my face. "Right now!" She tilted her head back and screamed, the sound utterly shattering.

I heard Liddy in the barn, neighing, turning, trying to break out of her stall, to reach Cleo.

She struggled out of my arms, her face hot.

"Help her!" Cleo shook my shoulders. "Help Mommy!"

"I can't help her anymore, Cleo," I sobbed, then bit my lip. "She's in heaven." Rozlyn had told her that that was where she would be, watching over Cleo like a "quilt-sewing angel."

"No, she's not. You lie." She hit me on the shoulder with her tiny fist. "Where is she?"

I could tell that the Cleo I knew was gone, disappearing into her hysteria. Liddy kept neighing, banging on the stall door with her hoof.

"Where is my mommy? You tell me!" She screamed again, long and raw. It reached up into that bright blue sky and the puffy white clouds. "You tell me right now!"

That did it for Liddy. She broke out of her stall, the door crashing open, and galloped over to Cleo. I put my arms around Cleo to protect her, but I had nothing to worry about. Liddy stopped before us, her nose to Cleo's wet cheeks.

"I want Mommy!" She hit my shoulder again, not hard. "She's here, she's here, she's here!" Cleo took a deep breath, then let all her grief and anger and desperate sadness out again. I swear her scream raced through the meadow, then bounced off those mountains, pummeling both of us. "Mommy! Where are you?"

She collapsed in my arms, and I sank to the grass and rocked her until she had screamed herself out, limp and lost, Liddy neighing softly beside us, agitated and nervous. I could hardly sit up, my body a wall of searing pain.

"Mommy! Where are you? *Where are you?*"

Watching a child grieve takes your breath away.

53

Cleo and I moved into Kade's house about two months later. It was not a hard decision. I tried living with Cleo in her home, and she couldn't stand it. She looked for her mother everywhere. I think, for some, living in the home of someone who is gone is a comfort. Cleo is a child. It was not a comfort. She was haunted.

Kade said, after he made us pancakes one morning at his house, and Cleo was outside, walking Liddy, "I want you two to come and live with me."

"Live with you?"

"Yes. That doesn't sound romantic. Will you live with me? But when I've talked about marriage, you freeze up. You look worried and nervous. I can see you withdrawing from me, so that's obviously not in the cards."

"You got that right."

"I want marriage, in the future. I want brothers and sisters for Cleo. I want the dog. But I'll wait until you're ready."

I ignored all the happy tingling in my stomach.

"I want to be with you, Grenady. All the time. I want to sleep with you, wake up with you, take care of you, laugh with you, the whole thing, baby, until we're old and out on that deck in our rocking chairs."

"You'd get sick of me."

"Never, Artist Lady." He leaned over and kissed me. "I will never get sick of you."

It was tempting. He was tempting.

"Please, Grenady, think about it. I want you and I and Cleo to be a family together. I am begging you. I don't like living apart at all. I'm lonely without you. I don't like sleeping here alone. I don't like driving up to the house and not having you both here."

"I'll think about it." I kissed him, and he picked me up and put me on his lap in his leather chair.

"Okay, I thought about it."

He laughed. "And?"

"Yes."

The day we moved in I noticed something new in Kade's yard. It was a white picket fence in a rectangle. He was building a gazebo in the center of it. In the fall he would plant bulbs. Lilies, for my mother, and in the summer, daisies for daisy crowns and roses for Mr. Lee.

It's hard not to be madly in love with that man.

He bought me a ring. It's gold, with a row of sparkly diamonds. I love it. "So it's a promise, Grenady, that when you're ready, you'll marry me."

"That's a yes."

My pink, ceramic rose box for my lily bracelet is right at home on the nightstand next to his bed with the married bald eagles.

Rozlyn made me the spy girl quilt. I found it wrapped in Christmas paper, in her room, with my name on a card, after she died. She made one for Eudora, too.

Three women, butts way in the air, slinking through the grass wearing night goggles, miniskirts, and bikini tops over well-endowed bosoms. I hung it in my new studio to honor her and our friendship. I still cry about her. One wonders how much pain a body can take before it breaks, but I am determined not to break.

Kade, Cleo, and I decorated Cleo's bedroom together. We hung up Rozlyn's heart quilt on one wall and the quilt with the woman climbing a mountain in a purple leotard and pink tennis shoes on another. She used two others for her bedspreads.

Kade built Cleo an exquisite desk. In the front he carved a replica of the heart quilt, which I painted.

Cleo and Kade were friends immediately. She clung to his hand, wanting him to read her stories or play space alien dress up or do science experiments. He held her, or I did, or we both did, when she cried. Cleo was a different girl after her mother died, as expected. She was more serious, introspective. She cried often. She would miss her mother her whole life, no question.

But with time, her light, her joy, Rozlyn's fierce, crazy love of life came shining through again.

I will keep my word to her mother: I will love Cleo as my own daughter, and I will love Cleo's children, Rozlyn's grandchildren, with everything that I have, everything that I am.

That's a promise.

Epilogue

~

When I'm done at Hendricks' I go home and work in my studio. The windows let in all the natural light I need, and I can watch the weather roll by, like a moving collage.

I've replenished my art supplies and I've painted shelves, chairs, and tables all the colors of the rainbow. I've bought more art books. I bought two bonsai trees and plants. I light candles on the cold days and paint on enormous canvases. For some reason, it's the bigger the better now, I don't know why. I have a new website, and my work is selling again.

I started teaching an art class once a week, after school, at the local elementary school.

It started out as a one-hour class. Now it's over two hours, as before. I have two classroom teachers who help me, the music teacher, a custodian, a secretary, a classroom aide, and the vice-principal.

We have about sixty kids, including Cleo. Hendricks' Furniture pays for all the art supplies. Kade uses his muscles and helps carry it in. He stays for a while, too, and the kids love him. He's an excellent father figure to them.

I know that part of my life's purpose is to teach kids art, so they can find joy and peace, and create and build, and find themselves somewhere within the color, the texture, the layers. The kids love the class. They call me Miss Grenady. When they see me in town, they run up and hug me, as do their parents. I feel included. I feel liked. I feel like I can hold my head up.

I know that Kade and I will become foster parents in the future. I have to. I want to.

To say that I am "fine" is ridiculous. I am not. I trigger back to my past in all sorts of ways and probably will all my life. Dark forests, fog, empty cupboards, disorganization, ugly rooms, chaos, dog kennels, ropes, even loneliness and aloneness, will set me off. I still have to control Alice, My Anxiety. I will probably always need my black charcoal pencil and my sketch pad to push the past back.

But I like me again. I like making collages and paintings. I like using whipping cream in my coffee, and I like whipping it up and using it on Kade.

I know who I am.

I've had tragedy in my life, and miracles. But isn't that life for all of us?

Some darkness, some rainbows?

Some fear, some courage?

Some love, some loss?

Yes to all of it.

It is life.

I am Grenadine Scotch Wild Whitney O'Malley, daughter of Lilly Maybelle Whitney and Liam Marcus O'Malley, granddaughter of Gene and Linda O'Malley, and Elizabeth Maybelle and Peter Whitney. Second mother to Cleo DiMarco.

The love of my life is Kade Hendricks. I will marry him some day very soon.

Together we will watch the lilies and daisies grow while sitting in our rocking chairs that Kade has made for the three of us. When other sons and daughters come along, he tells me, he will make them rocking chairs, too.

I am looking forward to the rockin'.

In my dream I saw my parents placing the red, crocheted shawl around my and Kade's shoulders as we slept. My mother was carrying lilies, and she wore her flowered skirt. My father carried his guitar and pointed up to the Big Dipper.

We love you, Grenadine.

We love you.

Peace.

WHAT I REMEMBER MOST

Cathy Lamb

ABOUT THIS GUIDE

The suggested questions are included
to enhance your group's reading of
Cathy Lamb's *What I Remember Most*.

DISCUSSION QUESTIONS

1. What did you think of *What I Remember Most*? What three scenes best depict Grenadine Scotch Wild's character?

2. Which character did you most relate to and why? Was there any part of the book that made you laugh or cry? What was your favorite scene?

3. If you could spend the day with Grenadine, Kade, Rozlyn, the Hutchinsons, or Eudora, who would you choose and what would you do?

4. Grenadine says, about herself, "I'm a crack shot and can hit damn near anything. . . . I'm a collage artist and painter. . . . I used to have a little green house. I sold it. That was a huge mistake. . . . I can smash beer cans on my forehead. . . . I fight dirty. Someone comes at me, and my instinctive reaction is to smash and pulverize. It has gotten me into trouble. . . . I have a temper, my anger perpetually on low seethe, and I have struggled with self-esteem issues and flashbacks for as long as I can remember. . . . I can wear four-inch heels and designer clothes like wealthy women, make social chitchat, and pretend I'm exactly like them. I am not like them at all . . ."
   Write down, and then share, how you would describe yourself.

5. Grenadine speaks in the first person. However, there are also police and children's services reports; memos, letters from a doctor, a teacher, and Grenadine; a report card; a court transcript; and third-person passages from the point of view of Bucky. Did the structure work for you? Why?

6. Marley, a customer at The Spirited Owl said, "Women are so picky. If you don't look like Brad Pitt or you're not rich, they don't want you."

    Grenadine said, "No, they don't want you, Marley, because you look like you have a baby in your stomach, you're unshaven, you drink too much, and all you want to do is talk about yourself and whine in that whiny voice of yours. Would you be attracted to you? No? Then why would a woman be?"

    Why did the author give Grenadine a job at a bar? Is she a good bartender? If she gave you advice while you were drinking a margarita, what would she say to you?

7. Did the author portray Grenadine's journey in foster care and the children's services division workers accurately?

8. Why was Grenadine attracted to Kade? What did Kade have in common with her? Kade had spent time in jail because of gang related activities when he was younger. Would his record have stopped you from dating him?

9. From Bucky:
    She never should have gotten away.
    That was a mistake. He had not expected things to take so long. It had always bothered him. He liked things neat. Planned. Perfect.
    He wanted to see her again. Before.
    He would do it! He would think of a way. He pulled four strands of hair out of his head, then made a design on the table in front of him.
    He giggled. He twitched in his chair.
    He told himself a nursery rhyme. He changed the words to create a new rhyme. He sang it out loud. He wrote it in his rhyme book.

He giggled again, then he hurdled his rhyme book across the room, tilted his head back and screamed.

What element did Bucky bring to the story? Did it fit?

10. What did you think of Covey? Was there any good in him?

11. Did you learn anything about living and dying from Rozlyn? Would it have been more realistic, or a better ending for you, if Rozlyn had lived? Why do you think the author chose for her to die?

12. Grenadine said, "I paint what's in my head. I paint whatever I'm thinking about at the time. I'll twist it up, spin it out, add color, add layers, add collage items, and I keep going until it feels done."

If you were to make a painting or collage that would tell the story of your life, what would it look like? What materials would you use? What would it say about you? Grab the artist in you and sketch it out. . . .